Of Blood Exhausted

JEMAHL EVANS

TABLE OF CONTENTS

For Caryl Morgan and the coven, my first fans.

CROSS DEEP, TWICKENHAM 1720

This principle is old but true as fate,
Kings may love treason but the traitor hate.
(Thomas Dekker, *The Honest Whore*)

I looked up from my scribbling. My idiot great-nephew was in the doorway holding a scrap of paper. I have told him often enough not to disturb me when I write my apologia.

'What is it? I am trying to remember a dear old friend. It was November 1644 when we first met.'

'A carriage has been sent for you, and a summons.'

'Tell them to bugger off.'

'It is from Windsor, Uncle, from the Duke of Marlborough.'

'Ah.'

There is only one Duke that matters in all of England. A summons from him is not to be sniffed at, even at my age, and particularly when a carriage is sent. I wrapped myself in a heavy coat, hat, cane, and warm gloves, and shuffled outside. The Duke's footmen helped me up the steps, and then tucked me in with a smuggled bottle of brandy and a blanket. That was exceeding kind, but patronage and favour always come with conditions. There is some plot afoot, and I shall do my damnedest to keep out of it. Pouring a large cup of the spirit, I sat back and watched the world through the plate windows.

The ride was comfort itself, with cushioned seats and sprung wheels, rattling along at a fair pace. Hampton, Shepperton, Chertsey and Virginia Water: busy little villages and hamlets filled with industrious and prosperous families. Winter snow is cleared from the new turnpike roads and cobbled streets. When I was a child, roads were muddy tracks of potholes and ruts, and even kings did not own carriages like this. It is a new age of luxuries, an age of colonies and empire; an age of merchant princes, usurers and moneylenders; an age where honour and chivalry are scorned.

We arrived at Byfield's old house before midday, sweeping up the drive and shuddering to a halt in front of the grand red-bricked building. It has grown over the decades, three stories, even as I have shrivelled. Byfield built a modest home (he was an excruciatingly modest man) but now it is a fine manse with tall chimneys. There were figures standing at the portico: servants and retainers. They helped me down from the carriage and into the building, ushering me along and showing me to a chamber off the main hall. A footman opened the door to the room as I shuffled in with my cane, and announced me.

1

'Sir Blandford Candy, Duchess.'

Duchess? Not the Duke? That was disturbing.

She sat in her parlour dressed simply in a blue dress with no ostentations or ornaments – she needs none to accentuate her beauty. The Duchess must be nearly sixty yet looks half her age, and that is no flatterer's cream, but pretty eyes and a sweet smile have always been her most dangerous weapons. She was smiling at me now.

What am I being dragged into? I know she despises me.

I bowed before her, as low as my decrepit limbs would allow, waiting with my eyes down until she spoke. She left me bent and crooked, just enough time to see my discomfort; just enough time to see my weakness. This one has always been a spiteful, vindictive hoyden.

'Oh, do arise, Sir Blandford,' she said, finally.

I stood up but kept my eyes down.

'I came at the Duke's summons, Duchess.'

'The Duke is indisposed, Sir Blandford. It is I who summoned you.'

'The men did not see fit to mention that, Duchess.' I looked her in the eye.

'Would you have come had you known?'

'Of course, Duchess, I am your servant.'

I am a liar.

The Duchess laughed at my deceit, she knew it for what it was. This one has always been too-clever-by-half. There is poisonous intellect behind the beauty. I told the Duke that often enough, but boys never listen when their cock twitches. Yes, yes, I know, hypocrite.

'Please be seated, Sir Blandford.'

There was only a low cushioned stool to sit on, another deliberate slight. I perched as best I could, cross-legged like a creaking spider. She gave another half-smile at my discomfort.

'Chocolate?' She waved at a valet.

I despise chocolate.

'Yes please, Duchess.'

I told you, I am a hypocrite.

The valet poured frothing sweetened dark chocolate into a bone china cup from a great silver pot. The Duchess waited until both cups were filled and then gestured for me to drink. I picked up the cup and sipped, burning my lips on the boiling bittersweet liquid. Biting back a curse, I put the china down. She smiled again; I noted she had not drunk her own froth. I was being played. I hate being played.

2

'You have a renowned talent for trouble, Sir. It follows you like a dark cloud. Even in your dotage, you spend your days baiting Mr Alexander Pope with vexatious court cases and suits.' She smiled. 'That is, when you are not writing your memoir or paying delinquents to abuse his horse.'

I had paid the Cleland boy to shove a stick of ginger up the horse's arse, and been fined and bound over by the magistrate for the act.

'Young Cleland is an enterprising lad,' I said. 'He has a great future ahead, I am certain, Duchess.'

'Indeed? What of your nephew's future? He works for the Craggs, I hear. It is unusual for one of yours to be working for a Tory, and friends of Mr Pope to boot. It cannot do his prospects much good, your *petite* feud?'

There is something of the night about the Craggs, both father and son. Craggs and Craggs; they should be a firm of funeral-undertakers. Instead, they hold the nation's purse-strings in their nasty grubbing digits. I told the idiot not to involve himself with such creatures. Craggs the Younger is a Twickenham neighbour. I am not welcome at his house. I am not welcome in many of my neighbours' houses. The idiot is, of course, they dote upon him as he sells them South Sea stock.

'My great-nephew is, I am most ashamed to admit, an idiot, Duchess, politically naive,' I said. 'He works for the Company but in a minor position of little consequence. He is no Tory, and no Jacobite either,' I added. I could see where this wind was blowing.

The Duchess smiled again. I disliked that smile, no matter how sweet.

'But treason runs deep in the Candy family, does it not? How you have managed to avoid the scaffold over the decades is an undoubted wonder. His father was convicted as a traitor, I recall.'

'Kit was no more a traitor than others not so far away, was he?' I said. 'I may be ancient, but my memory is undimmed, Duchess. Some got transported; some got a title.'

She frowned at that. My tales could be dangerous still to some, and she knows it better than most.

'Perhaps some things are best left where they lie, Sir Blandford, like sleeping dogs. Lest they bite...' She changed tack. 'I approve of your baiting Mr Pope.'

'I am pleased that you approve, Duchess.'

'You are protected by the King's favour, and Mr Pope was most unpleasant about my husband. As you vex him, so you please me.

You are still loyal to the Duke?'

'Till my dying day.'

'Then perhaps your nephew may be of use to us.'

'Duchess?'

She cannot wish to buy some Company stock?

'All in good time, Sir Blandford. Why do you have His Majesty's favour? I have been unable to discover.'

I cannot tell her the truth of His Majesty's favour, else I lose it. Some memories can be deadly.

'I did some service long ago for King George's late mother, Duchess,' I said. 'During the civil war.'

'The Last Roundhead served a Cavalier princess during the civil war?' An arched eyebrow.

'Princess Sophia was a remarkable individual, even as a young girl, and she kept her promises.' I gave a wry smile. 'A rare thing indeed for royalty; her brother did not like me.'

I glanced at the signet ring on my little finger; a rampant lion in yellow gold with a single diamond as an eye. It was Princess Sophia's ring.

'Prince Rupert liked you well enough, as I remember?' she said. 'He was not renowned as a judge of character.'

That was sly.

'Not Prince Rupert, Duchess. The eldest brother: Karl Ludwig, Prince Elector of the Palatine. Charles Louis if you prefer, he preferred it.'

'How fascinating, tell me about them.'

The Duchess was not fascinated; the Duchess was scheming. Whatever her plot is, I must keep the idiot out of it. So, I sat up and told her how a Roundhead captain once served a Cavalier princess, and the princess's arrogant, pig-headed, treacherous grasper of an elder brother.

1. The Office of Ordnance and Armouries: London, October 1644.

Who was the first that forged the deadly blade?
Of rugged steel his savage soul was made,
By him, his bloody flag ambition waved,
And grisly carnage through the battle raved.
(Tibullus, *Elegy XI*)

London smouldered with fevered imaginings. Discontent and rumours fanned the flames of vicious division. Higher and higher taxes imposed to pay for the cost of the war sent the apprentices and shop-boys wild as wages were cut. There were riots, foreigners abused in the street and beaten for Papist, or Royalist, or Covenanter, and more and more radicals flooded into the overcrowded city. They brought zealotry in the name of tolerance and hatred in the name of love.

'Twas a miserable time of contradiction.

I had hired a hackney to take me from Bedford Street to The Tower. Around the bridge, there was a crush of people: carts, sedans, and carriages barely moving. Workers and shoppers were disembarking from boats at the wharves, and wagoneers fighting to get to the shops and stalls in the city. It caused collisions and fights and arguments; every morning and evening the same. At the junction with Thames Street and Fish Street Hill, everything ground to a halt. I was going to be late.

I stuck my head out of the window of the hackney and called up to the driver.

'Can you go up by St Laurence Pountney?'

The man looked behind; we had just gone past the church.

'I cannot turn now, pretty, we are fixed here.'

He was looking at my face. The barely sprouted moustache and beard did not cover the fresh scar dissecting my top lip. That pricked my vanity.

'A pox on all London porters and their vehicles!'

I gave the driver his fee, even stumping up a gratuity though he deserved it not. Stepping down from the hackney, I walked briskly down Thames Street to the Tower, ducking past people, horses, carts, and bullocks.

'Damn, damn, damn! I shall be late.'

I almost landed in a fat pat of steaming cow shit as I rushed, stopping myself at the last, teetering over it with one leg until finding my balance. I stepped over safely, breathed a sigh of relief, and a woman emptied chamber pot slops from an upper story garret all over me. I looked to the heavens with stale piss and turds dripping down the brim of my fine hat.

'Why? In the name of God! Why?'

The woman merely closed the window and left me drenched and reeking. My efforts at presentation were ruined. There was a shine on my boots; my golden ringlets fell loose about my shoulders. A new blue suit, woollen cloak, and an expensive beaver pelt hat; all now splattered in faeces. I sighed, my head dropped, and I trudged disconsolately on to The Tower – so much for making a good impression.

I had been ordered to present myself to the Office of Ordnance and Armouries. My incarceration was at an ending. The new Clerk to the Office was one Mr Haslerig (his predecessor Darnelly had collapsed and died of a stroke in the summer). My friends had warned me that he was filled with true godliness of the cause, which meant that I was certain to dislike him. He was unlikely to be much enamoured with me, it must be admitted. Being covered in shit and bearing a scarred visage and scraggly beard was not going to improve the situation.

The guards at Middle Tower wrinkled their noses at the stink but let me pass and I arrived at the Office of Ordnance well past nine of-the-clock; well past the appointed time. Clerks and secretaries were industriously moving bits of paper around the room, or scribbling furiously with their heads down, all in silence. There was normally a hubbub of conversation in the room but not today. One of them nodded at the door to Mr Darnelly's old chamber; Haslerig's chamber now. I rapped on the wood firmly, rat-a-tat-tat.

'Come.'

Haslerig was sitting at the desk writing. A slight man with dark curls tied back from his face, and a wispy moustache under a very large Roman nose. Such a stunning proboscis made me pity the grindstone. He looked up and lifted the snout at me, like a hungry dog sniffing at gravy, and spoke first without any polite introductions.

'Since I have taken over this position, Captain Candy, you have been involved in an illegal duel, injured, arrested and subsequently incapacitated for near a month.' He started low and built the volume slowly. 'Now you are late when summoned, and you stink, sir, you stink! Like a privy on a summer's day! It is NOT a good beginning!' He stood up bellowing, red in the face, spitting his bile and gripping the desk tightly with both hands.

''Twas a woman with her night soil, she.'

'I did not give you leave to speak, sir.'

'But.'

'Silence!' He slammed his hand down on the desk.

'Yes, sir.' I added snippily.

Haslerig glared at me; I half-expected him to start frothing at the mouth again.

'You have tarried in this city for far too long, Candy, like an ungodly man diggeth up evil, but your uncle deems it unwise for you to return to the army with the current cloud of shame hanging over you. So, you have been given over to me.'

Uncle Samuel had used his influence as Scoutmaster General to quash any talk of charges, but the duel with John Hurry saw me in disgrace. I would have to endure the indignity of this prick-weasel for a time. I tried to be charming.

'I am certain that I can be of some assistance, sir.'

'I do not want you, sir. You are a fop, a jackanapes and a wastrel!'

Now, that was a tad unfair. I was all those things, I grant you, but I had proven my worth to the cause.

'My predecessor seemed to labour under the illusion that he was your uncle's to command. That is not the case. This is the Royal Office of Ordnance and Armouries, not a Covenanter dwarf's resource to be plundered. It is time it worked efficiently for the godly cause.'

'Sir?'

I was certain that there was a contradiction somewhere in that statement, but decided not to press the point. Haslerig picked up a piece of parchment from his desk and handed it to me along with a glass. It was a bill of landing for arms and powder.

'Your uncle insists that you are intelligent and resourceful, though I can scarce believe it, but also that you understand the shipping trade?'

'My father, sir, he had shipping concerns, but I would not.'

'I did not ask for an explanation, Candy. A simple yes or no will suffice.'

'Yes, sir.'

'What is wrong with that docket?'

I studied the paper for a few seconds; the writing was tightly spaced and tiny. Without the glass, it would have been unreadable. Columns of goods paid for and delivered, and demands for monies sent to London. I am no clerk, and certainly no mathematician, but I could see the discrepancy. It must have been a scribe's error. Instead of eighteen barrels of powder delivered only thirteen had been landed, but the numbers were written so tightly that it was barely noticeable even with a glass.

'There are five barrels of powder missing?'

'Indeed, a simple mistake perhaps, but there is a pattern in all of the dockets over the last few months. There are lots of these simple mistakes. Guns and powder have been stolen from shipments crossing from Amsterdam to King's Lynn; two thousand pounds worth since the summer.'

'That is enough to outfit an army.'

'There is no need for a commentary, Candy. You will have to go to Amsterdam and find out what is happening.

'Go to Holland?' I had expected him to send me to King's Lynn.

'Yes, Candy, Amsterdam is in Holland. Perhaps some time away from London and temptation will redeem you. Our factor in the city is called Septimus Hutchinson. You know him, I believe?'

'Beeston.'

William Beeston was a crooked schemer who sometimes used the Hutchinson alias. A talented actor and theatre manager, whose family was entwined with my sister Elizabeth through shared ownership of the Cockpit Theatre. His scheming had made London too hot for him and he fled to the continent the previous year. I might add that he left my sister to pay off his criminal creditors.

'Why Darnelly employed the man I have no idea,' said Haslerig. 'If he has been shaving some off the top, put a stop to it!' Haslerig looked down, picked up a pen, dipped it in the inkwell and started to write. 'Your man Coxon has been loitering in Whitehall for days with criminals and rogues,' he said not looking up. 'Take him with you.'

'Whitehall? He is supposed to be in Wapping.'

'Whatever he is doing, Candy, put a stop to it! The clerks have your orders and passports outside. There is a ship leaving in three days, your passage has been paid for.' He looked up at me. 'And wash, man, wash!'

I did not like Put-a-stop-to-it Haslerig. I silently mourned Darnelly as I collected my papers. From the clerk's face, I could tell he mourned his old master as well.

*

I walked from The Tower to Uncle Samuel's townhouse. The Luke manse was next to Baynard's Castle; four stories tall, brick built, with rows of expensive glass windows, stables, and its own private wharf on the river. There was also a new manor near Cople, but my uncle and ageing grandfather were both Members of Parliament and currently in London. My grandfather had returned to the city in the summer and spent time with my sister, but I had met him only once on my sickbed. An old man in his seventies, normal sized not like his tiny homunculus son, white hair, big belly, and the same beak as Uncle Samuel. I found them both in the study, seated in comfortable chairs with miserable looks upon their faces.

'Who has died?'

Uncle Samuel sighed, but Grandpapa's face brightened at the sight of me.

'Hello, my boy,' he said.

'When did you last wash, Blandford?' said Uncle Samuel. 'Go and clean yourself up, quickly, we have things we need to discuss with you.'

That sounded ominous.

I left the study and walked through the empty house to the stables out the back and gave myself a scrubbing. My doublet, cloak, and hat would need to be cleaned by Figgis, but once in my shirt sleeves, I was fresh enough. I returned to my uncle and grandfather, pausing at the door to listen to their conversation.

Yes, it is a bad habit, creeping at doorways in search of whispered secrets, but you will perhaps hear things to your benefit.

'I would trust Blandford with my life, Father.' My uncle's voice. 'He is loyal and brave.'

Sometimes you hear words that flatter.

'But he is a godless fop that cares nought for the Covenant.'

Mostly you hear unkind truths.

'He looks like his mother, they all do,' said Grandfather.

'He has his father's temperament,' said Uncle Samuel. 'Charming and irritating in equal measure; it is a dangerous combination.'

'You have never forgiven Bess for running off to Wiltshire.'

'No, I have not, but that does not blind me to Blandford's abilities, or his faults. He is stubborn and wilful and holds a grudge just like Christopher. He would cut off his nose to spite his face if he thought it would prove him in the right.'

My grandfather laughed as Uncle Samuel continued.

'He certainly has a sharp intellect, just like Bess and his sister. He is well-educated and resourceful, but he wallows in vice and debauchery, and his reputation is such that he will be watched as soon as he disembarks.'

'Yet, I fear that he is the only one we can trust in this matter, Samuel. He is family, and St John is insistent that there is more to these weapons going missing than mere embezzlement by a corrupt factor...'

There was a creak of a floorboard behind me. I had been caught in my eavesdropping.

'Master Blandford.' The words came from behind my back before I could about-face. 'Ye's raised better than that.'

I turned to face my accuser. Harry Figgis: in his late forties, bandy-legged, thin-faced and scrawny; a long nose, buck-teeth, and a cow's lick that sent his sandy hair sprouting in different directions. All topped off with a lazy brown eye that left one unsure quite where he was looking. 'Twas a face that could rust gold. He had been my late father's manservant, my eldest brother's valet, and then responsible for depositing my little nephew with Elizabeth in the summer.

'What are you doing here, Figgis?'

'Sir Samuel and Sir Oliver wished to hear o the journey from Wiltshire, Master Blandford. What bout ye? In trouble again?'

To this day I cannot decide if Figgis was a simpleminded loiter-sack, or a dark and twisted genius. He was lazy and insolent with not a whit of respect for my rank, but he had taught me to shoot and ride, and I was fond of him despite the regular beatings he doled out. I almost certainly deserved them. The Figgis family served my father and Candy grandfather, and Harry had brought Kit across England with no harm to the boy and no trouble to himself (that took some doing in those bitter times), but he gave not a glimmer of intelligence, mostly. Every so often a word or an act made you wonder.

'My hat, doublet and cloak are in the parlour. See if you can get the stench out of them, Figgis. There's a good fellow.'

'Splattered, Master Blandford?'

'Just do it, Figgis.'

He grunted and walked down the hall towards the kitchens and parlour. I turned and opened the door to my uncle's study and entered. Uncle Samuel waved for me to be seated and then leaned forward in his chair.

'You met with Mr Haslerig today?'

'Yes, Uncle.'

'What did you think?' asked my grandfather.

I paused before answering. 'He is an Independent; irritatingly officious, and with an overblown sense of his own importance. I did not like him.'

My grandfather roared and Uncle Samuel nodded.

'I did not think you would appreciate his zeal, but with Beeston's involvement it seemed apt that you should investigate. There is more to this than some scheme of the actor. Two of my agents have been killed in Amsterdam in the last month, on top of the weapons going missing.'

'You believe a Royalist plot is afoot in the city?

There are always Royalist plots being hatched in Amsterdam,' said my grandfather. 'It is a city full of Cavalier émigrés. What we fear is a Dutch intervention.'

'For or against Parliament?'

'That is a good question,' said Grandfather. 'Amsterdam is a republican city, but the Dutch Stadholder supports King Charles. The Winter Queen is only miles away in The Hague, and her eldest son appears in London claiming to support our cause against the King.'

The Winter Queen was King Charles's sister: Elizabeth of the Palatine, mother to Prince Rupert the Royalist general. Her eldest son, Karl Ludwig, had arrived in London that summer claiming to support Parliament. He had been granted a pension and apartments in Whitehall by politicians overawed at the foreign prince's celebrity.

'Why did Haslerig not explain this to me?'

'Because he is an Independent,' said Grandfather. 'They have been taking over committees in Parliament and appointing officers favourable to their cause. Haslerig is one of many and cannot be trusted. There is some talk of a new army. The Independents see it as an opportunity to strengthen their power in the country.'

God save me from all Independents and Covenanters and their interminable bickering. We would never beat the King whilst squabbling amongst ourselves. Uncle Samuel and my grandfather were Covenanters but had always been pragmatists: defeat the King first and then settle the country. Since Marston Moor, the moderates were all-a-fluster fearing the radicals might seize control and truly remake England.

'As far as Haslerig is concerned you are there to investigate the missing weapons,' said Uncle Samuel. 'He is punctilious enough in his new role and desires to do a good job, but your grandfather is correct that he cannot be trusted.'

'This matter becomes ever more complicated, Uncle.'

Uncle Samuel nodded. 'Coxon has been playing in Whitehall when he is supposed to be watching the docks in Wapping. Take him with you to Amsterdam, and impress upon him the importance of his work, will you?'

'Yes, Uncle.' That was the second complaint I had received about John. What had the impudent ragabash been up to?

I stayed a little while longer with my uncle and grandfather, but the talk was dismal misery of the war. The King was badly weakened by the loss at Marston Moor, but our leaders were reluctant to push the advantage. 'Twas little wonder that the godly autem-cacklers wanted a new army and new generals to finish the war, and the King, for good. My uncle provided me with funds for Amsterdam, and I walked with Figgis back to my sister's house on Bedford Street.

2. Beggars and Kings: London, October 1644.

THE glories of our blood and state
Are shadows, not substantial things;
There is no armour against fate;
Death lays his icy hand on kings.
(John Donne, *Death the Leveller*)

A livid red scar, near half an inch in length, ran from just under my nose through my top lip. The flaps of skin had been sewn carefully back together by the surgeon, but the scar still disfigured my pretty looks. I cursed and put the mirror down. I had been endeavouring to grow a full cathedral-dangler to hide my face. Over a month without a barber, and it was still patchy and wispy. Amsterdam was going to be a sorry place to visit looking so injured. Yes, I am vain, you know that already. The snotnose was screaming again.

'Figgis!' I shouted. 'Figgis!'

Every time I screamed for Figgis, the brat bellowed back in response.

My little nephew Kit was a new addition to the household, brought from Wiltshire to safety in London. His mother was sick, and my brother Henry was fighting for the King. The little beggar was not two years of age but already had a boisterous set of lungs. How could something so small make such an unholy caterwaul?

'Figgis! Where are you, man? Figgis! Damn your eyes!'

The baby had stopped crying. I listened out; there were steps coming towards my room. The door opened and my sister Elizabeth entered, dressed plainly like a servant in a blue wool dress and white cap, carrying the brat. They looked like a vision of the Madonna and child, both with blonde hair and so pretty. The child was cherubic in her arms, big blue eyes with long golden lashes and ruby red lips.

'I have had no sleep since you brought that noisy, stinking, snot-nosed, flea-ridden, pissing, shitting, vomiting, guttersnipe into the house,' I said.

'He is family, Blandford, and he has no fleas.'

'Why does he have to make such a din?'

'His teeth come through and he has the wind.'

Elizabeth put Kit on my bed where he sat grinning at me, burped, and started giggling to himself. Elizabeth smothered him in praise and kisses for the belch.

'He is a child, Elizabeth, children burp, fart and shit constantly; this one more than most. 'Tis no grand achievement. Where be Figgis? I am to Amsterdam on business for Uncle Samuel in but two days.'

'Good, 'tis long past time you stopped lazing in bed and whining about your face.'

'You have been my gaoler. Where be Figgis?'

'You were hurt for the first week, Blandford. Since then you have malingered. How long wilt thou sleep, oh sluggard? I thought the medics and potions would shift you, but the fouler we made them the more you snivelled. At the least, Uncle Samuel has found a way to move you.'

'That is not kind.'

She sniffed. 'Mr Figgis is running errands for me this morning. You shall have to look to yourself. Spend some time with Kit; he adores you.'

Figgis would have to attend to the packing when he returned. The child was lying on his back picking his nose and chortling happily along with my sister.

'The brat is not yours, you know,' I said.

'Now who be unkind? I have looked over you all since I was eight.'

Our mother had died when Elizabeth had been eight, and my sister became a self-appointed martyr. She never let us forget it.

'And, well...' She looked pointedly at me. 'We cannot be certain who the father is, can we? So you spend some time with the boy before you gad about to Amsterdam. He may not be mine, but he could be yours.'

The boy's paternity was not something I wished to explore too deeply. If my oversized witless monkey of a brother found any proof of it, he would carve me up into little pieces. Kit crawled up the bed to me and began looking in the mirror. He pointed at himself and licked the glass.

I laughed. 'The boy is clearly an idiot, Elizabeth; he can only be Henry's. What of breakfast? I will need to fortify myself for the sea voyage.'

'The North Sea is hardly a voyage, 'tis barely more than a pond. I will send a maid with something for you.'

She left me with the boy happily rolling on my bed. He pointed at me with his tiny forefinger.

'Unc.'

'That is correct, Kit, I am your uncle. Never forget that, my boy. And your best uncle too; your mother's brother be nought but a drunken wastrel.'

Pots and kettles.

Kit giggled at me. I reached for the deck of cards in my trunk and showed him some of the pictures, laying them out and explaining the names and numbers. The deck had images of the parliamentary leaders engaged in a variety of vices. 'Twas cruel sedition but amusing.

'That be a knave, the knave of pikes.' An image of John Pym in hell being tortured by demons.

He picked up the card, made some gurgles, and put it in his mouth. I took it off him.

'They are for cheating the unwary, Kit, not eating.'

He looked at me in askance at that, nodded to himself and picked up the knave of hearts.

'I shall teach you how to play Put,' I told him. 'Now, I will have to mark down any losses and take them away from your allowance, I am afraid, but I will hold the debt until you come into your inheritance.'

Do you think I was jesting? It is always good to have some insurance for the future.

Kit's eyes went wide and he giggled again. Perhaps I should teach him how to count first, and talk, walk, and shit in a privy.

I spent the next few hours playing with the boy and trying to teach him some words, with little success. By the time Elizabeth returned the boy was starting to stink, and I happily handed him back to her for cleaning and changing. I had much to do if I was for Amsterdam, and first on the list was the whereabouts and activity of my man John Coxon.

*

My sister had provided John with a large chamber on the top floor, well-furnished with a good strung bed and thick soft mattress. 'Twas nearly as opulent as mine, I mused. Elizabeth spoiled the lad like he was family. He had been absent for near a week, supposedly watching the docks in Wapping for my uncle, but I now knew better. John had been in Westminster playing cards with criminals. I sent word to his friends that he was required for a mission. That would bring him cantering home.

I sat waiting quietly in the darkness until I heard a creak outside the room. The door opened quietly and he tippy-toed into the room.

'Good evening, sir,' he said in the darkness.

'How did you know I was here?'

'Your perfume. 'It is most pungent, assaulting my nose like a Gypt in a prize-fight.'

I had doused myself in the stuff earlier. A lesson there, you have five senses so use them. Your eyes alone can deceive.

'What have you been up to, my lad?' says I, ignoring his snipe at my expensive scent. 'You were told to sit in Wapping and pick up information from the docks.'

'I have been in Wapping, sir...'

'Do you know why I always beat you at cards, John?' I said, and sparked a lamp.

The oil-soaked wick fired and the lamp spluttered into life, filling the darkness with a dull orange light. John was well dressed in his blue woollen suit, but wore neither cloak nor hat. He looked as if he had been running hard: beads of sweat glistening on his forehead. His dark mulatto features were flushed, long black curls wild and coat unbuttoned.

'You cheat at cards,' he said.

'I always beat you at cards,' I said, 'because you have a tell when you aim to deceive.'

I won at cards because I cheated. John was a consummate liar and mostly I had no idea (I did not want him to know that). This time, however, I knew where he had been. It is an exquisite delight to know that someone is lying and about to be exposed.

'When I aim to deceive, sir?' His innocent face was a practised weapon.

'But in this instance, I am forearmed with the knowledge that you have been carousing in Whitehall with associates of a rather unsavoury character.' His eyes widened with surprise for just a second. It was a picture that delighted me.

'Ah,' he said. 'Well, this is awkward.'

I raged at him for a while: about his duty, about his disobedience. He had been entrusted with a great responsibility and had betrayed my uncle's, and my, trust. At least he had the good grace to stare disconsolately at the floor at that. When I had finished with my ranted admonishment, he looked up.

'I was playing at cards, sir. I won.'

He poured out a purse of coin onto the bedcovers: silver mostly, but some coppers and a couple of gold pieces. It was indeed a fair prize for a trick or two.

'That is all very well, but you still have your duties,' I said. 'I have half-a-mind to confiscate the winnings for your impudence.'

His eyes narrowed. 'That would certainly be half-a-mind's reasoning, sir.'

'Yes, well,' I said. 'We are off to sea, my lad, to foreign parts, and mayhap you will need the coin.'

John's eyes brightened at that news, and he gathered together his haul of money.

'We are going to sea?'

He looked remarkably pleased to be leaving London. A wide grin broke out on his face at the thought of a journey.

'We are set for Amsterdam,' I told him. 'With tomorrow night's tide.'

Being the Fast day.

This morning, Haniel Boswell the King of the Beggars (as they call him) was found dead against Whitehall, by the Guard of Court there. Of Boswell's death, I shall give no other account but what is reported by many that saw him the night before. All agree that he had spent the evening with some malignants, drinking hard because it was the fast day, and in mockery of the law. But, he drank so much that he was soundly drunk, and left behind by his comrades. He was found the next morning dead in the streets. Whoever pleases to enquire of those that live thereabouts may hear more of it at large, if they be not satisfied that which I say is truth.

Let all drunkards and mockers that jeer at our fasting, and make it their sport, consider well of it; there hath been many examples of this kind.

God will not be mocked!

Nehimiah Wallington. October 22nd, 1644.

3. Captain Jakes: London to Amsterdam, October 1644.

Drink today, and drown all sorrow,
You shall perhaps not do it tomorrow,
Best, while you have it, use your breath,
There is no drinking after death.
(John Fletcher,*The Bloody Brother*)

Captain Nathanial Jakes was a shabby creature dressed in grey and covered in muck; a dirty wool bonnet on his head, creased-skin leathered from age, and the stink of whale blubber and piss. Jakes looked nought like a ship's master, but he treated the sea like his lover and knew me well enough from past association. He had my trunk loaded aboard his little tub, and told us to stay out of the way until the night tide.

We retired to The Red Cow on Wapping High Street. A fine inn: three storeys high with red roof tiles and white rendered walls. There was an old musician with a grey beard in one corner playing some type of Spanish gittern.[1] It was warm and friendly, busy with locals, sailors, and travellers.

The innkeeper's wife was a jolly sort with white hair. She brought a warm mutton stew with thick gravy and white flour dumplings. I worried about vomiting it all up as soon as we were at sea, but the flavour was good. Another coin bought a bottle of good sack for me and ale for Figgis and John to drink. I finished my food slowly, sipping the wine and listening to the music. The other two shovelled theirs down their mouths like pigs at a trough. After eating my fill, I belched and pushed the plate away. My top lip itched to buggery; I started scratching at it.

'My beard and moustache are not growing as quickly as I would like,' I said, to no one in particular.

'Ye need to warm ye bollucks with a pan, Master Blandford,' said Figgis.

He was smoking a pipe, with his back to the wall at a table on the other side of the fire, tapping his foot in time with the player's music.

---

[1]Guitar.

'Be not always the imbecile, Figgis.'

His parochial gobbets of village wisdom were mostly risible nonsense.

''Tis very true, Master Blandford. The more heat in the balls, the quicker yer whiskers will come out. Sit on a bedpan and heat em up. Ye shall have a cathedral-dangler before ye know it.'

I had learned as a child not to argue with him about such things. The damn fool was as stubborn as a mule!

'Why does Mr Figgis not sit with us?' asked John.

'Because he thinks me a drunken wastrel and believes servants should not sit with family.'

'Not true, Master Blandford. I *know* ye be a drunken wastrel,' he said. 'And I sits here because I likes my arse to the wall; I can rub back and scratch my itch.'

The arrival of Captain Jakes and his first mate put a stop to that conversation, thankfully. The first mate was a slightly built man named Duggan: a competent sort with dark hair and eyes, and immeasurably cleaner than Jakes. He was also an Irish papist, but I would not hold that against him – others would. The woman brought a bottle of rumbullion, which I paid for. Jakes took it eagerly and poured us both a cup. I noted Duggan took only ale.

'Let us drink to Poseidon, Sugar,' said Jakes.

'Will you be fit to sail?'

'I sail better soused.'

The first mate rolled his eyes at his captain's words.

Kill-devil is not a drink for the faint-hearted. I would not normally touch the stuff; a fiery thick black liquid that burns your throat and belly, and leaves behind a most hideous morning head. I decided the warmth would fortify me against the bitter North Sea winds.

*

The trouble started with the musician. More and more sailors had arrived demanding their rum, rowdy and with money to spend. They did not take so kindly to a foreign string-scraper playing his 'Spanish' strains. A wiser player, or one with a more common repertoire (and by common I mean base) would have obliged them, but the man seemed oblivious to the complaints. He ignored them, lost in the music, plucking hard at the strings so they pierced through the grumbles. It was an extraordinary performance of virtuoso skill, had the ingrate sailors but the wit or wisdom to realise. Instead, they were enraged, their moaning becoming louder and louder.

By this point, I was already fuddled and slurring. The noise the sailors made was disturbing the equilibrium of the evening.

'Gad! Those fellows are damned irritating,' I said to Jakes and Duggan. 'The player is extraordinarily skilled.'

I poured out another cup of rum as Jakes nodded his agreement. The boy was busy charming some girl by the bar, and I knew not where Figgis was. Shouts of complaint started up again as the player seamlessly switched to a French dance. Glaring at the sailors, I took a great gulp of the rum; the more I took the sweeter it became.

'The musician is deliberately baiting them,' said Duggan.

Jakes shrugged. 'They have been at sea for months and have money to spend on ale and trouble. It would not take much.'

'Coarse clay-brained whip-jack sea mongrels,' I slurred. The words tumbled out too fast for my tongue to keep up.

'Ye be drunk, Sugar,' said Jakes. 'This rumbullion is too much for you.'

'The rumbullion be too much for me?' I finished my drink off with one gulp. 'I have not had enough.'

The sailors had started throwing more insults at the player; a couple stood up to berate him, waving their fists. They were large menacing buggers, and I do not like bullies. I lobbed my empty cup at one of the louder sea-dogs, catching him right behind the ear. He and his friends turned back to face me.

'Be silent or be damned!' I shouted at them, standing up.

A wave of nausea came over me from rising too quick; dizziness and sudden blurring of my vision. I fell forward, flat onto a food-laden table. The crash sent drinks and dishes flying: platters, cups, bottles and knives hoisted up in the air then clattering to the flagstones. I banged my head hard as I hit the table, but barely noticed. There was a stunned silence in the inn at my display, even the foreign minstrel had stopped plucking his strings as everyone turned to stare. I waved weakly at my audience from the floor.

''Tis of no matter,' I said. 'I am very, very, drunk and can barely feel the broken crown.'

Then somebody stamped on my back.

I managed to climb to my feet and stood, swaying, looking about for my assailant. Whoever had stamped on me was nowhere to be seen in a mass of fighting men and women. I noted the minstrel in one corner of the room, still being menaced by a couple of sailors. I charged over to help him, knocking one of the sailors out of the way and turning to face the other. He held a knife in his hand.

I grabbed the gittern from the player and swung it at the sailor, smashing him across the face.

'Not the guitarro!' screamed the minstrel behind me.

The fragile wooden instrument exploded into bits at the strike, knocking the sailor down. A great blow from behind threw me to the floor, and I spewed up my guts and passed out.

Figgis and John carried me from the drunken mêlée. Jakes's crew fought off the sailors, with only a few bruised heads and cuts, and the ship took to sea on the midnight tide. I was thrown senseless into the hold.

*

The first day at sea I spent in a stupor; hung-over and sweating, with a throbbing lumpen headache, a bitter taste in my mouth, and a foul temper to boot. On top of that was the presence of the old minstrel from the inn: a melancholic Dutchman by the name of Hugo. He coolly informed me that I had destroyed an excruciatingly expensive gittern and owed him nearly ten pounds. He continued to whine about it for the rest of the voyage.

'It was made by Morisco craftsmen,' he told me again. 'You will have to pay for the replacement.'

'Which I will most assuredly do,' I said. 'As I keep telling you. Will it be easy to find another?'

'In Amsterdam, you may find your heart's desire,' he told me. 'But in Amsterdam, a heart's desire comes costly.'

I threw a quick prayer of thanks for the two purses of coin I had hidden in my trunk. It was beginning to look like the Dutch city would be an expensive excursion.

'Are there great ships in Amsterdam?' asked John. He had been disappointed that we travelled in Jakes's tub instead of a grand galleon.

'The greatest ships in the world,' the minstrel assured him.

The boat cut due east across the North Sea for three days. The slate grey waves tossed the ship about, but the crew worked in perfect tandem as they trimmed sails and pulled on sheets; Jakes or Duggan always at the tiller barking orders to them. Figgis, the minstrel and I contented ourselves under the scrap of canvas at the stern. John Coxon would sit high up by the prow of the ship as it cut through the waves, the spray drenching him, with a great wide grin across his chops.

Jakes came and sat next to me, opened a bottle of porter, and pointed at my man. 'I have told you before, Sugar, that one is a sailor born.'

'He is a thief born,' I said.

21

'Aye, well, that an' all,' said Jakes. 'I knew his father.'

I turned to face him. 'Truly?'

'Another born sailor and thief. He buccaneered out of Barbados in the thirties.'

'They hung him, so John says?'

'Aye, well he crossed the Gypt tribe. 'Tis a brave man or a fool that makes an enemy of the King of the Beggars. The Boswells turned him over to the magistrates and the hangman stretched his neck.'

I shrugged. 'The boy has changed his stars. He knows to stay away from the Boswells. My sister would carve off his pizzle and force feed it back to him after the last time.' John had previously tried to stab King Boswell over the family feud.

Jakes laughed. 'Aye, I think your sister most probably would.' He paused and then. 'There's one thing more I will say about Tom, he was a stubborn bugger. The boy is assuredly cut from the same cloth.'

The Walter Raleigh made good time crossing the North Sea. We came in sight of the Den Helder harbour and fortifications on the third morning. Jakes guided the boat through the shallow channels, past sandbanks and mudflats, to the inner sea beyond.

Anne Candy to Elizabeth Candy.

Dear Elizabeth,

Oh, how this horrid war drags ever on.

There is much that I would say to you, if I could, but to commit to paper in such times would be too perilous. I miss your kind words and advice, sister. Mistress Margaret Lucas is sweet comfort, but I confess we both yearn for our homes and families, and it is only our duty to the Queen that keeps us in France. I understand your fears and concerns, being so far removed and safely ensconced in your London manse, but they are baseless. I can you assure that I am more than ever in the communion of the true English Church. I wonder, dearest one, if you can attest to the same? Our party's may be different, but *my* devotion is undimmed.

I have made arrangements for travel to Antwerp and then onto The Hague and Amsterdam, where I will see to your affairs. By the time this reaches you I should already be there, and I will send further. This I do for you out of love and respect, but I thank you most earnestly for the funds and line of credit for me to draw upon. I am able to carry letters from many in the Queen's court. 'Tis but a small task but may alleviate their concerns. So many noble hearts are forced into degradation; they pawn their plate and jewels to maintain themselves in this foreign land. Even the highest in rank and the gentlest of character are afflicted with the baseness of poverty. I am, by your grace, spared such an indignity. I will travel onto Hamburg in the company of virtuous and gentle servants of the Queen. A task I also undertake out of love and respect.

No, I do not intend to marry the first Papist to batter his eyes at me, nor am I so fool as to mistake seduction for devotion or lust for love. It seems, with my beloved siblings at the least, I am ever the youngest despite having travelled the furthest!

I am fain to recount one incident of note at court that is of interest, regarding the Queen's Dwarf Hudson. Will Croft's brother, recently arrived from England, took Lord Minimus to task over his impudence. He mocked the dwarf and knocked off his hat. When Hudson called him out, Croft laughingly agreed to the duel. Mr Croft treated the whole event as a jape, but he was to be dismayed. Croft armed himself with a squirt intending to give the dwarf a soaking. He declared that *'no midget could ride as well as he'* and that *'Hudson would perhaps drown in the squirt's puddle.'*

He reckoned not with Hudson's horsemanship. The Dwarf kept his seat better than many a taller man, and Croft's splash went wide of the mark. Hudson then took out his own pistol and shot Croft right between the eyes. Mr Croft fell stone dead and Mr Hudson is in the custody of the French King's officers. Her Majesty has pleaded for clemency from Cardinal Mazarin, and it is believed the dwarf will be exiled.

This is all because of the war.

I will write more when I have settled your affairs in Holland, and before I travel onto Hamburg. As always, sweet one, I hold you in the highest esteem, respect, and love.

Anne.

Paris, October 22nd, 1644.[2]

---

[2]The duel between Hudson and Croft caused a minor scandal in the court in exile. William Croft, the Queen's Master of Horse and commander of her Lifeguard, was understandably furious at his brother's death and demanded justice. Hudson was soon forced to leave France, but he was captured by Barbary pirates and taken into

slavery for over twenty years. Hudson's release from captivity in North Africa coincided with Blandford Candy's service in Tangier with his cousin Samuel Luke Junior. Whilst there are documents in the archive related to Blandford's time in the colony, but they are still awaiting restoration and transcription.

4. The Monkey House: Amsterdam, October 1644.

If Egypt's ancient goddess deigned to favour me,
As long ago she granted Iphis' desperate plea,
Then – England notwithstanding – I'd have a weapon made,
And 'Knight of this New Garter' would be my accolade.
(Catharina Questiers: To Miss Cornelia van der Veer)

Hundreds of merchantmen could be seen from the deck of the Walter Raleigh. From great galleons whose wooden walls towered over our tub, down to little fishing skiffs the size of a rowboat. Cranes on the wooden wharves lifted great bales from the holds, and carts and mules whisked the goods off to storehouses and shops in the city.

A longboat came out to meet us, pulled by twelve men and with officials on board. Lines were cast to tug us into a mooring, and the customs officer came aboard. The man knew Minstrel Hugo (I was increasingly suspicious of that fellow) and was surprisingly easy to deal with. Officials are most normally corrupt prick-weasels after a bribe. This one checked my papers, questioned me on my business in the port and asked about my servants. All of which I answered easily enough and relatively honestly. With my commission from the Office of Ordnance to hand I was granted some status. When all was said and done, the customs officer doffed his cap.

'Welcome to Amsterdam, Captain Candy.'

Jakes told me that he would be staying in the port for a few days, if I needed to send messages back to London in that time. His load had to be checked and unloaded before he could pick up a return cargo. He pitched us up on the narrow wharves with our luggage.

'Where are you staying?' asked Hugo. 'It will not take me long to find a new instrument.'

I had not considered that question.

'I know not, as yet,' I said. 'We are new to the port.'

Hugo sighed disconsolately. 'Do any of you speak Dutch?'

'I speak French,' I said, and seeing his frown. 'Some Spanish, Latin, a little Italian.'

'No, is the short answer.' He shrugged. 'I know of a place. Come with me and start no more brawls.'

John and Figgis were told to bring my chest, and I followed the miserable musician into the city. Amsterdam was a building site. The great canals had already been built around the old town. A spread of stone and brick houses rose in newly cleared land. The eastern half of the city was still mostly gardens and some warehouses, but as the population increased the people would fill the space. Spreading from the west with new homes; all well designed and constructed. It was clean, and organised, the people friendly and welcoming, and businesses flourishing. It was what London could be, had we English but the wit to plan things instead of merely muddling through. That made me ill-disposed to the foreign city out of sheer patriotic bloody-mindedness.

Hugo led us to a flea-ridden monkey infested rat-hole, not far from the ships. It was full of drunken sailors but had spare rooms and was cheap if not clean.

''Tis a tad, shall we say, insalubrious?' I said.

'Given you have to pay for my new guitarro, can you afford better?'

'Twas a very good point. Hugo's new gittern would cost me nearly half the coin I had secreted away.

The innkeeper was a big man; the type who would brook no insolence from the drunks. He spoke some broken English and despite the fleas, monkeys, and drunks, he kept an orderly house. The screeching animals had been acquired from whip-jacks unable to pay their bills, so he told me, and then pointed to John.

'Will you leave the mulatto to pay your bill?'

'I am an Englishman, sir,' said John, offended. 'I was born in England and my father was an Englishman.'

The innkeeper just laughed as if he had made a great joke (mayhap he had but 'twas at John's expense) and showed us up to our room. A large well sprung bed and two cots for the servants. He sent for a girl to make up a fire in our room as Figgis and John brought the trunk up. The musician left us, promising to return that night with news of his new instrument.

*

Hugo turned the gittern over in his hands and stroked the long slender neck. The instrument was beautiful: the face a deep reddish brown colour with swirling patterns of grain exposed, varnished, and polished. The mouth and body were inlaid with delicate ebony and ivory roses. Five pairs of sheep's gut strings ran the length of the neck, fixed with more ivory pegs and frets. The back and sides were black mahogany, patterned with entwined ivory thorns running up the neck. I would not be able to find the like in London, of that I was certain.

The musician had wasted no time locating the instrument. He returned only hours after depositing us at the Monkey House, and dragged me to a small dark cellar shop in the old city. The vendor was a Frenchman; a Huguenot émigré, by all accounts.

'C'est magnifique,' said Hugo to the vendor.

''Tis expensive,' said I.

'It is made from Brazilian rosewood and mahogany,' said the vendor. 'Crafted by Sellas in Venice; it is unique, a work of art.'[3]

'Your other one came from Spain,' I said.

'The other one was made by Morisco craftsmen in Granada a century ago,' said Hugo. 'I could not find a replacement for that even in Amsterdam, and even if I could you could not afford it.'

'But twelve pounds...'

'I also lost my fee after you caused the brawl,' he pointed out.

'You playing caused the brawl.'

Hugo ignored my protests and began to play a slow song, plucking out the melody with his calloused fingers; he picked up the tempo, playing faster and faster, hands becoming a blur as they moved, fashioning a beautiful noise as sweet as any songbird. He stopped mid-tune.

'The tone is not as good. Perhaps it will mellow over time, but 'twill do.'

'A pound less? Because of the tone,' I said, hopefully.

The vendor shook his head. 'I will give you the case for free.'

'Damned right, you will!'

Grudgingly, I handed over the full fee; the seller looked delighted at his extortion. I was left with less than six pounds in mixed coin

---

[3] Matteo Sellas (c1580 - 1661) was a German musical instrument maker renowned in the Seventeenth Century. Originally apprenticed in Bologna he set up shop in Venice in 1630, and produced instruments made from rosewood, ebony, and inlaid with jewels and ivory. There is a stunning example of one of his Baroque guitars in the New York Metropolitan Museum of Art , and the Paris Museum of Music has a large collection of his instruments.

(Dutch and English), some in my purse; some in my trunk. Together with Hugo, I walked back to the Monkey House. Our arrival was greeted by cheers from the patrons and demands for the musician to play.

The minstrel sat on a short stool and took out his new gittern. He began to play a soft wistful romance, hushing the crowd as they listened enraptured. Soon he was lost in the music, oblivious to the audience as in Wapping. He picked up a stylus, striking all the strings and ringing out a loud deep tone, and then began a fast dance. The crowd in this tavern adored him, stamping and clapping a beat as sailors and whores danced. He played sea songs and folk strains, tunes that were common enough to all. It was a repertoire that would have averted the brawl in Wapping. Duggan had been in the right, Hugo had baited the sailors.

'Had you played like that in Wapping there would have been no fight,' I told him when he took a drink.

'That is true, but the sailors were coarse, and it gave me the chance to meet you.'

'Meet me?'

'Who would not wish to meet Captain Blandford 'Sugar' Candy, the Golden Scout?'

'You are a Dutch spy?'

'Spy is such a dirty word, and I would be a poor one to just give myself away. I am a musician; I travel from place to place and play my songs. Today it is a dirty little monkey-infested firetrap on the Amsterdam waterfront, next week it may be a great lord's manse, or theatre in Paris, or Hamburg. People tell me the news wherever I go, and there are those here who will pay richly for such information. Word of you was worth a pretty penny and the free passage home a bonus.'

'You have already informed the authorities?'

'They already knew, Captain, the moment you arrived and showed your papers, remember? Had you travelled under a false name the information would have been worth more, but I received a fair fee from my clients.'

The deception annoyed me, and the fact I had spent twelve pounds on the man's guitarro whilst he took thirty pieces of silver behind my back. It was infuriating but I had done nothing wrong, and my purpose on disembarking had been clearly stated. The question for me was whether Beeston would have been forewarned of our arrival. We would find that out on the morrow, until then I could enjoy myself.

Hugo began to play again, to the crowd's delight. I ordered some Spanish wine and winked at the maid who brought it. She blushed and hurried back to the bar. John had already found his paramour for the evening, or at least he was busy trying to charm a pretty young girl. I expected that it would be a transactional arrangement in such an establishment. I scratched my top lip (the whiskers were somewhat thicker) and poured myself another cup of sack.

'I told ye, Master Blandford, heat up the bollucks and it'll grow.'

'Thou art a simpleton, Figgis.'

He sat down at the table and ordered an ale.

'Ye thinks me a simpleton, Master Blandford, but mayhap ye flatters me. The factor's house, this Mr Beeston, be just a short walk from here.'

'Where did you hear that snippet?'

'The boy found out, from his girl.' He nodded to John and the maid. 'They be a very blunt-spoken people these Dutchmen... When you understands what they say.'

'Damned rude, I call it. Polite manners cost nought.'

'What you call polite manners they calls insincerity, Master Blandford.'

'We have been here less than a day, Figgis, but you have already deduced the Amsterdamer's character?'

'As I said, you thinks me a simpleton but mayhap ye flatter me.'

I frowned.

'You do realise that phrase actually means you are simpler than a simpleton?'

'Do it?' He looked at me in surprise. 'Then the devil take me for simpler than a simpleton, Master.'

Arguing with an idiot is like being a spit-dog in a wheel – round and round you run, never getting anywhere. I turned back to Hugo and his music, and listened to a virtuoso musician perform for the coarse audience. By the end of the night, I was deep-cut and taken up with a blonde trull that warmed my bed and stole my small purse. I was not enjoying Amsterdam.

For the much honoured William Lenthall, Esquire, Speaker of the Commons.

We gave you an account in our last letter of our proceedings in the West, and our return to Basingstoke. There we met with his

Excellency[4] and the Lord Manchester's forces. A happy union which the Lord hath blessed.

We marched to Thatcham, quartering beyond the town, and that evening we disputed some hills for our security, which we gained. The next morning (being Saturday) we drew up our Army within view of Newbury. The King's Army stood between two rivers blocking our passage to the town. They were strongly guarded and fortified, and the difficulty of assaulting them there was easily perceived.

We understood that the King soon expected supplies from Prince Rupert, and that two brigades of his horse were gone to Banbury, so we thought it not fit to delay. We resolved to divide our Army and to fall upon the King from two ways.

That night, His Excellency's Foot and all our horse marched out about 4 miles. The next morning (being the Lord's Day) the rest of us advanced early, and by two in the afternoon we were within a mile and a half of the town and arrayed upon a large heath. We fell into the lands and hedges and came upon the enemy. They blocked up our way with a strong breastwork and fine pieces of cannon, and for their better advantage they were under the cover of Donnington Castle. Their best cannon being sited there.

At our approach, the enemy played hard upon us. The hedges hindered our Horse very much, and their cannon made our ground very hot. There was no way left but to fall on without delay. His Excellency's Foot (both officers and soldiers) went on undauntedly, and never did men fight better. Your Horse advanced with the Foot; the enemy's Horse sallied out and fell upon us, but we beat them back. We took the Earl of Cleveland, his Lieutenant Colonel, and two of their standards.

We fell in with the Enemy into their works, putting their whole Army into an extreme confusion. The enemy would have been totally routed, but for their reserves in the hedges and breastworks which held us long in dispute. They prevented our prosecution until nightfall. It not being possible to distinguish friends from enemies in the darkness, we gave off shooting and waited for the morning.

In the night, the Royalists drew off to the castle with carriages and cannon. We expected to find their Foot and Horse upon the castle hill next day, but we quickly found that their baggage was secured with the cannon at the castle, and that their soldiers were shifting for

---

[4]The Earl of Essex

themselves in the dark. Some informed us they went Wantage way to Oxford, others to Wallingford, others Hungerford, and others Winchester.

The greatest enemy party fled to Wallingford, and we followed with as much speed as our Horse could march. The less able Foot marched very hard, the horsemen carrying their arms, and we gained Wallingford early the following morning.

The King had ridden away from the battle half an hour after sunset, entering Oxford early next morning. Some say about one hundred and fifty of his best horse attended him.

Whilst we battled, the Earl of Manchester went on for his assault, but it proved very difficult, we hear great commendations of the gallantry of his Foot. The enemy's works were well fortified, and ours went on with resolution, but the enemy killed some brave officers and soldiers. The City Regiments did well. Of those killed dead on both sides, the number is uncertain. Some of your officers and soldiers are wounded, but not very many.

We desire to give God the glory. He was our God at Cheriton in the spring, and now at Newbury in the fall. We pray this is a great step to the conclusion of the Kingdom's misery. We entreat that as God hath heard our prayers, so we may all return him our thanks.

We are now at Newbury and will improve this mercy to our utmost. The season of the year is unfit for constant abiding in the field. The patience and suffering of our soldiers is beyond expression, we presume your thoughts are upon them. Let us but receive your commands and we will obey as becomes.

Your faithful servant,

William Waller. Newbury, 28th of October, 1644.[5]

---

[5]The Second battle of Newbury (27th Oct 1644) was as indecisive as the first. Despite a numerical advantage of nearly two to one over the Royalists, the Parliamentary forces were unable to secure a victory, despite William Waller's claim at the end of the letter. The decision was taken to assault from two directions in order to overwhelm the King's force that were arrayed in strong defences. A failure to co-ordinate the attack effectively, and lethargy in pressing any advantage by the Earl of Manchester's assault, compounded by

allowing the King's troops to escape was a devastating blow to Parliament's commanders. Waller's letter does not mention the acrimonious command meeting on the night after the battle, where Cromwell accused the Earl of Manchester of deliberately failing to attack. An inquiry into the disaster was set up by Parliament to look into the defeat, and consider the Self Denying Ordnance (to exclude politicians from military command) and the suggestion from Waller earlier in the year for a new independent army that could act nationally rather than be tied to local associations. The King meanwhile gathered reinforcements and returned to Donnington castle, rescuing his baggage and artillery train before returning to Oxford for the winter. The Parliamentary forces were so riven with disagreements in their High Command they could merely watch on.

5. Mr Beeston: Amsterdam, October 1645.

Mark but this flea, and mark in this,
How little that which thou deniest me is;
It sucked me first, and now sucks thee,
And in this flea our two bloods mingled be.
(John Donne, *The Flea*)

The problem with a bed in an inn is that you share it with every former occupant and their lice. There were bites all down my legs and around the ankles. I bent over, dementedly scratched at the red pocks through my stockings, and then hurried after John.

'Damn fleas are enough to drive a man into bedlam,' I told him.

Beeston's lodgings were in a side street off from the Damrak, on the east side. We had walked straight down from the Monkey House. Even the narrow streets put London to shame, easily wide enough for two carts to pass each other. The upper stories of the tall houses jutted out with each level, but they did not lean and make dark tunnels of the narrow lanes. Even worse, the shopkeepers, traders, and hawkers were all smiling and Goedemorgening, and greeting all who passed. Try that on Borough High Street and you're liable to get robbed and bashed. I missed London. Amsterdam was too sober, too respectable, and too welcoming.

'I think this is the place, sir.'

A nondescript brick house in a nondescript cobbled street. I rapped on the door and stood back waiting for a response. Moments later it swung back to reveal an old woman dressed in brown wool. She smiled with false wooden pegs.

'Goedemorgen?' she said.

'Twas at this point the realisation that I spoke no Dutch came crashing in once again. I was about to begin speaking loudly and slowly in English (throwing in a few wild gesticulations) and expecting the poor local woman to understand. My man butted in with a sentence that sounded like garbled up German.

'Leeft Septimus Hutchinson hier?'

The old woman nodded and gestured for us to follow her into the narrow building. She turned and shuffled off inside.

'Where did you learn that?' I said to John as we followed her.

'Evy taught me.'

'Who the devil is Evy?'

'The maid from the Monkey House. I did introduce you.'

I grunted; the boy was enjoying himself far more than I on this little foreign adventure. The crone led us up some steep stairs to Beeston's chambers on the second floor. She did not bother to knock, merely pushing the door open. The woman frowned and said something in Dutch to us. John nodded.

'She says he is drunk.'

A fetid smell of sour wine hanged in the air. Beeston lay sprawled face-down on a dirty bed with stained clothes and stinking sheets. There were wine bottles around the room, all empty. I kicked the senseless actor a few times until he groaned and rolled onto his back. He looked terrible: no makeup, red nose and flushed spider-veined cheeks (a sure sign of drunkenness). His dark hair was greasy and lank, and green snot dribbled drying from his snoring nose. A broad, tall man, but he looked shrunken.

'Awake you drunken devil-spawn histrionic.'

John disappeared with the woman as I tried to slap Beeston into sensibility, all to little avail (other than the personal satisfaction of beating the blaggard). The boy returned carrying a pail of water. I stood back as he tipped it over Beeston's head and left for another. That finally brought some consciousness from the actor. He sat up spluttering and coughing, but still barely sensible. The boy came back and dumped another bucket on his head.

'Enough,' cried Beeston.

'Sir?' said John.

'Best to be sure.'

The boy nodded and left for another bucket. I turned back to Beeston.

'Are you some vision from hell come to taunt me?' he said, and fell back on the sopping bed, groaned and covered his eyes with his arm. John returned and poured a third pail of water onto the prone actor. Beeston sat bolt upright.

'I am awake, Sugar; call off your damned bucket-boy!'

'You were correct, sir: third one is always the key.'

It still took time for Beeston to come fully to his senses. I slapped him once or twice more and held nought back, and John threatened another bucket of water. Eventually, Beeston sat on the edge of his stinking bed, shivering and wet, but with his wits somewhat restored. The old woman had watched our bullying with a wide smile, now started to castigate Beeston. She began beating him around the head with her fists and shouting at him in Dutch.

'The woman says he owes her money,' said John.

'You spent too much time talking to that wench, my lad,' I said. 'And not enough time bedding her. I hope she did not charge you for the linguistic lessons?'

'She said she liked my tongue, sir.' He smirked at me.

I handed the old woman a silver coin to cover Beeston's debts and to silence her caterwauling. She swiftly buried the coin in her smock and put her hand out for another. I sighed and put another silver shilling in her palm, which seemed to satisfy her. She turned and shuffled out, leaving us alone with the actor.

'What are you doing here, William?' I asked him

'What are you doing here, Sugar?'

'Tormenting you, and if you do not answer I swear I shall cut off your fingers.' I tried to look fearsome.

Beeston burst out laughing.

'Oh, Sugar, you are too damned pretty to be threatening, even with that itty-bitty scar. I did hear that Hurry cut your face up.'

My hand went up to cover my mouth automatically, and Beeston laughed at me again.

'Vain, vain, vain. The moustache covers it not, you realise?'

'I may be vain,' I said. 'But I still want an answer.'

'Darnelly employed me to watch on the Royalists in Amsterdam,' Beeston said. 'I have been sending reports back for the last five months, as well as arranging shipments of weapons for him.'

'And taking some coin off the top?

'Of course I take some coin off the top. Everybody takes some coin off the top. Darnelly was pleased enough with my work, but I have heard nothing this month past. I have papers to send to him but decided to wait until he paid his dues.'

'Darnelly is dead,' I told him. 'Last month; it was sudden.'

'Ah, that explains why I have no funds.'

'You never have any funds. What of this information on the weapons that you have been accumulating?'

'Tis Davenant's plot.'

'Davenant? The poet?'

Sir William Davenant was a pox-ridden cavalier poet and gun smuggler. He was also embroiled with the Theatre Company, along with Beeston and his stepmother, and my sister Elizabeth. I knew that there was bad blood between the actor and the poet that went back before the war. Davenant had been given the company to run and Beeston imprisoned, but the syphilitic poet had in turn been accused of treason and fled to the continent.

'So what be this plot of Davenant's about?'

Beeston told me that the poet had arrived in Amsterdam during the summer and started gathering funds and weapons. He had arranged for the ships from Amsterdam to deliver weapons and powder from their cargoes on the Norfolk coast. The weapons were then hidden on the Le Strange estate in Hunstanton in readiness for an uprising.

'Davenant and Le Strange plan a rebellion in King's Lynn soon enough,' Beeston said as he finished the tale. He reached under his bed, pulled out a tattered box full of papers and handed some of them to me: delivery dockets and a list of weapons stored in Hunstanton.

'And what be your part in this plot? I can scarce believe you are some innocent observer.'

'Darnelly pays better than Davenant.'

'Darnelly is dead,' I reminded him

He ignored that and carried on. 'I have been making note of all the King's Lynn shipments, and what was being taken. You have that there.' He nodded to the papers. 'I can get the names of Le Strange's conspirators in Norfolk,' he said. 'Meet me tomorrow night at the Schouwburg of Van Campen, and I will have it all for you.'[6]

'Why the Schouwburg?'

'I have something to *show* you.' He smirked at his pun.

'What?' Beeston would be one of the last people I would trust with my security.

'You will see; it could be to both our benefit.'

'Why should I trust you, William?'

He looked me straight in the eye and answered. 'I want to go home, Sugar. I miss London. I am sick of herring; they eat it with

---

[6]The Schouwburg of Van Campen was the first purpose built theatre in Amsterdam, built in 1637 by the Dutch architect Jacob Van Campen. The theatre was based on the surviving Teatro Olimpico in Vincenza in Italy. It was replaced in the 1660s with a larger venue, but the original gates to the Schouwburg remain at Keizersgracht 384.

everything, pickled and by the bucket load. I'm sick of canals; sick of not hearing my own tongue around me. I just want to go home.'

He looked most forlornly at the floorboards as if he were about to burst into tears.

The problem with William Beeston was that a more convincing liar I cannot imagine. He was born on the stage and a master of dissembling and deceit. Despite my reservations, we arranged to meet the following night at the Schouwburg. I tucked the incriminating papers away in my doublet and walked with John back to the Monkey House. There was a plan forming that would neuter Beeston's turncoat devilry.

Once we arrived back at the inn, I grabbed Figgis and explained my design to him. He would take Beeston's papers, and a note I wrote for Uncle Samuel in code explaining what we had discovered. Beeston may be able to get the list of the conspirators, but I was convinced that Uncle Samuel had enough wit and informers to foil the Le Strange plot without it. I deposited Figgis at the Walter Raleigh with Captain Jakes and his crew. If Beeston betrayed me (and I was passing certain he would try in some way), Figgis was to take the documents and letter back to my uncle. Jakes would take the first tide back to London. When all my plans were laid and set, I sat back, ordered some wine, and listened to Hugo entertain the inn's patrons.

*

John and I took a boat to the theatre the next night, as arranged. The watermen, big and bulky fellows, swiftly ported us from the seafront into the rings of canals that encircle the old city. Rich new houses of stone and brick lined the sides of the waterways as we sped under ornate bridges, deep into the new city.

'This is certain to be a trap,' said John.

'There is always the faintest possibility that he will be honest.'

'This is Beeston, sir. He has never managed much honesty in the past.'

That was true enough; both of us knew Beeston of old; both of us took concealed pistols and wore our swords. If the theatre manager tried to play Judas, he would not find us accommodating the betrayal.

The boat pulled up at stone steps carved into the canal side. I paid them and we both climbed up to the street. A triple-arched Romanesque gateway with a cobbled courtyard beyond greeted us. The central gate gave out a hideous groan as I pushed it open and entered. John followed with his hand on his sword hilt. We were both wary, but the courtyard was as quiet as a cemetery. There was a crack of light behind the double doors. We both drew our swords; I pushed open the doors and stepped inside.

I was immediately struck by how grand and large the Schouwburg was inside compared to our own Phoenix. There was more space for seating, and the pit was three times the size. Two levels of opulent boxes for the richer patrons, with velvet curtains and upholstered seating, and another open seated gallery above. The main stage was raised six foot above the pit and covered with rich stucco decoration. It was wide with two hidden trapdoors to hell. The pillars and portico of the upper stage decorated with gilded gold leaf and paintings. Above us, the ceiling was painted in the image of a night sky, with candles hoisted up like stars in the firmament. You could pick out the constellations in the tiny flames. Standing in the centre of the stage, illuminated by the candlelight, was Mr William Beeston.

'It is enough to make you jealous, is it not?' said Beeston. 'If the Phoenix were like this we would make a fortune.' He spoke quietly but his words carried around the open space.

'Indeed we could, 'I said. 'If it were not for the obvious problem.'

'Problem?' said Beeston.

'What was it again, John?'

'The playhouses are closed and all performances are forbidden, sir.'

'That's correct, John,' I said, with all my sarcasm directed at the actor.

'The war cannot go on forever,' said Beeston. 'And land is cheap now; we could buy some and begin building in preparation.'

'With whose money?'

'Your sister has more than enough coin,' said Beeston. 'She could invest, she invested before.'

And that was the nub: Beeston hoped for my sister to build a brand new theatre on Drury Lane as big as this Dutch behemoth. I told him, in no uncertain terms, that if he wanted to return to London best he forget this foolishness, and hand over the names of the King's Lynn conspirators.

'I have something even better for you, then,' said Beeston. 'A gift...'

I heard a noise above in the galleries, and behind us two ruffians armed with cudgels rose out of the shadows to attack. We turned to face off against the bashers. Mine was a stout fellow with a blue cap. He swung the cudgel at my blade, trying to smash it out of my hand. I stepped back and to the side to avoid the blow, and cut at his wrist but missed. The basher thrust the end of his cudgel at my face, and I stepped back again. This one was no fool. I made to stab at his throat, but before I could move his mouth drooped open in surprise. We both looked down at the blade emerging from his stomach. The basher slumped to the floor dying. John had despatched his own enemy and mine in moments. I was more than shocked. The boy had been swinging a sword for barely four months and me two years, but he was already the superior blade.

'You really should learn to use that weapon,' he said. 'Sir Samuel showed me some.'

I sniffed. My uncle had tried to instruct me in swordplay.

We turned back to Beeston on the stage. The manager had a pistol to hand, pointing the muzzle at us. In the upper stage behind him, two new figures had appeared: a slender man in a blue suit wearing a scarf across his face, and a stocky bald man in brown wool who pointed a carbine at us. I dropped my blade and raised my arms in surrender; my page did the same.

'I told you, Hodgson, we have captured the traitors,' said the masked man in an Oxford accent. 'And you thought the plan would go awry.'

The voices easily carried down to us in the pit. Beeston was in the right, the building was fabulously constructed.

'They did kill the bashers, Master.'

'A minor detail.'

The bald man grunted but kept his carbine aimed at me. I was about to begin a soliloquy whilst I thought desperately of an escape, but before I could say ought the double doors to the theatre were thrown open.

'Halt! Halt! You are all under arrest.' A thick foreign accent.

Armed men in sky-blue uniform coats, some carrying torches, marched into the theatre. Others had halberds and muskets to hand and there was a richly dressed officer at the front.

'You are all under arrest,' he said again.

'On what charge?' I asked.

Always ensure that you know why you are being arrested before they cart you off to the compter. They are supposed to tell you, but I find officers of the state are oft unrevealing types.

'Trespass, bearing illegal weapons, a breach of the peace and espionage,' said the officer.

''Tis a reasonable summation,' I said, and handed over my sword and pistols.

John was similarly disarmed and our hands bound. Beeston and his conspirators were held by the other Dutch guardsmen. They held us together in a group and led us out of the theatre into the cobbled courtyard. The guards bustling us across the street to the canal where covered barges waited with more soldiers.

Close up, I saw that the man wore his silk mask for a reason: he had the pox. I could smell the rotting flesh from his nose.

'Sir William d'Avenant at your service,' he said, insisting on a faux French air. 'We would bow, however, we are restrained.' He turned to his bald companion. 'It seems the plan has gone awry, Hodgson. Yet I can hardly be blamed for the attention of the authorities. I am sure I shall be released soon.'

'Yes, Master,' said Hodgson.

That was the first time I met Davenant. I thought him pompous, grandiose, and unthinking. Puffed up and convinced of his genius. I grew to know him well over the next twenty years and count him somewhat of a companion, but I never changed my opinion. Oh, he was clever enough and could craft a decent enough ditty if he put his mind to it. Yet, he could never foresee the obvious consequences of his actions, and would never believe you if you tried to explain. He was also a crooked swindler and stole a fortune from me.

John nudged me as we were loaded onto the boats. 'Did you see him with the guards, sir?'

'Did I see whom?' I had noticed none.

'The Dutch minstrel.'

Hugo was clearly some sort of Dutch agent whatever his claims to the contrary. At least I had planned for a betrayal, forewarned is forearmed. Beeston's information about the Le Strange rising in King's Lynn would be in London in a few days (Hugo did not know about that). I smiled grimly as hoods were thrown over our faces, casting us into darkness, and the boats pushed off into the night.

Cross Deep, Twickenham 1720.

Since Death's a Buccaneer and the World will Rob
As well of Wits as the dull common Mob,
Though not much learned, I have Philosophy,
Enough to teach me 'tis in vain to Cry.
(Thomas Shadwell, *The Stockjobbers: A Comedy*)

I talked for hours with the Duchess, dredging every detail from my memory. My back ached in agony being perched upon the short stool, but I grimly carried on with the retelling. It was getting late, shadows were lengthening; a footman lit lamps and candles. It must be past four in the afternoon, I thought. She has to send me home soon, and I have given her nothing of value. Finally, the Duchess held up a hand.

'Have you read Galland's One Thousand and One Nights, Sir Blandford?'

Of course, I have read it; anyone with any claim to wit has read it.

'No, Duchess?'

Yes, yes, I am a liar; there is no need to dwell upon it.

The Duchess sighed. 'Is this going to be a long story?'

She sees only my lined face, bald pate, and creaking body. She forgets my vanity, she thinks my faculties dimmed; she sees me as no threat. Whatever she wants, it is my nephew that is the nub. I warned him; I damn well warned him.

'A story is only as long as it takes, Duchess.'

'You have not even mentioned Princess Sophia.'

'I am setting the scene, Duchess.'

She reached over to the slender French table next to her chair and picked up a silver bell. It gave out a dainty tinkle as she waved it about. A flunkey appeared in an instant.

'Have some cold cuts and bread brought for us, and my drink.' She looked at me perched on the stool. 'Bring a chair for Sir Blandford, and some wine and brandy.'

That was a small mercy. Why is she not summoning the carriageman to take me home to Twickenham?

She turned back to me. 'You will stay the night, Sir Blandford. Rooms are made ready for you.'

41

'I would not wish to impose, Duchess.'

'It is not an imposition. Please continue, Scheherazade.'

Sarcastic viper.

The footman brought a chair for me before I could carry on with my tale.

'Thank the Lord,' I said. 'My arsehole be as painful as a bishop's favourite choirboy's.'

She clapped her hands together in delight and gave a deep throaty chuckle.

'Oh, Sir Blandford, I had forgotten what a crabbed pettish fellow you are.'

A maid brought a tray of cold meats, soft white bread and a crock of butter. The Duchess took a wine syllabub sweetened with cream and nutmeg, and sat back in her chair studying me. I made a great show of stuffing my face with food and pouring out sack and brandy. She said nothing as I gluttoned.

Some people are born wrong. They understand not true love or passion, there is no real connection with others. They use you then discard you like an old toy in favour of the newest glitter. The Duchess of Marlborough is such; Lucy Hay was another. Both could make a man feel like he were a god with their glorious attentions, then crush him with disdain and silence on a whim. I have seen it happen: strong men brought to their quivering knees by cycles of flattery and cold fury. It has happened to me. 'Tis not love nor friendship; it be the hunter stalking their prey. Oh, take me not for a misogynist; my gender is no better, we are worse. My brother James was a glaring example of the type. Man destroys with violence and cruel words; how many wives do you see broken by their husband?

What has always surprised me of such hunters, is how weak they actually are; vulnerable and driven by fear, terrified each and every one. No matter how jewelled and golden a facade they present, no matter their success or intellect, martial prowess or beauty, they are always broken inside. It makes them no less deadly. They always want something.

'Now,' I said when I could eat no more. 'Where were we?'

She leaned forward. 'I wish to hear of Princess Sophia.'

'Ah, yes, Princess Sophia.'

6. Princess Sophia: The Hague, November 1644.

The gates of hell are open night and day,
Smooth the descent, and easy is the way,
But to return, and view the cheerful skies,
In this the task and mighty labour lies.
(Virgil, *The Aeneid*)

The five of us in the cell were not happy companions. Beeston suffered the most, such was his need for wine: sweating, and shaking, unable to sleep, and every word Davenant spoke seemed to grate upon him. John and Hodgson were mostly silent. I had decided that Hodgson was a melancholic sort; he seemed resigned to his fate and mostly desperate for tobacco. His master was an irritant. The prison was clean enough, however; a thick wooden door bolted from the outside with a hatch for guards to look in, and plain whitewashed stone walls. They had taken our boots, but I have seen worse cells in my lifetime...

'Will you, for the love of all that is holy, stop telling us about all the different prison cells you have seen,' said Beeston. 'We have all seen worse prisons.'

'Actually, we have not,' said Davenant. 'Sir William d'Avenant does not get arrested and imprisoned of a habit. He has more wit than that.' The poet insisted upon the faux French twang to his name.

'Do you know how pompous talking about yourself in the third person sounds?' snipped Beeston. 'You are not in a royal court now.'

'Gentlemen,' I said. 'Bickering amongst ourselves is as futile as fishing turds from the Fleet.'

Everyone grunted and there was silence for a short while.

'Perhaps this is a time to talk about my theatre,' said Davenant.

'*My* theatre!' Beeston and I chorused together, which raised a scowl from the poet.

'As I see it,' said John. ''Tis Mistress Elizabeth's land; Mr Beeston's stepmother owns the building, and there is no active company to speak of for either of you to manage.'

'Sneak,' muttered Beeston.

'Mr Beeston has a warrant for his arrest in London,' the boy continued. 'And you, Sir William, have a charge of High Treason against you.' John gave a broad smile at the poet. 'There is also still the prohibition against acting and actors.'

'Tell your Barbary not to converse with us, Candy. We do not like his kind.'[7]

'I am an Englishman, Sir William. I was born in Wapping.'

Davenant turned away from John, who shrugged his shoulders and made a face at the poet's back. Silence fell on the room again.

We had been like this for nigh on two weeks: crammed in a tiny cell with only one bucket for our piss and shit, and only straw pallets on the floor for bedding. There was barely room to stretch my legs, and we all stank. A dim light shone from a small barred window high up, too high to reach, and cold blasts of air would make us shiver. Everyone's tempers had grown short with the incarceration, but the guards who brought us food and water each day said little. I was worried that we had been forgotten about. It was a tad similar to York the previous summer...

'I care not about your prison in York, or Ely, or Wood Street or Hell itself!' shouted Beeston.

'I need to take a smoke,' said Hodgson.

He was the only one of us who took tobacco out of insistent habit, and watching him as he missed the vice was reason enough for me to

---

[7]Concepts of racial superiority were very much in their infancy in the mid Seventeenth Century. The widespread involvement of British shipping in the transatlantic slave trade had not begun in earnest, and James I even pointed out how ridiculous it was to judge a man's intellect based on the colour of his skin (judging a man, even a king, on his belief in witchcraft is a different matter). By the Eighteenth Century pseudo biological or biblical theories were expounded to excuse the enslavement of literally millions of sub-Saharan Africans, and the vast amounts of capital that flooded into England and powered the Industrial Revolution. William Davenant's well attested prejudice stemmed from his syphilitic state: he had contracted the disease from a mixed race prostitute in Covent Garden.

never desire it. The first two or three days he had actually pounded at the walls such was the grip the weed had upon him. That had passed, but now he said the same sad words nearly five or six times a day. He remained mostly silent the rest of the time, occasionally answering his master when Davenant started jabbering. Give me a bottle of sack instead, I decided, although Beeston's suffering was a salutary lesson in bousy moderation.

'I will be released soon,' said Davenant. 'I have influential friends in The Hague; they will not leave Sir William to rot.'

'Your nose is already rotted,' said Beeston.

Davenant turned away from the actor at his barb and fell silent once more.

I stood up and stepped over to the piss bucket, emptied my bladder, then sat back down on my pallet. Figgis must be in London, I had reasoned. He would have taken the information on the weapons hidden in Norfolk, and Davenant and Le Strange's plans for the uprising. I was absolutely certain that Uncle Samuel would have dealt with that quickly, and passing certain that Haslerig would have been satisfied enough with my mission. How long would it take them to send someone to rescue me? Davenant did not know yet of Figgis. I decided to keep that little surprise for the poxy poet.

'Opera is not acting anyway,' Davenant started up again. 'It is an Italian innovation; a drama sung. We could put on shows of music and spectacular together. There could be no objections to that.'

'His sister would object,' said Beeston. 'She objects to everything.'

'You still owe my sister two hundred pounds,' I pointed out to Beeston. 'Had she not paid off Haniel Boswell, he would have gutted you like a fish. Have you forgotten that?'

'Boswell is in no position to object,' said Davenant. 'He is dead, found poisoned in Whitehall.'

'How do you know this?' said John.

The poet ignored my man's valid question, turning his back on us once more.

'How do you know, Sir William?' I said. It was the only way we would get an answer.

He rolled back over on his pallet and looked to me. 'It was in the London journals. I get them delivered in Amsterdam four days after they are published in England.'

John looked overly concerned at that; somewhat of a surprise given he loathed Haniel Boswell. What had the boy been up to? If he had entangled us with the Gypt tribe once more through some nefarious criminal scheme, I swore to God I would give him a damned good thrashing.

'Opera would bring a better class of audience to the theatre,' said Davenant.

''Tis plays people want, not Italian warbling,' said Beeston.

'Philistine.'

'Gentlemen,' I said. 'May I remind you that we are incarcerated and far from London.'

'We have influential friends,' said Davenant. 'We will not be here much longer.'

It was not a collective we.

The next day the guards took Davenant and Hodgson away. If he was to be released, then he would soon discover that I had foiled his plans for rebellion. That gave me some comfort, but the poet grinned an I-told-you-so at us as he was led off. The prison door slammed shut, and then we were three.

*

The bolts were drawn back in the locks outside our cell; the door opened and a lamp shined in at us. I blinked at the light; four guards were at the door dressed in sky blue livery.

'Candy?'

'I am Candy,' I said.

They stood me up and took me out of the cell. A bag was swiftly thrown over my head plunging me back into darkness. I was led through corridors and up steps, on and on. We must have gone outside at one point, as the air grew colder, fresher, and there was wet gravel under my bare feet. Then more steps and down a corridor until they stood me still and whipped off the bag.

The brightly lit room stung my eyes. People were staring at me: Hugo the musician, and two other greybeards in rich fashion and bearing swords. Two more stood behind with satin cloaks and fur-lined hoods hiding their faces. They were smaller, petite; women or children.

One of them threw back her hood to reveal elfin features: a young girl, barely more than a child, dark hair crimped and pinned with silver. She was pretty, with a mischievous smile and twinkling blue eyes. A large blood red ruby in a gold clasp sat at her breast, with a teardrop pearl the size of a hen's egg. That was a jewel of royalty.

I bowed low as quickly and as gracefully as I could manage, and remained down with my face turned to the floor. One of the guards said something in Dutch or German to the girl, and then a female voice came in English.

''Tis him, Princess Sophia.'

I knew that voice.

''Tis my brother Blandford the, so ridiculously named, Golden Scout.' The last was said with a hint of Wiltshire disdain.

I smiled at the flagstones; my little sister Anne.

'Arise, Captain Candy,' Princess Sophia said to me in perfect English with no hint of an accent. The girl was one of the Winter Queen's brood. I had fought against her brothers... That is never a good way to start a conversation.[8]

Anne stood behind the girl. She had thrown off her cloak and was richly dressed in green silks and satins. Our mother's pearl choker

---

[8]The Winter Queen was Elizabeth Stuart, daughter of James I and sister to King Charles I. She was known as the Winter Queen because of her husband's (Fredrick V Elector Palatine) involvement in the Thirty Years War. As Elector of the Palatine, he had taken the throne of Bohemia in 1619 sparking off the religious conflict that would tear Europe apart. His rule in Bohemia lasted only a winter before the couple were expelled by troops loyal to the Catholic Holy Roman Empire. They were quickly elevated to protestant heroes in the internecine religious struggles. Elizabeth was the mother of Prince Rupert of the Rhine and his younger brother Maurice who both took an active role in the Royalist war effort in the English Civil War. Her eldest surviving son Karl Ludwig, or Charles Louis, however offered tacit support to the Parliamentary cause. Her youngest child, Sophia, was born in 1630 and would become heir to the English throne after the convulsions of the Glorious Revolution and the extinction of the protestant Stuart line. Sophia predeceased Queen Anne by only a few weeks, and her son ascended to the throne in 1714 as King George I.

necklace was about her neck, and her golden hair fell in slender ringlets about her bare shoulders. Anne had always been the prettiest. She was also stupider than a stewed prune, and liable to turn my hoped-for rescue into a sudden sentence of death. She came forward and reached up at my face, at the livid scar.

'I like the moustache not, Blandford,' she said quietly. 'It looks as if a yellow caterpillar hath crawled beneath your nose and died, and there be more fluff on a peach than hair on your chin.'

''Tis witty for you; be you practising your lines, little sister?'

'What say you? I am not some dunderheaded child.'

'Spell dunderhead, Anne?'

'Coxcomb.' She turned to the little princess. 'Princess Sophia, whatever the London newsbooks tell, my brother is a feckless wastrel and unbearably arrogant. The stories are flights of fancy and lies; he be no Herakles.'

'But I can spell dunderhead.'[9]

Anne burst into tears, threw herself into my arms, grabbing hold of me and sobbing. She told me how worried she had been for me, how the war was dividing families, how she missed Elizabeth and England. I held my little sister and comforted her as if we were children. I stroked her golden hair, whispered to her that all would turn out as God willed; all would be well. She looked up at me, blue eyes shining through her tears, and stamped on my bare foot with the heel of her shoe.

'Ow! That damn well hurt.'

I had forgotten that she could weep upon a whim.

'That be for calling me stupid.' She tossed her head, poked her tongue out at me, and stood behind the princess again. 'You can trust him, Princess. In this matter at least.'

This war was breeding unseemly behaviour in young ladies of quality, I decided. I had not called her stupid, I had merely inferred it.

The princess stepped forward and looked me up and down.

'Can I trust you, Captain Candy?'

I paused before answering.

'In faith, Highness, I am a loyal officer of Parliament and I will not

---

[9]Whilst we are in pre-Dr Jonson days, the correct spelling of words and the great vowel shift was very much in vogue in the Seventeenth Century.

hinder that cause, even if it means I am back to the prison cell.'

Anne pursed her lips at that but remained silent.

'I do not ask you to do anything against your party,' said the princess. 'I have a delicate family matter that must be cared for. In that, you and your uncle may be of assistance, should you agree?'

'If it pleases you, Highness.'

Princess Sophia explained her design to me. Her eldest brother Karl Ludwig had recently travelled to London to court Parliament. I had read about it in the newsbooks and everyone knew he was angling for the crown himself. 'Twas a family squabble that had thrilled the journal writers with their gossip and scandal-mongering. Now, the princess told me that an assassin had been sent by the Holy Roman Emperor to dispose of Karl Ludwig. She wanted me to protect the prince and keep him safe from the assassin, with Uncle Samuel's help and assistance.

The international ramifications of this were not to be understated. The German war had dragged on all my life: Protestant against Catholic, mostly, with every state in Europe involved (one way or t'other and around about). Karl Ludwig's assassination could drive a wedge between the Protestant states, and perhaps even tip the Dutch Provinces into active war against the English Parliament.

'What do you know of this ravaillac?' I asked.

'Only his name,' said Hugo. 'Schwartzbar: the Black Bear.'

'And his reputation, which is fearsome,' said one of the greybeards.

'We will provide you with letters for your uncle and the leaders of your Parliament.' He paused. 'Whosoever that may currently be.'

I thought that an unnecessary jab given he wanted our assistance.

'Will you help me, Captain Candy?' asked the princess. 'Help me to save my brother? I promise you that I shall be eternally grateful, and offer the hand of friendship of my house.'

Well, I ask you, what would you have done in such a situation? A princess of the blood gives you a mission and offers you eternal gratitude? You would take it too. It could be dangerous, I reasoned, but the Black Bear did not want me dead. Of course, royal gratitude is one thing, but royal displeasure is something quite different. If I failed, I was certain to be in trouble. Nevertheless, I gave the princess my promise and kissed her hand. Beeston would return to London with me, as would the Dutch troubadour Hugo, and I would carry letters from Princess Sophia to Uncle Samuel. Once the decision was taken, I was not kept long. The princess left with her retainers and greybeards, and men were sent to retrieve John and

Beeston from the hole. I had but a short while to speak with my little sister.

'What do you here, Anne? Elizabeth told me you were in France.'

'I am here on an important mission...' She caught herself. 'I am not allowed to talk to you about that. Mistress Margaret says that I talk too much sometimes.'

'Mistress Margaret? This be Margaret Lucas, Charles Lucas' sister?'

'Oh, Blandford, I'm not going to tell you that; you be a Roundhead spy.' She giggled. ''Tis such a ridiculous notion. You, a Roundhead spy. You are more suited to court jester. I have papers for Elizabeth, for you to take to her.'

'Indeed?'

'They are written in unfathomable code so do not try to read them.'

'Would I do such a thing? I am not actually a spy, you realise. I am a captain of dragoons and scout-captain.' I declared my rank with some modicum of pride.

She giggled again and gave me a hug.

''Tis so good to see you alive, brother, even though I know you for a liar and dissembler. When I heard of James, I wept for days.' She touched my face again. 'The scar will fade.'

That raised more than a pang of guilt, I can tell you. Anne was not finished, however.

'I saw Henry before I left England in the summer. He knows about Kit or at least suspects. You should have a care.'

That was most certainly a concern.

'Do you think this war will be finished soon?'

'I hope so, Anne.' I said. 'Truly I do.' I held her tight.

The Parliament Scout: 10th November 1644.

A report was made of Colonel Hurry's desire to serve the Parliament. The House thought it better to let him travel to Scotland instead.

*

We have had the saddest news that came in a great while. To give you it in a sea-term – all our forces were *stranded* near Newbury. To relate the several discourses and reports, could not be contained in this sheet.

His Majesty, that he might deliver those dumb creatures, viz ammunition money, jewels, negotiations, etc, and having accommodated himself with what Oxford could afford (which was not powder enough to fight for three hours) went his way to

Donnington on Saturday morning and resolved to fight.

Our forces resolved to try one last bout before we went into winter quarters, but it seems we were not quick enough. His Majesty, having loaded all he desired, went away in the fair daylight with his carriages and sallied to Wallingford. Our unhappy oversight, it's to be feared, will hinder the free course of our propositions.

Some say the Lord General was not there – that's true, had he been we would not have let the enemy escape, so we dare swear.

Others say all the commanders in chief are godly men, which is not always a character of wisdom or valour, but if godliness and piety are the great eyesores, what then do we fight for?

Others say there was a plot; otherwise, the King would not have adventured against our great army with only 8000 men. Others that speak more divine and spiritually, say it was a just judgement upon us because we put confidence in the army of the flesh.

Oh, Poor England! Afflicted after all thy bloodshed, thou art in danger of this, wither to be as thou were most miserable, or to continue a war which is equivalent.[10]

---

[10]Charles actions a fortnight after the Second Battle of Newbury devastated the Roundhead leadership. The King waltzed into Donnington Castle, where he had left much of his baggage ordnance and powder after the battle. With the Roundhead leadership paralysed by internal squabbles after their failure two weeks before, the three armies of Parliament merely watched on as the King loaded up and carried off everything he could. The outcry that this failure caused would lead directly to the formation of the New Model Army, and the Self Denying Ordnance (SDO), that forced MPs to resign their military commissions. The SDO was organised by Henry Vane the Younger, one of the leaders of the War Party along with Cromwell and Oliver St John. It was initially thrown out by the Lords in December 1644, who realised it was an attack on their hereditary role as military commanders. An amended version of the SDO was then presented and passed by both Houses on April 3rd,

1645. Cromwell himself (with the radical London press over-spinning his achievements at Marston Moor to the fury of the Presbyterian Scots) was considered vital to the cause and exempted from resigning. He was not alone, there were four or five other exceptions made, including Blandford's uncle Sir Samuel Luke, who was considered too important in the short term to be allowed to resign. However, Luke, unlike Cromwell, was a Presbyterian and came increasingly under attack in his role as Governor of Newport Pagnell and Scoutmaster General. John Hurry had been present at the Second Newbury and involved in the battle, and his nephew had been killed during the fighting. However, Hurry's character and penchant for changing sides persuaded Parliament to send him back to Scotland to face Montrose. England had grown far too hot for the Scottish freebooter, a situation that cannot have been helped by his feud with Blandford. There is evidence in the State Papers that in September 1644 Parliament was going to allow Hurry to serve under William Waller, but after the duel, and general failure at Newbury, Hurry was deemed surplus to requirements.

7. The Elector Palatine: London, November 1645.

Those who have greatest cause for guilt and shame,
Are quickest to besmirch a neighbour's name.
When there's a chance for libel, they never miss it;
When something can be made to seem illicit.
(Molière, *Tartuffe*)

Westminster Hall thronged with people: booksellers and pamphleteers mixed with merchant company agents and food vendors. Members of the House of Commons rushed from committee to chamber. There were beggars at the gates, crippled soldiers and the like, petitioners from every county and town, clerks, secretaries and lawyers; all bustling about industriously. London is the beating heart of England, and the Palace of Westminster is the brain. The great stone walls, vast flagstone floor, and vaulted ceiling of Westminster Hall amplified the hubbub of whispered conversations to a dull roar. Schemers, liars, cully-humpers,[11] swindlers and spotted charlatans steeped in every vice and sin haunt the place.

Uncle Samuel scuttled along on his stumpy little shanks so swift that I was fain to lengthen my stride to keep apace through the crowd. His odious secretary Mr Butler was with us, waddling along, red-faced and puffing, and barely able to keep up. My return to London had caused some consternation among the authorities. The information on traitors in King's Lynn had been enough to see Beeston reinstalled in the Phoenix Theatre, and all outstanding charges dropped. My uncle had sent agents (Sam, Meg and Everard among them) to the Norfolk town to deal with the Le Strange plot when Figgis had arrived with our evidence. However, news that there was an imperial assassin sent to kill the only prince of the blood to support Parliament was the more pressing matter.

'You will mind your manners, Blandford,' said Uncle Samuel. 'And you, Mr Butler. I will have none of the customary childishness each provokes in the other.'

'Yes Uncle,' I said meekly, as Butler nodded.

---

[11]A prostitute's clients.

I was more concerned with my crotch which had been on fire since returning to London. The itching was as if the devil himself thrust hot needles into my pubis. 'Twas hard to focus on the business at hand.

He led us across St Stephen's Court into a suite of new apartments. A clerk in a grey robe noted our arrival and showed us upstairs. Uncle Samuel knew where we were going and skipped up the stone stairs. He paused before a carved oak-panelled door, as if to knock, but then decided to enter unannounced. Butler and I followed him into the room; a panelled affair with rich carpets, high ceiling and tall windows looking out on the court.

Mr Haslerig was in there with two other men, all of them in black as if for Sunday sermons. The taller of the two men stepped forward.

'Well met, Samuel,' he said, grasping my uncle's hand. 'Then he looked to me. 'God's teeth, he does look like Bess. Well met cousin, I have heard much about you.' He held out his hand.

I looked to my uncle for an introduction as the man shook my hand. He had a most firm grip.

'Blandford, this is Oliver St John, we are cousins on your grandfather's side. He was close to your mother.'

'Close? Bess was like a sister to me,' said St John and shook my hand firmly.

I had heard of Oliver St John. Everyone had heard of Oliver St John. He was a leader of the Independent faction in Parliament, along with Cromwell and Henry Vane. A vociferous critic of the King and determined to prosecute the war to the bitter end. His arguments with the Tremblers and Half-Measure men were daily in the London journals. I had not known that we were related, but it was a welcome revelation. A newly discovered and very rich relative should always be prized. My sister Elizabeth would have known, but presumably kept such jewels to herself in case I embarrassed her.[12]

---

[12]Oliver St John, pronounced Sinjun, (1598 - 1673) was MP for Totnes and had been a critic of the King during the 1630s. He defended John Hampden in the Star Chamber over Hampden's refusal to pay Ship Money, and his wife, Elizabeth Cromwell, was related to the future Lord Protector. During Stafford's trial St John made a speech that Clarendon would later describe as 'the most

St John introduced his companion: Mr John Thurloe. The secretary was a broad-faced man with a square chin, receding hairline, and bulbous oversized forehead that gave him the aspect of a toddler. The man's credentials put Butler to shame, which I am sure my uncle's fat clerk realised as he went a bright shade of puce at St John's words.

'Well, this is a very affair,' said St John. 'If the prince is killed whilst under our protection, it would sit badly in the courts of Europe. The Lord himself knows what the reaction would be.'

'The Office of Ordnance is at your disposal, sir,' said Haslerig. 'My brother fears this is a scheme to divide the House. Prince Karl has taken the Covenant, but we shall not hold that against him.' He grinned sycophantically at St John, but when there was no reaction he carried on. 'I have set extra guards on his apartments and he will be well protected, but a single determined assailant is almost impossible to stop.'

'We must then find this ravaillac before he gets to the prince,' said St John. My uncle nodded at that.

St John and the Haslerigs were Independents, but the threat to the

---

barbarous and inhumane ever made in the House'. St John became one of the leaders of the war party against the King, and was closely allied with Cromwell in the arguments that led to the creation of the New Model Army and the Self Denying Ordnance. The Lukes were related to the St Johns through Samuel Luke's paternal aunt who married St John's grandfather. Whilst Blandford may have taken little notice of his family's relations, it is clear from the archive that Elizabeth Candy was aware. The Luke family links to St John, Cromwell, Valentine Knightly, and particularly Charles Fleetwood made them very well connected indeed with the Independents, despite their own Presbyterianism. His secretary, John Thurloe, would become Cromwell's Intelligence Chief during the Protectorate, foiling a multitude of Royalist plots against the general.

prince gave them common cause with my uncle. The failures in the field unleashed a new sense of urgency in the fight against the King. Many in the Commons wanted a new army, removed from the aristocratic control of the magnates. The Presbyterian Covenanters and the Lords (who wanted only a settlement with His Majesty) thought it some plot of the Independents to seize control of the country. Arguments in committee and on the floor of the house had been bitter and vindictive. Uncle Samuel sided with the Independent party. A new army was needed if we were to win the war, and that was ever my uncle's desire and design. The votes were there in the House, but the murder of the prince could change the numbers. Karl Ludwig, by his mere presence, could bring disaster upon us all.

'What is this prince about, then, sirs?' I said, to stop myself from dropping my breeches and scratching my burning whirligigs in front of all. 'Have any of you met him?'

'You can find out for yourself,' said Thurloe. 'He has arrived.'

The secretary nodded to a window and we all crowded around to see, like schoolboys trying to spy the maid. I did not catch sight of our illustrious guest; however, 'twas only a bare minute before the door opened, and a fop dressed in a spectacular embroidered scarlet coat with silver lining entered. Was this the prince?

'Gentlemen,' said the fop. 'I have the honour to present His Royal Highness Charles Louis, Prince Elector of the Palatine and Knight of the Garter.'

Karl Ludwig strode in, dressed in a red velvet suit with a gold lace falling band. His garter sash and badge were prominently displayed at his breast (there was a dark irony in that Royalist honour). A longer nose and not as dashing as his younger brother Rupert, but the same dark eyes and brown ringlets tumbling loose beneath his wide-brim hat. The prince dripped in gold: rings, buttons, even his tall leather riding boots were patterned with gold thread, and at his waist there was a golden scabbard and jewelled sword hilt. We all gave a bow.

'I have been summoned,' he said, in perfect English. 'I am not accustomed to being summoned.'

'Forgive us, Highness,' said St John. 'We feared only for your wellbeing. You are aware of the plot?'

'I have my sister's letters,' he said. 'Sophia is rarely mistaken, about anything. At least so she believes.'

'We have devised a plan to protect you, Highness,' said St John. 'We will have agents as well as our own bodyguards watching over you, and Sir Samuel will use his organisation to find this murderer, this Black Bear, and bring him to justice. May I introduce you to my cousin Captain Candy? He will be responsible for apprehending the assassin. You will have heard of him, I am certain. An excellent officer; he brought the correspondence from Amsterdam.'

Cousin St John was laying it on thick, and nobody had asked me about any of this. I bowed low again to the prince and then stood straight to attention. His Highness looked me up and down.

'You lost the duel,' he said. 'To Colonel Hurry.'

'He cheated,' I said.

That was true enough, Hurry had stuck me after provosts called a halt, but I was already beaten.

'Will this Black Bear cheat, do you think? Or will he play by the rules?'

That was a palpable hit.

'Highness,' I said. 'When I am not personally guarding thee, I shall endeavour to find a master to instruct me in swordplay, so that I may better fulfil my duty.' I gave another flourishing bow to go with my flowery words.

The prince sniffed. 'See that you do, Candy.' He turned to my uncle and the others. 'How else will I be protected?'

'Mr Haslerig has put extra guards on you as well as your own retainers,' said St John. 'Candy and his associates will seek out this assassin, Highness. I have set my very own secretary to oversee all the arrangements.' St John nodded to Thurloe. He will report to you daily. With Sir Samuel's organisation helping, I am certain that we can foil any threat to your body. Your apartments here in Whitehall are well defended, and...'

'If you would consider moving to The Tower until the matter is resolved, Highness,' Haslerig said.

'I will not hide away from the people like a coward,' said Prince Karl. 'I will not gain the reputation of a trembler when threatened.'

That was the rub. His Highness cared more for the opinion of the London crowds than his own personal safety, and the reason for that was clear enough.

What means this shouting? I do fear, the people choose Caesar for their king.

The politics of this assignment were almost as dangerous as the threat from the Black Bear, and the prince did not strike me as a compliant charge. He questioned my uncle, Haslerig, and St John some more until he was finally satisfied that all was in order. Then he swept out with Haslerig and the flunkey following on behind.

'I will need men,' I said to my uncle. 'Sam and Everard, but some of the others too.'

'You shall have them; both will be here by tomorrow.'

'And coin.'

'And coin,' Uncle Samuel assured me.

'This matter is most serious, cousins,' said St John. 'Yet, if we can avoid catastrophe we may play out some advantage to our cause.'

And that was that.

*

The prince's carriage made its way slowly down the Strand to Whitehall. His Highness had insisted upon going to the city about his business, despite Thurloe and my protests. A troop of Horse with naked swords kept the cheering crowds at bay. The Londoners waved their hats and called out to the carriage as it passed, and Prince Karl sat with the shutters down so all could see. He nodded and waved at them, lapping up the adulation from a crowd long divorced from the pomp of royalty.

I scratched my crotch (it was still itching to buggery) and flicked Apple's reins to follow on behind the guards. Sam and Everard were amidst the crowds somewhere in case of an attack. They had both arrived the day before. Sam with a patch over his blinded eye, but well dressed. His sandy hair had been recently cut and beard neatly trimmed. Everard was in his usual ragged poacher's fashion. We all scanned the roofs and upper storey windows of the buildings in case of a gunman.

I felt the explosion before I heard it; the ground shook, buildings rattled, and Apple snorted and reared. The procession halted at the noise. Prince Karl's carriage was undamaged; there were no bodies strewn around. I kicked Apple into a trot and led him past the carriage. German officers surrounded the vehicle and the shutters were now up.

'Get him back to Whitehall as quick as you can,' I shouted at the captain of Horse.

He nodded and gave orders to clear the road. I felt someone tug at my coat and looked down. The shabby former poacher and my fellow scout, William Everard, in a green woollen bonnet and mismatched boots.

'Down Katherine Street,' he said.

The prince's carriage and guard took off (at a much-increased pace), and I turned and rode down Katherine Street. Sam and John were already there, as well as some city watch. A wood and plaster built building had collapsed in on itself, smoking and smouldering. The adjoining houses in the row looked ready to tumble down. Bystanders crowded around trying to lift debris and dig out survivors. I saw one little girl with red hair and wearing charred rags being lifted out of the wreckage and passed overhead to safety. A waiting woman grabbed her, bursting into tears. She was alive at least, others had not been so fortunate. There were broken bloodied bodies of children amidst the burning wreckage.

'What was this place?'

'Unlicensed foundling hospital,' said John.

Children would be given to the foundling hospital as babes; orphans or abandoned. An old matron managed the operation and employed a wet-nurse. When the children were of an age, they would be apprenticed out or indentured to pay for their upbringing. All done without the authorities' permission, of course, but it was a lucrative business. The old woman must have had at least twenty or so ranging in age from guttersnipe to brat.[13]

'What is black powder doing in a foundling hospital?' said Sam.

'Black powder?'

'Can you not smell the sulphur?'

He was in the right. The acrid smell of gunpowder hung in the air. How much would it take to destroy a building?

'A box of grenades going off or shell exploding,' said Everard, as if he read my mind.

'It still tells us not why the powder was here,' said Sam.

'No it does not,' I agreed.

John had gone to help the rescue attempt. We were close to the theatre here. I reasoned that the boy must have known some of the children. He would have run with them before taking my employment. Soldiers were arriving, dragoons. These were not militia or watch; these were veteran men with grim faces. The flames had quickly been doused by the street's residents. The thought of a fire spreading through their buildings fixed everyone's minds, but the officer in charge of the new men ordered everyone back.

'Who are you?' he asked.

---

[13]Whilst The Foundling Hospital was set up in the next century, unlicensed private orphanages had sprung up in London after the Dissolution of the Monasteries.

'Candy,' I said. 'From the Office of Ordnance.'

'Sugar Candy?'

I nodded.

'Is this one of yours?'

I looked at him quizzically for an instant, and then realised what he meant.

'No, we just happened to be passing on other duties.'

The Office of Ordnance was known for its strange powders and contraptions. There were regular explosions over at the Artillery Gardens where all manner of devices were tested. Darnelly's influence in the main; he had ever been fascinated with the mechanical.

'Well, you will have to away if 'tis not your business. We have been ordered to secure the premises.'

'Ordered by whom?' I had earned enough rank and gravitas to ask that question.

'The orders came direct from the Committee of Both Kingdoms.'

The committee would not have had time to hear about, debate, and order an intervention. It took hours for them to decide whether to shit or piss when they went to the privy. Such a swift response meant a flunky clerk showing incredible initiative (something generally frowned upon in government), or some other party's involvement.

I nodded to the officer and called John away from the rescue.

'The coal cellars are collapsed,' he told me. 'It seems that is where the explosion happened. There is black ash blown through into the neighbour's cellar. You really need to see a quack about your itch, sir.'

I was scratching at my cock again.

'Were there any survivors?'

'Not down there, broken heads and a mess of bodies.' He pointed to a man vomiting in the street. 'That one lives next door; he checked his cellar and found them, the partition wall had come down.'

'Did you know any of them?'

He nodded. 'A couple of the older boys who lived here; they were a lot younger than me, so not well. Both were in the cellar according to one of the girls.'

'How would they have got their hands on powder?'

'I know not; not enough for this anyway.'

'See what more you can find out among the survivors,' I told him. 'And see if there is any news with the Gypts on this. With Boswell dead, mayhap it is some argument in the tribe.'

He looked at me strangely, as if he were about to tell me something but then decided better of it.

I sent Sam off to Whitehall to keep his good eye on the prince, and Everard to Haslerig to tell him what had happened. Perhaps the Office of Ordnance would know who had access to powder in the city. Enough powder to make a bomb, at the least. I needed to see Thurloe, but I would speak to him on the morrow when I knew more. There was no guarantee that this was involved with the prince, but the explosion had happened far too close to Karl Ludwig's procession for my comfort. News of his travelling had been known for a number of days. Could this be an attack gone wrong? I wondered. Perhaps it was nought but coincidence, but I became ever more cynical by the day.

In the meantime, I was going to find a pox doctor.

*

A TRUE RELATION of the discovery of the
PLOT against KING'S LYNN in NORFOLK.

Master Roger Le Strange sent for Captain Thomas Leamon of Lynn to come to Appleton Hall. Le Strange did acquaint Leamon with a design intended against Lynn. He had a commission from His Majesty to surprise the town, which he showed Leamon and told him that if he would undertake to be assistant to him (and raise a party within the town to effect the design), that he should have one thousand pounds for his pains. He would also receive whatever preferment he would desire, either in the town or in His Majesty's Navy. Le Strange further told him, that the King did value the town as worth half his crown. His Majesty would send a sufficient power to their relief under the command of Lord Goring.

Captain Leamon, having taken the Covenant and well weighing the peace and good of the Commonwealth, seemingly gave consent to the plot. He then departed from Le Strange with promise to come to him again the next day. Leamon hastened to Lynn and went to the Governor Colonel Valentine Walton, and acquainted him with Le Strange's treasonous design. After a long debate, they resolved that Leamon should go back to Appleton Hall, taking with him a Corporal Everard clad in seaman's habit.

Master Strange demanded of Captain Leamon who it was that came with him. The corporal answered very discreetly, that he was a poor man from Lynn and kept an ale-house. He complained that he was forty pounds the worse off for the Roundheads taking Lynn. Master Strange replied, that when the design was accomplished, he would have one hundred pounds for it and a cannoneers place. Master Strange went immediately to a hole in the canopy of his bed, and produced the Royal Commission and read it to them; after he had read it, he put it in his pocket.

At this point, Lieutenant John Stubbing and Lieutenant Major Moll, with five soldiers in the garb of poor seamen, came begging to the door of the house. As soon as they came up to the door, the Gentlewoman of the house (Mistress Paston) came running up to Mr Strange and told him of the beggars, with her new maid who was secretly acquainted with Leamon's design.

Master Strange sent down twelve pence to the supposed beggars, wishing them to be gone. When the maid went down, instead of giving the alms she let our men in. Captain Leamon gave a wink to the corporal and a stamp with his foot. The men below knew that the commission was in the rooms above. Master Strange, believing that he was betrayed, gave the commission to Captain Leamon for safekeeping.

The Lieutenants, given entry by the maid and no longer in disguise, did arrest the said Master Strange as an enemy to the Commonwealth and demanded his commission. He denied having such. The Lieutenant, seeing Captain Leamon, demanded what he did there, and called him a stinking knave. They searched Leamon for the commission (which he gave up, as had been his design all along) and took it from him. They set a guard over Captain Leamon, and another over Master Strange, and would not suffer them to speak each to other until they were brought as prisoners to the Governor. Here Captain Leamon was released. Master Strange is brought up to London, and committed to safe custody.

Tuesday the 21st of *Nov.* 1644.

8. Pox Doctors, Swordmasters, and Assassins: London, November 1644.

Happy art thou, O Israel: who is like unto thee, O people saved by the LORD, the shield of thy help, and who is the sword of thy excellency! And thine enemies shall be found liars unto thee; and thou shalt tread upon their high places.
(Deuteronomy 33:29)

A good pox doctor is worth his weight in gold. If you find one, keep him close. My itching crotch had driven me to seek one out. At the bottom of Stew Lane (by the boats that carry passengers to Southwark's dubious delights) are a cluster of quacks, pox doctors, and charm peddlers. They will sell you dried deer pizzle, and pigs bladder sheaths with pink ribbons for a shilling.

'Perhaps 'tis the pox, sir,' said John.

That was certainly more than a fear. I was almost driven to distraction at the thought.

'Your nose might fall off,' he said. 'You would look like Davenant the Poet. Mistress Meg would be most displeased.'

Meg was my lover; a courtesan and a spy. She would be most displeased indeed, I thought. And she was due back in London. Uncle Samuel had sent her into the Le Strange house near King's Lynn after Beeston's information. Now that matter was concluded she was to return to London.

'You are enjoying this,' I said.

'It is somewhat amusing.'

Doctor Shootwixt's chambers overlooked the river. A smoke-blackened wooden shack, but it was the first building revellers would see as they disembarked after a night of pleasures over the river. Shootwixt was not his real name, of course, more an occupational advertisement: to shoot twixt wind and water. I am passing certain that he was no true physician. The rooms were dirty and there was a fetid smell of sour milk that lingered on the nose. Good Doctor Shootwixt himself was tall and brown-haired, of an age with me, and dressed in heavy grey wool robes. He looked me up and down.

'Let me see it, then?'

I looked at him blankly.

'See what?'

'Your pizzle, Captain Candy,' he said gesturing to my breeches. 'I need to see the offending member.'

That was embarrassing. I dropped my breeches around my ankles and stood exposing myself. He chuckled at my discomfort.

''Tis just like a little mouse,' he said.

''Tis very cold,' I said.

'Not that cold,' said John.

The pox doctor picked up a glass to study my pizzle with, which only outraged me further.

''Tis not that small.'

John Coxon doubled up with laughter; the doctor looked up at me.

'As I suspected, Captain Candy, you have the herodian visitation, phthiriasis pubis.'

'I have no idea what you mean?' I say, worrying that it was some form of deadly, or worse, disfiguring disease.

'Lice, Captain Candy, you have the lice. You will have to shave your pubis.'

John burst out laughing.

'And your servant will have to shave the hair from your anus.'

'I shall not,' he said.

'You shall,' I said. 'Damn your eyes.'

'Your clothes and bedding will need to be boiled,' said good Doctor Shootwixt.

How was I going to explain this to my sister?

'So 'tis not the pox?'

'It is not the pox, Captain Candy.'

I breathed a sigh of relief at that.

He sold me some pig bladder sheaths, and warned me against whores and low women.

'Perhaps 'twas the monkeys not the women, you were rather drunken that last night in Amsterdam,' said John.

'You are becoming altogether too impudent, young Coxon,' I said, scratching my whirligigs. 'Now, time to procure a new razor and soap methinks. You have a rather unsavoury task to attend to.'

The boy grimaced.

*

I determined to seek out a Swordmaster that Elizabeth had met at her weekly service in the city. A churchgoing Huguenot was not the best recommendation, but perhaps he would discount the lessons given Elizabeth's friendship. I needed to learn to fence. My experience with Hurry had taught me that I was an unskilled bumpkin with a blade. In Amsterdam, I had even failed to mark the bashers and had to rely upon John. Of course, I had also vowed to Prince Karl that I would seek formal instruction, but that was actually the least of my motivation.

 John and I made our way out through Bishopsgate to Spitalfields. Porters in the street pointed us to a crooked building off Brick Lane. A tall house with an old shingle roof, blue door, and paint peeling from the smoke-blackened walls. There were small stables and a cobbled courtyard to the side, and a walled garden to the rear. It was a grand building once, but now the house listed over the street like a shabby old man.

'The Frenchie lives o'er there with his daughter.'

There was a crooked man, in a crooked house.[14]

We walked over to the front door. John looked at me and shrugged. I knocked on the peeling blue paint, rat-a-tat-tat, and waited. It was only moments before I heard the sound of steps, bolts being drawn, and the door was opened. A young girl, perhaps sixteen or seventeen, dressed in a plain grey dress, long skirts, and linen falling band. She smiled, big brown eyes, and fine brown hair pinned back under a white cap. A pretty enough little thing.

'Can I help you, sir?' A French accent.

'I am looking for Mr Maupin.'

'My father, sir, who may I ask calls upon him?'

---

[14]This is a reference to the nursery rhyme, but it is very early. The rhyme was recorded in the 19th century but is believed to originate during the Civil War period. Frustratingly we do not know from Blandford if it was contemporary to 1644, during the war itself, or a later (pre-1720) addition. Blandford also misquotes the first line from the rhyme as we know it from the Roud Folk Song index.

There was a crooked man, and he walked a crooked mile.

He found a crooked sixpence upon a crooked stile.

He bought a crooked cat, which caught a crooked mouse,

And they all lived together in a little crooked house.

'Captain Candy, of the Office of Ordnance.'

We were shown into the house; the interior was as unkempt as the exterior. The girl led us down a dark corridor, past doors to the right and left. A grand faded stairwell in the centre of the building led to upstairs chambers, but she took us deeper to the back of the building. This is a big house,' I said.

'It is only my father and me,' said the girl. 'And our housekeeper, but she is at the shambles. We need all this space for Father's works.'

She opened another door and showed us into a hall, big and light with tall windows overlooking a private garden. This was a room for parties, gatherings, and dances; it must once have been a merchant's grand residence. Now, there were four full-length Venetian mirrors, one at each point of the compass, and a selection of swords on a rack along the outside wall. A wooden bench at either end of the room, a half-filled water bucket, greased rags for cleaning blades. There were strange markings on the floor in red paint, like a mason's compass, and chalk dust covered everything. A large wicker birdcage, for parrots or monkeys and the like, sat empty in a corner.

'I will let my father know you have arrived, sir.'

'Thank you, ma'am.'

The girl left John and me in the hall. The boy looked at the swords on the rack. Different sizes, grips, and lengths, some with basket hilt, some with merely a plain cross-guard. English rapiers mostly, a couple of longer Spanish blades with cup hilts, and a pair of ancient two-handed longswords all polished and shining. The swords were the only clean things in the house. My eye fixed on one blade (basket hilt with an inlaid decoration) shorter than my own sword, but an expensive weapon. German, I would wager, and new, it must have been worth a fortune.

'A lot of swords here, sir,' said John. 'Is he planning a rebellion?'

'No,' I said. 'Different makers and styles, this is a rare collection, not a store.'

'You are a devotee of the blade, Captain Candy?' A foreign accent said, with heavy stilted tones.

John and I both turned towards the voice: a slender grey-haired man in a white shirt and breeches. He was of middling height and clean-shaven. I noted that his shoes were scuffed and old, but light. He had been silent as he entered.

'No,' I said. 'Merely an unskilled soldier. You are Swordmaster Maupin?'

'Yes, I have been expecting you, Captain. Your sister did mention you might seek my services.' He pointed to a bench. 'Please take a seat.'

I sat at the bench as John continued to look over the weapons rack. He picked up one of the rapiers and started to swing it. Maupin minded him not and sat with me. He looked at my face, studied the fading moustachioed scar.

'That was either a very lucky blow, or Colonel Hurry is the most accomplished swordsman in history,' he said.

'He was rather good, better than me. How much do you charge to teach swordplay?' I had never had any formal training, and against Hurry it had shown.

Maupin held my gaze for a second, scrutinizing me with narrow eyes.

'Nobody is that good... Not even me. I will need to see how skilled you are first.'

He stood up and turned to the rack, where John still pranced and twiddled with a blade, and selected a shortsword similar to my uncle's favoured weapon.

'You wish to fence with me?'

'Goodness me no,' said Maupin. 'I wish to see your stance and balance and speed. Take out your own steel.'

I drew my sword. The boy watched on behind Maupin, his interest piqued. The Swordmaster glanced at my weapon.

'A good weapon but it is too long. You English always worry about the length of your sword.'

The boy sniggered at that.

'Take up the prima guard stance,' said Maupin to me.

I stood with my legs apart, (right foot forward, left foot back) and my left hand on my hip. I kept my weight on the back foot with the leg bent; front foot straight and pointing at the swordsman. The sword was held high above my head in my right hand, pointing at Maupin's face. Out of the corner of my eye, I could see the boy mocking me by mimicking my stance, bouncing up and down on his toes with a big grin on his face.

'Secunda!' called Maupin.

I kept my stance but held my arm out to the side, still pointing the sword at Maupin.

'Terza!'

I moved the sword in front of me, with the quillions perpendicular to the ground. It was the most commonly used guard, the others I was only passing familiar with. Maupin kicked me in the left leg.

'Bend your back knee more. When you straighten in the attack it gives power, like a spring.

He called me through the other guards (six of them in all) tutting all the while.

'Let me see you make the cut. Take the Terza position; that is the most versatile.' He stood opposite me to study my technique. The boy was still bobbing around behind him like a fool. 'Now, mandratto,' said Maupin.

I cut from the left shoulder to the right knee, swinging the blade from my elbow.

'Reverso.'

I reversed the movement, somewhat clumsily, from right to left.

He took me through the different cuts as he had the guards, and then it was thrusts and parries, and then combinations. I followed his orders like a raw recruit at drill until, after a perhaps ten minutes or so, he called a halt. The short exertion had me dripping in sweat and my shoulders burning.

'You fight like all English, no finesse or style, hack, hack, hack. Your grip is held much too tight, it is a pen not your penis; you have poor clumping footwork and no defence – pah! It will cost you ten shillings a week for instruction, every other morning barring Sunday. The Barbary I train for free.'

'Why for free?' I was a tad outraged by that.

'The boy has perfect balance. Even mimicking you he takes a better stance. He moves on the balls of his feet like a dancer and has quick hands. He could become a master with instruction. You? You will never be a true swordsman. I can improve your defence, teach you how to counter properly, how to parry a riposte. It will be enough against most men, if you stay calm. I heard of your duel with Hurry; you lost control.'

'Who told you that?'

''Twas in some of the newsbooks, sir,' said John. 'Royalist ones... They were not kind to you, and Mistress Elizabeth decided it would only upset you to see them.'

That was just typical of Elizabeth, interfering as always; I liked to read Royalist tales about my adventures (yes I am vain you know that already), they amused me with their bilious deceits.

'The Aulicus said your face was so cut and disfigured that the ladies of Southwark now vomit when you pass,' said John cheerfully.

'Berkenhead be a bastard!'

Berkenhead was the editor of the Aulicus; he knew how to twist vanity's knife. Elizabeth was in the right, reading that would have put me in a foul humour. I agreed to Maupin's terms and arranged to begin our sessions the next morning at ten. I would need time to banish Dionysus's curse. He called his daughter to take us out of the house, back to the front door.

'You are from the Africs, sir?' she said to John.

'I was born in Wapping, miss, I am an Englishman,' said John.

'Forgive me,' she looked horrified. 'I meant no insult.'

And then John started apologising over and over, begging her leave, blurting out words like an idiot. We reached the front door, but she just stood there making cow-eyes at him like a trull at the county fair. In the end, I coughed to get her attention.

'I am so sorry, sir.' She said to me and opened the door to see us out. She gave one last lingering peep at the boy, before closing it shut.

'Methinks that young girl is enamoured with you, Master Coxon.' I swear that the boy blushed.

'Pish,' he said.

We both heard the crack of shot, turning to the sound – towards the city. In the same instant, we were showered in stone splinters as an iron ball smashed into the wall behind us. We fell to the floor.

'Where?' I said.

'I cannot see. No gunsmoke.'

'It came from the south,' I said.

'I thought from the west,' he said. 'There!' He pointed.

There was a man, white-faced in an upper window, south-west towards the city. Perhaps fifty yards away. He was looking directly at us. As soon as he noted us noting him, he pulled away.

'Up and at him, then.'

John shot off like a dog from the traps. I followed on as quick as I could; down a lane and through the market, shoving innocents rudely out of our path.

'There he is,' said John.

The man had come out of a laundry. Drying linen sheets hanged from pegs outside. He saw us and bolted through the washing to the city.

'Get after him!'

John crashed through a stall of vegetables. Cabbage hearts and parsnips went flying as the boy raced after the fleeing man. I followed on after him, slipping on a crushed nip, banging my knee and scraping my elbow. Limping and cursing, I caught up with John at the corner of Petticoat Lane and Winford Street. The road was packed all the way to Aldgate with people, carts, and animals. It would be simple for the runaway to get lost in the crowd.

'Do you see him?'

'No,' said John.

'Damn.'

We made our way back to the fruit market. The laundry was in the northern corner. The smell of lye, stale urine and black soap assaulted the nostrils as we entered. Stout old women were bucking cloth whilst younger maids beat out the cheaper linen. They all stopped working as we entered.[15]

'The man who just left, where did he come from?'

One of the crones took a pipe out of her mouth and pointed it at a doorway with a wicker screen. There were steps to the upper level behind. John and I went up three flights to an empty garret room with an open window. It gave a clear view of the Swordmaster's front door.

'Sir.'

John picked up a ripped and scorched piece of paper. He handed it to me and I put it to my nose. There was a faint whiff of sulphur.

'Wadding?' asked John.

'Yes. It was him. Damn!'

'Sir?'

'I hate it when ravaillacs come after me,' I said. 'I wonder who these ones be?'

'You?' said John. 'I thought 'twas for me.'

Looking back, that is an answer that should have aroused my suspicions, but I dismissed it. I assumed it was a Royalist supporter taking a shot, or perhaps a vengeful husband. I had made more than my fair share of enemies over the years.

'I doubt it was for you,' I said. 'You are not so important.'

Yes, yes, I agree with you – pompous and vain. I try not to hide my youthful failings, you see. Think on that when you read Samuel Butler's poisonously penned poem about my uncle and me. Sir Hudibras and Ralpho be buggered.

---

[15]A method of bleaching cloth with urine.

9. Mr Thurloe: London, November 1644.

I HAVE been all day looking after,
A raven feeding upon a quarter:
And, soon as she turn'd her beak to the south,
I snatch'd this morsel out of her mouth.
(Ben Jonson, *The Masque of Witches*)

Mr John Thurloe was living proof never to judge a man on appearances. He looked like a toddler (all forehead and eyes) but behind his glassy smile was the most calculating mind I have ever encountered. My uncle's secretary Butler was efficient and intelligent, for all his cursed faults, but Thurloe was something different. He had an almost supernatural intellect. Indeed, if I knew no better I would say he was a witch. Thankfully he was ne'er my foe. Thurloe had his own office and bedchamber at Lincoln's Inn, when he was not abroad on business for his master St John.

'Madeira, Captain Candy, I hear you are partial to it?'

Thurloe handed me a cup of the wine and I sat back in the chair. He was dressed nondescriptly in lawyer's grey cloth, but his chambers were well-furnished: expensive if not ostentatious. The modesty was conspicuous, 'twas almost as if he deliberately shrouded himself in shadows.

'My thanks, Mr Thurloe.'

'Pleased to call me John.'

'Blandford,' I said with a nod.

'Your associate Mistress Powell will be arriving in London today, Blandford?'

Meg Powell was due to return from Kings Lynn that evening. Thurloe was well informed indeed. She had helped to break open the Le Strange plot with Beeston's information, but had finally sent word that she was homeward bound. I had told no one that news. I was looking forward to seeing Meg most impatiently. More so now that my crotch was clean, although I would have to explain the bald pubis to her.

'She should be here by tonight.'

'Good, she has contacts amongst the Gypts that will help,' he said. 'Three bodies have turned up in the last week alone. There is a civil war going on amongst the scoundrels of London.'

'There is no Beggar King since Boswell's death,' I said. 'I think some of the tribe are using the period of uncertainty to settle a few scores.'

He nodded. 'That still leaves us with the Black Bear at large.'

The guards on Karl Ludwig had been increased since the explosion at Katherine Street. His apartments were well-protected and he had decided that further excursions to the city were unadvisable (both Thurloe and I had told him, but this was his decision you understand). The foundling hospital had been destroyed by a shell, a cast iron hollow ball the size of a bull's cod filled with powder. Broken pieces of the casing had been found in the cellar room, along with the remains of four boys. The matron had been found drunk on ale in a local tavern, blissfully unaware that her home and illegal business had been blown apart.

'Where did they get a cannon shell from?' I asked.

'That is a good enough question,' he said. 'Mr Haslerig tells me it is of foreign construction, and there is nothing missing from our arsenals in the city. It was not designed to be fired from a cannon, according to the Office of Ordnance.

I frowned. That meant a specially made bomb.

'John has discovered nothing from his contacts among the Gypts,' I said. 'Perhaps Meg will be able to discover more.'

'I do hope so. This is proving a most perplexing problem.'

Thurloe had set his intellect on discovering the assassin before another attack took place (we were all treating the explosion as an attack foiled). He used my uncle's contacts – scouts, spies and informers across England – for any information. Samuel Butler, the oafish poltroon, was not taking the encroachment upon his territory well.

'Your uncle's secretary is quite...' He paused. 'Protective of his sources.'

'He is a fat, pompous, pig-faced, droopy-lipped grumble-monkey,' I said.

Thurloe gave a low chuckle and then continued.

'The Dutch musician has given me information from Holland. My Lord St John has written to his people in France and Germany. In the meantime, was must ensure than nought befalls the prince. If the bomb was an attack, we have been fortunate in the first instance.'

I outlined my plans: Hugo and John Coxon would watch the port at Wapping for information and foreigners. None of us trusted the

Dutch musician, he was clearly an agent of the Dutch Stadholder, but his presence satisfied Karl Ludwig. Meg would plumb the beggars, whores, bashers and cutpurses for news, and she had her own contacts amongst the quality. Beeston knew all of the Royalists in London as well as most of the scoundrels, and William Everard the radicals, fanatics, and autem-cacklers. Sam and I would follow up any information we received, and I would report back to the prince and Thurloe.

'I will see if Mabbot and Pecke hear anything, also,' I said.

Gilbert Mabbot was a journal writer and newsmonger with contacts in trade and Parliament, and Samuel Pecke his printer. Both would have useful contacts at home and abroad. I was more than passing friendly with Mabbot, even if he were an unashamed and outrageous gossip.

'Be careful what you say to Mabbot and Pecke,' said Thurloe. 'I do not wish to see this tale in the newsbooks.'

He did not need to tell me that, but 'twas reassuring that Thurloe knew what he was about.

'This shooting in Spitalfields? You lost the gunman.'

I had not told Thurloe about the shooting.

'We lost him in the warren,' I said. 'A Royalist, perhaps; I have enough enemies about. 'Tis of no matter.' That was blasé; in truth, I was worried about the attack.

'It complicates matters somewhat, Blandford. We already have one assassin to discover. I do not need another one on the platter.'

'My apologies for the inconvenience.'

'Oh, I blame you not. Princess Sophia wishes you to save her brother. You are a good officer, but I would not have chosen you. You are too visible, and, as you say, have far too many enemies.' He grimaced. 'And you too oft seem to find yourself in the newsbooks.'

That was something my uncle had been telling me for years.

'But perhaps we can use that fact to our advantage. Whilst every agency gazes at you and the prince, I can work in the shadows. It will do.'

I instinctively liked Thurloe. The contrast with my uncle's self-serving fat-arsed secretary could not have been more profound. I left the chambers and returned home to Bedford Street. With Thurloe's mind set upon his task, I was passing certain it would not be long before we found this foreign hired killer.

*

Now, this is where I was before I was so rudely interrupted:

November 1644.

It was cold, wet and dark; a miserable stormy night to be abroad in London. Sam and I hurried through the narrow streets to Butolph Wharf. A row of dark wooden houses at the head of the bridge, built at least a hundred years previous, formed a passage down to the river. Jutting upper storeys left only a small gap between the opposing buildings. Sheets of water poured down from above, feeding a grubby stream that ran through the middle of the alley. The walkway under the eaves was muddy and damp, like caves behind a waterfall. John waited there for us, crouched behind a drainage barrel overflowing from the rain. He had been watching the dirty tenement all day.

'Is he in there?' I asked as we arrived.

'Aye, sir.' He went in about an hour ago.

'Hugo says there be something strange about him?'

'He is French, sir.'

'Apart from being French?'

John explained that the man had been at Westminster Hall every day since he arrived on a ship from Calais. Prince Karl had been taking part in the endless arguments between the Divines on the religious settlement of England. It gave His Highness something visible to do, whilst also keeping him out of trouble. This Frenchman had been overly interested in the prince's attendance at the debates, it seemed. John had followed him for the past two days and found that he used this cheap tenement as a base.

'He has a servant with him,' said John. 'They take turns to watch over the prince during the debates, but 'tis only the master at home at the moment; the servant went out when he arrived back.'

That was more than annoyance. It would only be half a task if we arrested one but left the other at large.

'Where be Hugo? He could have waited here whilst you followed the servant.'

'He said he had to meet with someone.'

I sniffed at that.

I told Sam to stay down in the alley to watch for the man's servant. He nodded and stepped back into the shadows to load his pistol. That was optimistic given the weather, I thought. Drawing my sword, I led the way into the tenement with John following on behind.

'He is in the garret, Master.'

'That be just typical,' I said.

We tramped up the narrow wooden stairs, four flights in all. A woman's face appeared at a doorway on the third story, curious at the noise, but she quickly closed the door upon seeing our swords and grim looks. I paused at the top of the final flight of stairs to catch my breath. There was a door into the chambers at the front of the building and another to the rear. A rickety ladder led to a trapdoor and the rooftops. John nodded to the front chamber.

'That one, sir.'

I walked over to the door. It was cheap and rough-hewn. I banged on it a few times with my gauntleted fist, rattling it on the leather hinges.

'Ouvrez la porte, monsieur. Au nom du Parlement !' I called. (Open the door, sir. In the name of Parliament!)

There was the sound of movement from inside the rooms. They always decide to run; they never ever give up. I stepped back and gave the door a great kick on the lock. My boot went straight through the door panel, trapping me with my leg up in the air. I could see through the broken door into the chamber. There was a richly dressed man: olive skin, high cheekbones and broad chin, dark hair and eyes, a hook nose and slim moustache. He threw the front windows to the garret open, and then he turned and bowed to me as I struggled to get free of the door.

'Au revoir, monsieur.'

The Frenchman dived out of the open windows, straight across the gaping chasm into the opposite tenement, crashing through their hide shutter. I finally shook myself free of the door and burst into his newly vacated garret. Across the alley, in the opposite attic room, the Frenchman pulled himself to his feet. A shocked family watched on aghast; mother, father and children. He rushed to their front door yanking it open. I shouted down to the alley below.

'Sam! The building opposite!'

I could hear banging on a door start in the alley. Taking a deep breath, and a couple of steps backwards, I threw myself forward as fast as I could, diving over the alleyway into the opposite tenement. The poor family said nought, just watched as I crashed through their broken window, got up and chased after my quarry. Their home had seemingly become the Strand after Sunday service. Sam was coming up the stairs, but the Frenchman had gone up to the roofs not down to the streets. I cursed and followed him up the ladder with Sam at my heels.

The shingled roof was slick with moss and rainwater. Our Frenchman was making his way slowly along the rooftops towards the river. I could see him moving off into the darkness. Almost slipping, he teetered for a moment before regaining his balance. I took a deep breath and followed. Placing each foot carefully and holding onto the sloping roof. Gusts of wind rattled the shingles, blowing off my hat and nearly sending me over the edge; the driven rain stung my face. Looking back, Sam was still stood at the top of the ladder.

'Come on.'

'I cannot see.'

Cursing Sam's blind patch, I turned back to the Frenchman. He was further away now, closer to the river, climbing along the rooftops. I followed after him. John was on the buildings opposite. There was a flash from a pistol pan, but no explosion of shot following – a misfire in the storm.

I was getting closer, never looking down, always forward; shuffle, step, shuffle; curse, curse, curse. He had stopped just a sword's length away.

'Il n'y a pas d'échappatoire, monsieur,' I said. (There is no escape, sir.)

The Frenchman had reached the end of the rooftops; there was nought beyond but a forty-foot fall to the cobbles by the wharf. He turned to face me and gave a grin.

'C'est l'histoire de deux pommes. Une d'elles se fait écraser et l'autre s'écrie... "Oh purée!"' (This is the story of two apples. One of them is run over and the other one says... "Oh purée!")

He stepped back and dropped like a stone towards the street below, with the smirk still fixed upon his face.

I rushed to the edge of the building, expecting to see his bloodied body on the street below. I was disappointed: there was a two-horse cart packed high with dross. It had broken his fall. He waved up at me and shouted to the driver

'Allez, allez, Planchet.'

The driver snapped at the reins and the cart moved off at a trot. By the time we had climbed down, they would be long gone, lost in London's dark streets.

'Buggery, frig, and damnation!'

I turned and slowly shuffled back to Sam holding the roof. He was white-faced, still stuck at the top of the ladder.

'I could not do it, Sugar, not go out there, not with one eye.'

''Tis of no matter,' I said. 'The Frenchman had it all planned. There was no catching him.' We both climbed down from the roof into the tenement. 'This one is good, too damned good for my liking.'

'The Black Bear?'

'It must be.'

We climbed back down and met with John in the street below. I needed information, and quickly. This Frenchman was dangerous, and now he knew we were on to his tail. We would need to press every contact and informer in the city to chase this one down.

*

'I understand not the joke... What be purée?'

'It is a play on the two meanings,' said Hugo. 'A mashed paste and the exclamation of surprise: Oh Purée!'

The musician met with me later that night in Wapping. I had taken Apple and ridden over to find him. The Frenchman had me exceeding worried. If he was the assassin, then he was at large and dangerous. Prince Karl would not be impressed with our efforts thus far, of that I was certain. If the Frenchman was not the assassin; he was still a foreign agent and needed to be hunted down.

'Well, 'tis not a very funny jest,' I said. 'The French have no sense of humour.'

'Given the context of falling from a rooftop, it is rather amusing,' said Hugo. 'He has some wit.'

'You would say that, you are Dutch.'

'The Dutch and the French are not always happy neighbours,' said Hugo. 'But you know what we both say about the English?'

'No, what?'

'God clearly had a reason for putting you all on an island.'

My eyes narrowed at that.

'Have you actually managed to find out anything of use?' I said.

'My contacts tell me that the Black Bear is in England.'

That was a problem. We had people watching the ports and double checking any foreign visitors. If the assassin was already in England, then all that effort had been to waste. It did, however, point to the Frenchman being the assassin. Here in London and watching the prince.

'Do you have anything else?' It was not a great return.

'The assassin is an expert in powder, fuses and explosions,' he told me. 'It points to the explosion at the foundling hospital being tied to him. The people who would know more are your canting beggars, but they are all keeping their own counsel. Something is happening with them.'

'There is a succession dispute among the beggars.'

'Really? That is interesting information.'

I laughed. 'You should meet the journal writer Gilbert Mabbot. He has a similar fascination for news. I realised that Hugo would be selling information about the beggar king to his clients in Holland.

Hopefully, Thurloe would have found out something, or Meg would now that she had arrived. She could tap the tribe for information that they would not give to me, or even John Coxon. If this dragged on much longer, it could be disastrous. I was actually starting to worry that the murderer might get to the prince. That would not be a beneficial outcome; neither for the prince nor for me.

10. Hidden Sins: London, December 1644.

Then said Jesus unto him, Put up again thy sword into his place:
for all they that take the sword shall perish with the sword.
(Matthew 26:22)

Prince Karl's apartments at Whitehall overlooked the river. Thurloe and I had been summoned to give an account of our investigations. The watermen heaved at their oars as we approached our destination, a wharf on the river with stairs leading up to the palace. The secretary was unhappy.

'Could a gunman shoot him from here?' He gestured up at the apartments from the boat. The row of thick glass windows was easily visible from our boat

'He would have to be a remarkable gunman,' I said. 'You would not be certain whom you were aiming at, and the shot exceeding difficult from a riverboat bobbing up and down.'

As if to confirm my point the boat pitched to the side, and Thurloe and I were fain to grab the sides to remain dry. I had my best suit of clothes on, bought on my return from Amsterdam. Dark blue satins and silks; a beaverskin hat to keep my hair dry, and a cloak of fine English wool (off the shoulder) the colour of deep red wine. All topped off with an embroidered white falling band, silver buttons, high black musketeer boots polished to a shine by Figgis, and a sword at my hip. Thurloe, by contrast, was all in black, with a pressed white linen falling band, tall black hat, black stockings and shoes. All well-made and expensive, but dull. We looked like the puritan and the popinjay.

People nowadays talk about cavalier and roundhead as if the division was one of fashion and cut of hair. Such is nonsense. Thurloe and I were proof of that.

'Do you think this Frenchman is a good shot?'

'Almost certainly, but nobody is that good,' I said.

It was a phrase Swordmaster Maupin oft used and I had picked up. Whilst the Frenchman had me worried, nobody could make that shot. Thurloe gave a wry smile. 'Let us hope you are correct. If something happened to Prince Karl, I do not think it would help either of our stars rise.'

I pointed to men in the rooftops in red coats: musketeers only, no halberds among them.

'Any assault from the river could be repelled,' I said. 'A single assassin perhaps could make it from a boat to the apartments, but then he would be alone in a palace full of soldiers and flunkeys. In faith, it would be easier to creep into Whitehall from the street. There are enough people coming and going.'

He nodded.

We disembarked at the water gate and climbed the stairs. Again, as if to prove the point, guards and flunkeys thronged to the prince's apartments. However, none of them checked our credentials as we walked unhindered through the gardens into the stone gallery.

'Perhaps it is the guards and flunkeys we need to be looking at,' said Thurloe.

'Perhaps you are correct,' I said. 'They are not as diligent as I would hope.'

Indeed they were not. None of them were fighting men; these were pretend warriors. We were finally stopped by a pair of actual soldiers at the doors to Karl Ludwig's apartments.

'The security is not good enough,' said Thurloe as we were admitted.

'No, 'tis not,' I agreed.

Haslerig would have to answer for that. The prince's apartment guards were his responsibility.

Inside the private chambers, we were confronted with a spectacle of royalty at leisure. With the King and his court in Oxford and absent from the capital for years, for obvious reasons, the hint of a titled visitor to Whitehall had the city equally fascinated and appalled. When that prince happened to be the famed son of the Winter Queen and brother to the Royalist general Prince Rupert, well, it sent London's curiosity into obsession. The journals poured over every detail of his dress and speeches in Westminster Hall; the gossips dressed a few wild opinions as fact, and the prince ever played to the galleries. Parliament gave him an allowance worth thousands of pounds with barely a murmur of complaint from the parsimonious crew of scoundrels. There was n'er enough money for the army or the people, but always enough to spend on fawning sycophancy.

After showing our credentials to the guards, we were shown into an anteroom to await the prince's pleasure. He kept us waiting for an age, but eventually arrived with a pair of gentlemen companions armed with swords. We both bowed low and Thurloe outlined the past few weeks' investigations.

'You let this French assassin escape?'

'He was expecting us, Highness,' I said.

'We are also not certain he is the assassin, Highness,' said Thurloe. 'London teems with foreign agents. He is most probably a French spy, but what his purpose is we do not yet know.'

'The French are not my enemies,' said Karl Ludwig. 'But who can tell what Cardinal Mazarin will do?'

'He is a papist,' said one of the gentlemen.

Prince Karl turned back to me.

'Have you been practising your swordplay as you assured us, Captain Candy?'

'Yes, Highness. I have engaged a master to instruct me so that I may better serve thee.'

'I hope you are more diligent in that matter than you have been hunting our enemies, thus far.'

I bristled at that, chasing the Frenchman across the rooftops in a rainstorm had been no county fair. However, I bit my tongue and stayed silent at the admonishment.

He upbraided us a little further. Thurloe did his best to reassure him that we were both diligent and effective and would soon find the assassin. Then we were expelled from his presence without a word of thanks. The whole meet had taken less than ten minutes. That was a pointless waste of time, I decided. We made our way back to the water gate in silence.

'That was a worthwhile visit,' said Thurloe, as we climbed into our wherry.

'How so?' I said. 'The prince seemed singularly unimpressed.'

'The prince is safe for the moment,' said Thurloe.

I raised an eyebrow at that, but the secretary continued.

'Nothing but fortune can stop a determined assassin that is prepared to lose his life,' said Thurloe. 'Our advantage here is we know the Black Bear is no zealot; he kills for money. Thus he will need an escape. Whitehall and Westminster are too crowded, too visible, he could not be certain to get away, and you insist a shot from the river is impossible. I can see no way for him to kill and survive.'

'The Frenchman was witted enough to arrange for his escape from Butolph passage,' I said.

'Indeed he was, but I think there are far too many chances for capture if he is to strike so visibly. Felton, for example, or Ravaillac himself, both killed but both were quickly brought to justice. And

again, both were zealots.'[16]
'Then he will strike when there are few crowds about,' I said. 'When the prince is at his play?'
'Or when he travels beyond London,' said Thurloe.
'Then let us give thanks that the prince is no hedonist, and pray he does not decide to go-a-visiting before we find the Black Bear,' I said. 'In the meantime, I should away to my Swordmaster. Perhaps that will please Prince Karl.'

*

I was late by the time I arrived at the crooked house in Spitalfields. John was already stretching and playing with his sword, and talking in earnest to the Swordmaster's daughter. There was some budding romance there, I was certain. Her father berated me for my tardy

---

[16]John Felton (1595 – 1628) was an officer in the failed Cadiz expedition against Spain in 1625, and then the disastrous intervention at La Rochelle in France. Both expeditions had been backed by Charles I favourite the Duke of Buckingham. Felton stabbed the Duke in the chest in Portsmouth, believing that he was owed monies from his service, and probably suffering from PTSD. He then gave himself up for trial and was executed at Tyburn. Unfortunately for the authorities, Buckingham's unpopularity and the celebrations at his death by the general public, and Felton's posthumous popularity, hinted at the divide in England that would become a chasm by the 1640s. Francois Ravaillac (1578 – 1610) was a catholic zealot who murdered Henry IV of France. Ravaillac believed the former Huguenot monarch was starting a war against the Papacy, and (in shades of Archduke Franz Ferdinand three centuries later) stabbed the King to death after his carriage had been blocked in the street. As a regicide, his name quickly became a synonym for assassin in the Seventeenth Century.

timekeeping and told me to begin my exercises without delay.

The first half of the hour was always spent the same way, scuttling around like a crab with my feet at right angles in the terza position: backwards, forwards, forwards, backwards, step and pass from side to side; a dance with no music, only the call from Master Maupin and the tap of his cane against the floor. John moved in unison with me, but was undeniably lighter on his feet compared to my clumping. He treated the whole thing as a game. After my bout with Hurry, I knew 'twas anything but.

'He who moves is alive. He who does not move is dead,' called Maupin as we stepped around the hall. 'You must both practice this every day after rising: one hundred steps and passes before breakfast. Watch Mariette as she makes the guards.'

He pointed to his daughter, dressed in loose brown skirts, moving through the guards at tremendous speed but keeping her balance and stance perfectly. John could barely take his eyes off her. I am certain he was not admiring the technique.

Observing young love be uniquely nauseating and amusing.

We spent the next hour standing straight, swinging our swords to Maupin's direction: cutting from the shoulder or elbow and quickly back into a guard position, again and again and again; mandratto, reverso, mandratto, reverso. My shoulders and arms burned at the exertion, leaving me panting. Then he had us crouch with our backs to a wall, as if we were sitting in a chair, until there was a fire of agony in my thighs.

'You need to build up your strength and endurance,' the Swordmaster said. 'As you practice the body remembers, and familiarity will make you quicker.'

The end of the lesson was a bout between John and myself with practice swords. Both were made of wood, but had a lead core to give it the weight and balance of a metal blade. We faced off against each other every day, and, whilst I was certain I was improving, John was faster, better balanced, and just as strong. I could not land a blow near him. Even as we faced off, I was resigned to another beating. 'Twas damnably detrimental to my dignity, I decided, as I crouched into terzo.

John's blade was in my face before his body moved. I stepped back but the lunge caught me off balance. Three times he was able to make a touch before I could deflect or avoid his blade.

'The boy be lightning fast,' I said.

Mariette giggled but her father silenced her with a glance.

'Mr Coxon is not so much faster than you,' said Maupin, 'but he leads with the sword, not the body. You step then thrust, it shows your opponent the move before you make it. Watch.'

He ordered Mariette to pick up a practice blade and to take up a position facing my servant. John's grin fell from his face.

'I wish to hurt Mariette, not,' he said.

'Hurt me?' said the girl. 'You shall not even come close.'

Mariette thrust at him with the wooden sword. John jumped back before crouching into his guard. He tried a thrust at the face, as he had with me, but she simply parried his blade quarte to the side. I saw what Maupin meant, he led with the hand. Twice he tried to make a mark, each time Mariette parried and twirled away with a coquettish smirk on her face. The third time she parried and countered; her riposte a blur. John was quick, but not that quick. She struck him in the solar plexus with just enough force to wind him. He fell to his knees gasping for breath.

'Pride goeth before destruction, and a haughty spirit before the fall, young man,' I said, smugly.[17]

'Mariette's body and blade move in unison; there is no warning of her strike,' said Maupin. 'You must practice your footwork every day without fail. Hands and feet must be in perfect time.'

The lesson was finished for the day, and the housekeeper arrived with flagons of ale for us all. She was the quiet type. John told me she spoke no English, but looked damned fearsome with a stocky body and broad shoulders, and she never smiled. My limbs ached and I was hungry after quaffing the ale, so we arranged the next lesson with Maupin and returned to the city. I was to meet with Meg that night in Southwark. Hopefully, she would have some information on the Frenchman (he had seemingly disappeared like mist in the sun). I was most excited to see her. We had spent little enough time together since her return from King's Lynn, and I intended to enjoy her company – cropped pubis or no.

*

I looked up into two stunning violet eyes flashing with anger. Meg Powell stood with undisguised fury on her beautiful face. What have I done? I thought. I find it so very easy to upset a woman without even trying that I often lose track of my misdemeanours. Meg was older than me by a few years, tall and slender, pale skin, ruby lips, with raven black hair pinned beneath her tall hat. She was dressed in

---

[17]Proverbs 16:18.

long green riding skirts and woollen coat.

'Where is he?' she spoke quietly.

'Who?'

'The idiot, witless, jackanapes of a fart-catcher[18] that serves you? The damnable spawn of a pirate and a Nubian trull. They should have drowned him at birth, such is his mischief.'

A stream of bear-garden jaw[19] followed that would make a docker blush, her voice getting louder and more shrill. She spied John coming back into the taproom and leapt upon him, grabbing him by the ear. People in Vaughn's common room turned to watch the commotion as she dragged him back to our seat.

'Come upstairs; this cannot be public.'

''Tis already public,' I said, gesturing to the audience.

Meg ignored me. She slapped John twice around his head and continued to beat him as she led us up. I grabbed a bottle of sack and two cups, and followed on. The tavern customers went back to their drinks and conversations as we stumbled up the dark wooden stairs. Her room at the inn was on the first level, large, with whitewashed walls, polished wood floor and a wide well-strung bed.

'Tell him what you have done, Brighteyes,' Meg said.

She used John's Gypt moniker; that did not bode well.

'I have done nothing, Meg,' said John.

She slapped him right across the face, the sharp crack ringing out.

'Do not lie to me, John Coxon! Else I will peel off your skin and drown you in vinegar.'

'What have you done, John?' I said.

'I have done nothing, sir.'

'What has he done, Meg?' I asked.

She turned to me, and I swear I had never seen such anger in her look.

'He killed Boswell,' she said. 'He murdered the King of the Beggars. And he has started a civil war among the tribe.'

There was silence.

'Well, this is awkward...,' John said finally.

I cuffed him, as hard as I damn well could and more than once.

Now that his crime had been exposed John told us what he had done. A foul tale of black murder and plot it was too. Before we left for

---

[18]Servant – because they walk behind their master.

[19]Profanity and obscenity.

Amsterdam, when he was supposed to have been in Wapping watching the docks, John had purchased deadly powders at the Crosse Apothecary near the Strand. He then spent the fast day drinking and playing cards with Boswell and his gang at The Leg in Whitehall. The boy had slipped the beggar king poison in his wine when none was looking. Boswell had been falling down drunk and his criminal retainers propped him against a wall in his stupor, but he did not awaken. John insisted none could prove his crime. The boy was quite unrepentant.

'The crew have no proof yet, John,' said Meg. 'But enough people saw you there, enough know your quarrel with the Boswells, enough know you have tried before. All it would take is for one of them to speak to Widow Crosse.'

He looked crestfallen at that.

'Why in the name of Satan's fiery seed did you do it?' I said. 'I told you to stay away from him after the last time.'

'He killed my father.'

'Gad, boy! How many times do we have to go through this?'

'Well, he is now dead, so...' John shrugged. ''Tis most probably the last time, unless he is Lazarus.'

'Be not so damned impudent!'

'With no king to control them old quarrels are come to the fore,' said Meg. 'There have been killings and beatings. Eddie Boswell is too young for the crown and there is talk of the Burned Man returning.'

John did not look pleased with that news.

'Who be The Burned Man?' I asked.

'A foul miscreant,' said Meg. 'He is one of the King's old henchmen; one of the worst. I have been told that the gunman in the laundry who attacked you was Eddie's friend; an opportune killing and settling of an old score rather than any price on your head.'

'My head?' I asked.

'His head.' She nodded to John. 'You are not so important to Eddie Boswell, Sugar.'

''Tis a relief,' I said.

My man did not look so relieved. 'Which friend of Eddie's was it?' he asked, frowning.

'Do not even think about it,' I told him.

Meg sat down on the bed. I handed her a cup of wine, and she sipped at it.

'Best you pray none speak to the widow, John Coxon,' she said. 'Else you will be just as dead as Haniel Boswell. Eddie will see to that. I will try and find out what more they know.'

'What of the Black Bear?' I asked. 'Have you found ought of him?'

For me, that was the most pressing concern. Now, do not take me wrong. I cared about the boy, but there was little I could do. If the tribe discovered the boy's crime I would fuss then. Worrying about the imponderables of the future be an exercise in futility.

'The boys at the foundling hospital had spoken to a foreign gentleman. One of the girls that survived told me. They had a promise of coin, but she knew not why or what for. She did not meet the man herself, so we have no description.'

That was news indeed. It certainly confirmed Thurloe's suspicion that the explosion was the work of the Black Bear. Foreign could mean anything, of course, and the assassin was well-practised in disguise.

'My thanks, dear heart,' I said and touched her shoulder tenderly. 'We are fortunate to have you as a friend.'

'Indeed you are,' she said. 'The pair of you could not pluck a chicken without assistance.'

'We would be certain to *fowl* it up,' I said.

That raised a smile, finally, a beautiful smile; her violet eyes shining. I turned to John. 'You may leave now. I will speak with you on this later, Master Coxon, and tell you the cautionary tale of Arsenic Pelham.

'I have heard that one, sir. He sat down too quick on his sword and cut his bum.'

'Get out!'

I watched him leave in silence and then turned back to my lover.

First examination of Sir Arthur Haslerig before the Committee of Both Kingdoms.

That he was present at the Council of War when the Parliament's army was drawn out upon Shaw Field, and the King's upon Winterbourne Heath and marching away. That it was there urged as a motive for present fighting and engaging with the King's army, that if the King's army were now beaten it would prevent the bringing over of the French or of any foreign force which was the present design in hand.

Whereunto the Earl of Manchester answered, "Upon my credit, you need not fear the coming in of the French, I know there is no such thing." The Earl afterwards there said, "That if we beat the King 99 times yet he is King still, and so will his posterity be after him, but if the King beat us once we shall be all hanged, and our posterity be made slaves." These were the very words as this examinant remembereth, but he is sure words to this effect were there used by the Earl as a motive against engaging in battle.

Whereupon Cromwell replied, "My Lord, if this be so, why did we take up arms at first? This is against fighting ever hereafter, if so, let us make peace, be it never so base."

Signed, Arthur Haslerig.

6th December 1644.

11. A Self Denying Ordinance: London, December 1644.

If I freely can discover
What would please me in my lover,
I would have her fair and witty,
Savouring more of court than city;
A little proud, but full of pity;
(Ben Jonson, *His Supposed Mistress*)

St Stephen's Chapel sits at the heart of Westminster. Before fat Henry closed the monasteries it was the Chapel Royal. Now, 'tis the seat of government: The House of Commons. Thurloe and I stood in the lobby watching the proceedings inside. Back then, if you wished to see the Commons at debate, it was the only place to view them. They have built galleries now for the people to watch, but then it was a crowd in the lobby: cronies, newsmongers, and clerks peering through the open doors. The chamber was but a show of power making. 'Tis even more so now it has become public spectacle (viewing should be a privilege not entertainment). It is in committee that real decisions are made, but on occasion, a powerful oratory can light a fire under the rabble.

The Commons was packed to the rafters that day, with honourable and dishonourable members. The doors and windows were wide open, despite the cold season, but the chamber was still stuffy and hot. The members perched in the old choir stalls (four rows of hard wooden pews that encircled the open bearpit in the centre) like crows in their black cloaks and tall hats. Decapitated statues of saints stood as sentinels on plinths set into the walls above them, still coloured blue and red with Tudor roses. There were even some painted papist icons remaining high on the walls, giving testimony to its past use. Dull winter sunlight from the great leaded windows at the far end illuminated the chamber, but candles, lamps and torches above and around were already lit. It stank: a couple of hundred sweating men, shouting, farting, waving their hats and fists, drinking, eating, smoking, and giving off a foul vapour. So much for Parliamentary dignity, I thought, 'twas more the school refectory.[20]

Speaker Lenthall in his tall hat sat on his tall throne (a high backed chair with the royal arms atop) and directed the debates: calling members to speak, judging points of order, shouting for quiet through the uproar. He would twist his long grey beard as he listened to their arguments. In front of him there was a table covered in green cloth, and still bearing the King's heavy gold mace. Clerks busied themselves with papers, making note of the decisions and divisions. A new army had been proposed, with new commanders – commanders that were not politicians.

Cromwell stood up and took off his hat, holding it in front of him like a shield, his ruddy face flushed. Lenthall called out his name, and pointed to the Member for Cambridge.

'It is now a time for me to speak, or forever to hold the tongue,' Cromwell said loudly.

The other members hushed to listen to him. Oliver was a power in the country: a successful commander and leader of the Independents with my cousin St John. People wanted to know his mind; they wanted to hear his designs. Since the battle at Marston Moor, he was a hero to half of them and devil to the rest. I suspect he enjoyed the notoriety.

'This important design is to save this nation out of a bleeding, nay, almost dying condition,' he said. 'Without a more speedy, vigorous and effectual prosecution of the war, we make the kingdom weary of us. They begin to hate the name of a parliament.'

People did not like that. Nobody enjoys having their faults proclaimed and their reputations exposed. It disturbs the sense of

---

[20]The boorish behaviour in the House of Commons is not a modern phenomenon. Sir John Chamberlain noted in 1614 that *"many that sat there were more fit to have ben among roaring boyes then in that assemblie"*. Blandford's description of the old House in 1644 matches the few descriptions we have; the walls and painted statues would be whitewashed when Cromwell came to power. Wood panels and public galleries were built in the 1690s, which cannot have improved the stuffy hot conditions.

self, and most Members of Parliament are self-important graspers to the core. There were some shouts, but Lenthall hushed them.

'Order! Order!'

'Uncle Samuel said it was coming,' I told Thurloe. 'A new army is logical enough.'

'Does Oliver have to be so brutal about it?' The secretary replied. 'He does not win friends easily.'

Nol was indeed no great orator: brusque, bordering on arrogance if you knew him not, forcefully ramming his few words home in a deep booming voice, every now and then jabbing his hand forward, as if he were holding a sword, to emphasise his conclusions. Strange, I thought, he could be passably charming and good-natured in private, even witty if infantile with his jesting, but this was Oliver fired with self-righteousness.

'What does the Enemy say?' Cromwell bellowed to his naysayers on the opposite benches. 'What do many say that were friends at the beginning of this Parliament? They say that the Members of both Houses have got great places and commands, and the sword in their hands. They say that we will perpetually continue ourselves in grandeur. They say we do not permit the war to end, because we enrich ourselves from it.'

He gestured contemptuously at Denzil Holles and the Half-Measure men on the benches to the right of the speaker. They bawled and jeered back at him. St John was sitting with my uncle and grandfather behind Cromwell. That was not their usual place in the chamber. Alliances were shifting around the House. Cromwell went on upbraiding the recalcitrant members.

'I do conceive if the Army is not put into another method, and the war more vigorously prosecuted, the people will enforce us to a dishonourable peace,' he said, looking around. 'Be it ever so base.'

There was uproar at that: men shouting and waving their hats. Lenthall called for order again, banging on the arm of his chair. My uncle nodded; Grandfather leaned in and said something to him and St John. This was not merely a new army, I thought, they were up to something. Oliver carried on, raising his voice above the tumult.

'This I would recommend to your prudence. Let us not worry about past complaints of any commander upon any occasion whatsoever. I acknowledge myself guilty of oversights, so I know they can rarely be avoided in military affairs. Instead of strict inquiry into the causes of these things, let us instead apply ourselves to the remedy.'

They all hushed at that. He even sounded reasonable. The past weeks had been full of bitter complaints after the failings at Donnington. Cromwell had eviscerated Manchester and Essex for their vacillation and lack of fighting spirit. They had made him out to be some kind of monster: a rebellious insubordinate. Now he offered himself as a sacrifice, he would resign his commission as would all Members of Parliament, Lords and all. Oliver had trumped the tremblers. How could he be seizing command when he offered to stand down?

Cromwell continued as the chamber quieted at the proposition. 'I hope that we have such true English hearts, and zealous affections towards the general wellbeing of our mother-country, that no members of either House will scruple to *deny* themselves and their own private interests for the public good.' Nol looked directly at Denzil Holles and the others who sat across the chamber from him. 'Nor should any account it dishonour done to them, whatever Parliament resolves in this weighty matter.'

He sat down and put his hat back on, nodding to the speaker's chair. There were shouts of approval from his supporters, and as many moans of shame or nay from his enemies. Members stood to speak, trying to catch Lenthall's eye and be called from the chair. A new army and new generals was a revolution indeed.

'They have to resign commands for *the public good*?' I said. 'The tremblers will see this as nought but a way to remove Manchester and Essex from command.'

'But Cromwell offers to resign his commission as well; they cannot object to that.'

'It would be a disaster if he resigned. He wins battles.'

'Losing him is a sacrifice, but losing Manchester and Essex is thrice the bonus' said Thurloe. 'But I do not think the Lords will stand for it, even if it passes the Commons.'

'Uncle Samuel would have to resign too?'

'Yes,' said Thurloe. 'Yes, he would.'

My uncle and St John came down from the benches once Oliver finished, and we followed them back into Westminster Hall. Word of the speech had already preceded us. Gilbert Mabbot and some of the other journal writers crowded around St John, but he waved them away. Instead, he led us to a small corridor and down some steps into a well-furnished chamber. A table laden with food greeted us: freshly baked bread, a crock of butter, Welsh cheese, dried apples, small pies with mincemeat and prunes, foaming jugs of ale, even a leg of ham. My stomach growled at the sight; I had not eaten properly for two days.

St John noted my slavering.

'Eat cousin, eat,' he urged. 'You should refresh yourself.'

St John had a reputation for being cold and aloof, but with me he was the model of friendliness; he perhaps saw some gain in cultivating me. I needed no second invitation to eat from him, taking a pie and biting into it, then pouring a full cup of ale and quaffing away. Thurloe told them our news.

'The Frenchman's name is Charles Ogier de Batz de Castelmore, Comte d'Artagnan,' said Thurloe. 'He is an agent of Mazarin; a renowned blade, and an expert with powder and fuses.'[21]

---

[21]Charles Ogier de Batz de Castelmore, Comte d'Artagnan (1611-1673) was a spy and agent of Cardinal Mazarin. His real life was the basis of the semi-fictional *Memoirs of Monsieur D'Artagnan* by the French novelist Gatien de Courtilz de Sandras published in 1700. It should be noted that Sandras's novel was certainly familiar to Blandford as two copies (one in French and one in English translation) exist in the archive with his name on them. Alexander Dumas used Sandras's work and other records left by Francois De Le Rouchfoucald as the basis of his classic *The Three Musketeers,* and its sequels. The real d'Artagnan had joined the King's Guard in the 1630s not 1620s as in Dumas account, and had seen considerable action by 1644. Some of his real-life companions in the French service also formed the basis of his friends in the books (Athos, Porthos and Aramis) although their backstories were somewhat more invented by Sandras and Dumas. D'Artagnan began working for Cardinal Mazarin in the 1640s (the de-facto ruler of France during Louis XIV minority). According to Sandras's account, d'Artagnan was in England the year before, fighting on the Royalist side at the first battle of Newbury (1643), but Blandford is the first source to mention him in London in 1644. D'Artagnan served Mazarin and

'Is he the assassin?' asked my uncle. 'I see no benefit to France in murdering Prince Karl. Is there not a new envoy from France in London?'

'He arrived separately to Monsieur Sabran, the French envoy,' said Thurloe. 'The Dutch musician managed to get d'Artagnan's name from his contacts in London.' He sniffed. 'He has not seen fit to introduce me to them. My sources tell me that he was with the King at the first Newbury fight. But we know not what his purpose is in visiting now, nor for certain where he hides.'

'For certain?' said St John.

Thurloe nodded to me. I swallowed a mouthful of pie too quickly, nearly choked, coughing, and had to drain another cup of ale to clear my pipes. Uncle Samuel had a resigned look on his face when I finally composed myself.

'His servant has been seen going into Somerset House,' I said. 'Thrice this week. I watched for the last two days with my men scouting the place out. The man comes in and out the same way, by boat, once barely an hour after he had been seen first going in. We did not see him leave this last time, and I have people on every gate, postern and sneak-house.'

'Whose apartments has he been seen going into?' asked St John.

'Lucy Hay,' I said. 'Milady, the Countess of Carlisle.'

'Envoy Sabran has also been meeting with the Countess since he arrived, but he is currently in Oxford paying court to His Majesty,' said Thurloe.

'Perhaps I should take charge of this, Oliver?' said my uncle.

'Yes, indeed, I think so,' said St John. 'You know what to say?'

'Yes,' said Uncle Samuel, with a nod. 'Come along Blandford.'

I dropped the bread and butter that I had been about to stuff into my mouth, wiped my hand on a napkin and followed my uncle as he

---

later Louis XIV as a trusted agent for over thirty years, particularly during the Fronde rebellions, and it was D'Artagnan who arrested Nicholas Fouquet for Louis in 1661. He was given the Governorship of Lille but returned to action during the Franco-Dutch War (1672-78). D'Artagnan was killed during the Siege of Maastricht in 1673 by a musket ball to the throat.

scuttled out of the room.

*

William Everard had become miserable and morose. When I had first met the shabby poacher two years previous, he had been happy and quick with a jest. He had always been too godly, and pondered matters far too deeply, but now a deep anger burned within him. It was a barely concealed fury 'neath his calm facade. It concerned me. He was no violent man; a rustic and a dreamer, who yearned only for the simple pleasures of life and God. He was ill-suited to this war. It had consumed him and forged him anew into a zealot in the vanguard of the godly. At least he still counted me a friend in spite of all my sinning. We both sat with my uncle in the study on Thames Street, and Everard outlined what he had heard amongst his radical comrades.

'There is a plot afoot amongst the Covenanters and Presbyterians,' he said.

My uncle sighed. 'What plot, William? I have heard nothing.'

'There have been meetings with the Countess of Carlisle,' said Everard. 'You are for the new army, Sir Samuel, Covenanter or no. I think they keep it from you because of that. Mr Holles and the Earl of Holland met with the Countess and the French envoy last month. The Earl of Northumberland feeds information from the Committee of Both Kingdoms to his sister, whilst making pretence of Independence, and the Countess feeds every snippet to her other brother Lord Henry Percy in Oxford.'

He looked my uncle straight in the eye when he said that. My uncle and grandfather were both Presbyterians, but they were not in favour with Holles and the Tremblers. If you read Clarendon or Holles' self-serving memoirs, they would have it that Parliament was divided by religion. The Presbyterians and Covenanters wanted peace, if the King would abolish Bishops. The Independents wanted no national church and religious toleration for all: barring Anglicans, Catholics, Turks and Jews, of course. Toleration can only go so far else it will become intolerable oppression, apparently. I have never understood such an argument. There was no neat division of religion in pursuing the war against Charles Stuart. I know of Catholics who fought for Parliament, and Independents who fought for the King. The dividing line for the Houses of Parliament, in truth, was war or peace, be it ever so base.

'The Percy family always play their own game, not the nation's,' said Uncle Samuel, after a pause.

'They will try to stop the new army and force a peace with the King,' said Everard.

'Then we shall have to ensure that cannot happen,' said Uncle Samuel.

The problem for the Peace Party was the lack of votes in the House of Commons. Only the Lords could block this new army or Cromwell's self-denying ordinance: Presbyterian Lords like Lucy Hay's brother the Earl of Northumberland, Lords like Holland, Manchester, and Essex who saw their commands being snatched away and their influence diminished. If the King had any fortune or wit, he would drive a wedge between his enemies, but he had the wit of a turnip and the fortune of a Jonah.

'I want you to stay close to Denzil Holles, Mr Everard.'

'I have already acquired a position in his household, Sir Samuel. A footman, as you asked of me.'

He had a look of disdain on his face when he said that. Servitude did not come easy to William Everard, but it was a role he had played more than once for my uncle.

'Good, I thank you, William,' said Uncle Samuel.

William left after that; we both watched him leave in silence. I was growing more than frustrated by William's intransigence.

My uncle got up and walked over to one of the wall panels. Pulling it back revealed a cupboard inside. He took out a long polished wooden box, and turned back to us with a smile on his face.

'I have something of interest for you.' He handed the box to me. 'Call it an early present for Christmas.'

There was a lock on the box and no key. Uncle Samuel was patting down his pockets.

'Darnelly procured it before he died. He was ever fascinated with new inventions and weapons, and thought of arming all the Scouts with these.' He smiled grimly. 'Mr Haslerig does not countenance such an expense. It is the Office of Ordnance's property, but I do not think they will complain.'

He found a letter in his coat and passed it to me. The key was inside, and a brief note from Darnelly giving the address of a gunsmith in London who could repair the mechanism, should it break.

'Colour me intrigued,' I said.

I unlocked the box and flipped the lid back to reveal a short barrelled carbine, perfect for horseback or a siege, lying in a blue silk cloth. It had a rifled barrel and new flintlock mechanism, but the trigger was fashioned strangely. I looked at my uncle. He picked up the weapon and flipped a hatch on the action to reveal two empty chambers and a rotating drum.

'The top chamber contains powder,' he said. 'The other contains the shot. You lower the gun and push the guard down, thus.'

He pushed the trigger guard mechanism forward as if it was on a hinge, the drum turned and there was a click. He lifted the gun and pulled trigger guard back and there was another click.

'Now 'tis primed and loaded, if there were powder and shot in the chambers.'

'What?' I said. 'How is this possible?'

'As you push the guard, the drum in the mechanism turns. It has two slots: one small and the other the size of charge and ball. As the drum turns, priming powder falls into one slot, then a charge and ball in the next slot, and it clicks. When you snap the guard back, the ball and charge falls into the barrel and the priming powder to the pan, and it clicks again. Ten balls, specially made, and you need the correct grind of powder to both prime and charge.'

'That means I can make ten shots in a matter of seconds?' I said.

'Indeed, however, then you have to take considerable time recharging the chambers, and the mechanism is fragile. Maintaining it in the field will be difficult.'[22]

I took the weapon happily; such a rate of recharge could be deadly. I promised myself to head to the range at the Artillery Gardens with it as soon as I could. My uncle looked to me again.

'Now, Blandford, I think 'tis high time we paid the Countess of Carlisle a visit.'

*

---

[22]Blandford is describing a Kalthoff Repeater: a type of carbine developed in the mid Seventeenth Century that had an unmatched rate of fire until the late Nineteenth Century. The weapon was excruciatingly expensive and easy to break or foul, so was never used for general issue. The Royal Guards of Denmark were issued with a hundred Kalthoff repeaters which they used at the siege of Copenhagen in 1658. The others were mainly used by private, and very rich, individuals for hunting and exhibition.

Lucy Hay's power had always lain in her seductive charms, but they no longer held sway with the rulers of England. The Court, once her playground, shunned her as a rebel, and the rebels no longer paid her court. Cromwell, Vane, and St John had no time for her, disdained her and condemned her as wanton and scheming. Once, she had shared the beds and counsels of the great and good, now she pottered in her apartments with phantom plans and greying hair. I think she was glad to see us, glad to be relevant, glad for the attention.

'Sir Samuel, it has been too long since we supped together. Have you come to wish me the merriest of Christmas?' she said. 'And your pretty nephew too. Will you both take some wine?'

She looked tired, but her doeling eyes had lost none of their sparkle. She smiled and I was enraptured. She was still a great beauty.

'I fear it is not a social call, Milady,' said Uncle Samuel. 'I am here on official business.'

'Official business?'

'We are seeking a French agent, Milady,' he said, 'and his servant has been seen coming to these apartments, on numerous occasions.'

She looked at me 'Oh, Blandford, have you been working as your uncle's little watchman again?'

'Watching over you is ever a pleasure, Milady, never work.'

She beamed with delight at that comment.

'Your nephew is always so very charming, Samuel.'

'So people tell me,' said my uncle. 'I do not see it myself.'

'Oh, you are too dour, sirrah.'

'Perhaps, Milady, but to the question at hand?'

'Which question was that?'

I could see my uncle was starting to get vexed with Lucy Hay. She was deliberately playing the vacuous courtling to brush him off, but he knew her games far too well.

'The French agent, Milady?'

'Oh, you must mean Monsieur Sabran? I am afraid he is in Oxford with the King. But he is an envoy of the French Crown, Samuel, no spy.'

'Not Sabran, Milady. This Frenchman's name is d'Artagnan.'

'Well, that is a relief,' she said. 'Sabran leans far too closely to the Independents for my taste, but I would not wish trouble upon him.'

'As I said, Milady, it is not about Monsieur Sabran.'

Well, I have heard nothing of this Dirty Nan, not at all. Are you certain he has been seen coming here?

Was that a deliberate double negative?

'D'Artagnan,' said my uncle. 'His servant has been seen coming here.'

'Oh, I have little to do with the servants, Samuel. I am a Percy, don't you know?'

'Yes, Milady. I do know.'

'Perhaps my secretary will have some knowledge.'

She picked up a little silver bell which tinkled as she shook it. Moments later the door opened and a young man came in: tall, muscular, and well dressed in tight breeches and a new doublet. A good looking lad; I could guess what his chores were.

'Justin,' she said. 'Now, have you spoken to a Monsieur Dirty Nan recently? Has he visited here?'

'No, Milady,' the man replied.

He looked confused; he was clearly not employed for his intellect then.

'The servant's name is Planchet,' I said.

'Oh, what a silly pair,' said the Countess. 'Dirty Nan and Plant It. Are they rogues?'

'D'Artagnan and Planchet,' said my uncle.

'Well, Justin, have they visited here? Have they spoken to you or any of the servants?'

'No, Milady.'

'Very good, Justin, you have done well. I shall reward you later.' She turned back to us. 'It seems, Samuel, that we have no French agents here. I will, of course, let you know if that changes.' She gave us both a beaming smile.

There was no arguing with her, slippery little shrew.

'Then Milady, we shall take our leave. My thanks for your attention to the matter.'

The Countess smiled benevolently at us as we bowed. Uncle Samuel nodded to me and I turned to leave.

'I do tire so easily these days, I find,' she said. 'Perhaps I should send to the apothecary for some rejuvenation potions. Widow Crosse makes such wonderful tinctures that I would quite believe she casts a spell upon them. Do you know Widow Crosse, Blandford?'

There were a hundred or more apothecaries in London. Three that I knew of were closer to Essex House than Widow Crosse's shop. This was no random polite query. Could she know about John Coxon's crime? Surely the lady did not move in such circles.

I half turned. 'Yes, Milady, I know her.'

'She is such a gossip, think you not?'

99

'Gossips never prosper, Milady.'

Uncle Samuel snorted and I turned and followed him out to the courtyard. Her secretary Justin watched us from a downstairs window as we left. The hackney driver opened the carriage doors and Uncle Samuel settled into a seat. I stood at the door to speak with him before he left.

'That was unproductive, Uncle. She said nought of worth.'

'Oh, I think not,' said my uncle. 'We know that d'Artagnan has been with Milady, she would hardly have played the simpering simpleton otherwise. And she let slip an important note about the French envoy Sabran.'

I looked at him quizzically. 'She did?'

'Sabran leans towards the Independents, so she said. The King of France is for the War Party. Or Cardinal Mazarin is, which is the same thing. That is news indeed, if it be true. Nevertheless, we are no closer to finding this d'Artagnan, nor if he is the Black Bear.'

'The Countess has become Covenanter?'

Uncle Samuel laughed. 'I have told you before, Blandford, that the Percy family are only ever for the Percy family. Her brother Northumberland claims he is all for cousin St John, Cromwell, and the Independents. The Countess says she is a good Presbyterian and all for Holles and the Half-Measure men. And all the while her younger brother is in Oxford with the King. Everard was right in that. Whichever path the good Lord has ordained for England, a Percy will be in the winning party. Do you see?' I did see. 'What was that about the Crosse Apothecary?'

I did not want to answer that question, preferring to wait until I was certain. I had not told my uncle about John's part in Haniel Boswell's death.

'Emily Russell worked there for a while,' I said.

Emily Russell was my first love. I had acted badly; her brother and father ended up dead ('twas the turncoat John Hurry's fault, but I was not blameless) and she and her mother had left for the Puritan colonies in the New World. I knew Uncle Samuel would not want an angst-ridden conversation with me on that subject.

'Ah,' he said, quickly. 'Well, I should away to Derby House. Find the Frenchman, Blandford, and soon. We cannot keep Prince Karl cooped up in Whitehall forever.' He banged on the roof of the carriage with his cane. 'To Westminster,' he called. 'As quick as you can.'

His carriage rolled off, and I walked on to Drury Lane. It was not far, and I had decided to call on my sister and Kit before going home. Beeston would be there; perhaps he had some news from the Royalists in the city. D'Artagnan could not keep hidden forever. He had to break cover eventually, wherever he was. When he moved we would hear about it. At least so I prayed.

12. Spindles and Swords: London, December 1644.

Oh the distraction of this Factious Age!
Have not wile-men (who are stark mad with rage),
Brought this faire land to such a combustion,
That through their means we may feare confusion,
A horrid Tragedy is now begun.
(Traditional: *'Tis A Plaine Case Gentlemen*)

They were arguing when I arrived at the theatre. I let myself in through the garden gate from Wilde Street to the back door. I could hear raised voices coming from the stage. It was Beeston, by the booming sound of him, and Elizabeth. The redundant boxes of decorations, costumes, masks and staging gathered dust backstage at the Phoenix, unused since the closures. I paused in the crossover[23] before stepping out onto the stage to find out what the disagreement was over, and to gauge my sister's temper. Depending upon the mood, I might just sneak back out again.

'An investment now, while the price of land is cheap and London awash with workers, would set up the theatre for when they reopen. Our competitors are making plans for the same.'

Beeston was beating that tired old drum. Since the return from Amsterdam and the sight of the Shouwburg, he had badgered Elizabeth incessantly.

'I am not spending coin on a new theatre when this one barely covers its costs, said Elizabeth. 'If the prohibition is lifted, then perhaps I shall think again. Besides, your stepmother owns more of the lease on the building than I, why cannot she pay for some refurbishment?'

'My stepmother is not in London, and waiting for her to return is time ill afforded. You happily use the theatre for your purpose,' said Beeston.

'No time that cannot be made up; we will have lost nothing, and you have paid no ground rent in three years or more.'

I stepped out onto the stage. Elizabeth was sitting on a stool

---

[23]The lane behind the stage for actors to move unseen from one wing to the other.

downstage in her blue dress, white apron, and cap. There was a distaff wrapped in wool under left arm with the thread drawn across her body. She spun the drop spindle with her right hand and teased the thread with her left. She could have been Athena, or more likely Clotho.[24]

'You realise that we quite literally employ dozens of people in Wiltshire to do that?' I said as I arrived.

'Not so many now with the war,' she said, 'and this yarn be for Kit. I am knitting him a hat and robe for the winter.'

'Mayhap you can talk some sense to her, Sugar,' said Beeston. 'You saw the Shouwburg.'

'I did see the Shouwburg,' I told him. 'But I told you then that rebuilding is a waste of time and money. At least with the closures. When the war is over, perhaps you and Davenant can spend some of your own coin for a change.'

My sister looked surprised at my words.

'What?' I said at her look.

'Perhaps you be not such a feckless spendthrift, after all.'

'In the meantime, we use the most exclusive theatrical venue in London as a schoolhouse and nursery?' said Beeston. ''Tis ridiculous.'

'Can you not go back to drolls for coin?' I said. 'You can always perform at Vaughn's.' Vaughn's was the riverfront stew in Southwark where Meg stayed; Beeston occasionally plied his acting trade there.

'The Lord Mayor and Pennington are less obliging than they used to be,' said Beeston. 'Vaughn's has been raided twice in the last month alone.'

'Even less reason for me to spend my coin on a new theatre,' said Elizabeth.

Beeston sighed and gave up. He told me he was going for a drink if I cared to join him. I did not. He would have spent the night whining and nagging at me. I would stay with my sister and escort her back to Bedford Street instead. Perhaps her good opinion of me would last the evening when she saw me refuse some debauchery.

'What do you want?' she said after Beeston had left.

---

[24]Athena was the Greek Goddess of spinning, whilst Clotho was one of the Three Fates who span out the threads of life in Greek Mythology.

'What mean you?'

'What do you want? First, you show some modicum of fiscal responsibility, and then you refuse a night in the cups. What do you want?' she repeated. 'Do you need coin?'

'Actually, my sweet suspicious sister, I want for nought.'

It was the truth. I had coin given me by Uncle Samuel, and, being in London, I had received some of the monies owed to me by Parliament in pay. For once in my life, I had my own money. I had paid off the few gambling debts I had, and settled tabs at alehouses, stews and inns. I was still left with nearly a hundred pounds hidden away in my trunk.

'I thought I could escort you back to Bedford Street, when you are ready.'

She smiled at me; her face lighting up in pleasure at my words.

'Why thank 'ee Blandford. That be most considerate of you.' She looked at me conspiratorially. 'Have you spoken to John?'

'On what matter?'

'On the matter of him being in love.'

'In love? The boy be a fool. On whom has his youthful infatuated eye fallen?'

'Mariette Maupin,' she said. 'The Swordmaster's daughter.'

I tutted. 'That helps me not; Maupin already gives the boy his lesson for free.'

She rolled her eyes at me. 'You must not mock him, nor subject him to your scurrilous attempts at wit in this matter. Promise me.'

'That be unfair. The boy can be most impudent. 'Tis rare I get the opportunity to bite back.'

It would indeed be a nice change to see him squirm. He had told all my friends about Doctor Shootwixt as soon as he had an opportunity. Between Coxon and Figgis I was cursed with disrespectful servants. Mind you, they both saved my life on a number of occasions, so perhaps the respect was worth less than the life-saving. That gave me a notion. Elizabeth sometimes attended service with the Swordmaster on Tuesdays, in the city.

'I think I will attend the service with you on the morrow,' I said. 'Maupin and his daughter will be there?'

'Yes,' said Elizabeth, 'and John. He has been most diligent in his attendance of late.'

'I wager he has,' I said, grinning.

You have been less diligent, she said.

'There is something else,' she said. 'This was found in the willow tree today. I did not tell Beeston.'

She passed me a note. I had been receiving cryptic messages for over a year now, but none since the duel. They were mostly left in the willow tree at my sister's theatre. I looked at the paper. It was in the same bold hand as all the others. It was a hand I recognised but had not yet found the scribbler.

But the cowardly, the unbelieving, the vile, the murderers, the
sexually immoral, those who practice magic arts, the idolaters and
all liars – they will be consigned to the fiery lake of burning sulphur.
'I have no idea who sends these, or why,' I said. I tucked the note in my doublet.

'Perhaps it be a salutary warning about your behaviour,' said my sister. ''Tis from Revelations.'

'You would say that, though, would you not?'

*

There is a perfectly good church only a few paces from the house in Bedford Street (St Paul's, Covent Garden). The household attended there on Sundays, but Elizabeth did not like the rector and had argued with the churchwardens. Every other Tuesday, she walked into the city to St Mary's Aldermanbury; a small little chapel near the Guildhall.

I walked with her and John that day, all of us wearing sombre colours, and sat on the hard benches to listen to the speaker. I had little interest in the sermon or sermoniser, but perhaps Maupin would give me a discount if he saw my protestant piety. Normally it was Henry Burton (a dissenting malignant of the worst kind) spouting his nonsense in the dull candlelight. That eve it was a moustachioed Gloucester man in a black robe and skullcap. I remember not the name, but he was no less divisive and carping. The congregation lapped it all up: blame some foreigners and Papists for all of England's ills. Throw the Queen in for good measure, and fan the flames of hatred just enough to fill your purse in the name of God's truth. These preachers were barely disguised hatemongers profiting on our misery and madness.

'One thing have I desired of the Lord,' said the man. 'That I may dwell in his House all the days of my life, and mine head be lifted up above mine enemies who are all about me.'

'This is going to be a long sermon,' I whispered to Elizabeth.

She scowled at me and turned to listen to the speaker. On her other side, John kept glancing over at Maupin's daughter, and she back, batting her eyelashes and pretending all coy. She noted me watching them, blushed and turned away. John glared at me. I sighed and turned back to the preacher.

'It is clear to me that the Pope in Rome is the Anti-Christ and his city nought but Babylon rebuilt.' The man gripped at his lectern so tight his knuckles went white, and he was quite literally frothing bile at the mouth. 'The deceitful workings and enticing means of the Babylonish whore intoxicates the kingdoms of the earth. She hath sent her agents into our three kingdoms for this end: to entice, and beguile, and seduce with wine and fornication.'

In all honesty, the papist whore of Babylon sounded an interesting companion for an eve. Who enjoys not the wine of fornication...? Yes, yes, I know – blasphemy.

The preacher carried on with his irrational ranting, wildly gesticulating, waving his arms and rolling his head. I worried he was having a stroke.

'They win souls to them, every day in England, hoping greatly to undermine us by little and little; and grow to greater numbers.'

That was a stretch. Most people in the country were quite happy with the King's church. The godly radicals were always in the minority, but they always shouted the loudest, and, for such parsimonious souls, always seemed to have the most funds.

'The papists are strangely cunning in their carriages. They take the shapes of physicians, that in a more covert manner, they may visit the sick and pervert them. I have seen it myself,' declared the zealot, and carried relentlessly on. 'They take the habits of beggars, soldiers, captains, and of countrymen, and they will be our servingmen too, if occasion gives way.' He was coming unhinged, spitting as he ranted. 'There is scarce a house, that looks like a house, which they have not fitted with secret doors and conveyances.'

'This be nonsense,' I whispered to Elizabeth. 'Are papists shape-shifters and wizards?' She was frowning, but not at my words.

'Have no fear.' The preacher raised his voice, and arms to the heavens. 'For the Popish Religion and all the power of Rome shall decay. It is foreshadowed by symptoms of its death. All these great commotions that hath been raised in England, Scotland, and Ireland are but the pangs of dying Popery amongst us.'

'Well, that be reassuring,' I said.

My sister pursed her lips at that. I am not sure if she was angry or trying to stop herself from laughing. The preacher was spouting nonsense, even to her. I sat back and dozed whilst he ranted. Elizabeth elbowed me in the stomach as he drew, finally, to a climax.

'The destruction and extirpation of Anti-Christ shall make way for the setting up of the Kingdom of Heaven on earth, in all its glory and beauty.' He paused for dramatic effect, and in a quieter tone. 'That alone should maketh a people or a nation truly happy. For Babylon is fallen; Babylon is fallen.'[25]

I looked around at the congregation sitting in raptures at his speech. These fanatics had forgotten their wits, their reason. I think it was the war, so desperate were the people for a respite, for peace and an end to division, that any half-brained cozener who promised them God's grace had a captive audience. There is no point in rationalising with such people, everything is about how they feel and reason matters not.

Afterwards, I spoke to Maupin briefly, but he was eager to return to Spitalfields. He was quite obliging when Master Coxon asked to accompany him and his daughter home (to see them back safely, you understand). Most men would have baulked at such an idea, but Maupin seemed quite happy. He was a refugee and a stranger in this land, I concluded, but remarkably sanguine about it all. Some people are simply made such. Others are right miserable bastards from birth to death. Hugo the musician was cut from the latter cloth.

'John be in love,' said Elizabeth, gleefully clapping her hands.

'What is this? Do you plan on marrying him off so young?'

'I plan to marry you off first.' She pulled her cloak around, straightened her hat, and linked her arm in mine. 'Though heaven help the poor unfortunate I manage to cozen into it.'

I burst out laughing. 'I think I am not yet ready for such a sacrament. You need not fear, we have Kit to carry on the family line, and I am sure Henry and James will crap out some more.'

Elizabeth's eyes widened; I realised what I had said.

'You have not mentioned his name since he was killed.'

I paused before answering. 'There is little to say; we were not close.'

She took my hand as we walked. 'Do not let the war consume you. There be too much madness and hate in this land because of it. A new wife will bring back the sweetness in your soul.'

'It do be the war,' I conceded. 'If the New Army ordinance passes I may resign my commission. I think I will be glad to do it. Mayhap that will bring my sweetness back, else they start calling me Sour Candy instead.' I grinned.

---

[25]Revelations 14:8

'Resign? I expected that not.' She looked surprised.

'Uncle Samuel would have to give up his rank,' I said. 'He would become but a Member of Parliament once more. Perhaps they would give me a troop of dragoons in the new army, but I would get little else.' I paused. 'This fight cannot last forever. I think I have played my fair part.'

*

John and Mariette moved like a blur, both thrusting dodging and parrying at a speed I could only dream of matching; both of them grinning from ear to ear as they fenced. The boy was stronger, and nimble on his feet, but Mariette Maupin could match him.

'They are evenly balanced,' I said to the Swordmaster.

I had spent the morning practising my footwork and then parrying thrusts from Maupin, over and over until my arms ached. John had spent the lesson fencing with Maupin's daughter. The boy seemed to be enjoying himself inordinately.

'She is fighting left-handed,' said Maupin, with a smile. 'I have seen none so gifted, except for your mulatto. He will be better than her, if he practices.'

'He be a freeborn Englishman,' I said. 'He was born in Wapping.'

Maupin turned to me. 'I think it was your King James who said to judge a man on the darkness of his skin is ridiculous. He was correct, I believe.'

'Yes, well,' I said. 'King James also believed in witches and warlocks.'

'Do you not, Captain?'

'I have seen no evidence of them. No real evidence, at least. 'Tis but an insanity overtaking all.' I gestured to the duel with my sword. 'The boy wins.'

John's strength and endurance were too much for the slight girl, and perhaps her skirts not best suited for such exertion.

'Switch, Mariette,' called Maupin.

The girl flicked the blade into her right hand and stepped to the side to avoid a thrust from John. Then she attacked, stabbing at his face so he was fain to step back else risk losing an eye. She gave him no respite, dancing forward on tiptoes and thrusting at his belly. John did not hold his terza guard position; he was off balance with his sword raised too high. The blow caught him square in the stomach.

'You still leave your belly exposed, Master Coxon,' said Maupin, and called a halt to the lesson.

'May I have permission to take Mariette into town?' asked John of her father.

He nodded his acquiescence and the two of them bustled together making ready to leave.

'Make sure you are back by this eve, Master Coxon,' I said. 'We have work to attend to.'

'Yes, sir,' he said as the hurried off.

'You are busy with the Office of Ordnance, Captain?' asked Maupin. 'There always be something,' I said.

'Mariette told me,' said Maupin. 'A threat to Prince Karl of the Palatinate?' He must have seen my look. 'The boy told her.'

I cursed my cock-happy scout with his pillow whispers. I would have words with him about that. Maupin was a decent enough sort, but our business was supposed to be secret. Then I remembered all the times I had unwittingly done the same.

'It is not so serious,' I told Maupin. 'Hopefully, it will be resolved soon, perhaps even tonight.'

I left the Swordmaster's and headed home to Bedford Street, after promising Maupin that I would pass his fond regards onto Elizabeth. They were meeting at some sermon or lecture at least once a week, I noted, and Maupin was good looking enough. Was there a budding romance there along with John and Mariette?

Cross Deep, Twickenham 1720.

And what's a life? A weary pilgrimage,
Whose glory in one day doth fill the stage,
With childhood, manhood, and decrepit age.
(Francis Quarles, *The Brevity of Life*)

The Duchess of Marlborough is not a patient woman. My tale dragged on late that night, quite deliberately on my part, and in the end she called a halt. I thought that would be the end of it, but someone had told her that I write my memoirs (one of my treacherous servants, no doubt). I am instructed to continue my tale by hand, and forward it on to her when it is done. She packed me back home with instructions to not tarry in my telling, lest I expire (insolent harridan). She realises not that the arthritics limit the time I spend with a pen. I shall have to hire a scribe. The Cleland boy can do it. His parents have seemingly given up on him as a lost cause, and they have two other sons. I know how that feels. He be off to school in the autumn so his penmanship needs the practice.

The idiot is seemingly unconcerned by the attentions of nobility. He thinks it is all over company business, but I am not so certain. There is something else; something to do with Princess Sophia. I fear the Duchess knows already.

'I make no claim to understand stockjobbing,' I told the idiot as we sat down to supper. 'But I understand the value of things. One single ship cannot feed the masses who have invested. There would not be enough profit in one hundred ships; one thousand ships even.'

I heaped up my plate with veal pie and fricassee of egg from the table. I considered adding a roast squab, but Doctor Barrowby tells me that too much food in my belly strains my heart. Bugger Barrowby; I added the squab to my plate. The idiot raised an eyebrow.

'I do not think you understand, Uncle.'

'Understand what? If I own an estate, I have an income based on the value of the land and my industry in exploiting it. It is there in bricks and mortar, blood and earth. Your company has no assets to speak of, and only speculative profits that can never be realised.'

'A nation is hardly a country estate, uncle.'

'The principle is the same.'

'Actually, Uncle, it is not. Have you heard of Colbert?'

'Of course, I have heard of Colbert, witless boy. He was a scheming, grasping, parasite, and he was French. I had heard of Colbert long before you were born, and I wager he had heard of me. I was comrades with his best intelligencer. What of him?'[26]

The idiot had the good grace to blush.

'Mr Craggs the Younger is using some of Colbert's ideas with the company, and Mr Law the Scotsman's notions.'

'Mr Law the Jacobite,' I pointed out. 'Mr Law the traitor. I warned you about the Craggs; they cannot be trusted. Why would this be of interest to the Duchess?'

'The company will present a plan to Parliament, very soon,' he said. 'All of the nation's debt will be secured against the company's stock. The Duchess seeks advantage before the bill is passed.'

'She be just another schemer, then. What of Walbrook?'

'The company will take over the Bank of England, eventually.'

'Madness.'

He sniffed. 'Madness of no, it will pass in the House. Make sure you tell none, Uncle. I tell you only to end the complaining.'

I sniffed right back at him. 'Who would I tell? The Cleland boy? His interest is in bawdy jokes, not the national purse.'

'What is the interest in the King's late mother?' asked the idiot.

'I know not.'

That is a lie.

---

[26]Jean-Baptiste Colbert (1619 - 1683) was Louis XIV Finance Minister.

13. The Comte d'Artagnan: London, December 1644.

A virgin most pure, as the Prophets do tell,
Hath brought forth a baby, as it hath befell,
To be our Redeemer from death, hell and sin,
Which Adam's transgression had wrapped us in.
(Traditional Christmas Carol: *A Virgin Most Pure*)

London is peaceful when the snow falls. A calm shroud of white descends upon the city, driving people indoors and magicking the smoke-blackened buildings clean. It does not last long: the sun comes out, carts cut muddy ruts, dark lines like ink across parchment; the powder melts into an icy slurry, mixed with piss pot emptyings and horse-shit, and the delightful enchantment is broken.

'He be in there?'

'Aye, Sugar,' said Sam. 'And his manservant. They are not hiding themselves, spending money like water, drinking and wenching.'

'They must be up to something.'

The Tabard is a dirty broken down old stew in Southwark, not far from the bridge. It is built around three sides of a cobbled courtyard open onto the street. A couple of stories high with covered galleries. Inside, there is a large open taproom full of punks and pimps, a long polished wooden bar; tapsters, maids, and ale barrels. They have dancing, music, and games of chance, and an old grey-haired whore by the bar will take out her wooden gnashers and suck on your cock for a silver sixpence. Out the back are rooms overlooking the river, with higher stakes card games and skittle alleys. Even the falling snow could not give such an establishment a pristine gleam. This was where our quarry, Monsieur d'Artagnan, played. He had women waiting upon him, and Hugo playing music to entertain. Food had been served and sack poured; all of it conspicuous and extravagant. I had people all around the building. Meg was one of the servers and John played at potboy. We had the Comte d'Artagnan cornered, but I have lost enough money on baiting to know that a cornered beast is most dangerous.

'This be far too easy,' I said. 'He keeps himself hidden for two weeks, even with us scouring every tavern and flophouse in the city, and now he suddenly appears in one of Southwark's more popular if insalubrious stews?'

'You think it is a trap?'

'I know not. Let him not go upstairs,' I called to the men. ''Tis a warren of rooms and twisted corridors to get lost in.'

One of the soldiers gave a knowing grin: upstairs at The Tabard is still infamous. A set of crooked wooden steps lead up from the taproom to private chambers for special patrons. If you pause on a landing, the sound of couples fornicating in the rooms will whisper on the air, or the slap, giggle and gasp of those with more... exotic tastes. We could find anything or anyone happening up there.

'We go in when the bells ring out?' said Sam.

The old priory church was only a stone's throw from the inn. Seven bells that would ring out across the south bank of the river. At eight-of-the-clock every night they sang out the curfew peal to mark the end of the day, and all of London knew the stews, taverns, and alehouses of Southwark were open for worshippers.

'Yes,' I said. 'The men know to hold the entrances?'

Sam just nodded.

I checked the repeater carbine to make sure it was charged and ready. Whilst I hoped that the arrest would pass off simply and without incident, there was a part of me that was excited to see how the weapon performed in action. I had not yet tried it on the range at the Artillery Grounds, and promised myself to test the weapon properly as soon as possible.

'Meg is in there,' said Sam. 'Have you told her of your feelings yet?'

'That be blunt.'

'Franny used to say how you could not see what was right under your nose when your cock was involved, Sugar.' Sam smiled. 'Sometimes we need to point it out to you.'

'The married man must turn his staff into a stake,' I said.

'What nonsense is this?' said Sam.

'One of Figgis's,' I told him. 'He does not have Franny's wit.'

'Nobody expects you to get married, Sugar, but in times like this 'tis best not to leave love unsaid.' He looked doleful. 'Take it from one who knows.'

Sam's heart had broken when Franny was executed. I realised that it was almost a year to the day since Hurry hanged him, but Sam's heart was not yet mended.

The ring-of-bells from the priory pealed out their clear tone across Southwark. It was our call to arms. Sam nodded to the men, and we walked across the cobbled courtyard, up the wooden steps and through the double doors. The taproom was full of people who looked at us in silence as we entered. John appeared from the throng. 'This way, sir, he is out the back.'

We followed my valet down a couple of steps and into a narrow corridor with a door at the end. None of the drinkers in the main room intervened, nor the staff, they just turned back to their drinks and conversations. The Tabard was like that; Cromwell could have ridden through the bar-room buck naked on a billygoat, and the clientele would have barely raised an eyebrow. John paused at the door.

'In there, sir.'

I opened the door with my carbine in hand. It swung in to reveal a big room with large windows overlooking the river at the far end; a table laden with food and drink and the Frenchmen sitting and smoking pipes. Hugo was in a corner stamping his feet and playing a fast dance on the guitarro whilst three maids, with their skirts lifted up around their waists, waved their naked arse cheeks at the Frenchmen and his servant. They shook up down in time to the music and sang along.

> *My dame is sick, and gone to bed.*
> *I'll go and mould my cocklebread!*
> *Up with my heels and down with my head,*
> *That's the way to mould cockle-bread.*[27]

We marched into the middle of the room. D'Artagnan did not move as I pointed the repeatable at him. Hugo stopped playing his tune, and the girls paused in their jig. I noted, with a start, that one of the girls was Meg. Her skirt was around her waist showing off her legs, and barely concealing her cuckoo's nest now she had stopped shaking. She ushered the other two girls out of the room. I waited for them to leave before dealing with Monsieur d'Artagnan. He was more presumptuous, speaking before Meg closed the door behind the punks.

'Bonjour, Captain Candy. I have been expecting you. Would you care for a drink?'

I turned back to the French spy. He had a wide grin across his face.

'You speak English?' I said.

'Apparently so, Monsieur. You speak French so very badly, that I

---

[27]Moulding the Cockle Bread was a 17th Century version of twerking that would make Miley Cyrus blush.

feel 'tis the better tongue to converse in. Madeira?'

Did every man know that I drank Madeira out of preference?

'I speak French badly?'

'And have a habit for stating the obvious.'

'I state the obvious?'

'And tend to repetition, Monsieur.'

I honestly did not know what to say. I stood silent, dumbfounded. I had expected him to run or to fight, not to offer me a glass of wine whilst taking lascivious glances at a woman I was... very fond of. I sat down and his tubby grey-haired manservant handed me a glass of the Madeira. I sipped at it, swilling the sweet nectar around my tongue. This damnable Frenchman was too-clever-by-half. John and Sam kept their carbines on him. Megan came back in with her skirts still hoisted up. D'Artagnan's grin grew wider at the sight of her.

'Are you looking at my legs, sirrah?' she said, pulling her skirts down.

'Non, Mademoiselle, I am above that...'

Megan actually blushed at the outrageous French swine. He turned back to me once again before I could say anything.

'I surrender, Captain Candy.'

'You are under arrest,' I told him.

'But I have already surrendered, so I cannot, therefore, be arrested.'

'That be sophistry,' I said, even more irritated.

There was something about this man; there is something about all French men: a Latin temperament with a smug superiority that infuriates English reserve. Do not mistake me for Xenophon. French women are intoxicating and enchanting, 'tis but the men that are most difficult. The servant spoke to d'Artagnan as he topped up my glass of sack.

'Avez-vous à les irriter, maître?' (Do you have to irritate, Master?)

'Oh, Planchet, you are une rabat-joie.'(a killjoy) The grin fell away from his face and he looked serious. 'Take me to your uncle, Monsieur Candy. I have some information of interest to him, I think.'

*

My uncle and grandfather were still in London. The arguments about Cromwell's Self Denying Ordinance had rumbled on through December. The House of Commons finally voted in favour of the bill two days previously, but the House of Lords were taking their time to consider the design.

Uncle Samuel and Thurloe had both questioned d'Artagnan about his presence in London and had now called a conference at the manse on Thames Street. I noted that Mr Haslerig was not in attendance. Sadly, Mr Butler was there, along with my grandfather, Everard, Thurloe, and the Frenchman. None of us held out much hope for the new army.

'The Lords will throw it out,' my uncle told me. 'They pin their hopes on a new peace treaty. The King has agreed to yet more talks; a fruitless diversion.'

'Mr Holles hopes that the King will see sense and compromise,' said Everard. 'But he has other treasonous irons in the fire.

Everard had been working in Denzil Holles London household as a servant and had picked up some valuable information. He explained what he had uncovered.

'The Countess of Carlisle plots with her brother and Holles. They plan to use Prince Henry, the King's youngest son, or perhaps Prince Karl if the boy should prove too obstinate.'

'What plan?' asked my uncle.

'Peace and Presbyterianism,' said the Everard. Everything you would desire, Sir Samuel, even if the Godly do not.'

That was most bold of Everard; I glared at William for his insolence.

'It would not settle the governance of the Kingdom, William,' said my grandfather. 'His Majesty cannot be trusted to govern wisely and justly. If he could, we would not be where we are.'

I noted the Frenchman smiled at our discussion. I did question the wisdom of his attendance (everything we said was certain to find its way to Cardinal Mazarin in France), but I trusted my uncle and Thurloe's judgement. D'Artagnan was not, it seemed, The Black Bear. He had been sent to protect Prince Karl from the assassin by the French Cardinal.

'Find out more about this plot, William, if you will,' said my uncle. 'I think the King will welcome it not; the news from Scotland and the failures at Newbury and Donnington give him renewed hope of victory in the field.'

'Yes, Sir Samuel, said Everard, glaring back at me.

The Earl of Montrose was sweeping all before him in Scotland. Covenanter armies had been annihilated one-by-one. If Scotland be lost to the King, I thought, the north of England would be threatened again. All the gains won in bloody victory at Marston Moor would be lost.

'Monsieur Sabran, His Most Christian Majesty's envoy, tells a similar tale,' said the Comte. 'He is not in favour of these...' He paused as if searching for the word. 'Plottings. However, the Countess and her noble supporters already seek to have him dismissed by Paris. The Cardinal will, of course, oblige. Nobody wishes to upset King Louis' Aunty Henrietta, but a new envoy will only arrive after this treaty is decided. It is not in Paris's interest to interfere for either side in this guerre Anglais.' (English war).

'Cardinal Mazarin has promised the Queen that the Duke of Lorraine will bring ten thousand men to serve the King,' Thurloe pointed out.

'Indeed,' said the Comte smiling. 'But sadly we are unable to procure the necessary ships to transport Gaston's phantom army.'

'Well,' said Butler. 'What do you here then? What is your papist cardinal's interest in good Prince Karl and England?'

D'Artagnan smiled at my uncle's moon-faced secretary. We all knew that it was in Paris's interest that England remained in turmoil, leaving the Cardinal and France free to re-order Europe as he pleased.

'His Eminence the Cardinal has many interests, Monsieur Butler,' said d'Artagnan, opening his arms widely.

'If the Comte would forgive me?' said Thurloe. 'I can give a reasonable summation for you, Mr Butler.'

Butler blushed red at that. He had thought to look clever in questioning the foreigner, but now Thurloe made him look uninformed. The Frenchman nodded for Thurloe to continue.

'France is stirring up trouble against Spanish influence in Milan and Naples,' said Thurloe. 'French agents are all over Italia, from the reports I have received. The new pontiff in Rome is also Spanish and particularly unreceptive to the cardinal's designs.'

D'Artagnan grimaced but Thurloe carried on regardless.

'Denmark is likely to sue for peace after losing their fleet last month, which leaves the Hapsburg Empire with few allies of worth. The Swedes can assert their authority over the North German princes, and France will gain the Spanish Netherlands and influence in Italy, and perhaps even the next pope.'[28]

---

[28]The naval Battle of Fehmarn was fought in October 1644, not November as the memoir states, but news of the Swedish/Dutch victory probably arrived at the start of November. The result left the Swedish and Dutch in complete control of the Baltic Sea and the

'What does Prince Karl matter in this?' I asked.

'As a bargaining chip,' said d'Artagnan. 'He claims the Palatinate; who rules along the Rhine is of interest to France.'

'Paris wants the Palatinate as a buffer to the Empire, not as an Imperial province,' said Thurloe. 'Prince Karl would be such a buffer; his religion matters not to France. Cardinal Mazarin is a pragmatist, as was Richelieu before him. At the moment France controls the Rhine valley. It is unwilling to relinquish such control. So the Empire sends an assassin to kill the prince; it opens the Palatinate question once more, drives a wedge between their protestant enemies and distracts the French. The assassin will be expensive, but for such an outcome it would be a cheap investment. The Black Bear could turn the war in their favour once more.'

'Do we have any information on who this Black Bear actually is? Is he German then?' I asked.

'He can speak many different languages, by all accounts,' said d'Artagnan, unhelpfully. 'He could pass as a native of many lands. In the past, he has been a Turkish Mamluke, a Jewish doctor, a Frenchman, a Spaniard, Catholic and Protestant. He is une fantôme.' (A ghost)

'Not English,' said Butler, as if it were a matter of pride.

'Not English,' agreed d'Artagnan. 'It is such a... unique petite country, after all.'

Butler blushed red again. He had enough wit to see the barb.

'We also know that he has been in England for some months,' said the Comte. 'Since at least the summer; I was rather hoping that you would know more by now.'

'That he is already here changes things somewhat,' said my uncle. 'There is less need to watch the ports and more need to focus on the City. He will be in London, somewhere. Blandford.' He looked to me. 'I want you to assist our friend the Comte, along with Mr Thurloe. It remains imperative that we find this assassin. I shall see what I can find of this plot of the Countess and Holles.'

The meeting broke up at that. We all had our tasks to take care of. Thurloe left to report back to Oliver St John. Everard was quickly out of the door, not waiting to speak with me. I confess that irked, as

---

Danish government sought peace terms, leaving the Holy Roman Empire on the defensive.

did his rudeness to Uncle Samuel. Presbyterian and Independent; the bitter fault lines were cutting deeper by the day. D'Artagnan's podgy servant was waiting in the parlour with John and Figgis as we all emerged from my uncle's study.

'Do you have chambers?' I asked them.

'We have been staying with... friends,' said d'Artagnan. 'But I do not think we can return.'

'I know where you can stay,' I said.

Bread Street was only minutes away, and I still had the key to my old lodgings. It was empty by my design. I had asked Uncle Samuel to leave it thus in case I needed refuge from Elizabeth. I had also used it as a chamber when I was late or soused in the City. I saw d'Artagnan and his servant in and settled, and then headed home to my sister.

Anne Candy to Elizabeth Candy.

Sweet Sister,

I am presently in Antwerp and set to sail to France on the next available ship. There is much to recount of my journey so I shall begin at the beginning. In my last to you, I told of my travel arrangements. I have been exceeding fortunate, and give thanks for the Lord's blessings that accompanied my journey.

In the first, I arrived in Amsterdam at the start of November. I saw your letters delivered to factors in the city. The results of which should be sent on to you presently. On my journey, I was accompanied by an officer of the French Crown set to protect me by our Queen herself: Henri, Seigneur d'Aramitz Musketeer of the

Maison du Roi.[29]

Seigneur d'Aramitz is most gentle, gracious and kind. He be a papist, but his father is a loyal and devout Huguenot. Fear not for my eternal soul, sweet Oizys.[30] From Amsterdam, we travelled onto The Hague, where I delivered much correspondence and was presented at the Winter Queen and the Dutch Stadholder's courts. Seigneur d'Aramitz was known to many in The Hague and provided introductions. You cannot imagine my surprise upon discovering our own Blandford languishing in the dungeons. It was not that he was under arrest that shocked, of course, more the detail that he was abroad only three days before being so detained. Even for him, that is swift work indeed.

Seigneur d'Aramitz said he knew of our brother's exploits and had heard tell that he was an efficient agent of the perpetual parliament. I told him such was surely scurrility and rumour for Blandford be a vain spendthrift. Seigneur d'Aramitz smiled and told me that he was certain our brother was much more than that. It was on his influence that I was presented to the chamberlain of the Winter Queen, to plead clemency for Blandford and his mulatto. The results of which I shall not recount here, for they are of the utmost secrecy, and I am certain our brother will have told you anyway; he being an unashamed gossip and storyspinner. It was bittersweet to see him and then part so soon, but there is a new hardness about him that worried me. I liked the moustache and beard not.

From thence we returned to Amsterdam and took ship for Hamburg. The weather was exceeding cold with ice on the ship's decks, and icicles dangling from the ropes and sails. When they fell all were at

---

[29]Henri, Seigneur d'Aramitz (1620-1674) was the historical basis of Alexandre Dumas, Aramis, in the Musketeer books. He joined the Musketeers in 1640 and was a close associate of the Comte d'Artagnan, alongside Armand d'Athos and Isaac de Porthau. D'Athos was killed in a duel in December 1643 whilst de Porthau survived until 1712 and often corresponded with Blandford before his death.

[30]Greek goddess of worry and distress.

risk of a skewering. The ship's master ordered us women below, and I was happy to go in the conditions. Yet, when a school of leviathan was spotted I took up a serving boy's breeches, doublet and cloak, tucked my hair under a Montero, and wrapped my face up in a scarf so as not to draw notice. Then I went up onto the deck to watch the whales with Henri. There were five or six of the beasts swimming along with the ship, and nearly as long as it. They would rise up out of the water and blow their spouts. It was a most delightful sight of God's creation. There was some talk of hunting the beasts, but the ship's master said that it was a good omen that they accompanied us and would countenance it not.

We soon spied the mouth of the River Elbe and took the waterway to Hamburg. I disembarked to find many English in the city; more even than Holland or Paris, but they are longer in exile. We delivered our letters to the Marquis of Newcastle's household and awaited our replies. A crowd waited on the words we brought, and all wished to write back to Paris. Henri and I waited a week or more in the German city, and were offered much hospitality and welcome.

The return to Antwerp has been of less enjoyment: a week of rough seas and vomiting until we arrived here. I would travel overland from here to Paris, but it is through Spanish lands and Henri says our letters are too important to risk. When the weather turns we shall take for ship. I enclose this with a London bound merchantman, but the master is well known to Henri so I have all faith that these words shall reach you swiftly.

I shall write more when I am safely returned to Paris.

Your ever loving sister,

Anne.

December 12th, 1644.

Postscript. Merry Christmas to all, kiss Kit for me. A.

14. Beware The Burned Man: London, December 1644.

Let Kings beware how they provoke
Their Subjects with too hard a Yoke,
For when all's done, it will not do,
You see they break the Yoke in two.
(Anon, attributed to T.B., *The Rebellion of Naples*)

'Twas but the two of us for supper: my sister and I. John would ordinarily have been there but instead he supped with Mariette Maupin and her father. Elizabeth regaled me of what a good match it would be for the boy and how besotted he was with the girl. She then told me that the Swordmaster had been oh-so chivalrous and generous of spirit, and pious too; piety always mattered to my sister.

'More herring pie?' She carved me off a slice before I could answer and topped up my syllabub from a jug.

'We have servants, you understand? What do we pay them for?' This was becoming a regular complaint.

'I pay them,' she reminded me. 'The servants are eating, it has been a busy day and seeing to ourselves is no hardship.'

I shrugged; it was, after all, her household and her money. Figgis would be stuffing his face by the fire in the kitchen, pronouncing his gobbets of witless wisdom to the cook and maids. I decided to make small talk.

'Have you thought any more on Beeston and the Phoenix?'

'No,' she said. 'The theatre can wait; the lease runs another ten years but I think I will sell my share, if a buyer could be found.' She paused as if deciding something. 'I am considering an investment in the New World.'

'In the New World? Damn me, why?'

She frowned at me. 'Do not swear, Blandford. It is most unedifying to God. My late husband left me with concerns in the Dutch colony south of Boston. There are opportunities for investment with the Massachusetts Company.'

'Massachusetts,' I stumbled over the unfamiliar word. 'I barely know where that be.'

'Many men have come back with the war, to fight against the King; the colony needs money and land is cheap.'

'That is because it is full of murderous savages unhappy with the new landlords,' I said. 'Just how rich are you?'

It was something I had oft wondered recently. Elizabeth had embezzled a few hundred pounds by forging my father's signature many years before – with the connivance of her doddering lawyer. From that, she had managed to buy failing businesses across London and transform them into thriving little shops, mills, and bakers. My sister had a talent for spotting and organising gifted craftsmen and traders, who were utterly incompetent and inept at managing their money, and transforming them into prosperous concerns. Her short-lived Dutch husband had also been wealthy enough to build this fine house on Bedford Street, but I had never inquired into the source of his coin. Elizabeth explained that his investments were quite extensive in the Americas and the Indies through Dutch companies.

'I think it would be wiser to move assets into English companies,' she said. 'A Dutch war would be most concerning.'

'Little chance of a Dutch war,' I told her. 'Are you as rich as Father?' She had not answered my original question.

She smiled. 'I have coin enough, Blandford. But I do not like all my eggs in one basket. My late husband's legacy is extensive but I need to spread it out. I have begun that process of late with Anne's assistance. Perhaps there may be some employ for you, if you be interested? You will need some estate of your own if you are to marry'

'For me?'

It sounded like a trap; I knew Elizabeth. I would get some gentle offer that would turn into devilish trouble. And she had been most insistent on marriage of late. I knew she liked Meg Powell, but I did not see her welcoming a courtesan and spy as a sister-in-law.

'If you are to resign your commission along with Uncle Samuel, you will need to find something to do. You showed some good monetary sense with Beeston the other day. You are not witless; mayhap you could be of use to me in the Americas?'

'You plan to ship me off to puritan colonies to fight heathen savages for the Godly? Have I not done enough fighting? And who are you planning on marrying me off to? Will you lead me from farm to farm like a bullock at stud?'

'Be not so overdramatic, Blandford. I send you not to fight Indians, but to buy land and arrange a factor in Boston, perhaps in Bermuda as well.'

'I will think on it,' I told her.

It did not sound an attractive prospect. In faith, I had planned on some extended debauchery and drunkenness without the beat of a drum to answer to: marsh sickness, savages, slaves and shipping sounded like hard work, and dangerous. I did recall that Emily Russell, my first love, was somewhere in New England, but then felt a pang of guilt over Meg Powell.

I have heard tell that you can love more than one person at the same time. I believe it to be true, but it does sound like an excuse for infidelity.

'Before I forget,' she said. 'Another message came in the willow tree yesterday. You did not return until very late, Rosie tells me, and you had not arisen afore I left this morning.' She handed me a folded paper.

Rosie the maid was a sneak: a short, fat and warty Gloucester hog. I had been drinking in a chop house off Cheapside with d'Artagnan, and had been soused and unsteady on my return. The maid had complained all the while of me waking the household. I took the note off my sister. It was in the same bold hand as always with no sigil or mark.

If any man's work shall be burned, he shall suffer loss: but he himself shall be saved; yet so as by fire[31].

'It is from Corinthians,' she told me.

I tucked the note into my doublet.

'I have no idea whom these be coming from or why. 'Tis most frustrating, and this one be just as meaningless.'

'They only come when you are in London,' she said. 'When you went to Yorkshire in the spring only one was sent, and that found just after you had left; it could have been placed before and missed. After that, they ceased.

'Until the one that led to the duel,' I said.

'Then nothing for months until these last two come in short order.'

'So, they wait for my return to start again, whoever it is?'

'Or when you left the city, they also did.'

That thought was a much more concerning notion. Could I have been followed to York and back? I knew the writing was none of my companions on that journey. Or had the scribbler gone somewhere else when I was in the north? Why the long gaps between delivery, and what had sparked the two most recent missives?

'Even more for me to ponder on,' I said. 'Tonight at least I shall be

---

[31]Corinthians 3:15

early to bed to sleep on it all. I have swordplay with *Chevalier* Maupin in the morning.' I winked at her. Was there the hint of a blush? 'Afterwards, I need to see Thurloe before he reports to Prince Karl.'

'Find out what happens with John and Mariette. I wish to know.'

'Is gossiping not a sin?'

''Tis not gossip to look to the affairs of my household,' she said with a toss of the head. 'He that is ungodly, swears, drinks, and profanes the Sabbath, can hope for no salvation in Christ. Anne is in the right, there be a new hardness about you. A good wife will set Master Coxon, and you, on the path to heaven.'

'I have been to Heaven,' I said, glibly. ''Tis a wild stew near Charring Cross, and the drinks are damnably expensive.'

She sighed in despair.

'I have had news from home,' she said, changing the topic.

'From home?'

'From Dickon Candy in Wiltshire; he plans to join the new army. I have written to him.'

I remembered the boy, a few years younger than me. He was the one with the puppy.

'More fool him,' I said.

*

I found Dickon weeping in the hay meadow behind the hall. He was sitting in the tall grass holding the puppy in his arms; he shielded it from me as I arrived.

'You shall not have him,' he cried.

'I want him not, Dickon.'

'James says he be a runt; he will drown him in the Avon.'

My hateful elder brother had found a new victim to bully. The arrival of my Uncle, Aunt, and seven cousins had been an opportunity for James to prey on the young boy. Richard was only a year or two younger than I, but shy and quiet; the perfect quarry for James's particular penchant for vindictive spite. One of the stable dogs had birthed a litter not long after they had arrived. The old bitch spawning three little beggars, but this one was the least: tiny in size compared to its siblings, flopping oversized ears too large for its head, lolling tongue and gangling legs. 'Twas an ugly beast indeed.

'In truth, it do be a runt, Dickon. I think not that it will survive.'

'You shall not murder the animal, it be sinful. I will keep him alive.'

My young cousin was determined at the least.

'What will you call him?' If he wished to waste his energies keeping

the animal alive, who was I to complain?

'Goliath,' he said.

'Goliath? That be a misleading name. You should call him Tom Thumb.'

'He will grow,' said Dickon. 'I shall feed him.'

I could see James coming over the field and had a choice to make. On the one hand, this was not my fight, and anything I did to help my cousin would be returned ten times over by my brother. At the least the eldest monkey was away, else he would have joined in the torture. On the other hand, James would not be at home long to torment me, he was up to Oxford soon, and I was better placed to protect myself than my young cousin. And, well, I enjoyed upsetting my brother. We were at war long before England fell out. That decided me. James had a riding crop in his hand, but he would not dare use it on Dickon. That would bring down my uncle's wrath, and my father's displeasure at the embarrassment caused.

'Give me the animal,' said my brother as he arrived. ''Tis a cruelty to let it live.'

''Tis a cruelty that we suffer you,' I said standing in front of him. 'But the good Lord works in mysterious ways, so Elizabeth tells me. Are you so ill-formed in character that you now take pleasure from drowning small puppies? That be moon-struck strange, James.'

'You dare to challenge me?'

He tried to push past me but I stood my ground. Dickon huddled back away from us holding the hound. James raised his crop to strike. He whipped the crop across my face; stinging agony in my cheek and breaking the skin. My hand went to my face. I could feel the welt rising.

'I will tell father,' I said, trying to fight back the tears.

'I care not.' he raised the crop again

Nor would our Father, I reasoned. He would tell us to drown the runt as well, and then give me another thrashing for wasting his time.

'I will tell Elizabeth!'

That gave him pause for thought.

'And I will tell her that you steal coin from the church pot. She knows some is missing.'

I had been saving that bit of blackmail for when I really needed it. I took coin from the church pot, but endeavoured to return it before Elizabeth handed it over to the rector. James stole from the pot without caring, and I had caught him red-handed.

James pulled back, his knuckles whitened as he clenched on the riding crop. I was expecting a beating, but he just laughed. Perhaps the thought of a scene and the familial consequences restrained him. Perhaps the thought of Elizabeth in a righteous dudgeon with him was enough.

'I will remember this, Blandford. Just you wait and see.'

I sighed; that was the kind of promise he always kept. As my brother stalked back across the grass to the hall, I turned back to Dickon.

'Keep the dog away from James,' I said. 'Stay near your father for the rest of the visit.'

The boy looked up at me with shining eyes and a smiling face.

'I thank you, Blandford. I shall forget this not.'

*

Most mornings after swordplay, I would take a leisurely walk beside the new ditch and rampart that surrounded London home to Bedford Street, but Thurloe's chambers were at Lincoln's Inn, so John and I went through the City instead. It was a quicker route: in through Bishopsgate, cut through St Paul's churchyard, out of Ludgate and down Fleet Street. I knew the city well enough to use the maze of tiny back streets, narrow passages, and alleys rather than the crowded main thoroughfares.

'I cannot be late,' I told John. 'I want to know if Thurloe has heard anything.'

Two men stepped out of a doorway into our path. Both had swords in their hands: broad bladed and short, sailors' weapons. I heard a movement behind and saw another coming out of a side lane.

'Now, fine gentlemen,' said one of the sailors. 'This is nought personal, just business. Hand your purses o'er if you please and there will be no trouble.'

Footpads; John and I drew our swords in unison.

'I shall take the first two, sir.'

I nodded and stepped to face the man coming out of the lane. He was barefoot and bandy-legged, and his skin had been burned by a hotter sun than England's. A grubby blue doublet and loose canvas breeches. He grinned and swung a wild overhead slash at my head. I blocked with ease, surprising myself with a new-found speed. The sailor's face fell. They had been looking for an easy mark, a fop and his servant, but instead got two trained men. He crouched into a defensive stance but his inside line was wide open. I thrust, stepping forward in a single movement, just as Maupin had drilled into me, and pinked the tough in the chest before he could parry. My blade cut through his doublet, ripped a hole in his breast, scraping off the ribcage, piercing his heart and lung, and spraying blood when I withdrew the sword. He was dead before he hit the floor.

I turned to help John but he needed no assistance. One of the bashers already lay face down on the cobbles; a dark pool of blood spread out beneath him. The other footpad backed away from John, as he stepped forward with bloody blade in hand. 'Twas clear that the boy outmatched the sailor and was merely testing his guard. John made a half-hearted thrust at the sailor who stepped back, and parried the blade aside. He had only needed to make a single defensive move, even I could see that. John made a feint to his left, and thrust at the man's chest. The tough stepped back again out of range, but still jerked his blade to parry.

The basher was sweating; he must have known he was dead. I had experienced that sinking feeling when I fought Hurry. The man looked increasingly desperate as he stepped back again from John's blade, but the boy followed him up relentlessly keeping in perfect terzo guard. The sailor stepped forward and ventured a single thrust of his own. I saw his foot move before his hand and knew what was coming. John saw it too, parrying the blade to the side and riposting. He drove his blade into the man's chest and out of his back.

The sailor's legs gave way and he collapsed, blood bubbling from his mouth and a gush of red as John withdrew his blade. The boy leaned into the dying sailor, and the scoundrel reached up a bloody hand to pull him down. He was trying to say something, gasping and croaking, but I could catch it not. Then he was silent. John turned back to me, blood on his face.

'He is dead,' he told me. 'I saw the thrust coming.'

'As did I; he whispered something to you at the end?'

'Beware The Burned Man. He said it three times.'

I sniffed.

'What?'

''Tis damnably irritating,' I said. 'Everyone has to be so mysterious: The Burned Man; The Black Bear, Old Robin, The Prince Robber; all such ridiculous names. It is enough to drive a man into Bedlam. I begin to think all England is become insane.'

'The Golden Scout?'

'That was Mabbot's doing and design.'

I turned one of the bodies over and rummaged in his pockets. There was nothing but a couple of copper coins on him; the one who had faced me the same. The robber who had spoken at the start (and died the last) had a purse of silver and gold on him, at least five pounds. I threw it at my valet.

'You earned it,' I told him. 'Do you think the tribe know?'

'These were not ravaillacs,' said John. 'They were nought but street bashers, sailors ashore looking for coin. If the Burned Man was after us...'

'After you.'

'If the Burned Man was after *me*,' he said. 'Then I think it would be a better quality of killer.'

'Let us hope so.'

15. Guns and Poison: London, January 1645.

So the herbs virtue stole into his brain,
And kept him off; hardly did he refrain,
From sucking in destruction from her lip,
Sin's cup will poison at the smallest sip.
(John Chalkhill, *Thealma and Clearchus*)

The magical carbine that Darnelly had bequeathed to me had sat in its walnut box in my room in Bedford Street since arresting d'Artagnan. After Christmas (which had been a cold and miserable affair with few of the usual festivities), I waited for a bright day and took Figgis and the weapon to the Artillery Gardens past Moorfields. The wide-open field had long been used for gunnery and archery practice, and there were always butts and roundels set up. The Office of Ordnance used it regularly to test new weapons. As we arrived, I could see some companies from the trained bands drilling away. There was a small huddle of men by the range at the far end of the field. I led Figgis over.

'Ye need to marry and sire children, Master Blandford.'

'Elizabeth got to you did she, Figgis?'

''Tis the way of things, Master. Think now, if your mother and father had no children, chances be that you will sire none. Now, ye want that not?'

'Figgis, if my parents had no children, I would not be here to sire my own tadpoles.'

'Exactly, Master Blandford, then you sees my point.' He grinned triumphantly like a taproom advocate.

'Oh, witless loiter-sack.'

There be a salutary lesson there: argue not with an idiot. They will drag you down to their station and beat you with experience. The men at the range turned at our approach. With dismay, I recognised Haslerig and a couple of ensigns from the Office of Ordnance. One red-haired one I knew as a supercilious arse-goblin. It was too late to turn back, they had seen us.

'Captain Candy,' said Haslerig. 'What do you here?'

'Mr Haslerig.' I nodded. 'I wanted to test out this German invention of Darnelly's.' I gestured to the box in Figgis's arms.

'Ah yes, I remember. It did not seem worthwhile or effective to me.'

I shrugged. How did he expect me to respond to that? Figgis placed the box on the table at the end of the range, and I took out the Kalthoff. Flipping the charge pan open, I filled the chambers with powder and shot.

'Go set up a roundel, Figgis.'

'Yes, Master Blandford.'

I could see Haslerig whispering with his minions as Figgis set up the mark at twenty yards. There were a couple of laughs and chuckles at one murmured comment, but I could not catch the words. Figgis took his time strolling bandy-legged back to me. The roundel was set up on a pole with sandbags behind to stop accidents.

'You have an audience, Master Blandford.'

I could hear more giggles and laughing from Haslerig and the others. Breathing deeply, I calmed myself. I lowered the muzzle and pushed the trigger guard forward until it clicked and then pulled it back to the second click. It was charged. I lifted the muzzle, stared down the sight and squeezed the trigger. The powder in the pan ignited sending fire to the charge with a hiss, and the carbine kicked spitting fire and shot. I waited for the white smoke to clear.

'Go and get it then.'

Figgis wandered down to the butts and brought the paper back. I had clipped the roundel at the top of the outer ring. It lifts high and to the left, I thought. Haslerig and the others were watching me intently. Figgis took the roundel back to the butts.

'Let us see what this piece is about then,' I said, as he returned.

I set the charge once more, hearing the clicks, took aim and fired. This time I waited not for the smoke to clear. Push-click-pull-click-aim-fire and round and round again. Five shots before the mechanism fouled.

There was stunned silence from the audience.

'Let me have a look at he,' said Figgis.

He took out some thin copper wire to clean the chambers and drum. I went to see how good my aim had been. All five balls had hit the mark; all clustered together just to the left of the bull. That was phenomenal accuracy. Now, mark me. I was an excellent shot, counted among the best in the Scouts, but this weapon was bewitched. I walked back to Figgis and the gun.

'The drum spring will not hold out much longer,' Figgis said.

'Do we have spare?'

'Gunsmith have ee.'

'Let us see how much longer it lasts.'

I took the piece back off him and recharged the chambers with powder and shot. Once again I raised the carbine, stared down at the mark and pulled the trigger. Without a pause, I went through the same routine: push-click-pull-click-aim-fire. Six shots before it fouled once more. Something had caught in the mechanism.

'Spring broken,' said Figgis.

'Go and get the roundel then,' I said.

The audience was watching on open-mouthed. Whatever they had expected, it was not a display of such speed – or accuracy. Once again the roundel was peppered with a cluster of holes, two even cutting the bull. I showed the paper to Haslerig.

'It seems most effective to me, sir,' I said. 'Of course, I have no way of assessing its worth.' I looked to my valet. 'Come, Figgis, let us away. I think we have seen enough for today.'

In truth, the weapon was more than effective, but it was too fragile and easy to foul. I would not want it in a battle or a desperate fight. My uncle had been correct: it was a show weapon. I would send Figgis to the gunsmith to get it fixed and find out how to replace that spring. My valet packed the Kalthoff away and we left the range. As we walked away, I had a distinct feeling that Haslerig was discussing my performance with his officers.

'Do you ever get the notion that people are talking about you behind your back, Figgis?'

He tried to fix me with a look, but his lazy eye did not catch up.

'There be a simple solution, Master Blandford. When the bowsers talks behind thy back.'

'Oh?'

'Fart.'

*

Someone was hammering at the door. The room at Vaughn's was on the second floor; it was too early for maids. I tried to ignore the banging and curled into Meg's naked body. It had been a late night, my head hurt, and I could see that it was still dark outside. Meg nudged me.

'Get the door,' she mumbled, still half-asleep.

'Bugger off!' I shouted at the door.

She giggled.

'Captain Candy! Open up, if you please.'

That sounded official. I sat up with a sigh and Meg pulled the blankets over herself. Whoever it was started banging at the door again. I got up, pulled the bolts and yanked it open. There were three men standing in the corridor: two in uniform white coats. I recognised the other. Haslerig's red-haired sycophant from the Artillery Gardens the day before.

'In the name of Satan's sulphurous arsehole, what is wrong?' I said, standing naked in front of them.

'You can come with us now, if you please, Captain Candy,' said Red. 'Mr Haslerig commands your presence.'

''Tis not convenient,' I told him. 'I have female company.'

'Then pay her for her time and bid her farewell,' he said. Presumptuous bastard.

'The woman is most dear, I would have you know.'

'Dear? Then you should have haggled better, should you not?' said Red.

I was actually somewhat taken aback by that. I am well used to my poor reputation travelling before me, but this was damned insolent.

'An insult from a fool be as good as a compliment from a king,' I said.

He was not cowed.

'There has been a murder, Captain. At Westminster.'

That woke me up.

'I had best get dressed then,' I said, and slammed the door in his face.

My clothes were strewn about the room and I made some noise as I located my breeches and dressed. I sat down on the bed and let out a loud sigh as I pulled on my stockings and boots.

'You can be as noisy as you please, I am not getting up,' said Meg.

'There has been a murder.'

''Tis your business.' She rolled and pulled the blankets over herself. 'I am not so foolish as to awaken for you to then leave.'

'Foolish women are more amenable,' I muttered.

'I heard that.' A disembodied voice from the blankets.

'It be a compliment.'

I tucked in my shirt, buttoned my doublet and straightened the falling band. Throwing on my cloak and hat, I returned to the waiting guardsmen.

'Come along then,' I said.

They led me down to the river where a wherry awaited us in the early morning gloom. I climbed in and the boat pushed off upriver into the mist. I turned to Red.

'So who has been murdered?' I prayed it was not the prince.

'Mr Haslerig will tell you everything,' he said.

There was no conversation forthcoming after that. I sat in silence as the boat cut upriver. My head hurt and I felt sick. We arrived at Westminster Stairs and they led me up into Palace Yard and onto King Street. The Bell Inn was an excruciatingly expensive tavern, oft used by the Divines who debated a religious settlement in Westminster Hall. Some kept chambers there, others would sup there of an evening. It was not the kind of establishment that I would frequent, but I suspect that is more a judgement on my character than the facilities.[32]

There were armed men outside, but Red led me past them. Haslerig was in a backroom with the prince's moustached officer. A white-haired man was slumped in a chair, dressed in black robes and a skullcap. His dead face fixed in a grotesque grimace. The table before him was laid out for a meal for ten or more people, but all untouched. Fetid vomit pooled on the floor and on his robes, and it smelled as though he had loosened his bowels in death.

'Good Morning, Candy,' said Haslerig. 'I thought it best to summon you. Mr Thurloe is still in Uxbridge, but it seems we have a poisoning.'

'Poisoning?'

'In the wine.' He gestured to a bottle on the table.

I picked up the bottle and smelled the mouth. It was a sharp fragrant smell. There was a shattered wine glass on the floor in front of the corpse.

'His Highness came because of the wine,' said Moustache. 'It is a Bohemian grape but Mr White had somehow acquired a bottle. He

---

[32]King Street as Blandford describes no longer exists. The old layout of Westminster was changed when Westminster Bridge was built and King Street and the alleys and lanes around were pulled down and Parliament Street was created as a new thoroughfare. The Bell Inn was a well-known tavern, convenient for Westminster, and with a reputation for expensive wines and food. It was one of Samuel Pepys favourite establishments, and later an informal base for the Tory party.

invited His Highness for a late supper. When we arrived, we found him in this state.' He gestured to the body. 'The prince returned to his apartments and I sent for the authorities.'

It sounds a strange thing, but I had never tasted a Bohemian wine. I was half-tempted to take a sip even though I knew it be death.

'Who is he?' I asked.

'Jonathan White,' said Haslerig. 'A Welsh Divine and lawyer. The last thing we need is a scandal, Candy. News of this must be kept quiet.'[33]

I wondered how Gilbert Mabbot and his ilk would feel about that, but I agreed with Haslerig.

'Where did good Mr White acquire the wine?'

'From a foreign woman according to his servant,' said Haslerig. 'She approached him with it and suggested the meal.'

'Description?'

'Pretty and young.'

'The Black Bear is a master of disguise,' I said. 'But I think even he could not pass for a maiden. An accomplice perhaps, or unrelated?'

'It is too much of a coincidence for it to be unrelated to my master's security,' said Moustache.

In faith, I agreed with him.

'Well, the Black Bear is most certainly ruthless, then,' I said.

'Why say you?' asked Haslerig.

'He may not have planned to kill children, but the bomb at the hospital would have caused enough damage to onlookers had it been tossed under the prince's carriage.' I looked at the laid cloth. 'Had you eaten and drunk together as would be customary, then all at the

---

[33]Jonathan White's death at the end of January 1645 is recorded, but not with poison as a cause. White (1590 - 1645) was a radical Presbyterian and had produced polemics against Bishops and the Episcopal system. His family hailed from Tenby in South Wales, but he was buried at the Temple Church with a number of MPs in attendance. Bohemian wine was known but not widespread during the Early Modern period. Based, even then, on the Riesling grape it produced a number of sweet white wines.

table would have been killed. He does not care whom he murders with the prince, or how many. We can count ourselves fortunate that Divine White decided to take an early taster.

'When does Mr Thurloe return from Uxbridge?' asked Moustache.

I was slightly affronted by that, but granted that Thurloe's mind was sharper than my own.

'He should be back soon,' I said. 'The talks at Uxbridge are not going well, by all accounts.'

'His Highness desires to see you both as soon as Mr Thurloe returns,' said Moustache.

I had expected that. I can determine when a thrashing is coming, and in truth, this one was well deserved. The Black Bear had got within a whisker of killing our charge.

I thanked God for an impatient Divine overeager to sip at the Bohemian vintage.

*

Giving a full and true Relation of all the remarkable passages this present Year, January 1645.

The Uxbridge Propositions from the King are these:

- That His Majesty's Revenues, Magazines, Towns, Forts, and Ships, that have been taken or kept from him will be restored. That whatsoever hath been done or published contrary to the known Laws of the Land, or derogatory to His Majesties legal and known Rights be renounced and recalled, that no seed may remain of the like to spring out for the future.

- That whatsoever illegal power hath been claimed or exercised over His Majesty's Subjects, as imprisoning and putting to death their persons without Law, stopping Habeas Corpus, and putting Impositions upon their estates, (without Act of Parliament) either by one or both Houses, or by any Committee of both or either Houses, be disclaimed, and the persons committed be forthwith discharged.

- That His Majesty will consent to make a Law to establish and to maintain the Protestant Religion: and for the firmer establishing thereof, desires there may be a Bill drawn up for the continuance of the Book of Common Prayer, and to maintain it from all soon and violence.

- That there be a Bill to ease tender Consciences, in such particulars as shall be agreed upon: and that there be a National Synod called legally, with all convenient speed.

- That all persons which shall be excepted and agreed upon on either side to be excepted out of the General Pardon, be tried per Pares, according to the usual custom, and known Laws of the Land to be either acquitted or condemned.

- And to the intent that Trade may not suffer, nor any interruption to the Treaty, and that there may be a Cessation of Arms, and a free Trade with all possible speed concluded.

- And as to what shall be debated, His Majesty gives power to his Commissioners to agree and conclude upon them.

LONDON, Printed for *Richard Harper,* and are to be sold at his shop in Smithfield.

16. Our Unhappy Guest: London, January 1645.

Difficile est non saturam scribere
It is difficult not to write satire.
(Juvenal, *The Satires*)

The prince met us in a large empty stable at the palace of Whitehall that was being used as a Gymnasium. The stalls had been removed, creating an open space with a high ceiling, wide unglazed windows and sawdust on the earth floor. Prince Karl and his flunkeys were exercising, practising with their swords in shirtsleeves, as Thurloe and I arrived. His Highness kept us waiting as he watched a bout between two of the gentlemen. A wide circle formed around the combatants with a cluster about the prince. I turned and watched the fight with interest.

They both fought with long curved practice swords. I had not seen the type before: made of wood and leather. As long and curved as an Ottoman scimitar, but with a basket hilt and broad blade almost a handsbreadth in width. The weapons were perfect for cutting and slashing. Maupin preferred to use the point of the sword, and keep your opponent at length, but these strange blades looked no less deadly.

'The prince chose this venue deliberately,' whispered Thurloe to me. 'There is some point to this.'

I nodded; from the furtive glances the prince and his gentlemen cast our way, I could tell Thurloe was in the right. His Highness was up to something.

The two swordsmen seemed evenly matched: both of middling height and of a similar age to me, more gentleman retainers of the prince I assumed. They would have followed him over from some part of Germany or Holland. One was the moustachioed gentleman from White's poisoning. The other combatant was clean-shaven. I took to judging their stance and footwork, trying to see if they had a favoured move or weakness.

It did not take long to realise that both had received a different training to me. Maupin would have beaten them with his stick they seemed so wild with their swords and open stance. Their left arms were tucked tightly behind the back or on the hip, but the guard positions were unusual: holding the sword behind the head or behind the back, with their open side exposed to their opponents.

'I have not seen this before,' I muttered to myself.

These men were skilled and trained, but it was acrobatic. They tried to overwhelm an opponent with a flurry of cuts and thrusts from different angles. Their curved blades were perfect for such a style, but I was certain they would quickly tire.

We did not find out. After less than a minute, the clean-shaven gentleman slipped and took a vicious crack to the head from the Moustache's practice sword, knocking him senseless. I tutted as the bout came to an end. The prince heard me sucking my teeth.

'You think you could do better, Captain? You have been practising yourself, I hope?'

'Of course, Highness,' I said, with a bow.

'Then let us see how your lessons are progressing.'

This had been the prince's design. Did he wish to humiliate me? He waved for me to choose a practice sword. I took off my cloak and hat, and handed Thurloe my real sword. The practice weapons were made of wood with a lead core and strapped in leather, much like Maupin's. I found one that closest resembled the rapier I used in my daily exercises, and turned back to the prince.

His Highness called for Moustache to come forward and face me. We were of a similar height, so there would be no advantage in reach, but my sword had length on his wooden bludgeon. I was not confident, so decided to concentrate upon my footwork and defence as I had been taught.

'Are you ready, Captain Candy?' called one of the Rhinelanders. 'I will act as Director.'

'I am.'

Prince Karl whispered something to Moustache before he came at me. The swordsman looked flustered by his words, but came forward and assumed his strange crouched guard position with sword behind his head. He had neglected to salute me. Forgetfulness or a deliberate insult, I was unsure, but my sister had brought me up better. I saluted him as he waited, taking my time so the audience knew why. I stepped into terzo stance: side on, feet a shoulders-width apart with my right foot pointed forward and back foot sideways. My back knee bent and foreleg straightened, and my sword held to the front.

Moustache leapt into action. He cut at my head with a wide swing, and I blocked, with ease. He stepped back then forward again, stabbing at my chest. I parried his sword to my left (the inside line) and struck reverso with my blade, cutting at his body. He jumped back and crouched into guard again with the blade behind his back. All of Maupin's tedious exercises and moves had built a new speed, strength, and instinct with a rapier. To be fair to the prancing popinjay swinging his stick at me, he had just fought one bout and had little time to catch his breath. As he cut and stabbed and slashed and swung, I merely stepped aside, blocked or parried, and conserved my energy as I had been taught. I was not particularly fast, nor particularly skilful, but I was well drilled and only riposted out of the parry. A master would have cut me down in seconds, but Moustache was not a master.

I noted that he favoured a cut from behind his head, swinging the blade mandratto down across my body from left to right. When I stepped back his cut went too far, leaving him overstretched and open.

Once I had seen the pattern, I waited. He repeated it twice more. That was his weakness. Moments later the pattern started again: a crouched guard with sword lying over the shoulder. He twisted his body into the cut, but this time I stepped to the left and his weapon whipped past the outside line. His back was open. I thrust my sword at his shoulder blade but my aim was too high, and I caught him on the on the back of the head. The practice blade scratched a deep cut down his right cheek. I had drawn blood.

'Halt! Halt!' The Director stepped in to check the wound.

The blow finished any more talk of swordplay, and was certain to leave Moustache with a scar on his face. Prince Karl did not look happy with the result. He called Thurloe and me over to him at once. Since I had beaten his man, the prince chose to ignore me, not even a word of polite congratulations – *ingratus*[34].

'You still have not found the assassin?' He said to the secretary brusquely.

'No, Highness,' said Thurloe. 'The Frenchman is not The Black Bear, but he has proven helpful.'

'Cardinal Mazarin is a good friend of the Palatinate,' said the prince. 'There has been a bombing and now a poisoning. And yet you are no nearer to discovering the man. How can I be assured of my safety after such?'

'I promise your Highness that we are doing our very best to apprehend the man,' said Thurloe.

---

[34]Unpleasant or disagreeable.

I winced at that answer; it was not one to inspire confidence after the repeated attempts thus far.

The prince paused for a moment, looked to his gentlemen and then back to us.

'I mean to travel to Windsor next week,' he said. 'I will ride there on the Wednesday and reside in the castle before, perhaps, journeying on to Uxbridge and the talks.' He must have seen the look of horror on both our faces. 'You object?'

'Highness,' I said. 'It is not that we wish to restrict your freedom to travel, but is this wise with such an immediate threat. Whitehall is defensible and close to the Divines and Parliament. Is there an urgent need to visit Windsor?'

'I am tired of Divines and politicians and their arguments, and it is not so safe as we have seen. Perhaps if you were more diligent in neutralising the threat, Candy, there would be no issue.'

I noted he did not answer my question.

'Perhaps if His Highness would consider travelling by barge?' said Thurloe. 'The river is quicker, after all.'

The prince glanced over at one of the gentlemen – older, a grey beard and streaks of white in his hair. The man nodded and Karl turned back to us.

'That is acceptable to me.'

I took more note of the greybeard now, was he a backroom advisor? I did not recognise him from earlier visits. Was he new?

'I will arrange the transport personally, Highness,' said Thurloe.

'Then best you return to chasing our phantom assassin in the meantime,' said the prince to me and turned away.

We were dismissed. The Prince Palatine stalked off with his retinue of flunkeys and guards, leaving Thurloe and me alone in the stables. The secretary let out a huge sigh of relief once the prince and his staff left.

'You were supposed to fight the loser of the first bout,' he told me. 'The moustachioed gentleman had to take his place, but is not as skilled. Then you went and beat him up. The prince is unhappy his design went awry.'

'He was trying to humiliate me?'

'No, merely to remind you that he is still a prince. He expected us to protest more over his journey to Windsor, beating you up would have tempered our resistance. As it is, I now get to arrange the travel. That is good. We could not keep him cooped up in the palace indefinitely.'

'I am glad I could be of assistance,' I said. 'There is less chance of an attack on the river?'

'Let us hope so, since you shall travel with him.'

*

The stout housekeeper brought a frothing jug of ale and four tankards on a tray into the hall, and Maupin called a halt to our practice. We had spent the morning training and now I regaled the Swordmaster and my valet with the tale of my victory over the German fop. The boy had already heard it numerous times, and Mariette sat shyly whispering to John as we relaxed, but Maupin was interested in his student's progress and the German's style.

'They were using leather dusacks,' he told me. 'It is a practice weapon, not for duelling, but a sharp blow can break a limb or crack a skull. I prefer Cappo Ferro to Meyer, but a metal dusack wielder is a fearsome enemy, indeed. You did very well... Do you see your mistakes?'[35]

'Mistakes?' I said, somewhat deflated.

'I do,' said John.

Maupin smiled indulgently at the boy.

'You were not even there,' I said. 'How can you know?'

'After you realised he overstretched with the cut, you waited, what was it? Four or five blows. You should have finished him sooner. And you stepped to the left, if you had stepped to the right his blow would have still missed and his neck would have been open.' He had a smug look on his chops.

'What say you, fopdoodle?'

'The boy is in the right,' said Maupin. 'When you see an opponent's weakness, exploit it, and a move to the right perhaps more effective for the counter.' He smiled at the boy. 'However, Master Coxon, never rush straight in as it may be a trap; a deliberate show of

---

[35]Ridolfo Cappo Ferro was an Italian weapons master who published his fencing manual in 1610. He is regarded as the 'grandfather' of modern fencing. Jochaim Meyer (1537-1571) came from a German tradition of weapons mastery. The dusack used by the Palatine retainers against Blandford was a popular weapon in the Sixteenth and Seventeenth centuries.

weakness to draw you in. Over-eagerness for the killing blow can be just as deadly a mistake as waiting overlong to strike.'

'Thus by these lessons ye may learn good cheap: in weddings and all things to look ere ye leap,' said Mariette with a saucy smile at the boy.

The boy smiled adoringly back at her. Elizabeth was in the right, he was besotted. As long as he offended Maupin not with his infatuation, I minded not. I wished for no trouble with the Swordmaster. My sister's growing fondness for the man was another factor. 'Tis always best to keep a prospective brother-in-law happy; they may come in useful someday.

'That reminds me,' I said. 'I will not be able to train next week.'

'Business?' asked Maupin.

'I travel to Windsor with the prince,' I said. 'He has some meetings at the castle. At least I cannot get seasick on the river. I apologise that I will be unable to attend, but the boy will remain in the city.'

'Then, Master Coxon, we shall have to think of something special for your training days,' said Maupin with a smile.

Whilst I had graduated to competent with the sword under Maupin's tutelage, John's progress had been remarkable. He was quick of hand, fleet of foot, and clever. All of Maupin's knowledge was poured into the boy. I concentrated on my single blade whilst John learned two-handed styles, how to fight with or against a sword and dagger, or cape. Sometimes Maupin talked of putting on display bouts with the boy for an extra income, perhaps even a travelling show when the war was finished.

When the war was finished... I heard so many people declare their dreams and designs for when that happy day came. Most were never realised; most dreams never are. Cherish the ones that you fulfil.

'Perhaps we could put a display on at the Phoenix,' I said. 'It would raise funds and we could bill it as an exhibition of martial skill. There is no prohibition on such.'

'Perhaps,' said Maupin. 'How would your sister feel about an exhibition in the theatre?'

'I am certain I could talk her around, if she has any objections,' I said.

17. A Shot in the Dark: London, February 1645.

But now this mighty flood, upon his voyage prest,
That found how with his strength, his beauties still increased,
From where brave Windsor stood on tiptoe to behold
The fair and goodly Thames, so far as eer he could.
(Michael Drayton, *Polyolbion*)

The Thames is a cold bitter highway in winter, even when the sun shines. Twenty rowers in synchronised rhythm sped the barge upriver from Westminster, hauling at the oars, billowing clouds of steam at their exertion; pull, pull, pull; splash, splash, splash. They were warm from their work, at least. Amidships a canopy covered the prince and his flunkeys, drinking hot spiced wine, dicing, and smoking their tobacco pipes; all in high spirits. The boat's master stood at the stern-tiller in a thick coat and blue wool scarf. Every now and then he would bark orders at the rowers. The men chanted a work song as they pulled at the oars.

'Aloof! And aloof! And steady I steer!
'Tis a boat to our wish,
And she slides like a fish,
When cheerily stem'd and when you row clear,
She now has her trim,
Away let her swim.'
Aloof! And aloof! And steady I steer!'

I sat in the bow in high dudgeon as they sang, wrapped up in a cloak and hat, but still shivering in the cold, and squinting through the winter sunlight reflected from the ripples. There were four of Haslerig's men, heavily armed, sitting silently with me. The five of us scanned the brown reed banks, bare trees, and frostbitten fields as we passed looking for any sign of danger. 'Twas unlikely, I had concluded: there was too much traffic and too many armed men aboard the barge for it to be boarded, and we travelled through solid parliamentary lands.

'Think you a lone assassin could attempt a shot from the banks of the river, Captain?' said one of the guards.

''Tis a fair distance,' I said, 'and would need to be an excellent shot, with no guarantees of success. But best we are careful.'

If there was to be an attack it would be on the road to Uxbridge, if Prince Karl persisted in his design to ride to the negotiations. There was certainly some plot afoot: the prince had given no reason for travelling to Windsor, and a winter's boat ride was hardly a pleasure cruise. I glanced back at the courtiers drinking and dicing. They were enjoying themselves; five in all, mostly young aristocrats and gentlemen of an age with the prince. They were perhaps a couple of years older than me. I noted that Moustache, my opponent from the sword ring, was not present. The old greybeard was sat on cushions beside the prince. He played no cards nor dice, merely sat watching the riverbank intently, sometimes leaning forward to whisper a word in Karl Ludwig's ear.

Westminster to Hammersmith to Brentford: palaces and mansions, ornamented gardens, frosted fields, sleepy little villages and ancient mills. On the north bank, a lone heron waded in the shallow brown reeds and mud; long beak, grey, black, and white feathering. It stood fixed as a statue, and then stabbed its spear beak down, skewering its prey. A splash, a flash of silver scales, and it took to the air with its prize still flapping. The boat slipped on past one of the little islets that dot the river, and I tensed fearing an attack, but nought happened.

'Captain Candy!'

One of the prince's gentlemen beckoned to me to attend His Highness. I sighed to myself; what did he want now? I gingerly made my way past the rowers, trying not to pitch myself or them out of the boat until I got to the revellers. The prince was reclined on cushions drinking wine, with Greybeard beside him. I doffed and bowed unsteadily before them.

'You have been training with a Huguenot Swordmaster, Captain Candy?'

'Yes, Highness.'

'He has certainly improved your skills?'

'Indeed, Highness. I would not have beaten your man only a few weeks past,' I said.

A frown crossed his face as I reminded him of Moustache's defeat.

'Perhaps I should meet this man who has had such a transformative effect. He could train my armies.'

By all accounts, the prince had no armies of his own left, but I was not about to remind him of that. Royalty are apt to take offence at the slightest provocation.

'Master Maupin plans an exhibition soon, Highness,' I told him.

'Bouts and entertainments, food and drink.' That was somewhat of an exaggeration; I had merely made the suggestion to the Swordmaster.

'Where will this be taking place?' asked Greybeard.

'At the Phoenix,' I said.

This was also something I would have to explain to Elizabeth, but I was certain that the attendance of royalty would prick her mercantile sensibilities. An exhibition of swordplay was not prohibited, and with the right audience could be most lucrative indeed. It may even put a smile on Beeston's sorry visage. My mind worked overtime at the financial rewards such a show could present.

'You will let me know when this performance will take place,' said the prince. 'We will not be travelling to Windsor today.'

'Not going to Windsor, Highness?' What was he up to?

'We shall stop in the Syon House; I have a meet there.'

Syon House was a gleaming white jewel in the winter sunlight, all plated glass windows and faux crenellations. It was the palatial home of the Earl of Northumberland, the brother of Lucy Hay, just outside Brentford. The Percy family was plotting.

The barge pulled in at the Earl's grand residence. There was no mooring by the river. Instead, the boatmen jumped into the ice cold muddy waters of the Thames, dragged the boat up onto the banks and laid down a gangplank. The prince and his gentlemen could disembark without wetting their boots. I stood up to get off the boat with the Karl Ludwig and the others, but Greybeard noticed me and said something to the prince. His Highness turned before I could reach dry land.

'You shall remain with the watermen and guards, Captain Candy. I will not require your protection here, methinks.'

'My uncle and cousin were most insistent on my accompanying you, Highness. In case of any trouble.' They had been.

'Do you suspect the Earl of Northumberland of plotting, Captain?'

Of course I did, but I could not say that to a prince of the blood. I knew my station well enough.

'No, Highness.'

'Then you will remain here until I return.'

'Yes, Highness.'

I watched as they walked up to the gates to the great house. Servants and flunkeys came out to meet them, and the prince entered. The gates slammed shut behind his party leaving us alone on the riverbank.

'Open unto me the gates of righteousness; I shall enter through them, and I shall give thanks to the Lord,' I said to myself.

We sat waiting for about an hour for the prince to return. The boatmen played cards and smoked pipes whilst Haslerig's guards stood about redundant. The day was still bright, but the sunlight would not last long and 'twas already past noon. I did not fancy a boat back to Westminster in the dark when I had planned on the night in Windsor. There was a sweet girl in the Mermaid Tavern, I had hoped to see.

'Bugger and damnation.'

The walls around the great house, and guards and servants, made it impossible to try and sneak into the house and discover whom the prince was meeting there. Then the gates opened and a procession of servants came out carrying food and ale for the boatmen. There was a middle-aged valet with them, dressed in red and black livery and directing the operation.

My memory is no better than the next man's, but with a start I recognised his face, and remarkably recalled the accompanying name – Richard. I had met him years ago on my very first adventure.

I waved at him and fixed a false smile on my chops.

'Richard! Well met.'

He doffed his hat and bowed, clearly overjoyed that I had remembered him. There be a lesson here: cultivate other people's servants as they will always know their master's secrets.

'Captain Candy, I am honoured you remember me. Your star has risen high these past years. We have brought some victuals for the boatmen.' He nodded back to the house. 'They have only just begun.'

I took a chance

'Her ladyship was late as always, I wager?'

Richard laughed. 'As always, sir, but she and Mr Holles have arrived now. There is time for some mutton and ale before you return to London.'

The maids were handing out platters of food and flagons of frothing ale to the men. I nodded to the guards that they could partake and they gratefully grabbed their share.

'My thanks to you, Richard,' I said. 'My men appreciate the consideration. Please convey my gratitude to His Grace.'

He beamed with delight. 'I will indeed, Captain Candy. Good day to you.'

He led the servers back to the great house, assuring us that a boy would come to collect tankards and platters. I watched them go through the gates, and grinned with satisfaction. Lucy Hay, the Earl of Northumberland, Denzil Holles and the Prince Palatine. All were plotting in the house, 'twas a snippet both my uncle and St John would find of interest.

The peace talks in Uxbridge were pointless. The King may have lost York and the north the summer previous, but the war was still finely balanced. Scotland was in chaos, as Gallant Montrose rampaged through the Kingdom. The Scots army, our allies in the north of England, now looked to home. Meanwhile, the King shipped troops from Ireland to replace his losses at Marston Moor, and the failure to beat him at the Newbury and Donnington left our leadership paralysed with infighting. It would be months before any new army would be ready for the field. In the meantime, His Majesty looked to gain the advantage. The talks at Uxbridge were just a way of spinning out the winter months until the campaigns began anew. An annual cycle that had been repeated for the past three years.

'Twas dark by the time the prince and his party returned; laughing and joking and in high spirits. The meeting had obviously concluded satisfactorily. Karl Ludwig ordered us back to London, and the boat's master and men soon had us flying over the water. Lanterns were lit at the bow, stern, and amidships to light the way and avoid collisions with river traffic and flotsam.

I sat in the bow and relaxed. We would be home in a couple of hours. I considered my proposed exhibition at the Phoenix. If I could get Beeston to manage it, and Maupin agreed, it could prove very lucrative indeed. I began fixing admission prices in my head, costs for refreshments, sack and the like, and how much I could pimp them out for. I would have to speak to Meg about punks for the quality. I watched the banks slip by and dreamed of my fortunes.

The flash came before the crack of shot. I marked it, high in the trees on the north bank. I heard shouts from the prince's party, prayed to God that he was unharmed, and started discharging shot from the repeatable at my reckoning of the mark: push-click-pull-click aim and fire: crack, crack, crack, crack, crack, crack – then it clogged and I cursed. Haslerig's guards started firing blindly at the shore. I screamed at them to halt.

The boat was turning towards the riverbank. I shouted to the boat's master.

'What in the name of all that is holy are you doing, you witless baboon? Pull for Westminster, your fortunes and lives depend upon it. This could be a trap!'

The master was no fool. He ignored German orders to go ashore at my words, pulled the tiller into his body and directed the barge back midstream. I scrambled over to the prince. He was unharmed, they all were. That was a relief. The shot had hit the gunwales, sending splinters flying, shocking all but harming none.

'What is that weapon, Candy? Let me see it,' demanded the prince, as I clambered towards him.

'Are you unharmed, Highness?'

'I am unharmed, now that piece? What is it, you shot but did not reload.'

One of Haslerig's guards passed the Kalthoff gun up to me and I, in turn, showed it to the prince.

'I have clogged it, Highness, with powder. It will need a gunsmith. 'Tis from the Kalthoff armouries.' I did not actually know where that town lay, but it seemed the prince did.

Greybeard looked at the weapon. 'Think what our men could do with such guns, Highness.'

'It clogs easy, and breaks too,' I said. 'I fear it is not suited for battle.'

'May I take this to study, Captain?' asked the prince.

You cannot really refuse a request from Royalty, no matter how much you desire to tell them to stuff their anointed head up a bovine orifice.

'Of course, Highness, but 'tis the property of the Office of Ordnance, and so not mine to give.'

That bothered the prince not.

'Oh I am certain that Mr Haslerig will approve,' said Prince Karl, holding out his hand.

Glumly, I had to agree, and handed over my weapon to the Germans. Then I returned to my berth in the bow and sulked all the way back to Whitehall. His Highness did not return my weapon when we disembarked. In fact, I never did see it again. I hear he gave it to the King of Denmark as a coronation present. Karl Ludwig was a thieving bastard.

*

His Royal Highness had been busy in Syon House before the attack. He had managed to insert a clause into the Uxbridge settlement. It was perhaps the most glaring lesson in his character. My uncle and grandfather, Mr Butler, Thurloe and I were sat around the table in my uncle's oak-panelled study later that night. I sent word to Thurloe as soon as I disembarked from the barge, and he met us at Thames Street. Uncle Samuel passed the papers across the table for me to read. I glanced down; the relevant clause was circled Butler's red ink.

That your Majesty will give your Royal assent to such ways and means as the Parliaments of both Kingdoms shall think fitting for the uniting of the Protestant Princes, and for the entire restitution and Reestablishment of Charles Lodwick Prince Elector Palatine, His Heirs and Successors, to His Electoral Dignity Rights and Dominions; Provided that this extend not to Prince Rupert, or Prince Maurice, or the Children of either of them, who have been the instruments of so much bloodshed and mischief against both Kingdoms.

'He is not fond of his brothers,' I said.

'Twas a notion I understood better than most, perhaps.

'He is not,' agreed Uncle Samuel.

'I do not see how this helps the negotiations with His Majesty?' said Butler. 'He is exceeding fond of Prince Rupert.'

'It helps the negotiations not at all,' said my uncle. 'I must confess I do not understand it. Denzil desires accommodation with the King, but they forced the clause through committee this morning.'

Thurloe was secretary to the delegation at Uxbridge. He told us what he had observed.

'The prince has many admirers in Parliament,' said Thurloe. 'He has been entertaining and flattering the Half-Measure men, recently. My master St John is concerned that the prince may try to broker some agreement with His Majesty. The negotiations in Uxbridge have not been going at all well.'

'If there was to be peace,' said my grandfather. 'This clause would solve the problem of too many armed men in the country. Pack them all off to Germany to fight against the Emperor.'

'You think that is the prince's design, Father?' said Uncle Samuel.

'I think the prince has many designs. Men for his army is most certainly one, but perhaps he aims higher than a prince-elector's coronet. Perhaps he aims for a royal crown.'

Thurloe nodded. 'It would take the King's death or defeat, and a number of other cards to fall correctly, but Prince Karl would have a claim to the throne. If Parliament and the Divines supported him, it would be an exceedingly strong claim. Henry Vane and my master both believe the prince would take the crown, if it were offered.'

'Is this not all rather tendentious?' I said. 'The King would have to die, and surely the Prince of Wales would be more pliable to Parliament?'

'The King is in arms against us,' said my grandfather. 'So are his sons. Prince Karl's religion is in his favour, and there is enough romance around his family that he could make claim to the throne.'

'That would be setting aside our rightful King,' I said, somewhat outraged in spite of being a rebel in arms against the current monarch. That may seem a contradiction in reason, but I was not alone in it.

'It would be better than no king at all, perhaps,' said Thurloe. 'Could the attack on the river be unrelated to the Black Bear? Could it be to do with the Prince's meddling with the treaty?'

I noted they were looking at me.

'I dared not risk taking the boat to shore to investigate,' I said. 'So have no way of knowing. I will ride out in the morning, but I doubt we will find ought of the gunman. I must confess, we are no closer to finding this assassin. He be as elusive as smoke. I have been similarly unable to find the woman who provided the poisoned wine.'

'What of the Comte d'Artagnan and the Dutch musician?' asked Butler. 'They are foreigners. Can we truly trust them to deliver up the assassin? Or even not to be him?'

It was a fair point, but the fact that Butler asserted it riled me somewhat.

'Have no fears, Mr *Timorous* Butler,' I said. 'I wager my reputation that they are not assassins.' On such statements are reputations broken. 'But they are most certainly foreign spies.' I added as a caveat.

18. Grand Designs: London, February 1645.

Ladies of London both wealthy and fair,
Whom every Town Fop is pursuing,
Still of your Persons and Purses take care,
The greatest deceit lies in Wooing.
(Anon., *Advice to the Ladies of London*)

Elizabeth gestured around the theatre. There were benches and tables set up in the pit where her street urchins were daily instructed in reading the catechism, piled high with chalks and slate. The galleries above were dusty and full of cobwebs; the plush seating in the higher levels covered in sheets, and the gilded paint was cracked and peeling. It was over a year since there had been any sort of performance or games. The Phoenix looked shabby and unloved; like an ageing roué dressed in fading breeches and cross-braced garters.

'It will have to be cleaned and painted,' said Beeston.

My sister nodded at him as she thought of details, I could see her planning. Elizabeth had been most enthused by my suggestion of an exhibition of swordplay. I suspected 'twas more her interest in Master Maupin, for she had little care of the vagaries of fencing, and no need to stage a spectacular for extra income. When I had suggested it in Beeston's back room, she jumped out of her chair, rushed out onstage and started formulating a grand design.

'We could set up the exhibition here on the stage,' she said. 'With vendors and servants taking food and drink up to the galleries from the pit.'

And gamblers, punks, pickpockets and all, I thought to myself.

'What think you, Mr Beeston?' Elizabeth asked the actor.

''Tis a better use than schoolhouse for your gutter brats,' said Beeston. 'But will cost to make it fit and will take two or three weeks for the work to be complete. You know that some of them have been carving their names into the gilding in the galleries?'

'So you see no problem?' She ignored his complaint.

He pursed his lips at her. 'I see a problem...'

'Be not so impertinent, Mr Beeston.'

'There is the Mayor,' he said. 'You keep insisting that performances are forbidden when I suggest them.'

'I will not stage musical spectaculars because the authorities would close it down and fine us. This is an athletic spectacle, and 'tis not blasphemous.'

'That was sophistry, pure and unabashed sophistry. Elizabeth could find some justification in scripture if need be to pour salve on her soul. Personally, I saw little difference 'tween baiting, theatre, musical performance, or athletic spectacle. I doubt God cares much about the distinction either.

'The Beggar crew,' said Beeston. 'They will want their cut. There is a new king.'

'The Burned Man can go fu...' I paused, glanced at Elizabeth. 'Fund his sins elsewhere. We shall have soldiers all about the theatre to protect the prince and deter the street-scum.'

'They can still burn the theatre down the day after, or the day after that,' said Beeston. 'And I sleep here. 'Tis better we pay them a share. Look now, we will take perhaps thirty pounds a night in entrance fees alone. Then there is food and ale, wine for the quality; that is where we make most coin. Even with expenses and staff, 'twill be nigh on five hundred pounds profit for a week of performances. We can afford fifty pounds to keep The Burned Man happy.'

'Why does he call himself the Burned Man?'

He looked at me. 'He calls hi'self the Burned Man on account of his face being broken and scarred by fire. He looks as if he was smashed on the head with a burning tree.'

'When did you see him?' I asked, curious.

'There is more of an immediate problem,' said Elizabeth, before Beeston could answer. 'Swordmaster Maupin is injured.'

'Injured? When did this happen, and why did nobody think to tell me?'

'He was set upon by a crowd near Bishopsgate because of his French way of speech last night,' she said in disgust. 'They thought him a papist. I would have told you had you been home at a decent hour, or up this morning to break your fast.'

Maupin had been attacked by a gang of bashers whilst I had been paddling up and down the Thames with Prince Prickly. The Swordmaster walked home alone after a late night sermon and had been set upon. He managed to escape and make it home to Spitalfields, but took a shallow wound to his side. When John had arrived for his training that morning Mariette had told him of her father's hurt. I had actually been up and out early that morning to ride the Thames shoreline in a fruitless search for the gunman, but I did not bother to inform my sister of that. I was more concerned that the performance could be cancelled.

'You have seen Maupin? How badly is he injured?' My dreams of fortune were evaporating.

'Not badly,' she said. 'Mariette told John 'twas but a graze. Monsieur Maupin fought them off, but he needs to rest up a while. I plan to visit this evening after I have been to the apothecary.'

Elizabeth was building a still room in the house in Bedford Street at incredible expense. For all her austere claims of Puritanism she could be as much a spendthrift as any Candy when she deemed it a necessity.

'I will need money to make this place fit for the show,' said Beeston, bringing the conversation back to the theatre.

'Twenty pounds to clean and make fit,' said Elizabeth.

'I will need fifty,' said Beeston. 'It will need painting and re-gilding.'

'We are not painting it in solid silver,' said Elizabeth. 'Besides I can procure the paints.'

'I still need to pay the workmen.'

'Will you hire Master Ruebens to do it?'

'Ruebens is dead,' I chipped in. They both glared at me. I am certain they were enjoying their exchange.

'Forty pounds, then,' said Beeston. 'We will need to arrange the work quickly.'

'And London is overflowing with men looking for work who will jump at the employment,' she countered. 'You shall have twenty-five pounds, Mr Beeston, and be thankful for it. Unless you wish for me to organise the renovations and workmen myself?'

That was enough to end the discussion. The last thing Beeston desired was Elizabeth poking her nose too deeply into his management of the building. When all their grand designs were set, I walked Elizabeth home to Bedford Street and then begged my leave. There were people I needed to see, and an assassin still to find.

*

Monsieur d'Artagnan and his servant Planchet seemed to do little more than drink, revel and feast at the Tabard. They were waiting on orders from Mazarin, so they said. Personally, I found it irritating, but the news of a sword exhibition at least piqued the Frenchman's interest. I met with him in the backroom overlooking the river, and took Figgis along to keep him out of my sister's way. The table in front of d'Artagnan was piled high with different dishes of food and a pitcher of wine, and he lounged in a chair with one leg over the arm as Planchet poured the sack. St John had agreed to pay the Frenchmen's tavern bill, and they were making good use of the account.

'An exhibition of swordplay?' said d'Artagnan. 'Finally, something to break the boredom of this godless city.'

I started to laugh; 'godless city' was a phrase William Everard used often enough, but I wagered the radical puritan poacher meant it for completely different reasons to a papist French spy.

'Pourquoi riez-vous de moi?' said the Comte. (Why are you laughing at me?)

'London is the greatest city in the world,' says I, proud of my adopted home.

'Mon Dieu, Candy! For a city to be great, Monsieur, the food and wine needs to be glorious, the people engaging, the conversation stimulating and the women enchanting. London has none of this. Come to France; you will find good food, better wine than this piss, and prettier girls in every village.'

'Pas Gascogne, maître,' said Planchet. 'Les Gascons sentent mauvais.' (Not Gascony, master. Gascons smell bad)

'Silence, Planchet,' said d'Artagnan. 'Planchet is from Paris. Even the poorest Parisian thinks himself better than a Gascon comte, even when that comte is his master.'

'Surtout quand le comte est son maître.' (Especially when the comte is his master)

Planchet grinned at Figgis. The blackguard clearly understood the English tongue. He was more than the Comte's mere servant, I was certain. My rustic valet opened his chops as if to say something.

'Ye know...'Figgis began.

I interrupted him before he could embarrass me.

'I have similar problems with witless and impudent servants,' I said, glaring at Figgis to be silent. 'And what be wrong with the wine and food? You seem to have enough of it.'

'Ah the wine: it is Spanish, sweet, sickly and thick, at best. The good wine is never sent here. Instead, it is barrels of poor quality vinegar, that you quaff and quaff, caring nothing for taste or body. You cannot even pour it properly, always right to the brim to get as much as possible in your cup.'

'Ils doivent être très assoiffés, maître.' (They must be very thirsty, master.)

'And the vegetables, you murder the vegetables. There is a reason God put the English on an island: it is to stop you poisoning the rest of us.'

'What be the matter with the vegetables?' I liked pottage.

'There are farms nearby. I picked a leek, fresh and crisp and full of taste. You English turn it into this.' He pointed to the dish of pottage on the table. 'You boil the flavour out of the food. I would rather eat rat meat; C'est dégoutant.' (It's disgusting)

'You ate a raw leek? That be disgusting.'

'And what is the jelly? Aspic? You put a boiled egg in aspic then choke it in spice: ginger, nutmeg, and cardamom; tres dégoûtant!' (very disgusting). And then you encase it in a pastry so tough it could be made of stone. Pastry should crumble and melt like butter on the tongue.' He sat straight in his chair and pointed to some salted fish cooked in cider and honey; another dish I was partial to. 'You live by a river yet there is no fresh fish anywhere in the city, it seems. Why is that? Salted fish, spiced fish, smoked fish, dried fish, and pickled fish, but no fresh fish at all?'

'Well, you would not wish to eat ought that came out the Thames near London,' I told him. 'The poissonis liable to be poison. You are supposed to be seeking out an Imperial assassin, not on a culinary tour of England.'

D'Artagnan, waved his hand dismissively at me. 'Believe me, Monsieur Candy, nobody would come to England on a culinary tour. The ravaillac runs out of the most precious commodity,' he said. 'Time for him is pressing. Perhaps your theatre event will be the place he next chooses to strike.'

'Why think you?' I did not want anything to spoil our grand design.

'If the prince can be killed before the spring it will sow confusion and discord in the alliance, and here in England. By May, France will be invading the Hapsburg Empire, and your new Parliament army will face King Charles. Ferdinand[36] is losing the war; thousands were lost in a battle in Brandenburg last November.' He picked up a chicken leg, bit into it and spat it out again. 'Quelle surprise, even the bird is dry and overdone. The only thing you English can cook is roast beef.'[37]

---

[36]The Holy Roman Emperor; Ferdinand III.

[37]Roast Beef is a very old stereotype. English cuisine was famous for spit-roasting during the Early Modern period.

Planchet started to chuckle.

'Stop whining about the food,' I snapped. 'Dip it in the bread sauce if 'tis too dry.'

'Je ne recommanderais pas la sauce, maître,' said Planchet. (I would not recommend the sauce, master)

D'Artagnan sipped at his sack instead, grimaced at the taste, and continued. 'The Bavarian war is almost finished, the Empire nearly broken, and their ally Spain is bankrupt. King Charles must defeat you Roundheads in the field this year, else he is finished too. This assassination is a last desperate political gamble for Emperor Ferdinand before His Most Glorious Majesty's armies invade; before England can send veterans of civil war against him. Before he is forced to sue for peace.'[38]

---

[38]D'Artagnan's assessment of the situation in the Thirty Year War is perhaps overly optimistic and pro-French in outlook, but the war was certainly turning against the Holy Roman Emperor. The Catholic league had been beaten badly in 1644 at the Battles of Jüterbog and Jankau by the Swedes, and French invasions of the Spanish Netherlands and Bavaria co-ordinated with a Swedish attack from North Germany were planned for 1645. Even so, the Empire was still able to field significant troops and Spain was far from beaten. Karl Ludwig's presence in London was both an attempt to secure funding and troops from Parliament, but clearly also positioned him to claim the throne of England, should it be offered. Veronica Wedgewood asserts that the German Prince lacked the courage of his convictions, and the ruthlessness to really push for the English crown, preferring to wait in England for the situation to develop. Charles I's pro Spanish foreign policy before the Civil War, in spite of the Palatinate being overrun, had certainly alienated his eldest German nephew, and upset the radical puritans in Parliament who viewed the Winter

'His Majesty?' says I, confused for a moment.

'King Louis,' he said in explanation. 'Since Prince Karl stays in Whitehall surrounded by guards, without even women brought to his chamber for entertainment, opportunity for The Black Bear to strike has been unforthcoming. The poisoning was messy and failed, and he becomes frustrated and desperate. That is why he was willing to risk a shot at the prince's boat. It was, as they say, a very long shot. Now, your theatre is public, but with a performance in a dark space there is every chance of success and escape. You think this Huguenot Swordmaster will let me take part?'

'Can you use a sword?' That was perhaps a touch hubristic.

'Better than you, Monsieur Candy. Better than you.'

'Maupin may not be well disposed to a papist,' I said. 'He was at La Rochelle.'

'He was at La Rochelle?' D'Artagnan grinned. 'Donc étais-je.' (So was I)

*

Gilbert Mabbot was a journal writer and newsmonger; a slender well-dressed man who haunted the Fountain on Fleet Street, when he was not in Westminster or Whitehall. Information was his currency, bought or sold. He had contacts across London and the Kingdom who would receive his weekly newsletters. Some of his tales would appear in the *Perfect Diurnal*, but the best titbits had to be procured in person. I liked Mabbot, he was friendly and pleasant company of an evening, but I would not trust him. Since taking the assignment to protect the Elector Palatine I had kept my distance, seeking not to appear in his newsbook. Now, however, I wanted information and I had a task for him.

'You wish me to place news of this sword exhibition in my letters?'

''Tis newsworthy.'

Queen and her brood as Calvinist heroes. However, the offer did not come from the Commons and after Charles I's execution, and the abolition of the monarchy in January 1649, Karl Ludwig finally returned to his homeland. It does perhaps suggest something of the prince's ambitions that he waited in England despite being restored to some of his lands at the Peace of Westphalia in 1648.

'Sugar, I like you; you are a decent enough fellow, but you simply want me to tell my readers such to sell more seats at higher prices.'

'Well, yes, but that does not mean 'tis not the truth.'

'What is truth, Sugar? Is mine the same as yours?'

'Pilate asked that of the Messiah.'

'Oh, I do not deny the veracity of the report. I merely point out that your intent is not to inform but to profit.'

'Makes that some difference?

'Not to those who read it; nobody ever wonders on the purpose of the news, but that is rather the point is it not?' he said. 'I sell information, Sugar. A good story is always worth more. Had you come to me with a tale of a foul murder, or better, some lascivious scandal amongst the quality, I would be paying you the gold. As it is you come to me with a tale of mild interest to my readers, but of profit to yourself.' He held his arms open, palms up.

'How much do you want?'

He smiled. 'How much importance do you wish me to give to the news? A shilling will buy you a line.'

'I have a sovereign. What will that buy?'

'That will buy a most excellent preview of your exciting display of martial prowess,' he said. 'The audience will be treated to the best blades in town demonstrating their skill, at the most spectacular venue in London. We can call the winner the champion of the city.' He pulled out his journal and scratched the words down with a pencil bit.

I burst out laughing and handed over the gold coin. Gilbert reached inside his suit and pulled out a copy of Pecke's newsbook. He cast it across the table at me.

'There is today's news,' he said. 'It will be on sale in St Paul's and Westminster on the morrow. Your uncle is a clever man. Even if the Lords block the denying ordnance, the new army will be formed under Fairfax. The earls of Essex and Manchester may keep their commands but will receive no funds for them. Their armies will wither on the vine starved of resources. It was your uncle's design. I believe they call it checkmate.'

The Perfect Diurnall.

This day the Commons spent many hours in debate of the new army which is to be raised. Although the ordnance for displacing members from command was rejected by the Lords (as you heard last week) the Commons held it fit in their judgements, for the good of the Kingdom, to proceed anyway. Having previously agreed upon the number of Horse and Foot for the new army to be 21,000, and how they should be paid, they proceeded now to the nominating of the Commander in Chief. They nominated Sir Thomas Fairfax to command, and Major Skippon to be Sergeant-Major General (two such persons of valour and fidelity; the kingdom can hardly find two braver gentlemen). They proceeded to name the Colonels of Horse and Foot for the said army. Col. Hoborne, Col. Middleton, Col. Fortescue and Col. Barkley are four of the colonels agreed.

The Commons, in the next place, took into consideration the good service of the Lord General Essex, and appointed a committee to consider what honour should be conferred upon him for his fidelity and good service to the public. The like was also done for Sir William Balfour for his faithful services. And also considered was how to settle the payment of arrears of such soldiers as should not be employed in the new establishment.

January 21st, 1645.

Cross Deep, Twickenham 1720.

Every Bridegroom does then what he please,
And the lovely Brides their flames appease,
I need not name what young Lovers do,
For 'tis known to every one, to I and to you.
(Traditional Ballad: *Cupid's Victory*)

The Idiot is to become a father. There has been much joyous celebration at the news, and it has meant a stream of well-wishers to the front door. His wife, of course, has treated the whole situation as an excuse to retire to her chambers. Doctor Barrowby was summoned to give his verdict on the incarceration. That was a pointless exercise. I told the idiot that there is a perfectly good midwife that lives on King Street, and a well-regarded wetnurse in Whitton. What need was there for a doctor? What do they know of childbirth? Barrowby is no fool; he took his fee and agreed with me. So, the midwife has been sent for to tender to the woman's complaints.

'What will you call the babe?' I asked.

'If it is a boy then Christopher,' he said. 'If a girl then Elizabeth.'

'Kit would like that,' I said. 'As would your Great Grandfather, but the less said of him the better.'

He smiled. 'I have wondered on him more since the news. I wish I had known him.'

'Your Great Grandfather? He was a miserable drunken bastard.'

'No, my father.'

'Ah, well, you and Kit could be peas from a pod to look at. You are more thoughtful, perhaps, less impulsive.'

I heaved myself over to the sideboard and took out two glasses. There was no brandy; we would have to wait for the weather to turn and the smugglers to ply their trade. I cracked open a bottle of Madeira and poured us both a glass. Turning back, I handed one to the idiot and collapsed into my chair.

'Kit would have been overjoyed,' I said. 'And your mother too. She would have taken charge of the household and organised us like a regiment.'

He laughed.

161

'I jest not,' I said. 'Your mother was a formidable woman when she was in a temper, and woe betide any who did not follow orders. She was much like your Great Aunt Elizabeth, in that. We could do with one of them here now.'

'You have been a father to me all these years,' he said.

I could feel the tears in my eyes.

'Oh, witless boy, you are a sentimental fool,' I told him, and took a great gulp of the sack to cover my embarrassment. 'We will need help.'

'Perhaps we should employ a housekeeper to organise us,' he said. 'I will be spending a lot of time in the city with the proposals for Parliament. What think you?'

Evenings in Covent Garden are one way of passing the time while your wife is indisposed, I thought. Perhaps I should tell him of Doctor Shootwixt and his sheaths.

'As long as the housekeeper tries to organise me not, and I do not have to pay, 'tis your choice and money.'

'If Parliament accepts the Company plan, Uncle, then we will soon be as rich as Croesus. I will be able to afford ten housekeepers; one for each day of the week and four on Sunday.'

I am ever suspicious of such pronouncements, and it ended badly for Croesus. None ever seem to remember that.

'Here's to a new babe, wealth beyond imagining, and a new housekeeper then,' I said, raising my glass. 'Let us hope the Company delivers on its promises. For all our sakes.'

19. Bad Omen: London, February 1645.

Though I am young, and cannot tell
Either what Death or Love is well,
Yet I have heard they both bear darts,
And both do aim at human hearts.
And then again, I have been told
Love wounds with heat, as Death with cold.
(Ben Jonson, *Though I am young and cannot tell*)

The Swordmaster's injury was not serious, just a graze, so he said. However, it did mean that any display would have to wait a few weeks until he recovered. I thought it a measure of the man that he complained little at the witless rogues who knew not the difference twixt papist and puritan. Such was the sorry state of England. Malignants and scoundrels preyed upon the innocent, but none thought it unusual or strange. Foreigners were being beaten daily in the streets, papist or not, it mattered little to the rabble.

Maupin was enthused about the exhibition at the Phoenix (not least because my sister had promised him a quarter of the profits) but he was reluctant regarding d'Artagnan's participation. Welcoming one of Richelieu and Mazarin's bullyboys stretched even his accommodating nature. I had sparred with d'Artagnan since his suggestion and knew he was an excellent blade, certainly better than me. Other students would make up numbers in the exhibition, Maupin assured me, and the matter was closed.

John and I went through our morning exercises under his watchful eye but the Swordmaster was fain to observe only, and dismissed us early with apologies.

'I want you to speak to Hugo,' I told John as we left. 'It is about time he did more than sit in taverns playing music and supping ale. I want this assassin found before the exhibition. The last thing we need is an incident at the theatre.'

'Sir?'

'Murder is bad for business. His Dutch contacts should have found out more by now.'

'Yes, sir.' He turned to head to Wapping and then turned back. 'There is a dance tonight at the Wheatsheaf... Mariette wished to go?'

I sighed. He was spending more and more time with that girl. The boy was fortunate that Maupin was not discriminating. Even Everard could not claim that as providence.

'I wager you are smitten, John.'

'I wager you are jealous, sir,' he said.

You know, that barb actually struck home. Mariette was a pretty thing, but she had not given me a second glance, fascinated only with my man from the start. I was not used to such disdain. It pricked at my vanity and John knew it.

'If you can get to Wapping and back in time for the dance, then you are welcome to the evening off,' I told him.

A grin broke over the boy's face.

'And since you are passing by, you can pop into The Tower and see if Mr Haslerig has any tasks or information for us.'

John's face fell, and I burst out laughing.

'On your way, my lad; you had best hurry if you wish to be back by nightfall.'

He was muttering under his breath as he went off to the Tower and onto Wapping. I walked through the gardens at Moorfields, chuckling to myself, and followed the wall round to Smithfield. I was soon lost in thought, letting my feet lead the way home.

I confess that dreams of a regular flow of coin into my purse were enticing me. I pondered more and more on resigning my commission. It looked certain that Uncle Samuel would be forced to resign his rank as Scoutmaster General and Governor of Newport Pagnell. Without his patronage, there would be little chance for my further advancement. The generals for the new army were not well disposed to me. Black Tom Fairfax was to be Captain General and bore me an unfathomable dislike. Skippon, the Lieutenant General of Foot, believed me to be an impudent and heretical fop. Leonard Watson was the new army's Scoutmaster; I did not trust him and he did not trust me (I was passing certain that he had betrayed me and caused my incarceration in York the previous summer). All taken, a commission under Fairfax did not seem an attractive proposition.

I looked up as I passed through Smithfield, planning to cut through the warren of tenements and over the Fleet River. Someone smashed the back of my head with a fearsome blow that stunned me and forced me to my knees. Turning to try and mark the attacker, a hobnailed boot caught me square on the jaw snapping back my head, and I slumped to the ground swooning. I could barely take note of the voices as a bag was thrown over my head, and my hands and feet were bound.

'Stay quiet, Candy,' someone hissed in my ear. 'Else you die.'

Not a sound did I make. They threw me onto wooden boards, into a handcart by the feel, and I was trundled off half-senseless.

*

I was carried bound and hooded from the cart and thrown to a hard floor; scraping my knees and banging my face again. I prayed that I had not broken my nose. The hood was shipped off. I blinked trying to clear my sight and looked around. It was a small cell with earth floor and two rough vagabonds staring at me. One was small and wiry, perhaps thirty years of age. The other was older, fatter, and ugly: a gap-toothed smile, heavy jowls and thick lips, with dirty straight brown hair under his red woollen bonnet.

'Forgive me, gentlemen,' I said, wincing at my bruises. 'There was no time for introductions. Whom might you be?'

Gap-tooth looked to the small fellow at my words. Jack-a-dandy[39] was in charge, then. They were both likely from the Gypt tribe, I decided. A wave of fear came over me when I realised that. Had they discovered John's hand in Boswell's death?

'You will find out when all is good and ready,' said Jack-a-dandy. 'Stay here, Sid, and make sure he tries nowt.'

He left me and gap-toothed Sid alone in the cell. Given my hands were bound and my weapons taken there was not a lot that I could try, other than perhaps bait ugly Sid. When I was younger (before I had endured incarceration in York) I would have happily crafted some insults for the situation. That could get you a slit throat at worst and a beating at best. I rolled up onto my arse with my hands still tied behind me, and remained silent.

'Ye are Candy, sire?' said Sid, after a short period of silence.

'Yes.'

'Ye own the Cockpit?'

'My sister does, amongst others.'

If this was some fault of Beeston's, I would geld the scoundrel. That I had most assuredly decided, and John Coxon would not escape my wrath if 'twas his transgressions responsible. I was cursed with disobedient servants and scheming business partners.

'I worked in the Cockpit,' he said. 'Before the closures.'

'Oh?'

---

[39] A small, impertinent, and insignificant fellow.

'I am a Fool, sire.' He bowed and doffed his bonnet at me. 'Sidcup Buttermeadow at your service.' He gave a little jig and doffed his cap once more.

Sidcup Buttermeadow? I thought. God give me strength. I noted a little white furry head poking out of his shirt as he bowed. It was a tiny mouse sniffing at the air.

'You have acquired a tenant, Mr Buttermeadow,' I said, nodding at the offending rodent.

He looked down at his breast.

'That is King Arthur, sire.' He tucked the mouse back inside his shirt. 'Once he was monarch all the land over, but turned into a mouseling by the machinations of Morgan the Fey. 'Tis said that that there are witches abroad again in England, sire, and the *divil* hi'self rides out.'

Stories of monsters and strange omens, phantasms and magic were all over the pamphlets. Whispers of the Witchfinder General had already reached London. Though most dismissed it still, a wild insanity was overtaking even sensible Englishmen. The horror of the war drove belief in anything, blame in anything, if only the madness would end.

'Do you truly believe in witches, Buttermeadow?' I asked.

I thought it nought but primitive superstition, but Sidcup struck me as the type who would. I did not tell him that in some parts of England 'King Arthur' could be enough to see him convicted for possessing a demonic familiar.

'Aye indeed, sire. I have seen the witches. Hubble bubble toil and trouble.'

'That be a play,' I pointed out.

'And I am the eighth child of eight children, sire; seven sisters and me. That is a powerful charm against witches and warlockery.'

'Eight children? Your mother must have been exhausted.'

'Was till she sewed up the flap in my pa's britches.' He gave me a gap-toothed grin. 'Ye know what they say, sire?'

'What?'

'A stitch in time will save nine.'

The Fool actually had me laughing as I sat trussed up like a hog in a shambles. Sidcup was pleased with my response. I knew his type, they needed the adulation of an audience; Beeston was another.

'Mr Davenant wrote that line special for me,' he said. 'I told ye, sire, I am a Fool.'

'I have not seen you at the theatre?'

'I was fighting for the King,' he said quietly, the laughter in his voice gone. 'But I am a Fool, not a soldier. I will fight in no more wars. Billy Beeston says there is no place for me at the Cockpit.'

'So instead you bash innocents in broad daylight for coin?' Sidcup had the good grace to look ashamed. 'What of your friend, another actor?'

'No, sire, he is a rogue. I had been selling hot chestnuts in the cold, but the Lord Mayor's men gave me a day in the pillory for wormy edibles. If ye look for workers, sire. I wish only to return to the stage. The Phoenix is my life.'

''Tis an unusual way to gain employment,' I said. 'Assault on the King' highway?'

''Twas not my notion...'

The door swung open and Jack-a-dandy came back in with another basher. I recognised him; he was the Gatekeeper to the King of the Gypsies.

'The Burned Man is ready for him now,' said the Gatekeeper. 'Put the hood back on his noodle.'

Sidcup Buttermeadow plunged me into darkness once more, and they stood me up and led me out, pushing me to the right. I had been dragged to the Hall of the Beggars once before, but when they took off the hood 'twas a different vision of hell. A small cell, lit with tens of flickering candles, smoky, and a thick musky perfume in the air. A man in black hooded robes like a Benedictine monk sat in a high backed chair, wreathed in incense and shadows. His face was a mask, quite literally: a porcelain white fashioning from a Venetian tragedy, with a long pointed nose and narrow slits to see out. The blood-rimmed eyes behind watched me intently. It reminded me of Mephistopheles in Marlowe's play.

Were these men all players? I wondered briefly, but dismissed that. The shadows and smoky perfume were staged to disorientate, but the beating had been no act.

How can they see anything but the shadows, if they are never allowed to move their heads?[40]

'Leave him with me.' The Burned Man spoke with a harsh rattle in his voice. 'You can wait outside.'

The Gatekeeper, Jack-a-dandy and Sidcup said nought as they turned and closed the door behind them. I was left alone with the King of the Beggars. He pondered me in silence for more than a few

---

[40]Plato, Allegory of the Cave

moments. It was uncomfortable, standing with my hands bound and being measured by this masked man.

'There is a singular irony that masks are created for actors to show their deepest emotions,' I said. 'To an unmasked audience who are obliged conceal theirs. What think you?'

I was nervous, I sometimes blurt out foolish things when I am nervous.

The Burned Man sighed. The first audible sound since he had dismissed the others.

'Your legendary wit is undiminished, I see. You owe me, Sugar Candy.'

All of this could not be over a share of the sword exhibition.

'A tenth part of the profits be insufficient?' I said.

There was a hoarse chuckle from behind the mask.

'Beeston told you would pay only a twentieth part.'

I was going to find a smithy and get him to hot-hammer Beeston's whirligigs on an anvil. The Burned Man continued before I could conjure a suitable answer.

'You also owe me for three men killed.'

The sailors who attempted to rob John and me.

'Surely that be the risk a footpad takes when they pick out armed men to bash?' I said.

There was a blink behind the mask, and a nod. The footpads had been knuckle-dump turnips. Perhaps this demon would be satisfied with the increased monies. I saw a glimmer of hope in the shadows.

'And finally, there is the heinous murder of Haniel Boswell by your man, a proven traitor to the Tribe.'

'Ah,' I said.

He sat and stared at me again, surveying me. I tried to hold that cold calculating gaze, but in faith my wits had deserted me. John had killed the King of the Beggars. If the tribe had discovered that and The Burned Man wanted to avenge him, John was dead. I wondered if he had even made it to Wapping. Had they taken him running errands for me?

'What think you the penalty for such a vile sin?'

I opened my mouth as if to say something, thought the better of it and closed it once more.

'A penny for your thoughts?' He was smirking behind the mask, you could tell from the tone.

'Do you have any proof of this accusation?' I said finally.

'I need no proof. This is not a court of law.'

'What be this, then?'

'This is hell.'

That was more than a tad histrionic, I thought to myself. I wondered again on the acting and the theatre of this encounter; looking around the room, trying to note the illusions.

'This cannot be hell,' I said. 'My brother and father would be here complaining about me.'

He laughed again; 'twas not a pleasant sound.

'If I give you your man's life, what will you give me?'

I paused again before answering. After all, what do you offer a man who can have most anything? Money or women would entice most men, in some form or other, but The Burned Man would care nothing for such. Information is costly, but I would not spy for him and determined I would sacrifice my man on that point.

'I would be eternally grateful,' I said.

He sat back in his chair.

'A favour for a life, at the time of my choosing?'

'Yes,' I said.

'If you renege, I will take both your lives. That is my sworn oath.'

'Yes.'

John Coxon was going to spend his lifetime scrubbing pisspots for this bondage.

'Then there is one more condition,' said The Burned Man.

'What?'

I grant you I was quite curt in my answer, understanding well enough what it was to be in debt to this creature.

'You will take Buttermeadow and give him employ in the theatre. He is next to useless as a beggar, too faint-hearted to bash, too clumsy to steal or burgle, and too distractible to even keep out an eye for the watch.'

'He be a Fool,' I said.

'In more ways than one. I owe him a debt, and, Sugar Candy, I keep my promises...' He left that hanging on the air.

I agreed to the condition. What would you have done? Spit in the eye of the Beggar King and been taken outside stabbed and dumped? It was not a difficult decision, if I be honest. The Burned Man frightened me.

*

'No,' said Beeston. 'I will not have him. Do you have any idea what he is like? He is a fool.'

'So he told me.'

169

'He is a fool by nature and design. None like him.'

'Woe to you when all men speak well of you, for according to these things their fathers used to treat the false prophets likewise,' I said.[41]

Beeston sniffed. 'Sidcup has a penchant for falling and breaking people and props. The last time he performed at the Red Bull, he fell through the stage onto a seventy-year-old porter and broke both his legs.'

I started to laugh.

'It is not funny; the man died a week later. Sid is clumsy and foolish, but worse he is unlucky.'

'Oh, pish posh.'

'When the Duke of Buckingham came to see a play, back in the twenties, Sidcup managed to spill half a barrel of red wine over him. The Duke was murdered by Felton only days later. Sidcup Bad Omen they started to call him. Plays fail, takings get stolen, the actors refuse to act; the theatre gets burned down. He is a good sort, kind-hearted and all, but he is a Jonah.'

'That be just poor fortune and superstition,' I said.

'Actors are the most superstitious creatures under heaven,' said Beeston. 'If there are damages or losses because he is in the theatre, you are liable. I am not paying for his malefic presence.'

'You will not use his *malefic presence* to avoid your own duties, Beeston. I do not forget your design to cream a twentieth part from the swordplay monies with the Gypts caused this.'

'I was merely trying to get the best price from the tribe. If you go and offer The Burned Man extra that is your decision,' he said, quite unrepentantly. 'In fact, I should be reimbursed for the loss incurred by your negotiations.'

'Or perhaps I should tell my sister all, and let her decide how best to proceed. You may guarantee she will desire only to help poor Sidcup.'

She would, I thought. It would be her Christian duty.

'Yes, well, I do not think we need go that far,' said Beeston. 'I will find something for him to do. You know they left him guarding the latrines with the Royalist Army under Hopton, such was his worth, and he still managed to burn them down? The stench of smoking shithouse choked the whole camp for two days.'

That made me laugh again.

'Then keep him away from the privy and the fire,' I said.

---

[41]Luke 6:26

I had left Buttermeadow waiting in the gardens of the theatre. He had told me Beeston would not be accommodating (although he had not explained the nuances of such emotion) and I had expected resistance from the theatre manager. I had waited till the right moment to threaten him with Elizabeth. Beeston understood that he was well looked after at the Cockpit, protected by Uncle Samuel's contacts and given some employ. All that was ultimately on my sister's sufferance: Sidcup Buttermeadow might be a fool by nature and design, but William Beeston was most assuredly not. I found Sidcup waiting for me in the garden, smoking a pipe and kicking at some dry leaves piled under the trees.

'Beeston will find you some employ,' I told him. 'Be careful not to vex him.'

Sidcup tapped out his pipe on a tree trunk, gave a big grin, and tugged his forelock at me.

'Thank ye, sire. You shall not regret it, I assure you. I shall do whatever Billy Beeston desires.'

There was smoke coming from his feet. The burning tobacco was smouldering on the leaves. Sidcup had noticed not.

I sighed. 'You be afire, Sidcup.'

He looked down and stamped out the leaves, then gave me his gap-toothed grin.

You are Beeston's problem, I thought to myself.

20. A New Modelling: London, March 1645.

The phoenix hope,
Can wing her way through the desert skies,
And still defying fortune's spite;
Revive from the ashes and rise.
(Miguel De Cervantes, *Don Quixote*)

The Cockpit was being transformed. Workmen were painting and fixing; the sound of hammering and smell of fresh paint filled the air, as busy labourers toiled to make the theatre ready for performance. The last time the venue had seen an audience had been for illegal cockfights and baiting. My sister had put a stop to that as soon as she discovered the activity. There were still street-brats running around, ostensibly to be taught to read the catechism, but they were more interested in Buttermeadow's tomfoolery. The Fool had found some painted wooden balls backstage and demonstrated his mummer's skills to the children. At first, only three balls were spinning through the air, but he called on Figgis to cast another in, and then another, till he had five flying higher and higher. Sidcup would spin and twist as he caught them, bending to catch one with his hat whilst his other hand would cast another in the air. He sat in a chair, got up and danced a jig, all the while throwing and catching the balls without a single one touching the ground. I turned to Beeston.

'You told me he was clumsy.' I gestured to the acrobatic display from the large man.

'You will see. He has not had time enough to wreak his havoc.'

'Elizabeth says he be kind-hearted, and the children adore him.'

'I do not say he is a bad person, Sugar, but misfortune wraps around him like a cloak. Sooner or later he will cause a disaster to someone.'

'Put him outside selling chestnuts when the exhibition is on. He cannot fall on a porter there.'

'He can start a fire,' said Beeston sourly. 'This swordplay could be lucrative; I see no reason to take the risk. Maupin wants me to announce the bouts and Dutch Hugo will provide musical entertainment in-between each match.' He saw my look. 'Music is not theatre.'

'I thought Maupin would do the announcements.'

'Better to have an English accent for the audience, I would say. A foreigner will only upset the crowd. The Swordmaster and I can adjudicate on the bouts. There will be other students as well. I wonder if we can get them to rehearse?'

''Tis not a play,' I said. 'If there are *rehearsals* some interfering imp will complain it be theatre. I am certain we can *practice*.'

Beeston grunted at that.

There was a cheer from the children as Buttermeadow bent backwards over the chair and caught the last wooden ball in his mouth. He stood up and took a bow.

'What of your sister?'

'What of her?'

'Is she likely to be in attendance? There are certain entertainments for the galleries that she might object to.'

I laughed at that. Beeston would be pimping sack and punks to the richer patrons like he was a stew-house gallant.

'You are fortunate,' I told him. 'Elizabeth plans on spending the evening with Maupin's daughter Mariette. 'Tis a shame, I would have liked to see the crowd when that girl fenced.'

'Bad?'

'Good,' I nodded to John. 'The boy comes close to her, by all accounts. If you be looking for a wager.'

'I have heard all about the boy coming close to her,' said Beeston, with a snigger. 'He talks of little else.'

'Young love, were you not the same with your wife?'

Not particularly, no. It would be unseemly for a woman to take part in the bouts, no matter how skilled. There would be complaints and we need that not.

I agreed with him. Beeston and I both saw the exhibition as a chance to earn some decent coin. If it was successful perhaps regular bouts and shows could be arranged. I had heard of the like in Italy and Spain, even Paris according to d'Artagnan. Mariette would have to spend the evening with my sister, no doubt being lectured on something or other, whilst we men played. 'Twas a transparent attempt by Elizabeth to talk with Maupin's daughter over John, but I was still convinced my sister was enamoured with the Swordmaster.

One of the street urchins arrived with cards requesting seats at the performance from richer sorts. The pamphlet sellers and journal writers had all been scribbling over Prince Karl's attendance. Mabbot had done his work well.

'If we get many more of these,' said Beeston. 'We shall have to put on another week of performances. This one is from the Countess of Carlisle.'

'Exhibitions,' I said, 'not performances.'

I pulled the card from Lucy Hay to me and checked the handwriting. It was an increasing habit. Whoever had been passing notes through the willow tree had a strong and easily recognisable hand. The testicle-twisting annoyance was my conviction that I had seen the writing before the notes began. I knew that it was someone I was acquainted with. The Countess's card was written in a neat, perfectly constructed hand. It was not the anonymous pen. Perhaps that was the secretary's handwriting, I mused. The Countess of Carlisle has always taken too much interest in my career. I endeavoured to try and get a sample of her hand.

John burst in through front doors to the pit, and Beeston and I both turned. The boy had a wide grin on his face and waved his hat at me.

'We have him, sir! We have the Black Bear.'

*

A tanner's yard is about the most nauseating establishment one can imagine. The process be quite foul, but everyone needs leather. Cow carcasses, stripped of edible meat, are delivered to the yard. The horns, hooves, and udders cut away and boiled down to glue, the hide trimmed and washed clean of blood and shit. Then the skin is soaked in stale piss until pliable, and every last bit of hair, fat, and flesh scraped off by children. They wash it again and soften it in dog shit. That be why, when you walk past a tanner's yard, 'tis all you can do to stop from puking. After that, it is a year of soaking in oakbark before the leather is ready for market. Rotherhithe has tanners, curriers, tawers, and parchment makers galore; I held a perfumed kerchief to my nose.[42]

---

[42]Curriers dyed, finished, and dressed the tanned leather before passing it on for production as shoes or saddles. Tawing was the same process as tanning but dealt with smaller hides of sheep, pig, and goats. Rotherhithe was well known for leather production in the Seventeenth Century. There were perhaps eighty tanning yards in Bermondsey and Southwark in the seventeenth century. Fifty years later the area provided 10% of all excise revenue on English leather.

'The information came from Everard,' said Sam. 'There is a foreigner staying here. Since he arrived last summer they have been stockpiling gunpowder. Five kegs of the stuff. It was easily enough to cause the explosion at the foundling hospital.'

I looked at John.

'The neighbours say the men are all strange and ill-formed. The two that rented the premises rarely leave the tanning yard, and there have been neither leather coming out nor carcass going in these past six months.'

'Ought else?'

'The foreigner has come from Germany, sir,' said John. 'He sometimes drinks in the Tooley Street brewhouse. Meg spoke with a punk he visits there. He is a soldier and knows fuses and powder.' He smiled. 'And he talks in his sleep.'

'Oh dear,' said I, with barely concealed glee. It had to be the Black Bear.

'There is a plan and a great fortune to come, so his punk says, but she knows no detail.'

I looked around at our resources. We had a squad of men, with swords, clubs and halberds; all were veterans. Some of them were ready to attack the yard from the river, some were with us to go through the gates. No firearms, the risk was too great with black powder stored, that was my great fear. The foundling hospital had not required much. I had inquired of the Office of Ordnance how much was needed for such an explosion. There were clerks there who made such calculations. Only two pounds in a tight casing was their answer. That meant there could be nearly sixty pounds of gunpowder in the yard.

'We need to be quick,' I said. 'Katherine Street would be but a mild fart in a tub if that went up.'

Sam and John both nodded.

'When the trumpet blows,' said Sam. 'At your order.'

I paused for a moment before giving the word. When you command men to risk their lives there is a responsibility. I gave a silent prayer that all of us would survive the day.

'Blow the horn,' I said.

It is as disgusting a process as Blandford describes, but the demand for leather remained high until the invention of plastic replacements.

The peal sounded out, and I led the soldiers into the yard with Sam and John behind me. In the gates were great barrels with curing hides soaked in piss. There were sheds and outbuildings around the cobbled yard and a brick house. A man standing in the yard turned as we all charged in. There was a look of surprise on his face, but he ran at us, screaming at the top of his voice.

One of the soldiers stepped forwards.

'Be silent, addlepate,' he said, and brought his club down on the man's forehead.

The man collapsed into a heap but three others came to the doorway of the main building with clubs in their hands. Two of them charged my soldiers starting a mêlée, but the other stepped back into the building. I went past the fight (the two malignants were already being overpowered) and into the brick building.

Inside was a small room with low beams. There was fire blazing in a grate, and five kegs with a match set in one corner. The man had grabbed a lit torch from the fire and was reaching at the match with his torch. I slashed down at his head. My blade glanced off his skull and cut away his ear. He howled, dropping the torch, and reached for his bloody ear on the ground. I kicked the torch across the room in a shower of sparks, but away from the match and powder kegs.

John and two soldiers came running in with swords in hand.

'Take him away,' I said.

The torch man was still kneeling in shock on the floor, holding half his face in his hand, with blood streaming from his wound. His shirt was soaked red, but he seemed oblivious to us. One of the musketeers walked up behind the man and clubbed him on the back of the head with his sword hilt. The kneeling man collapsed, unconscious.

'Makes it easier this way, sir,' said the other soldier to me. 'For him and us.'

They bound the man's hands and legs and carried him out, dripping blood all the way.

Hopefully, someone will bind his ear so he bleeds not to death, I thought.

In the yard, two of the miscreants were bound and under guard. The last was cornered, but waving a pistol at Sam and a couple of men. He had a distracted look about him: eyes wild, shirt torn. When his partner was carried out bloodied and bound from the building, he let up a great wail and discharged the pistol in the air.

'The Kingdom of Israel is at hand,' he called out. 'We rejoice in the

Lord of Hosts as we strike this blow. Our reward is the treasure of his love.' He spoke in a thick Scots accent. 'Babylon is fallen. Babylon is fallen!'

'Get him!' shouted Sam.

The two soldiers grabbed the Scotsman by the arms, but he did not struggle. I looked him in the eyes as they tied him up and took him to join the others.

'I am an illusion made of glass,' he said to me, quite cheerfully.

'Bugger,' I said.

He was not German; he was quite, quite, mad, and he was certainly not the Black Bear.

*

They were perhaps all mad (the Scotsman certainly was) and were likely for Bedlam not Tyburn. A belief they could set a fire under the Divines in Westminster Hall had inspired them. They wanted no bishops and no divines. Driven to insanity by the war and division, I concluded. Did they not realise that the balance of power in England had already shifted to the zealots? Their design was pure make-believe, but they had procured enough powder and that was a concern. The kegs were still sealed barring one set for the match, and that still full. That meant the Katherine Street explosion had not been their work. I had known such as soon as I looked into the madman's eyes. All England seemed mad.

I explained all to Uncle Samuel, my grandfather, Thurloe, St John and Butler in the study at Thames Street. I had met Thurloe beforehand. I had a plan, and he was only recently back in the city from Uxbridge, but he was intrigued.

'The Scots will return home,' said my grandfather. 'Mayhap that sparked these men's explosive intent. Montrose wins victory after victory against the Covenanters in Scotland.' He winked at me. 'Your friend John Hurry is not proving so adept at fighting the Earl.'

'He will turn coat again as soon as 'tis opportune,' I said. 'The man has no honour.'

He that is without sin among you, let him first cast a stone.[43]

'The new army will pass the Lords eventually,' said St John. 'Manchester and Essex pinned their hopes on the King being reasonable at Uxbridge after the loss of the north, but Montrose's victories in Scotland gives His Majesty confidence he can win a decisive victory this year.'

---

[43]John 8:7

St John explained how the treaty talks at Uxbridge had been a disaster. There was no desire for peace that could be given to Parliament. The Royalists had instead reorganised their armies ready for the campaigning season. The Lords left in London knew that their heads would be on a pike if the King was victorious. Cromwell laying down his commission was the political sacrifice they needed to support Fairfax's army. They had dissembled and prevaricated but the ordnance would pass. His Majesty's intransigence gave them no other choice. Uncle Samuel and Grandfather nodded at St John's words. I noted Butler scribbling furiously in a green ledger. I wondered what that was about; he rarely took a record of such meetings.

'What of The Black Bear?' asked St John. 'Are we any closer to discovering the man? If not these bedlamites in Bermondsey then who?'

Everyone looked at me. Thurloe and St John had been in Uxbridge at the talks, whilst Uncle Samuel had been in Newport Pagnell for weeks. They had only recently returned to the city for debates in the House about the new army, and I had only the time to speak and plan with Thurloe before the meet.

'He be a ghost,' I told them. 'The Prince is well protected, which is a blessing, and the poisoning and attack on the river are a sign of desperation. But of the man himself, we have discovered nought. We have raided and arrested nigh on fifty foreigners as well as the tanner's yard – French, German, Italian, a Pole, some Jews who entered the Kingdom illegally – and we have exposed a number of suspicious and criminal schemes, including the four madmen, but we have found nothing of the Schwartzbar.'

Butler coughed for attention. We all looked at him.

'Perhaps you are too distracted by your theatre's dubious entertainments to attend to this task diligently,' said the snivelling wretch.

'Au contraire, Monsieur Butler,' I said. 'I led the last raid myself, and the Prince has expressed a desire to attend the exhibition. The Dutch musician and Comte d'Artagnan both think that an attack there is possible.'

'So we shall bait a trap,' said Thurloe.

Butler coughed again.

'There is a great risk to that,' he said. 'What should happen if Candy fails to protect Karl Ludwig? If the prince is set on attending, mayhap we should refuse a licence for the exhibition. To protect

Prince Karl from himself, of course.'

'You really are an odiously spiteful goblin-turd, Butler...,' I began.

'Enough, Blandford,' said Uncle Samuel quietly.

'I think only of our duty to the Prince,' said Butler.

'I think the risk worth taking,' said St John.

'As do I,' said my grandfather.

Butler's smug face disappeared with those rebukes. He was ever the obsequious jam-trumpet.

'Mr Haslerig will have men in work clothes stationed on Drury Lane and in the gardens of the Phoenix,' said Thurloe. 'I have spoken with him and he too is in favour of the design. We will also put men around the prince's gallery seating. Added to that we shall have unknown agents in the audience.'

That was quick work, I thought.

'They shall have to pay an entrance fee,' I said, 'else 'twill look suspicious.'

Butler made another cough at that. Perhaps it was an obvious attempt to keep my profits high, but he would have acted no differently.

'Really, Butler, you should get that cough seen to,' I said, before he could make another sly comment. 'It could be the death of you.'

He understood that; his fat face flushed red and he said no more. St John nodded for Thurloe to continue.

'The prince will travel by carriage from Whitehall to Drury Lane. We will assign dragoons to accompany him and make sure nought happens en route. They will keep the crowds back when he arrives at the theatre, and get him to his seating safe and sound, if the Lord wills it.'

'We could scare the killer off,' said Uncle Samuel. 'With so many guards and agents?'

'He could be warned off. In this we balance the assassin's self-preservation against his murderous intent, Sir Samuel,' said Thurloe. 'I have made arrangement for bills for the exhibition to be distributed from the churchyard of St Paul's, Old Bailey and Westminster Hall. Mabbot and Pecke will advertise that the prince will be present, Blandford has seen to that. The other journal writers and pamphleteers will soon follow suit. All London will know the prince is to attend. The assassin must see it as his best chance of success before the summer.'

'At the least, we will have done our duty in keeping the prince safe,' said St John. 'I think this French Comte is correct in his assessment. If it cannot be done before the summer campaigns, the prince will be safe. This situation cannot carry on indefinitely.'

If it were done when 'tis done, then 'twere well it were done quickly[44]

'Cardinal Mazarin will be keeping d'Artagnan informed,' said Thurloe. 'But I do not think we can fully trust him, nor the Dutchman, they are both agents of foreign powers whose motivation is changeable.'

Everyone grunted their agreement at that point. Distrust of foreigners was running rampant in London. 'Twas little wonder Master Maupin had been assaulted. I wager we had not helped the situation by arresting any with a strange name or tongue. You reap what you sow when all's said and done. Once everyone had agreed to the design, after asking a few more petite questions, the meeting broke up. I walked with Thurloe out of the city and down the Strand. He was away to the prince to report, and I to the theatre on Drury Lane.

'Think you that the prince truly desires the crown?' I asked him.

He paused before answering, considering his response. I liked that about Thurloe; he never rushed to conclusions.

'I think he desires it,' he said. 'My master concurs. But I do not think he has the courage to reach out and seize it. In honesty, I do not think that the country would stand for it, and he does not have much wider support. Nevertheless, 'tis best we keep him alive.' He smiled and fixed me with those intense eyes. 'Just in case we need a new king.'

It was more than a jest. England was Bedlam.

*

The Information of Matthew Hopkins of Manningtree (Gentleman), taken upon Oath March 1645.

This Informant saith, that Elizabeth Clarke (suspected for a Witch) was watched certain nights, for the better discovery of her wicked practices. This informant came into the room where Elizabeth was watched, but intended not to have stayed long there. But Elizabeth told this informant, and one Master Sterne also present, if they would stay and do the said Elizabeth no hurt, she would call one of her white imps and play with it in her lap. This informant told her that they would not allow of it.

Elizabeth then confessed she had had carnal copulation with the Devil for six or seven years, and that he would appear to her three or four times in a week at her bedside, go into her bed, and lie with her. He would take the shape of a proper gentleman, with a laced falling band, having the whole proportion of a man, and would say to her:

---

[44]Macbeth Act I Scene VII

"Bess I must lie with you," and she did never deny him.

Within a quarter of an hour there appeared an imp as a dog, which was white, with some sandy spots, and seemed to be very fat and plump and with very short legs. Then it vanished away. Elizabeth said the name of that imp was Jarmara. Immediately there appeared another imp, which she called Vinegar Tom, in the shape of a Greyhound with long legs. Elizabeth then said that the next imp should be a black imp, and should come for the said Master Sterne, which appeared, but presently vanished. The last imp that appeared was in the shape of a Polecat, but the head somewhat bigger.

Elizabeth then told this informant that she had five imps of her own, and two of the imps of the old Beldam West (meaning one Anne West, widow) who is now also suspected to be guilty of Witchcraft. Sometimes the imps of the old Beldam sucked on the said Elizabeth, and sometimes her imps sucked on the old Beldam West. Elizabeth further told this Informant, that Satan would never let her rest, or be quiet, until she did consent to the killing of the hogs of one Mr Edwards of Manningtree, and the horse of one Robert Taylor.

This Informant further saith, that going from the house of the said Mr Edwards to his own house about nine or ten-of-the-clock that night, with his greyhound with him, he saw the greyhound suddenly give a jump, and ran as she had been in a full course after a hare. When this informant made haste to see what his greyhound so eagerly pursued, he espied a white thing about the bigness of a kitten, but the greyhound standing apart from it. The white imp or kitten danced about the greyhound, and by all likelihood bit off a piece of the flesh of the shoulder of the greyhound, for the greyhound came shrieking and crying to this informant with a piece of flesh torn from her shoulder.

This informant further saith, that coming into his own yard that night he espied a black thing, proportioned like a cat, only it was thrice as big, sitting on a strawberry-bed. It fixed its eyes on this informant, but when he went forwards it leapt over the pale and ran quite through the yard. His greyhound ran after it to a great gate. The imp did throw the gate wide open, and then vanished. The greyhound returned again to this Informant, shaking and trembling exceedingly.[45]

---

[45]Elizabeth Clarke (c1565-1645) was Matthew Hopkins' first victim in the witchcraft craze that gripped the eastern counties in 1645-46.

The self-proclaimed Witchfinder General and his associate John Sterne were appointed by local magistrates to investigate Clarke, after she was accused of witchcraft by a local tailor known as John Rivet in March 1645. Clarke, who was eighty years old and had lost a leg, was subjected to three nights of sleep deprivation before she made her confession, and her imps allegedly appeared. Clarke accused other women of witchcraft during her torture who were then subjected to the same treatment, with the same unsurprising result. Nineteen of the women were executed in July 1645 with another four having died in prison, and nine reprieved. In London, the Parliamentary journal the Moderate Intelligencer showed the distaste such activities were viewed with in the capital, by dedicating a critical editorial to the affair in September 1645. Hopkins and Sterne would go on to cause the execution of perhaps two hundred women in their short but financially lucrative careers as they travelled the eastern counties. It was so lucrative that a special tax had to be levied in Ipswich to pay for their investigations. Hopkins himself died of tuberculosis in August 1647 and Sterne retired from the witch hunting racket to his farm (although he did pen a treatise on witch-hunting that was very popular in Salem, Massachusetts, a few decades later).

21. Rehearsals: London, March 1645.

A sigh or tear perhaps she'll give,
But love on pity cannot live:
Tell her that hearts for hearts were made,
And love with love is only paid.
(John Dryden, A Song)

Love be a curious thing. If you listen to the poets (and I do not recommend it), they would have you believe it is a lightning bolt which sends you swooning and lumpen-headed. Love can be so much more. Sometimes it comes on like a slow dream, unnoticed until it is a passion; a fire that cannot be extinguished. To fall in love takes time, not an instant. To truly love another takes a lifetime; to love through the vagaries of the world in defiance of age takes devotion. What is youthful desire when compared to such, but a shallow imitation of Aphrodite's curse? I always preferred the Egyptian play to Romeo and Juliet, although both end in turgid misery. Elizabeth said to me once that love is two travellers on a road, 'tis best for both to look at the destination rather than gaze at each other.

'I love you,' I said.

'You lust after me, Sugar,' said Meg. 'There is a difference.'

She curled into me under the blankets, her leg wrapping around mine.

'With disdain you wound me.'

She was wrong. I did love her, even if it had taken me over a year to realise it. Franny would have laughed an I-told-you-so, but Franny was long dead. Meg and I had spent so little time together since Christmas. Uncle Samuel used Meg's skills as an agent, and she spent most of the time away. I had missed her, more than I had been willing to admit. I had even stopped wenching and strumping of late, and that was not like me. Meg had been the only one that I had dared to tell of my vow to the Burned Man. She knew enough of the Gypt crew, had her contacts among them, and warned me that the Boswell family were still to be reckoned with. If they found out about John's poisonous behaviour, the Burned Man would not be able to help the boy and he would still insist upon his favour.

'It was a fool's promise,' she told me again.

'What else could I have done?'

'Pack him off to the New World or send him to sea. Any number of things would have preserved his life.'

'I had to think quickly.'

'I do not think you thought at all. The Boswells are dangerous, Eddie may only be of an age with John, but he has uncles around him and he loathes your man. The two families have a history of bad blood.'

'I know of pater Coxon's death,' I said. 'Nat Jakes told me. It matters not, I fought at Marston Moor. I am certain I can cope with the Boswell clan.'

Those words were nought but braggadocio for my lover. In faith, I was severely worried about the Boswells and The Burned Man. Meg laughed at me.

'My grandfather fought against the Armada,' she said. 'He would not cease in telling everyone.'

'And the nub of this?' I said stroking her hair.

'You remind me of him.'

'I remind you of your grandfather? I am unsure such is seemly given our recent entertainments, my lover.'

'You declare your love for me,' she said. 'But what of Emily Russell?'

There was more than a hint of jealousy in her voice.

'Emily Russell is half a world away in the Americas, and you are here.'

It was the wrong answer.

'So am I but a consolation for the Golden Scout?' She pinched my nipple, and not playfully.

'Ow.'

'I am neither prize nor toy, Blandford Candy. When you understand that, perhaps you will deserve me.'

I laughed. 'Sometimes you remind me of my sister.'

'I am *certain* such is unseemly given our recent entertainments. Elizabeth is spending much time with Maupin and his daughter, I note.'

'She is enamoured.'

'I do not trust him.'

I sat up and looked at her in surprise. 'Maupin, why not?'

'He is a hunter, I have watched him. He presents a pleasant face, but there is a black fury in his eyes that no mask can hide.'

I lay back down and pulled her close.

'He has been harried from his home and family, chased to a foreign land by the King of France, and forced to live off scraps by teaching callow youths like me to swing a sword. I would be furious too, if I were him. He was unhappy with d'Artagnan taking part in the display. I did not press the point.'

'Now, I do like the Comte d'Artagnan,' she said. 'He is most witty and amusing.'

'He be French.'

'I know, 'tis a wonderful accent.'

Those words hanged in the air. Dryden was in the right: jealousy be jaundice for the soul; 'tis love's poison.

'I think the Countess of Carlisle will attend the exhibition' she said, changing the topic.

Lucy Hay was a meddler and a schemer, but her influence had waned. She rattled around her apartments, playing with her pretty secretary Justin, as her charms slowly faded.

'Why do you think she will come?'

''Tis not so long since her presence would have been the audience's object of desire; her beauty is passed but she knows not or believes it not. I watched it happen to my sister, it happens to us all. A pretty face will only last a year or two. Man or woman, you cannot escape time. You should think on that, my sweet.'

'I knew not there was a sister?'

Meg had revealed more about herself than night than in all the months I had known her – a grandfather, a sister.

'Her name is Lilith. She was once the pretty one.'

'Now, that I do not believe.' I lifted my hand to cup her breast.

'That is why I love you, Sugar. You have a golden tongue.' She reached to kiss me.

*

There were eight of us in all on the stage of the Phoenix. John and I, of course, a tall merchant's son from Aldgate; a lad named Arthur who I knew from the Gloucester march;[46] a pair of cornets from the city's Blue Regiment; a Northerner who worked for some Covenanter Divine in Westminster Hall. The last was the clean-shaven swordsman from Prince Karl's retinue, the gentleman I watched lose a bout in the stables. He was the prince's spy here, no doubts. Beeston stood in the pit with Maupin beside him and called up to us.

---

[46] See Davenant's Egg & Other Tales

'There will be four bouts initially, and the winners will progress to the next round. The losers will play off for consolation. Ten fights in all and the final bout will be the ultimate champion of the day.' Maupin nodded at the theatre manager's words.

'There will be breaks in between performances.'

'Bouts, Mr Beeston,' said Maupin.

'Well, of course, sir,' said Beeston. 'We do not wish for the audience to know the ending.'

'My students are well trained and matched, Mr Beeston. I cannot tell you who will win of a night.'

Beeston nodded and turned back to us.

'We have been granted a licence for three days of physical exhibition,' said Beeston. 'With the option of more if they are a success, less if the opening night is a failure. It would be good if we could have a different champion each evening, just to keep the audience guessing.'

Beeston was treating this as a theatrical spectacular, although I knew his desire to plan out each bout stemmed from the gambling that would accompany the evening. Maupin was having none of it. I smiled as the Swordmaster stepped forward, pushing past the stage manager.

'Gentlemen,' he said. 'You will all use the same style of blade.' He nodded to the collection of practice swords, blunted and strapped so we did not kill each other. 'We have basket hilt rapiers for all, no daggers. The rake[47] is not so steep and the stage is wide enough for the bouts, but you must stay side on else you risk pitching off...'

'And it looks better,' Beeston interrupted. 'Although one of you taking a tumble could please the crowds, if any of you know how to tumble?' He looked at us hopefully.

Maupin ignored Beeston. Instead, he set us to practising for the rest of the afternoon. We drew lots and faced off against our chosen opponent. I was given the Northerner first (from Durham, I think) who was quick but not well skilled.

I put on a quilted gambeson and took up the practice blade. It was the one I used with Maupin for sparring. I gave it a few swings and stood opposite the Northerner.

We both took the terzo guard position, our blades held in front of the body. We saluted, waited a moment, and then he made a thrust at my chest. I deflected it to the inside line and stepped forward to riposte,

---

[47]The slope of the stage towards the audience.

but he stepped back quickly before I could strike. We settled into guard positions again, but this time I tried to be clever and took up prima. My sword held high pointing at his face. Northerner settled into a standard terzo, and I thrust down at his chest. He parried quickly, pushing my blade low with his own, and then struck over the top of my sword with his riposte.

'Twas a fortunate mark at best, but he scored a touch on my chest. It meant I was fain to sit out the next round of contests. I sat in the benches opposite the stage and watched John demolish young Arthur in seconds. My man was frighteningly quick on the counter. I noted Mariette in the attic above the stage looking down on the fight. She was gazing adoringly at her paramour.

John and the German were the best out of us. Young Arthur was the least skilled but most enthusiastic; he had learned no swordplay on the Gloucester march. I wagered to myself that I could match most (not John or the German, theirs would be an interesting bout) but I was looking forward to facing the Northerner once more. Had Mariette been on the stage instead of watching from above, she would best us all. That would probably have the event closed down, however.

I turned as a voice came down from the galleries behind me.

'Monsieur Maupin, allez-vous pratiquer contre moi?' (Mr Maupin, will you practice against me?)

'Twas the Comte d'Artagnan with Hugo the musician. They must have crept into the theatre as we practised, and now sat on the benches of the second level watching the exercise. Maupin turned to see who the interloper was. His back stiffened as he caught sight of the Frenchman.

'We are in England, sir. I will speak the language of my new home, if you please,' said the Swordmaster. 'Not a nation that denied me.'

There was a bitter tone in his voice. D'Artagnan stood up, bowed and doffed.

'Of course, sir. I meant no offence. Would you care for a friendly bout? You were at La Rochelle in Thirty, no?'

'I was,' said Maupin, after a pause.

'So shall we spar in friendship where we once fought in anger, Monsieur?'

It was a clear challenge to the Huguenot with his students watching on. Maupin was obviously unhappy about the situation, but he shrugged and beckoned for d'Artagnan to come onto the stage. The Comte clambered along the benches and climbed down, and the

Swordmaster stepped up and handed him a practice sword. D'Artagnan took it in his left hand, then stretched and limbered. He was being deliberately ostentatious as he made ready. Maupin waited for him to take his place, sword held loosely in his left hand also, and then Beeston called out the en garde.

Maupin went into terzo, and d'Artagnan prima. The Frenchman struck first, a cut to Maupin's head. The Swordmaster merely stepped back and the Comte's blade whistled harmlessly through the air. Maupin stepped forward again and held his guard position. This was going to be interesting, I thought. They fenced for nearly ten minutes with neither making a mark on the other. It was a display of virtuoso skill from both men: parries, thrusts, quick hands and feet. I had sparred with d'Artagnan and knew he made no false boast about his skill. Maupin was older and his movement was slight, barely using any energy. D'Artagnan was showy, quicker, but he could not pierce the Swordmaster's defence. Maupin would riposte and counter at lightning speed, but he rarely took the initiative. He fought as he taught, defence was all.

'They are evenly matched,' I said to John.

He nodded. 'But Maupin is fighting left-handed when the right is his stronger.'

I grinned. 'So is d'Artagnan.'

*

A Perfect Relation of the Amazon of Andover

We told in the last of the rapid fall from grace of Lord Henry Percy, and that his lordship had so offended the King that he was sent into exile. It is whispered that the designs at the late conversations of Uxbridge, and the Queen's intervention, had seen to Percy's fate. His Lordship and some thirty Horse did retire to Andover, where, as we reported, he was captured by General Cromwell and General Waller, and held and questioned. General Waller ordered Cromwell to entertain such notable captives with some civility.

A friend in Oxford tells us, that amongst his Lordship's party was a youth of such fair countenance that General Cromwell declared he was a *'prettier fellow even than Sugar Candy, but Candy cannot sing.'* The general seeing through the Amazonian disguise ordered the youth to sing up for King and Parliament. It is reported that the youth instead sang *'Put me on a man's attire, Give me a Soldier's coat, 'I'le make King Charles's foes, to quickly to change their note!'* General Cromwell scrupled not to say to Lord Percy that, *'being a warrior, he did wisely to be accompanied by such Amazons.'* On which Lord Percy, in some confusion, did acknowledge that she was a damsel. It is reported that General Cromwell was much amused with the disguise indeed.

Finis

Gilbert Mabbot 2nd April 1645

*

My uncle leaned forward over the desk and passed me the invitation. The Countess of Carlisle was holding a gathering in her apartments, and we had been invited. It was written in the same small neat hand as her note to Beeston. I cursed myself for not having checked the countess's handwriting; I had been distracted by the Black Bear. Uncle Samuel explained that her design for the King to accept the covenant was not going well. Her younger brother Henry Percy had been exiled by the King for the designs around Karl Ludwig. I had already read that in Gilbert's newsletters, and Cromwell's snipe at my singing.

Everard snorted at my uncle's words. He was still a spy in Denzil Holles household, feeding useful information to my uncle.

'Holles believes in it,' he said. 'No Covenanter can be trusted to prosecute the war as it should be, but especially not Holles. He will be at the Countess's supper.'

'Well, I shall not be at the supper party, William,' said Uncle Samuel. 'I have a war to prosecute, Covenanter or no.'

My poacher friend at least had the good grace to look shamed by those words. His burning anger at injustice may have been righteous, but 'twas directed at a false mark in Sir Samuel Luke. I shall hammer that nail home. Without my uncle the war would have been lost, Naseby would have been lost, there would be no Cromwell; we would all have our heads cut off, and King Charles kept his. I will leave you to judge which outcome more preferable for England. For me, I like my head exactly where it be.

'Blandford.' My uncle turned to me. 'I want you to attend this event. Needs must that I return to Newport Pagnell to ready for the new army's campaign...'

'You should be resigning your command, Sir Samuel?' said William. Uncle Samuel paused before answering; I could see he was annoyed. The Self Denying Ordnance had not yet been passed by the Lords, but would be soon enough. My Uncle, by rights, should have resigned his commission. However, Parliament insisted he remains as Governor of Newport Pagnell for the time being. His scouts and intelligencers were too valuable a source of information to discard.

'I have a war to prosecute still, William, as I have pointed out. There are problems in the garrison I must address, and the House commands it. Now, if you have no further objection, may I continue?'

Everard glowered at his words but nodded. I was more than passing annoyed, I was seething at William's damned insolence and ingratitude. I listened as Uncle Samuel told me to attend the party, take names and listen. He wished to know who was involved in the secret cabals of the Countess of Carlisle. She knew he was a Presbyterian and her plans relied upon support from those, like Uncle Samuel, who desired such a religious settlement. The Countess's obvious problem was that few left trusted the King's word, even had he made such a promise, and His Majesty was in no way inclined to peace. Montrose was winning Scotland for the Royalist cause; the king had beaten Essex and escaped at Newbury. Had Rupert not lost the north at Marston Moor, the war would have been over. When my uncle finished outlining our orders he dismissed us, me to my tasks and William back to Holles' household. I said nought to Everard until we were on Thames Street, then I grabbed him by the arm.

'What is wrong with you?' he said.

'What be wrong with you? How dare you speak to my uncle in such a way, wretched man. How dare you question his loyalty to the cause?'

William was taken aback by my anger. I could see the surprise on his face.

'I meant no offence to your uncle, Sugar. But he is a Presbyterian and a gentleman. I have not spilt my blood for that cause. He should resign his commission.'

'I hear you not make the same complaint over Cromwell?'

Cromwell's commission was to be prorogued, like my uncle's, because he was the best General of Horse we had. Parliament made pretence of it being temporary, but all knew that Oliver was our only hope in the field against Prince Rupert.

'Cromwell is an Independent.'

'He is a gentleman.'

'But he holds himself not in high estate. Humilitate vero principium sit intelligentia.'(Humility is the beginning of true intelligence. – John Calvin)

'Quidquid Latine dictum sit altum videtur.' (Anything said in Latin seems profound) I knew his Latin was not good enough to translate.

'You regurgitate a heretical preacher's words like Kit regurgitates pottage, and with as little understanding.'

William's face twisted with anger. 'There is a levelling coming, Sugar. The world is turned upside down. None is so high in rank that they cannot fall, be they king, or prince, or the conceited third son of a Wiltshire tanner.'

He turned and walked away towards the bridge. I did not follow him. A few bystanders had observed our argument, but it was such a common sight in the streets that none remarked upon it. It was the madness overtaking all. I cursed and walked down to the wharves. Meg's rooms were at Vaughn's tavern, and I needed to escape the war for a time.

*

Letter of Remonstrance to Sir Samuel Luke from the Soldiers under his command.

Honourable Sir,

You are not ignorant of our wants and grievances in regard to our pay, which is so long kept from us. In the meantime, we find many commands from your Honour that will prove very disadvantageous to the State. As for those that concern our duties in martial discipline, it is best known to your Honour how ready we have been to obey, but for those that concern our quartering in the country, we have just cause to fear that the people may rise up and cut our throats.

They say we eat the meat out of their children's mouths, they pay their contribution but we never have any coin to recompense them, nor do they receive any abatement in their taxes. They have been too long deceived by fair promises (which are probably as great an oppression to the country as a Pharaoh's demanding the full tally of brick, without any allowance of straw). Your Honour may be pleased to consider the cries of the country which is daily in our ears.

We are not ignorant of the extraordinary sums of money that are allowed by the Parliament for the payment of the garrison (which we conceive should amount to above four weeks pay at 14s. per week). Our desire is that your Honour would speedily redress it, considering that we can neither have apparel for ourselves, nor fodder for our horse, nor much powder and bullet. How can we secure this place from the approach of the enemy without money or security?

Finally, we desire that your Honour may understand, that, if upon this reasonable declaration, we cannot have our pay upon reasonable terms, we shall appeal to the honourable High Court of Parliament. In the meantime, until we have an answer from your Honour, we rest at our quarters at Cosgrave.

Your obedient soldiers in all *lawful* commands,

THO. WEBB. WM. SEDWELL. JOSEPH FINCH. JO. LANCASTER. SAM. DAVIS. ROGER BEGERLEY. WM, FORETH. JO. HODGKINS. HEN. VICARS. RICH. DRAPER. RICH. PRENORTHERNERE. WM. OLD. RICH. BARRETT. WM. COWLEY. WM. PAKE. JO. MALORY. JO. ALLEN. THO. HAIKE. SAM. WRIGHT. ROBT. WIETT. ALEX. WHITNELL GEO. YOUNG. XTOPHER. SMITH. THO. CHAPMAN. RICH. PALMER. ED. SHRIES. WM. PINKARD. JO. ANDERSON. ROBT. NASH. LAUR. GOUTHER. SERNON KORKE. ED. BARBER. LUKE WILLIAMS. THO. MOORE. THO. BIRD.

Our demands is ten weeks pay at the least, and treat us not to the cocking of a pistol or stern threatening, as upon former like occasions.

April 14th, 1645.

22. Secret Cabals at the Countess of Carlisle's House: London, April 1645.

She has a sulfurous spirit,
And will take light at a spark,
Break with them gentle love.
(Ben Jonson, *Cataline his Conspiracy*)

Essex House is a ramshackle old mansion house off the Strand. The main buildings are at least three hundred years old, built around a courtyard with adjoining wings and stable blocks. 'Tis an untidy ugly mix of stone and wood, mismatched tiles and fading paintwork. Dubbed Cuckold Hall by the Royalists, half of the buildings were given over to the Earl of Essex (recently rendered unemployed by the Denying Ordnance and his own impotence). The other half was leased to the Earl of Hertford and apartments for Lucy Hay. Her parties and balls were renowned, but Meg and I were there for an 'intimate supper'. Intimate for Lucy Hay meant perhaps forty people sitting at long tables; the Countess at the top table with her flatterers and sycophants, and those that she sought to seduce.

'There are luminaries indeed here,' said Meg. 'She does throw the best night in London.'

My love was clothed in a dress of rich satin of the deepest blue that matched her eyes. Her raven hair was pinned up with silver thread, and a rope of pearls around her neck that must have cost a pretty penny. There was no point in inquiring of the source of such riches. I had learned that would swiftly cause an argument, through a combination of my jealousy and her stubborn streak.

'The last time we were here 'twas a debauched buttock-ball,' I said

By contrast, this night was sombre. Quiet conversations created a soft hubbub in the hall, as we were shown to our places by liveried servants in red and black. There were a few women in attendance: Lucy Hay herself, Megan, and others partnering fat politicians and rich merchants. Few looked like wives, at least not first wives.

I noted that the men were all influential Presbyterians, the peace party in Parliament. Holles was sat beside the Countess, to her right hand, and was deep in conversation with the former Lord Mayor of London, Sir John Wollaston. These were the Half-Measure men, the tremblers; those who had started this war but were now terrified to grasp the victory God presented. Along with Holles and Wollaston was the French envoy Monsieur Sabran. I noted d'Artagnan sitting at a lower table (higher than Meg or me in station). He waved his hand when he saw us, and winked at my companion. That assuredly made me jealous but I was fain to like the Comte, even though he infuriated.

'We do not fit in with these,' I whispered to Meg as we were seated. 'None are friends of Uncle Samuel. Why has she invited me?'

'There be a reason God gifted you two ears but only one mouth, Blandford. Listen and learn. She has spent a fortune on this little supper. There will be a reason for your attendance, but I doubt it is the only reason for this gathering. You are not so very important, my love.'

That was true enough.

The Countess kept a rich table. A cloth of the finest spun wool, dyed red, was quickly filled with the first course by liveried servants: Spanish olio,[48] ox tongue soup spiced with nutmeg, platters of roasted mutton with artichoke heart; kidneys topped with raspberries and redcurrants, and baskets of penny loaves and crocks of butter. I heaped my pewter platter and called for a servant to fill my cup with spiced wine. Meg gave me a nudge.

'Gluttony, Sugar?'

'We may as well enjoy ourselves whilst we are here,' I said. 'This be a rare feast in wartime London, and it stops my speech and opens my God gifted ears.'

She smiled at that and helped herself to a modest portion of the olio and bread. As I stuffed my face, I looked around to take note of the other guests, and to eavesdrop on their conversations. The talk was of the new army under Fairfax; the Lords were certain to pass the denying ordnance. The new army would be readied for war within weeks, and the moderates were gelded. Enough pragmatists like Uncle Samuel had decided the King could not be trusted and victory in battle was their only security.

Fairfax was a good enough general (that I knew even if he disliked me). The King had neither enough money nor men to keep up the war much longer. It meant a battle, all or nothing; the New Army against the best of the Royalists. There was no forgone conclusion to such a death-match, but there would be no more half-victories and

---

[48]A stew of beef, lamb, veal, and poultry with vegetables and herbs

half-defeats.

'This will be the decisive summer,' I said to none in particular.

'Why think you so?' asked a portly fellow a few seats up; a rich red-faced merchant by the look. 'You are Sugar Candy?'

'Money,' says I, nodding at his recognition. 'There be not enough to go around, so both parties will want the decisive stroke.'

'I can only pray so,' he said. 'Money is in the right. I am nearly made pauper with increased taxes and loss of trade. I care not who wins now, only that it is finished.'

He did not look as if he was suffering too much from the size of his belly, and the young girl accompanying was certainly no daughter, wife, nor even long-lost niece, but the sentiment was common around the hall. Peace at any price, be it royal tyranny or perpetual parliament. These merchants and businessmen cared only for profits. Others, higher in rank, sat close to Lucy Hay, but there was a palpable sense of defeat among them. As the first course was consumed, I noted the Countess had turned from Sabran the French envoy, and her flirtation had become cold disdain. The Frenchman seemed oblivious to the Countess's displeasure. I wondered what request he had refused.

Meg nudged me. 'Some design with the French envoy has gone awry,' she said whispered in my ear. 'The Countess is most displeased.'

'I noted. Sed convivatoris, uti ducis ingenium res adversae nudare solent, celare secundae,' I said. (A host is like a general, calamities oft reveal his genius)

She laughed. 'I sometimes note, sweetling, that your penchant for quoting Latin when you are worried is a marked tell. Do it not when you cheat at cards. Besides, I prefer Catullus to Horace.'

'That is about content not construction,' I said. 'Or so my Latin master told me.'

'Perhaps the Countess's brother being exiled for the plots around Karl Ludwig is a cause of the displeasure?'

'Perhaps.'

The second course was lighter meats, roasted partridge and squab which were consumed in a growing atmosphere of misery. Conversations hushed and whispered rather than raucous or entertaining, the feast was rapidly becoming a wake as the guests took their cue from the hostess. The third course was composed of fruits and cheeses. A swan of sugar and marzipan was brought out by the servants and presented to the Countess. It should have elicited gasps of wonder, but passed in front of the audience with barely a murmur.

Meg sniffed.

'What?' I asked.

'The cheese is poor quality for a countess,' she said. 'My sister Lilith would be appalled.'

When all the courses had been consumed and thanks and prayers given for 'King and Country' and much bewailing of the sad circumstances, we guests were dismissed. Whatever the Countess had planned for the night was curtailed, and it all seemed to hinge upon the French envoy and Comte d'Artagnan. Those two seemed blissfully unaware of the descending gloom; both wore wide smiles and proclaimed themselves 'most pleased to have attended' in broken English. I knew not about Sabran, but d'Artagnan's linguistic difficulties were a play-act. Lucy Hay, still mindful of her manners and station, made sure to bid each guest farewell personally at the steps to Essex House. Some she whispered quiet words to (Denzil Holles among other notables), but most received a perfunctory thank you before being whisked swiftly away by their carriage or hackney. The Countess fixed a smile as Meg and I were presented. She knew me well enough, but I introduced my companion.

'Lady Sarah...' I hesitated realising that I knew not Meg's surname in this guise.

'Vaughn,' said Meg, swiftly to cover my ignorance.

The Countess raised an eyebrow at that. I prayed she thought it nothing more than a vain man's thoughtlessness. Indeed, 'tis what it actually was.

'Vaughn?' asked the Countess. 'Are you perhaps related to the Vaughns of Golden Grove, Lady Sarah?'

'Cousins,' said Meg. 'My father's seat was at Glynhir in the Amman Valley. Not far from Golden Grove. I visited often as a child, Countess.'

Lucy Hay looked nonplussed at that. Meg's disguise was well constructed. The Countess turned to me.

'How are preparations for the exhibition of swordplay coming along?'

'Well, Countess,' I said. 'It should be an entertaining few evenings.'

'You will, I hope, ensure seating for myself and some friends? On the night that Prince Karl is in attendance.'

'Beeston is arranging the seating, but I shall explain it to him.'

'Please do.' The countess smiled and gestured to our Hackney where

Figgis stood waiting.

'A new servant, Blandford?'

'An old servant, Countess.'

'You should have kept Jacob,' she said. 'He was a good servant.'

'I remember, Countess,' I said. 'He was indeed a good servant, until I had to kill him for being a base traitor.'[49]

Lucy Hay laughed; a beautiful musical laugh.

'Kill him, Blandford? Why you did not kill Jacob. He was sorely hurt, a broken crown and terribly burned down one side of his face, but he lives still. He is a terribly burned man; a good evening to you.'[50]

I felt the blood drain from my face as she turned to speak to the next departing guest. Jacob lived? Jacob was The Burned Man? That was clearly her inference. He could not live, I was certain that I had killed him. Yet, that night was confusion, a battle in the darkness, a burning mansion, my father's death and Royalist regiments all about us. We had run without too much checking of the dead. If Jacob lived, if he be The Burned Man, then Lucy Hay knew of John's crime; Lucy Hay knew I had sworn an oath, and Lucy Hay would use it when she needed to. The Countess of Carlisle had purchase over me.

I said nothing to Meg as we got into our waiting hackney. Figgis closed the doors, swinging himself up with the driver, leaving us alone inside. Meg finally broke the silence as the carriage turned onto the Strand and headed for the city.

'I think the claim that your former servant is The Burned Man is but a fiction set to spin distrust,' she said. 'There is no need to brood on the subject, when 'tis a phantom.

'Why say you?'

She told me that the Burned Man was well enough known, and had been for some years. He was not a true Romany, not like the Boswells, but the tribe took him as one of their own (as they did with most the outcasts of London). He had earned his rank before the wars and retired. His return after Haniel Boswell's death and election to the crown had been unexpected, but supported as London's beggars wanted stability and Edward Boswell was too young for the title.

---

[49] See The Last Roundhead

[50] See The Last Roundhead.

'Jacob told me he was a soldier in the German wars,' I said. 'I know not if that be the truth or disguise.'

'I still think it not be him,' she said. 'However, that is of little comfort. The Countess is too well informed. She knows of your oath; that is certain.'

I said nought in response. Lucy Hay had my testicles in the palm of her hand and she had decided to give them a tweak, and not a friendly tweak at that.

'Will you give her the seats?'

'Yes,' I said. 'And I will pray it does not lead to trouble. Are you truly a Vaughn? A cousin to the Earl of Carberry?'

She laughed at me. 'Why are you suddenly curious? My name and estate have never concerned you in the past?'

'I knew not that I loved you then.'

She giggled again. 'You drip sweet words like honey from your tongue. 'Tis one of your better qualities.'

I took her hand and kissed it.

'Well?' I asked.

'My father was a Vaughn.' She grimaced. 'My sister and I were born on the wrong side of the sheets, so to speak. My mother's family come from near Gloucester; she lived with him as wife, but when he died my Vaughn cousins cast us out.' She spat the word cousins. 'My mother married the local miller who gave us the Powell name. They were both taken by Smallpox before the war. I came to London when the fighting started, and Lady Sarah Megan Vaughn became Meg Powell the whore. My sister Lilith lives still with my mother's father.' She gave a bitter laugh. 'She is married to a Royalist major no less.'

'I understand not the jest?'

'Lilith cares only about books and cheese; the making and selling of the latter. I love my sister, Sugar, but I am quite amazed she has married. The world is truly upside down.'

That phrase was starting to irritate me; 'twas on everyone's lips. The very problem was that it was the truth.

Anne Candy to Elizabeth Candy.

Dear Sister,

It has been overlong since I have written, for which I can only offer my sincerest apologies. Much has happened since my last to you. I did not return to Paris from Antwerp until the second week of

January. The last and least part of my journey took the longest. Since then, whilst there are ever visitors from England and London, there are so very few going in the opposite direction and none of those trustworthy until now.

It was a joyous return to see my dear friend Mistress Margaret Lucas after so much time apart. She is quite miserable at the climate and the country. In my absence, she has been afflicted with the purging flux, and was only saved by a strong tincture of opium and ground pearls (I have asked for the receipt, but the papist doctor is unforthcoming; my book is filled by strange remedies found on my journey which I will copy and send on). Were it not for her faithful maid Bess Chaplain, and her mother's insistence, Margaret would have come back to England before my return. Returning home is a question all here ponder upon. There are few here able to maintain themselves in any station, and the plotting and bickering of bored insolvent courtiers fills the Parisian streets. There have been more fights, and duels, and arguments since Hudson killed Croft. The Queen's decision to send an envoy to the Pope in Rome has infuriated all. The French hate the Pope for a Spaniard, and we exiles hate the Pope as the devil-in-chief. The Queen takes no notice. She is ever ensconced with her favourite Jermyn. So many here have given all they possess for the cause, but she disdains them in favour of papists and sycophants.

Her Majesty has been given over apartments in the Louvre Palace by the French, but it is a cold palace for show, not a place to live or home for our Queen and court. Her Majesty, like Margaret, has been most unwell through the winter, and I can only but blame the condition of our quarters for both illnesses. The French are disgustingly unclean within and without. They defecate in the corridors and halls with no thought of decency nor disease from the foul vapours. After Antwerp, Amsterdam, and Hamburg it is a striking contrast. The smell alone forces all to keep perfumes and scents close to hand. Henri d'Aramitz tells me that one mademoiselle caused a riot at the Theatre Illustre by pissing in a pot in her box, and then tipping the contents over the common seats below. Can you imagine such behaviour in your own theatre?

Margaret and I visited the cathedral at Notre Dame and saw more of the city, but were both unimpressed. Filth is piled high in the streets, disease is rife, and beggars, scoundrels and ruffians plague innocent travellers. We were fortunate indeed to be accompanied by the gentle Seigneur d'Aramitz; one sight of his Musketeer coat and the rough fellows left us be. I confess the excitement of Paris was jaded after good Protestant cities. Both of us talked more of returning home, but resolved to do our duty.

All our despondencies have been lifted by the arrival of the Marquis of Newcastle in Paris. He came to the Louvre two days past to present Her Majesty with a set of the finest carriage horses I have e'er seen. So tall and beautiful, with arched necks and purest white coats. I was told they are Holsteiners by Henri. Truly they make B's roan look like a ploughman's nag in comparison. Do not tell him such, you know how proud he be of the beast.

As I enthused over the animals, Margaret had been struck by a lightning bolt. In all the time I have known her, she has disdained all the advances of men. 'Tis one reason why they call her strange. At first sight of the gentle Marquis, Margaret could not raise her eyes from him, and it seems for Cavendish it be the same. I do not understand it myself. The marquis be so very old, perhaps thrice my age.[51] He could be our grandfather, and it shows, no matter how polished the boots or fine the suit. There is no accounting for taste in love or hats, for she be truly smitten. I wager they will marry.

I thank you for the monies that arrived today. Through your benevolence I am spared the indignity many here face. Henri informs me that a comrade of his will be in London with the French envoy. He is named the Comte d'Artagnan. I hope you welcome him in as a friend should you meet.

I will send on the receipt book soon, there is more I wish to add to it. I remain your loving and affectionate sister,

Anne.

The Louvre, April 23rd, 1645.

---

[51]The Marquis of Newcastle was 53 in April 1645. Anne Candy was nearly 19, and Margaret Lucas 22.

23. The Exhibition: London, April 1645.

It is the Sword doth order all,
Makes peasants rise and princes fall,
All syllogisms in vain are split,
No logic like a basket-hilt.
(Traditional ballad: *The Soldiers Fortune*)

The crowds blocked the road in Drury Lane, heaving at Cockpit Alley. The spring sunshine had brought them all out in their finery to cheer and shout in excitement outside the Phoenix. Barely one in ten among them would actually get inside the theatre, but a festive atmosphere had overtaken all. Beer was poured out of nearby taverns in foaming tankards, spiced wine was sold from carts, and it seemed every pie seller and sausage broiler in London had brought their wares. Perhaps it was some blessed release from the misery that so many cocked-a-snook at the authorities. They treated it as an afternoon Spring fair; a ray of rare delight cutting through the oppressive clouds of war. The good weather helped. There were guardsmen and soldiers mixed with the common folk, but they all seemed swept up in the collective enthusiasm for the exhibition. The pamphleteers and criers had done their work well. Beeston would be pleased. I certainly was; it was two sovereigns well spent.

Someone saw John and me pushing through the festival, trying to get to the theatre: shaking hands, kissing maidens, and thanking enthusiastic well-wishers. Shouts of encouragement and bawdy commentary soon accompanied our approach.

'Here comes The Golden Scout!'

'Are you going to best the German, Sugar?'

'Give us a sweet kiss, Candy!' That from a well-dressed old man thrice my age.

'I would rather lick a leper,' I told him.

'Stick the German with yer sword, Sugar!' called one.

'The steel sword, that is, not yer lady's friend,' shouted another wag.

'They say the mulatto is the better swordsman.'

I heard that voice off to my side as we entered the courtyard of the theatre. John heard it as well and grinned at me.

'Smirk not too much,' I said. 'I have ten shillings on you winning this night.'

I noted Hugo playing ditties to an audience of children, scoundrels, and misfits in the shadow of the theatre's red-bricked portico. Buttermeadow was wearing his harlequin suit with oversized shoes and giant cod, and juggled three painted balls in time to the music. A ragabash little girl passed a hat around the audience for payment at the performance. They were making some good coin.

The Fool had been sent by Beeston to sell his roasted chestnuts outside the portico entrance. His cart with untended brazier sat next to the walls of the building, smouldering happily away. That made me wince, a fire would be a disaster. I cursed *Jonah* Buttermeadow but only half-heartedly. He ne'r meant any harm.

'Sidcup!' I called as I arrived at the theatre entrance. 'Your cart is one mishap from disaster.'

He turned to me with his balls high in the air; the children screeched in delight as they came down one-by-one bouncing off his noggin: red, blue, and yellow.

I had come to the conclusion that Sidcup was but a simple man, not witless, but placid and overly eager to please which oft led to misfortune. He was also easily led, and Beeston bullied him unmercifully.

'Right thou art, master,' he said, and slipped on one of the juggling balls stumbling towards the cart in his giant boots. I held my breath as he righted himself before disaster, triumphantly twisted back to me with a broad smile on his face, and knocked a tankard of ale onto the roasting brazier. It hissed and smoked, spluttering out and ruining the cooking. Beer burnt and roasted chestnut smells most peculiarly fetid, even in London's stinking streets. Sidcup looked crestfallen.

'At the least, you doused the flames,' said John to him.

'This is all your fault, you know,' I said. 'He only be here because of your fool's act. So if he burns the theatre down, you can answer for it.'

Sidcup bowed and tugged his forelock at me, apologising most profusely for his clumsiness.

'Go back to your juggling,' I told him. 'It be less dangerous.' There were dark circles under his eyes. 'When did you last sleep, Sid?'

'Billy Beeston had me up all night getting the old girl ready,' he said, nodding to the playhouse. 'Then he said to sell food to the crowd till the show opens. I shall catch a nap when ye all are performing.'

'Competing,' said John.

We left Buttermeadow happily playing along with Hugo, who gave a wave and a grin but barely broke the rhythm of his tune-mongering. Instead of trying to go through the main entrance into the building, I led John to the back garden. The rabble was kept out of there by two burly bashers (The Burned Man's crew no doubt) that Beeston had assigned to watch the gates. They allowed we two to pass without question. The gardens were quiet, trees and bushes blossoming in the sunshine, and the noise of the crowds died away. Maupin was there on his own, smoking a pipe under the willow tree and supping at a cup of wine.

'The other combatants are inside,' he said. 'Art thou nervous?'

The question was directed at John, not me.

'No, sir,' said my man. 'I will best the German.'

He smiled. 'We shall see.'

'I knew not that you took tobacco, Master Maupin?' says I.

'I suspect there is much you do not know of me, Captain. I only partake of the leaf on occasion, lest it become habitual, but I find it soothes before a display.' He grimaced. 'Your Mr Everard has the most pungent taste in the weed.'

'That he does,' I said. 'Be he within?'

'Nay, he left with your sister and nephew. Mr Beeston upset him and he is away to his wife (Everard had married his widow after Marston Moor). Mr Figgis is about here somewhere helping make ready. Elizabeth and the babe are to spend the evening with Mariette.'

Elizabeth had little interest in the exhibition beyond commercial value. I doubted she would have attended even if women were permitted. She would certainly not countenance attending in disguise as practised by the Countess of Carlisle and others. Everard and Beeston were akin to oil and water; each repellent to the other. It was no surprise that the poacher had huffed off. I had spent little enough time with William of late, and had been affronted by his insolence to my uncle, but I worried about him still. I feared for his mind even then, but said nought. That is to my shame.

Maupin gave a little smile. 'My daughter enjoys Elizabeth's company, but I fear tonight it is of little consolation that she cannot compete.'

Mariette had the least of the evening's entertainment, I agreed. Kit would probably enjoy himself, but he was less discerning. I noted that Maupin used my sister's first name, also. Normally, it was Mistress Candy this; Mistress Candy that. Now 'twas Elizabeth; that was intimate. There be some affair happening.

John and I left Maupin with his pipe and peacefulness, and entered the hive of activity that was the Cockpit. It may not have been a performance of a play, but Beeston did not see it so. Half of the city's actors and playhouse men were inside (Royalists to the man) making the place ready for the doors opening. Since Marston Moor, the actors were returning to London, and the Cockpit was become their meeting house. I was more than passing suspicious of such.

The exhibition was set to begin at three-of-the-clock. The prince's seating was arranged and his arrival all planned out. Beeston, dressed in a full mask of makeup and finery, grabbed me in a bear hug as we arrived.

'Ah, Sugar, 'tis just like the old days on opening night. I feel most exhilarated by it all. Will the boy best the German, think you? The odds are shortening on him.'

'I have ten shillings on him,' I said.

The Phoenix had been transformed by Beeston's efforts, and my sister's coin. Freshly painted stalls and benches, great chandeliers with large wax candles ready to be lit for the competition, all gilt and glitter and polished to sheen. The other competitors were already on the stage waiting, a palpable sense of tension on the air as John and I joined them. The German kept apart but the others happily welcomed us.

''Tis a very crowd outside, said young Arthur.

'Are you nervous?' When I had first met Arthur, he had been naive and immature. No longer, it seemed.

'Nay, this is just playacting. I have grown up some since the Gloucester march.' He gave a sad little smile. I recalled his friend had died at Gloucester.

'Did you ever marry the girl?' I asked, curious.

'Yes indeed. My sweet pretty Isobel; we have a baby daughter not six months old. Mr Howis has me running the shop and warehouse now; I shall take over from him in time.[52] Is John ready? I have some coin on him beating the German.'

'As do I.'

The battle between the German and my man had enthused all. The two of them were evenly matched. I had faith in John's ability, but I knew from bitter experience that winning a duel, even a practice bout, was no sure thing. I was however certain that I would not beat the German nor John Coxon, not in a month of Sundays. I was an

---

[52]See Davenant's Egg & Other Tales

average swordsman at best. I should point out that so few in the world had any formal instruction, that I was better than most bashers on the street, and even most soldiers who know only the hack of battle. Beeston came to the front of the stage to talk to us all, part-reassurance and part-encouragement to put on a good show. He gave a final nod as he finished his speech.

'You have some time for tobacco or drink to soothe your nerves, but take not too much lest you cannot perform. We open the doors in half-the-hour.'

*

I felt an unexpected burn on my cheek, as if doused with spots of boiling rain. It faded as suddenly as it came on, but 'twas enough to distract. The crowd roared; the German caught my shoulder with his blade, and the bout was his. Beeston called it. He and Maupin alternated as the judge in each contest and I had drawn the short straw. I bowed briefly to my opponent and straightened. My hand went to my cheek as I turned to face the crowd. Hot tallow wax dripping from the chandeliers above had splattered me.

Now, before you go thinking that is an old man's excuse for youthful failings, I make no claim to victory stolen. In faith, I was well outmatched and would still have lost the bout barring some fortunate blow. The dripping merely made the action short, too short, much shorter than I would have desired. In truth, it was a humiliation.

My face burned as much from embarrassment as the wax, as I stood blinking at the front of the stage looking out at the crowd. 'Tis a strange thing to say but it is quite impossible to distinguish individuals from the boards. They are shrouded in shadows and darkness, whilst the blazing candles create a halo of blinding light for the performers. I knew the prince was out there, and would be cheering on his man's victory, and I knew the Countess of Carlisle would be a muffled observer. I bowed to them one-and-all, and left the German to his accolades.

He still had to face John.

'You could have made more of a match of it,' said Beeston as I exited the stage. 'I shall have to deliver an improvised monologue to make up the time.'

'You could have given fair warning about the wax drippings.'

''Tis an ill workman that quarrels with his own tools.'

'It be your tools I quarrel with,' I said.

Beeston shrugged and stepped up from the wings with Maupin, as the German retreated from the cheering. The theatre manager waxed lyrical for longer than needed about my 'martial trials and tribulations' and 'Sugar is renowned for a different blade.' The last raised enough chuckles from the crowd. Maupin finally cut him off and called out the next bout: John against the Northern Covenanter. The victor would face the German for the spoils. My man was the clear favourite in this bout, but I knew the Northerner could be dangerous.

Maupin acted the judge, and Beeston came offstage, after having a quiet word with John before he faced off against the Northerner.

'I hope the boy does better than you,' Beeston said, as he returned to the wings.

''Tis the Northerner you should concern yourself with. John will despatch him quickly enough. You may have to monologue once more.'

The bout did not run to my prediction. John was skilled enough and fast enough to have finished the Northerner in an instant, without difficulty. Instead, he was cautious, careful, as if nervous. His defence was immaculate but he hesitated over thrust and cut. 'Twas not the display that I or anyone had expected. Then I noted Beeston with an ever-widening grin as the bout dragged on. Nigh on ten minutes of sparring and both swordsmen were sweating like the Pope in hell. John stepped up, as if finally bored with the encounter. He parried a thrust at his head from the Northerner with quarte, knocking the blade to the left, and riposting over the top to pink him in the chest. Maupin called the bout for my man, and John took the audience's adulation.

'What was that about?' I asked as he came offstage. 'You could have beat him in an instant.'

'Beeston says the odds would lengthen on me the longer I took for victory. All wager on the German now. Put another couple of decus[53] on me at the better price.'

I gave him a quizzical look.

'You are certain?'

'Aye, sir. Mr Figgis knows the betmonger.'

There was time before the final bout. Beeston had called a break and refreshments for all, before John faced the German. Hugo struck up a strain on his guitarro, a jig of some sort, and the crowd stamped a

---

[53]Ten shillings: a decus was street slang for a five shilling piece.

beat. Wine and ale, oysters, pies, and wraps of candied almonds were taken around the seats in a veritable cornucopia of victuals. All sold by very pretty young girls. Beeston was milking this for every farthing he could get. I found Figgis outside serving at Buttermeadow's stall in the courtyard. There was still a crowd around Cockpit Alley and Drury Lane. Cromwell had a house barely fifty yards from the theatre. I thanked God he was not in London. He would have been liable to march in and close the whole event down, licence or not. The French Comte and his servant were with Figgis eating some sweets. I told my manservant to put another ten shillings on the boy.

'Where be the Fool?'

'He be sleeping in the attic,' Figgis told me. 'Poor man has had no rest in three days. I told he to leave the roasting to me.'

The attic was the large space high up in the theatre, above the stage. It had the gallery where Mariette had watched the practice bouts below. I was surprised that Beeston had sold no tickets for viewing up there, but fitting seating and emptying discarded playhouse dross would have taken more time and more money. Before the closures, it would have been used by musicians to provide songs and sounds to imitate the world playing below. Beeston mostly used it for storage now.

'I feel for Sid,' Figgis carried on. 'He be an orphan like you, me, and the boy.'

Harry Figgis's mother had only died a couple of years previous at the age of eighty, and he was father to a brood of four hi'self.

'Be not so ridiculous,' I said. 'You cannot call yourself an orphan at your age.'

'At my age one be most often orphaned, Master Blandford. ''Tis the very young that be most often orphaned, less.'

Figgis served up a portion of freshly roasted candied nuts in a hide cup for tuppence, and handed it to an old maid. There was a line of people building up, all wanting his wares.

'Just be sure to place the wager on, Figgis,' I told him.

'Aye, Master Blandford, worry not.'

'Monsieur Candy,' said d'Artagnan. 'A moment of your time.' He pulled me aside from any listeners.

'No sight of any danger thus far,' I said.

'Ah, but it has been tres excitement. I wonder, the gates at the back of the gardens, are they locked?'

'No,' I said. 'They never are. I doubt Beeston remembered, or if he even knows where the key be; why? There should be some of Haslerig's men out there.'

'Ah no matter, just curiosity. I have seen nought in the audience to raise concern.'

'Perhaps he will not strike.'

'Oh, he will strike, monsieur, I am just not sure how he will do it. It is, as your Mr Figgis says, a bejummery fuzzle-puzzle.'

I agreed and left him, making my way back into the playhouse. Backstage was filled with even more people: beaten contestants, Beeston's actors and retinue drinking and smoking, betmongers, women watching on in hoods and cloaks. I found John in the wings, waiting to go on.

'Are you ready?'

'Yes,' he said, a tad curtly.

Beeston was already at the front of the stage. Hugo had finished his song playing, and bowed to the rowdy (and increasingly drunk) audience. The theatre manager hushed them with a wave and a bow. Damn me, he had presence on the stage. He stood up and announced that the next contest would be the finale of the evening; to the winner the spoils – The champion of London town. He called John out onto the stage.

'Wapping's very own blademaster: John 'Brighteyes' Coxon!'

The audience went wild again, stamping their feet and cheering. There was vocal support for the local boy against the foreigner; mulatto or not. There always is whatever the contest. We English are a parochial sort. John had to fight his way through the crowd of well-wishers and watchers in the wings; all slapping his back, and urging him on. There was little hope of getting a good view of the battle from there. I had a full pound wagered on this bout, I wanted to damn well see it. The attic would be quiet enough with none but Buttermeadow sleeping up there. I slipped past the curtain and up the stairs to the space above the stage. It would be the best seat in the house. Beeston was just announcing the German (whose name I forget, so let us not concern ourselves with it), the fight was about to begin.

I stepped into the attic, my eyes getting used to the gloom. There was a figure kneeling at the bannister pointing something at the audience.

'Sidcup?'

The figure turned towards me, anger in her eyes and a crossbow in her hands.

'Mariette!'

Maupin's daughter with a weapon; I was dumbfounded, trying to understand what was happening.

'Yes, sire?' said Sidcup.

Buttermeadow rose up in the dark from wherever he had been sleeping, startling the girl. It all happened so quickly. She unloosed the crossbow bolt at me, missing, and charged. In the same instant a blow struck me full on the back of the head and knocked me to my knees, another blow sent me sprawling.

Master Maupin and his daughter: the Black Bear and his apprentice.

24. The Black Bear: London, April 1645.

For tho' I liv'd in Wickedness,
Yet since I come to die,
A hearty Sorrow I express,
For all my Villany.
(Anonymous Ballad: *The Mournful Murderer*)

Sidcup lifted me from the floor as I tried to gather my senses. My head hurt; I could feel a lump rising at the back of my skull and there was blood on my hands. The cacophony of noise from the fight below told me the duel had just finished. Was that a quick or slow bout? How long had I been stunned? I noted the crossbow bolt buried in the playhouse wall. Mariette had loosed in haste, but I wagered there was blade venom on that dart. The merest nick would be death. An aimed shot at the prince would have been certain to kill.
'Mariette! Where did the girl go?'
'She ran down the stairs with her pater.'
'Damn! Touch not the crossbow bolt, Sidcup, lest you die. 'Tis poison.'
I took off like a hare down the stairs, leaving behind the dumbfounded Buttermeadow. In the staging area, people were cheering and clapping as John came offstage. Where was the German? Where was Maupin? I grabbed Arthur.
'Have you seen Master Maupin?'
'Aye, he went off to the gardens. I think he had a woman with him. We won, Sugar!' He was jumping about like a giddy girl.
'Tell John that my sister is in danger. Tell him to follow me to Maupin's house. 'Tis urgent, Arthur, most urgent.' I hoped that got through the elation at his winnings.
It seemed to. He nodded without question and turned to make his way to John. I left the playhouse, out through the back doors not through the crowds, and into the back garden. Where in damnation are Haslerig's two guards? I thought. They are supposed to be watching here. The gates at the bottom of the garden led to Wilde Street; they were wide open. I made ready to run, cursing my riding boots.
'Monsieur Candy, a horse.'

The French spy and his servant were waiting on horseback.

'That be a timely intervention. You knew it was Maupin?'

'I had my suspicions, but I did not know for certain until tonight. We found Haslerig's guards dead; their throats slit.' He turned to his valet. 'Climb down, Planchet, the good captain will need your beast.' The servant got off the horse and I mounted up, thanking him. D'Artagnan carried on explaining.

'I was in the high seats and saw the girl in the gallery above the stage, and your own *timely intervention*. I made my way out and to the back, but they had already bolted. Planchet had our horses ready.' He gestured. 'They went to the north of the city wall on horseback.'

'To Spitalfields,' I said. 'Maupin has my sister and nephew at his house.'

'Then lead on, Monsieur Candy. You know this city better than I.'

John came running out of the garden gates, almost tumbling into us. He was carrying a brace of pistols as well as his sword.

'Climb up behind me,' I told him.

'I won,' he said, mounting.

'My congratulations.'

I kicked the horse into a gallop down Duke Street and across Lincoln's Inn Fields. Our quarry must have had a few minutes start on us. Maupin had been shrewd enough to hide his design all these months, and he was shrewd enough to plan his escape. The houses flashed by in the fading spring sun, long shadows in the twilight. It would be nightfall soon.

Holborn, Smithfield, and Long Lane; we charged on. Bystanders jumped out of our way, we spilt carts, and nearly crushed walkers without pausing. I am, was, an excellent horseman, and whilst Planchet's nag was not my own Apple, and it carried two grown men, I drove it hard. I cared not if it was broken at the end of the race. I would buy the Frenchman a new animal.

Barbican, Chiswell, and Finsbury; we cut down winding alleys barely wide enough for a man, let alone two charging kaffels.[54] 'Tis a wonder we killed neither ourselves nor some innocent in the mad dash. I wager we did the whole stretch to Smock Alley and Brick Lane within five minutes. Normally it would take four times that to

---

[54]Street slang for horse, but phonetically sounds the same as the Welsh word for horse – ceffyl.

get from the theatre to the Swordmaster's crooked house. Both steeds were sweating foam and drooling at the exertion, snorting hard as we dismounted. The blue front door was wide open to the crooked house; the lamps all lit up, and two saddled horses were left unattended in the yard.

'They are still here,' said John.

There was a crash from inside to confirm the truth to that. D'Artagnan and John both drew their blades and uncloaked.

'Take the pistols, Captain,' said the Comte.

I argued not and took the brace from John. Maupin and Mariette were both exceptional with a blade. The Frenchman and my boy might hold their own, but I would not survive a heartbeat. Mark you now, I was a damn fine shot with a pistol, and the guns were scout issued with rifled barrels and already loaded.

We entered through the front door, into a long corridor reaching into the middle of the building. D'Artagnan and John led the way to the central stairwell. A door to my right creaked and opened after the others had passed. A figure wielding a butcher's cleaver stood in the doorway – the stout housekeeper – I discharged my first pistol into her chest, and she fell down dead. A life snuffed out in a single shot without a second's thought or moment's guilt. D'Artagnan and the boy turned at the explosion and smoke, but I nodded for them to go on. We reached the bottom of the stairwell and Maupin's voice came from above.

'I have been expecting you.'

He stood at the top of the first flight of steps in his shirtsleeves with his sword in hand.

'Where be my sister?' I said, pointing my undischarged pistol at him.

'Shoot him,' said D'Artagnan.

I ignored the Frenchman.

'Your sister is safe, Captain Candy, and your nephew, but if you shoot me they will both die in a heartbeat.'

That gave me pause, but I did not lower my pistol.

'You cannot escape,' I told Maupin. 'The Prince is unharmed, and the authorities have been alerted. You will not get out of London. If you surrender, perhaps you can bargain your life.'

'This has been my first failure,' he said, ignoring my offer. 'I am most surprised a fop such as you has managed it.' He nodded to the Frenchman. 'Of course, you have had the inimitable Comte d'Artagnan to assist.' D'Artagnan nodded back. 'I thought Karl Ludwig's overweening arrogance would be the death of him, but you have kept him locked up safe like a father does a pretty virgin daughter. Mariette came close with the poisoned wine, but we did not count on English impatience.'

'The Divine was Welsh,' I said.

Maupin nodded his acknowledgement. There was a reason for this monologue; this was a distraction.

'Where be my sister, sir?'

'I waited all day in a tree for the barge to pass, you know.' He smiled. 'I should thank you for that information, even if the attack failed. I had expected him to go by carriage. A small chance of success but little chance of discovery, I assumed. I did not count on your mechanical gun. You winged me, Candy, near killing me with one bullet.'

'There was no attack in the street?'

That was my fault. I should have investigated the attack, but foreigners were assaulted so often that I thought nought of it.

'There was no attack,' he concurred. 'You grazed me in the side. Then there was the bomb. I had a boy ready to toss it under the Prince's carriage. I told him 'twas a firework and paid a half a crown for the work. Instead, he tried to set it off for his friends and blew them all to pieces. Why are you English so contrary? Finally, you offered him to us on a platter, and your witless Fool ruined it all by being in the attic. We should have struck and been away before the breaks.'

'Enough, sir!' I shouted at the top of my voice. 'Where be my sister and KIT!'

There came an answering cry from the practice hall. I smiled, that had been my design. Kit's bellowing lungs in response to my yelling, as if at home. A flash of dark fury crossed Maupin's face, and he came down the stairs.

'Save your sister,' said d'Artagnan, stepping forward to meet Maupin. 'J'ai attendu avec impatience cela.' (I have been looking forward to this)

John and I turned to the sound of Kit's cries, but the door to the practice room opened, spilling light into the corridor. Mariette came out with her sword in hand. My sister and nephew were in that room, but I could not shoot Mariette with John between us. The boy stepped up against his lover.

Qui in amore præcipitavit pejus perit, quam si saxo saliat[55]

I had missed the evening's finale between John and the German, distracted by assassins and a cracked head, but now I was treated to two virtuoso performances of swordplay. My head swivelled between the fights, like a spectator at Lisle's tennis court, pistol in hand, praying for an opening in one battle or t'other.

John and Mariette fought at a furious speed, both in silence, both trained by Maupin. Neither seemed able to mark the other in the narrow space of the corridor; using only terzo, thrust and parry and riposte, but no room for slashing or acrobatics. Instead, I was fain to keep my eyes on the other match: Maupin against the Comte d'Artagnan. Had Homer seen this combat, he would have scorned Achilles and Hector.

They were afforded more space in the stairwell and d'Artagnan used it all, bouncing from one wall to the bannister to another wall, like a monkey. I tell no lie when I say I saw the French Comte vault the bannisters and strike a blow from above, then somersault over Maupin's head, land lightly and strike out again. The Frenchman also fought dirty, kicks and headbutts; he even bit Maupin's hand at one point. The Swordmaster fought as he had taught: economy of movement to conserve energy, defence first, waiting, watching for an opening, and trying to keep the advantage of height on the stairs. When he did strike, d'Artagnan was forced out of his rhythm to survive, fain to avoid or parry. Through it all they chatted happily, as if over a pipe of tobacco and pitcher of ale.

'You knew it was me?' asked Maupin. He blocked a cut to the head from the Comte.

'I suspected,' said d'Artagnan. 'La Rochelle was finished by 1630. Anyone who was there would know that. I was only a boy, but it was not an experience easily forgotten.'

He swept a blow at Maupin's feet. The Swordmaster jumped to avoid, and thrust down at the Comte, who stepped back. There was a brief pause as both men caught their breath. Of the two d'Artagnan looked the most blown. Tiredness is the killer in a long duel.

'I knew I had made an error there,' said the Swordmaster. 'I was in Hispaniola until thirty-two. I thought you too young to know; it was careless of me. I should have checked my story better.'

---

[55]Plautus: He who falls in love meets a worse fate than he who leaps from a rock.

'The cardinal's agents received information from the Swiss about you,' said the Comte. 'It arrived this evening.'

'Ah, that would be because of Jenatsch's murder,' said Maupin.[56] 'I was also careless in Chur, but the Swiss paid exceptionally well for that act. Perhaps I am getting a bit too old for this business, but I have a successor.' He gestured to John and Mariette locked in their own deathmatch. 'I had hoped for another apprentice to join her, but I suspect that will not now be the case.'

He stepped forward with a determined look set on his face, and launched a blistering combination of blows on d'Artagnan. For the first time, the Comte was hard pressed to defend himself: thrust after thrust at lightning speed, using the point, playing on the Comte's weariness and forcing him to retreat.

Looking back to John and Mariette, I could see the stalemate continuing. Both were so evenly matched and knew only Maupin's style that it was a battle of attrition. John was the stronger; he should win.

'Ahhh!'

I heard the shout and turned back to the battle on the stairs. D'Artagnan was pinned to the floor by a thrust through his thigh. The Swordmaster's blade had cut straight through his leg, out the other side and into his ankle. Maupin stood on the steps above him,

---

[56]Jörg Jenatsch (1596 - 1639) was a Swiss political leader in the Grissons Canton. He initially fought against the Hapsburg power of Spain and the Holy Roman Empire, and was responsible for a number of murders in his career including that of Pompeius Von Planta in 1621. He converted to Catholicism and switched allegiance in the 1630s, negotiating a hugely personally beneficial peace deal with the Imperial forces. In January 1639, Jenatsch was murdered in Chur in Grissons allegedly on the orders of Von Planta's son. The assassination was carried out during the annual carnival by anonymous assailants led by a man dressed as a black bear.

drawing out the blade with a twist and a snarl. The Frenchman screamed in agony. I discharged my second pistol, taking Maupin in the chest and blowing a hole out of his back. The roar of the gun died, smoke cleared, and the Swordmaster toppled down the stairs over d'Artagnan.

'No!' Mariette screamed as she saw her mentor slain.

John's blade took her in the throat. A lightning thrust when she had been distracted; just as Swordmaster Maupin had taught him.

There was a look of surprise on the girl's face as the blood guttered in her mouth, turning into a scarlet gush when John withdrew his steel. She collapsed to the floor clutching at her torn throat, and then reached a bloody hand to my man. John fell to his knees, taking her in his arms and weeping as she bled out.

You may think me cruel, but I cared not a jot for Master Coxon's broken heart. I jumped past the crying boy and rushed into the practice hall. Elizabeth was trussed to a chair, a gag of rags stuffed in her mouth and roped. My bawling nephew had been placed in the wicker parrot cage like one of the monkeys in Amsterdam. He stopped crying and smiled when he saw me; a golden-haired little cherub with a snotty nose.

'Unc Bandy.'

Kit reached through the bars of his prison as I released Elizabeth. I began with the gag, although I was quickly obliged to regret that.

'You took your time.'

'I was a little busy.'

I started to untie the ropes that bound her.

'Do not untie them, simpleton, cut them with your sword.'

I drew my blade and cut her free.

'Where is he?'

'In the hallway. Worry not, he is dead, Elizabeth.'

I broke open Kit's cage and pulled him out into my arms. The boy gave me a great hug and promptly fell asleep. My sister in the meantime rushed out of the room. I sighed and followed her carrying my nephew.

John still knelt weeping by the body of Mariette. The floorboards were sticky with her blood. The boy said nothing as Elizabeth stepped past. D'Artagnan was sat against the wall bandaging his leg. He waved weakly as we appeared.

'Bonjour, Madame Candy.'

Elizabeth ignored him, rushing to the body of Maupin tumbled broken on the stairs. She spat at it, falling to her knees and pummelling the corpse, howling in unadulterated rage. I had never seen her in such a fury. She screamed profane insults and obscene curses at the dead Swordmaster, as if her voice could reach down into hell to torment him. I was taken aback at the venom, and the bear-garden jaw. Even if we Candys are all prone to the odd tantrum, it was a most spectacular display of anger. I put the sleepy boy down and went to her. Kit crawled over to d'Artagnan and climbed into his lap, making the Frenchman wince as he jarred his wounds.

'Elizabeth?' I said it quietly.

She paused from battering the corpse to tenderised meat and looked up at me. Her eyes shining and red from her tears.

'I gave myself to him. Do you know what that means when you seduce your harlots? We give into your animal pleasure, often with little reciprocation from you dullards who paw at us like cattle at market. For that dubious experience we risk childbirth and death. I swore I would never do it again, but he cozened me with his fine words; a pretence of godliness and flattery.'

She quite literally started snarling like a rabid dog, spittle flying from her mouth.

'He used me! How could I have been so foolish? How could I have been so beguiled? Death borders upon our birth, and our cradle stands in the grave.'

Elizabeth screamed again, a long, loud wail of agonised fury and frustration. 'Tis what a banshee sounds like, I thought. She pounded at Maupin's body again until her fury abated and her shoulders slumped.

'I did not realise,' I said, tenderly touching her shoulder.

In faith it had ne'r occurred to me. I worried about the pox, of course, but the odd bastard or by-blow concerned me not, but again it was not my life on the line. I knew well enough how many women died in childbirth.[57]

''Tis because you are too absorbed in your own vanities, like all of your species.' She sniffed and then smiled. 'I knew you would come for me.'

'You did?'

'You always do. Thou art reliable in such circumstances, at least.'

---

[57]About 12 women would die for every thousand live births in 1700; presumably the rate was much higher during the Civil War period with so much upheaval.

I raised her to her feet and she burst into tears, holding me and sobbing for a few minutes; her crying the only sound in the crooked house. Then she pushed me away, brushed herself down and went to John, still sitting by Mariette's body.

I understand women not.

'Odi et amo, John,' she said quietly to him. The boy did not understand Latin. 'Love and hate.'

She reached out, and the boy smiled shyly, his eyes red from his own tears. He took my sister's outstretched hand.

Men started arriving then: soldiers and the watch bursting in a quart-of-the-hour late. It all became a blur of officials and questions, and more arrivals. Thurloe and my grandfather appeared. Arthur had spread word of the attack to the authorities first, and then ran to Thames Street to rouse my grandfather; he told me all this in a rush. Prince Karl had been whisked back to Whitehall by his guards, claiming the evening's result was in question and his man still a champion.

Through it all, my sister never let go of the boy's hand, holding it tightly and keeping him by her side.

*

The French galleon towered over the wharf at Wapping. A four-masted monster, dripping with guns; a ship of war with golden fleur-de-lis on a royal blue field at its mast. The Comte d'Artagnan took my hand and shook it, whilst his servant doffed and bowed. Hugo stood beside them, with his guitarro in a case and smiling happily. The foreigners were homeward bound.

'I must say, Monsieur Candy, it has been a most enjoyable sojourn in your country. You must come to Paris, and I will offer you the hospitality of my home.'

'Un pauvre grenier humide, maître?' said Planchet. (A poor damp attic, master?)

I laughed and bowed.

'It has genuinely been a pleasure, sir. What will you do now?'

'Ah, Candy, I work for Cardinal Mazarin; I cannot tell an English intelligencer such.' He gave a fierce grimace.

I laughed again. 'I have the boy to protect me. You lost to his Swordmaster.'

'Did I, Monsieur Candy?'

'Well, yes?' I was surprised. I expected some weaselling from Prince Karl over the evening's results but not the Frenchman. 'Maupin demonstrably ran you through.' I gestured to d'Artagnan's wooden crutch.

'Indeed he did, Captain. An opening I offered, trapping his blade in mine own body and giving you the opportunity to blow a hole in his chest.' He grinned. 'You seized the chance most admirably, I thought. Je vous salue, monsieur.' (I salute you, sir)

'You took his blow deliberately?' I knew not whether to believe him.

'Of course, Monsieur. It was the only way for us to win.'

I shook my head. I knew not if that was the truth, but I did know that Charles Ogier de Batz de Castelmore, Comte d'Artagnan was a dangerous man, no matter how engaging. England was fortunate to see the back of him.

'And, Master Hugo,' I said. 'You leave for France too?'

'The Comte has a friend who owns the Theatre Illustre in Paris.[58] He has promised to introduce me, and France will be interesting at this time.'

It certainly will be, I thought, with an invasion of the Hapsburg Empire about to begin and a child on the French throne. Lots of profitable information for you to gather and sell on.

'Princess Sophia will be pleased, I think, Captain Candy. Some reward will come your way soon enough.'

'I do hope so,' I said. 'Prince Karl has been an ingrate over the affair.'

I shook Hugo's hand and bade him farewell, along with the two Frenchmen. The envoy Monsieur Sabran was departing as well. Lucy Hay's complaints to the queens of England and France had persuaded Mazarin to despatch a more royally inclined representative, but the replacement would not arrive for months. It mattered not: Sabran had done his work well; there would be no Covenanter compromise. Instead, as summer dawned wet and misty, Roundhead and Cavalier girded for battle once more.

There was a palpable sense on both sides of the great divide that a final decision was at hand.

News from Scotland: Letter from the Marquis of Montrose to Charles I

My Lord,

Since Sir William Rollack returned, I received one letter from you and another two nights ago dated 20th April. The carrier informs me

---

[58]Moliere.

that there is another on the way, which is not yet come into my hands. I hear that some may have been intercepted.

All here, praise be to God, goes well. Of Inverlochy and the burning of Dundee, I am confident you have heard. The rebels being somewhat strong, they having brought five or six regiments from England and Ireland. I thought it not safe to deal with all their forces together, but resolved to divide my forces to make them do likewise. Once I had made them do this, I marched from Forth to Spey (night and day) with long marches to force Major General Hurry to fight. Hurry was then lying at Spey. I plan to raise the North against Bailly and all other rebel forces should they come from the south.

At my first approach Hurry took the retreat, but I pursued him to Inverness and marched back again to Auldearn, some 14 miles from Hurry. Hurry, finding himself little concerned by my force, did not stay until Bailly and those rebels from the south could join him. Instead, he left Lavers and Buchanan's regiments in Inverness, and came marching back upon me to Auldearn. He had twixt four and five thousand men, and four of the best-trained regiments in the Three Kingdoms. I was in total about fourteen hundred (Horse and Foot). I resolved to fight, but chose my posts and all advantages of the ground to beat them at the defence.

So they, being confident both of their men and numbers, fell hotly on, but being beat back seemed to cool their fury. Instead, they tried to block us up till more rebels could come. Perceiving this, I divided my force into two wings (which was all the ground would suffer) and marched upon them most unexpectedly. After some hot salvos of musket, and a little dealing with sword and pike, they took to flight. They left three thousand of their Foot slain and all their Horse killed or scattered. I am now making for General Bailly.

I have received nothing of your Arms and Ammunition, but the enemy is my best magazine, and I never lack for supplies as long as it pleases God I beat them.

Your Most Affectionate Servant.

Montrose.

Cullen Aboyne, 17th May 1645.

Printed in the Mercurius Aulicus.[59]

---

[59]The Battle of Auldearn was fought on May 9th, 1645. John Hurry's force was destroyed by the Earl of Montrose. Montrose's account is clearly biased, Hurry had planned to surprise the Royalists, but

accidental discharging of a musket gave away his plans. After the defeat, Hurry resigned his commission with the Scots Covenanter army claiming ill-health. The King's defeat at Naseby in June was followed by Montrose's destruction at Phillipaugh in September, and the Royalist cause in Scotland, as in England, was finished. At the outbreak of the Second Civil War in 1648, Hurry changed sides once again, and joined Montrose to fight against his former comrades.

Cross Deep, Twickenham 1720.

Could man his wish obtain, how happy would he be,
But wishes seldom gain and hopes are but in vain,
If fortunes disagree.
(Traditional: *The Mournful Shepherd*)

I bundled the papers up in a thick envelope. The carriage will be here on the morrow to collect them. I insisted Cleland made a copy of my words: one for my library and one for the Duchess. The servants brought some sack for me and small beer for him. I placed the last sheet of parchment in the envelope, closed it and sealed the package, pressing my signet into the soft wax, and reached for some red ribbon to tie it up.

'Is that it?' asked Cleland.

'Is what it?'

'You have not finished the story.'

'I have,' I said, putting the package in a leather satchel for collection. 'What more do you want of the tale?'

'What of the Prince, and what of his sister Princess Sophia, our own monarch's mother? Did he remain in England?'

'Prince Karl stayed in London for a while, as I recall, but his influence waned. There was little point in setting aside one monarch only to encumber ourselves with another, and a German to boot.'

I realised what I had said. Our own King is a Hanoverian, and we have set aside more kings and princes in the intervening years; at least fifty to put German George on the throne.

'Of course, they were different times,' I said, before the boy questioned that. He is remarkably quick-witted, irritatingly so at times.

I put the Duchess's leather satchel to the side. I doubted that she would find what she wanted in my words. I wagered that I knew what she desired from Princess Sophia's shade.

'Did you receive the reward Hugo promised?'

'Princess Sophia was most grateful,' I said, sipping at my sack. 'I was passed one hundred pounds by the Dutch ambassador for my troubles, and a gold signet should I ever need the princess's help. This very ring here.'

I took off my signet and passed it to him: solid yellow gold with a crowned lion rampant sigil, and a tiny white diamond in the eye.

'An artefact of my life. Does that answer your questions?' I asked.

'Not in the least,' he answered, outraged. 'What of Mr Everard, and Meg Powell? What of John and your sister? Fell they in love?'

He always looks for the lascivious detail in my tales.

'They most certainly did not,' I said. 'John adored her, that be true, but Elizabeth saw him as a surrogate child or perhaps another brother, not a lover. She empathised with the boy. When you recognise yourself in others, you understand their pain.'

He frowned at that.

'That is a particularly morose attitude,' he said.

I laughed. 'A long life lends itself to a morose disposition,' I said. 'I was not so as a young man. Wait until you are my age, and you will perhaps understand.'

If Cleland lived as long as me he would see another century, another world. Meg Powell's grandsire knew a Methuselah as a boy who claimed to have fought at Bosworth Field. I knew others who fought the Armada, and that is now nigh on a century and a half ago. The past reaches long into the future. I wonder what influence I have on this boy. I wonder what he will take from our association. Is there enough time left in me to see the bratling born? I would like to see the Candy line continued.

'What about Cromwell and the new army?' The boy interrupted my musings. 'Did you go back to the war? Did you fight at Naseby? Was there a reckoning with the Burned Man?'

'Yes, I went back to the war for a short time, and fought at Naseby. And yes, there was a reckoning with the Burned Man.'

223

25. The New Army: Newport Pagnell, May 1645.

Wrapped up, O Lord, in man's degeneration,
The Glories of the truth, thy joys eternal,
Reflect upon my soul dark desolation,
And ugly prospects o'er the spirits infernal.
(Fulke Greville, *Wrapped up, O Lord, in man's degeneration*)

I did not plan on returning to the army. The Self Denying Ordnance had passed both Houses of Parliament, after much wrangling, and my uncle resigned his commission as Scoutmaster General. In turn, I handed in my resignation from the Office of Ordnance, in person, to Haslerig. You cannot imagine the thrill of excitement I enjoyed telling that rabid dog to bury his head in a cesspit. Technically, I was still commissioned as a captain of dragoons in the Newport Garrison, and my uncle was begged by the Committee of Both Kingdoms to remain as Governor of the Town, at least for a short time. Towards the end of May, I packed up my belongings, took up pistols, pot, and breastplate, and rode back to the war. John and Figgis came with me, and we were joined by Sam and Meg. Uncle Samuel called us all back to the colours, one last time.

'William has taken commission in the new army,' Sam told me. 'Ensign under Leonard Watson.'

'More fool him,' I said.

Luke's Scouts were no more. Most had joined the new army under Fairfax, William foremost among them. Others were hanging up their weapons and returning home. Necessity had drawn we few back. My uncle's command had been prorogued, extended for the duration of the current emergency. Fairfax had taken his new army to besiege the royal capital at Oxford, whilst the King's force was in the Midlands. Prince Rupert and His Majesty were certain to ride to the relief of Oxford; that meant a battle was coming.

We spent the first two days travelling with reinforcements on the Northampton road, and spent the nights in good inns with feather beds. On the third, we rode on ahead to Newport Pagnell – an easy ride in spite of bouts of drizzle. My blue roan Apple, a tall stallion with ambling gait and stubborn temperament, whinnied with joy at being on the open road. For too long his only exercise had been circuits around St James's Park, and I confess it had been Figgis who had done most of that work.

'Ye have neglected that beast, Master Blandford,' Figgis said. ''Tis not how I taught ye.'

He was in the right, therefore I did not respond.

John and Figgis had French nags bought off d'Artagnan before his departure; Sam his own bay mare. Megan rode her docile grey like a man, with her wide skirts all bundled up at the front, thick riding boots with a long stiletto secreted in one, and a pocket pistol hidden in her green coat. A wide-brimmed hat of black felt with a green peacock feather and wire garrotte in the rim topped off the ensemble – beautiful and murderous.

'The cathedral dangler does nothing for you, Sugar,' she said. 'It hides your dimples.'

My beard was finally coming out strong.

'Ha! Dimples,' said Figgis. ''Tis what his mother called him as a babe.'

'A good servant would be silent, Figgis.'

'A good servant would be, Master Blandford.'

I was more than passing pleased at the full beard and moustache I now sported, but to state that would lead to merciless mockery and banter for my piss-pride. 'Tis very characteristic of the Englishman, to express affection through cruel japes and jests. We will laugh at a mocking slight from a friend, that would lead to drawn blades were it from a stranger.

John Coxon had been quiet and withdrawn since Mariette's death. I understood that. Love is a difficult enough ocean to navigate without scuttling the ship yourself. That be an appalling metaphor, but you understand me?

'Who was Joan of Arc?' the boy said, breaking his silence.

'Why?' I asked.

'The Frenchman's servant prayed to her. I merely wondered.'

'I hope you think not of papist apostasy, young man. I fear even my sister would not forgive such.'

'Of course not. So who was she, this Joan of Arc?'

'Noah's wife,' said Figgis

'Simpleton, Figgis' I said. 'She was a common woman who helped the French win a war against England in centuries past, John. We burned her at the stake as a witch, but the French venerate her as a saint. That be a lesson in perspective.'

'She dressed as a man,' said Meg. 'That is why they burned her. 'Tis more a lesson in misogyny.'

'I know a fellow who likes to dress as a woman in the privacy of his home,' said Sam. 'Skirts, underskirts, chemise, stockings and paint; he makes a most pretty maiden.'

I shot him a sly look and he blushed. When they hanged Franny it had broken Sam's heart, but he seemed happier recently. I gave thanks to God for that. Time heals almost all wounds. None of us talked of the war. It was the one topic of conversation that did not interest. We all knew what awaited us at Newport Pagnell. I relished not the thought of being sent to siege Oxford, or worse to look for the King's army. The others felt the same, I would wager. It would be cruel ironic fate to be slain now.

It was mid-morning when we reached the garrison town. Tickford Bridge was defended with ditch and bastion, and cannon overlooking from the walls. On most days there was a steady flow of traffic across it, in and out of the town. Today, there was a commotion. Carts and walkers were waiting to cross the bridge; farmers and merchants and the like. There were soldiers charging a toll for passage across.

'What happens here?' I asked one of the farmers.

He spat on the floor. 'They are charging for entrance into the market. The governor should not allow it.'

The soldiers at the bridge were the worst type of skulking loobies and criminals. The best men of the garrison had been sent to Fairfax. This raggle were ill-formed and mismatched in their makeshift coats and hats, mudded faces and breeches,

'Dirtiest soldiers I e'er did see,' said Figgis. 'He be filthy that one.'

'Let us see what they are about then,' I said, guiding Apple around the waiting carts.

There were two men sat at a table by the bridge taking money – the coinage spread on the table before them. Two others with pikes slouched at the crossing, opening the gate and letting the carters over one at a time after payment. There were three more at the far end of the bridge watching the traffic coming out of the town.

I rode up and looked down on the two at the table. The one taking the money was thick set with a grey beard, dressed in dark woollen breeches and stockings, a dirty buff jerkin over a brown coat and a blue montero on his head. His comrade was thinner and taller, no hat, but similarly attired. Both wore fading orange sashes over their coats, but I did not recognise either from the town's officers. I had been absent for months. The two pikemen this side of the bridge wandered over when they saw us ride up – patched coats, scuffed boots, and rusting weapons. Was this the condition of all in the garrison?

'What goes here,' I said in as authoritative a tone as I could muster. 'Where is your officer?'

'Who asks?' said a redheaded pikeman.

'Captain Blandford Candy, nephew to the governor.'

Pick Beard looked up at that, finally taking note of us.

'Sugar Candy? The Golden Scout?'

'So they tell me.'

'Are you Presbyterians?' he asked.

'I give not a damn for bishops or divines, kirk nor congregation! This be insolence above your station.'

'Cost is twice for Presbyterians and Scots,' said Red. 'Thrice for Irish.'

'We travel under the auspices of the Committee for Both Kingdoms and my uncle is governor here. You are in no position to challenge us.'

'Maybe if you let us dally with your punk we shall let you cross freely,' said the other pikeman; he reached out for Meg's mare's bridle.

My lover did not stand for that. She struck the insolent scoundrel with her riding crop. The man fell back with a livid welt rising across his face. Drawing my first pistol from its holster, I pointed it at Pick Beard. He stood up, calm and cold.

'You are under arrest,' he said.

'I think not,' I said. 'You have no rights to raise tolls on the bridge, and your man just assaulted a noblewoman. I could have you hanged for this.'

Pick Beard looked around, he was used to bullying locals not standing up to armed men. The farmers and carters started shouting at him.

'Free passage! No tolls!' A few of them held cudgels or readied stones to throw.

'You shall pay for this, Candy,' said Pick Beard to me.

'String em up!' shouted someone from the crowd.

I turned to talk down the crowd, and Pick Beard and his companion both ran for the town. I let them go, they had left the money which tempted me, but I told the farmers to take back their fees and give the rest to the local church – that pleased them – and when they discovered my name from John, the cheers and adulation soon started up. Thanking me, shaking my hand, giving thanks to God and praising us to the heavens. I love flattery, but even I tired of it soon enough. We crossed the now unguarded bridge into the garrison town, with a flood of locals heading to market behind us.

'I do so love to make an entrance,' said Meg.

*

My uncle was in despair: dark circles ringed his red sleepless eyes, deep wrinkles and his swept-back hair was whiter; he had aged years in the few weeks since I had last seen him. The chambers in the Saracen's Head were cluttered with papers and scribbling. Normally orderly enough, that day it looked in chaos. Uncle Samuel's brows furrowed as I told him of the scene at Tickford Bridge. The tollgate had been set up that morning without his knowledge or authority.

'Mr Butler!' he shouted for his secretary.

Butler waddled in, fat face red and thick lips wobbling, like a rod-caught chub gasping for air.

'What?'

By frig he was insolent.

'What is this of news tolls on the Tickford Bridge, Mr Butler? My nephew has a most concerning report.'

The secretary shot me a vindictive glance.

'It was decided that market day could provide the garrison with added income to better defend the town, sir.'

'Decided by whom?'

'Mr Cockayne approved of it.'

Cockayne had been made deputy governor of the town before Christmas. I had not met him, but knew his appointment had come from House committees dominated by the Independents. He was supposed to take my uncle's place as governor after the Self Denying Ordnance, but Holles and the Tremblers had blocked the promotion. They had deemed any Covenanter better than an Independent as governor, even one determined to prosecute the war to victory.

'There will be no tolls to enter the town on market day, or any other day,' said my uncle. 'Please remind Mr Cockayne that I am governor still, and such decisions require my approval. He will have my seat soon enough and will be free to fleece the local populace for funds then.'

My uncle turned back to Meg and me, but Butler stood there as if waiting to say something.

'That will be all, Butler,' my uncle said without looking back.

The fat secretary waddled out in a dudgeon.

I wagered he had some stake in the toll-taking. Turnpikes are, after all, a very way of making coin. I myself have investments in two. Take my advice, if you be aged, spurn South Sea imaginings and settle for a small steady income instead. If you be young, well, what is youth for but making and breaking fortunes?

'This garrison is no good,' said my uncle. 'Cockayne will be welcome to it. The best men are gone to the army and the remaining dross are mutinous and malignant. I have had no monies at all sent this last month and pay is nearly four months in arrears. If the King comes here we are doomed. I fear the men will not fight.'

I did not know how to respond. I had never seen my uncle look so browbeaten and weary.

'Where be the King?' I asked.

'Near Burton on Trent at the last report, but that is two days since.'[60]

Rupert was fast on the march but not so fast. It would still be days before the Royalists could reach Newport Pagnell or Oxford. Our Scots allies were withdrawing home to their own lands. The Marquis of Montrose had destroyed another Covenanter army under my nemesis John Hurry. It was rumoured in the newsbooks that Hurry had turned coat once more (I could believe it). The Royalist army was free to turn on the army at Oxford with no Scottish threat from the north. An attack on Newport Pagnell would draw Fairfax away from the King's capital; a direct march to Oxford would mean a battle. I prayed that the Cavaliers chose Oxford, but my uncle's garrison was a ripe plum waiting to be picked. They could sack the town and cut the army's communications with London.

'What of Butler?' I said.

'Mr Butler has been informed that his services will no longer be required once my command is finished. Parliament has extended my commission for another twenty days. After such, I will hand over my command to Cockayne. The decision will have been made by then.'

'You think that it will be the end?'

'The beginning of the end,' he said. 'One way or the other.'

He explained why he had called us back. The garrison was weak enough and needed experienced officers.

'You are better used as intelligencer than soldier,' he said. 'But I need those I can trust if the King comes here.'

I could have refused the commission, returned to London and made arrangements for my voyage to the New World. Uncle Samuel

---

[60]The King was at Burton on Trent on 26th May 1645

would have forgiven me, I think. I would not have forgiven myself for such a betrayal. I agreed to his design and prayed the King went to Oxford. Uncle Samuel smiled at my response. He had worried that I would not agree. There is more loyalty in me than that. He told me rooms were kept for us at the Swan, and asked to speak to Meg in private. I knew what that meant: he had some secret mission for her to undertake.

'Your sister is married to a subordinate of Sir Edward Nicholas, Mistress Powell,' my uncle said as I left the room. 'Perhaps you could...'

I closed the door behind me and stepped out. I desired not to know what danger Uncle Samuel placed my love in, and she would not thank me for my concerns. The Swan was but a short walk away from my uncle's residence. Sam and the others would be waiting for me there. I passed recruits drilling in the High Street. They looked so damn young, and me still only twenty-one. There were fifty or so, in two ranks, holding pikes. They were being taught how to set them to receive Horse, still dressed in their ordinary clothes, with no matching coats or colours. This was the garrison now, callow youths and criminals, unwanted by any battle commander and sent to Newport to rot. The best men of our age were being wiped out.

The sergeant started bellowing at one who kept dropping his pike. A scruffy lad with a dirty wide-brimmed straw hat, brown coat, patched breeches and scuffed boots.

'It slipped, Sergeant.'

'It slipped sergeant? It slipped? 'Tis thicker than your pizzle, Bunyan! Slips your hand on that?'

'Does when I greases it up, Sergeant.'

The rest of the company started laughing. The sergeant, realising control was slipping away, went red in the face and started screaming at them as I passed.

Yes, that was my first sight of John Bunyan: a rude lazy scoundrel. There was no hint of godliness in him, then. I am passing certain that such zeal only became fervent when coin started flowing from his sedition; else he would have ended his days as a poor tinker.

I turned away and walked to the tavern. I had little hope of survival if the King came to Newport. The innkeeper had set aside an attic room for me. I bought some sack and took myself upstairs to get drunk. Sam, John and Figgis were waiting in the garret, and the stink of rotting feet hit me as I entered. Figgis was sat on the floor with his boots off picking at his toenails. I handed the wine to him to open and pour.

'By all the toads of hell, be that stench your stockings, Figgis? Change them, by god.'

'I change my stockings regular, Master Blandford,' said Figgis, outraged.

''Tis a very shame you can change not your feet, instead.'

Figgis got the bottle open and handed around cups for us all. Sam started to pack his pipe and lay back on a straw pallet.

'What said your uncle?' he asked.

I explained the situation to them, as best I could. The King could be coming here to raise the town and we were left with base types to defend. Only one troop of dragoons – mine now – remained in Newport, and them not paid in months.

'So we wait?' said John.

'Yes, we wait for the King to make his move, and pray it is to Oxford and not Newport,' I said. 'If they come here, the town shall not hold.

'How long to wait?' said John.

'Not long, I fear.'

A Perfect Relation of the Taking of Leicester Town.

SIR,

TO satisfy the request in your letter touching the condition of Leicester. I have endeavoured to inform myself from the most moderate and understanding men that were sufferers in that general loss, and eye-witnesses to the sad business. They are since fled hither for refuge.

In the night of Wednesday, May the 28th, a strong party of the King's Horse faced our own, and hindered the supplies from the county. On Thursday, enemy artillery were drawn up near the town, and by the direction of some malignants (who had formerly been put out) their great guns were planted against some of the weakest places of our works.

By Friday night the enemy had made wide breaches in the walls, which by the industry of the men and women of the town were made up again with woolpacks. However, the enemy pressed upon them, and about the town the defenders were hard put to it; the enemy being numerous without, and we but few within and the works very large.

The foot soldiers in pay in the town did not exceed 450 men, with the townsmen in arms, and some of the county that came into their assistance, altogether about 1000 men. By reason of the smallness of their numbers, the enemy were able to keep them in constant alarms, which did so tire out the townsmen.

The enemy had about 4000 foot, who stormed in so many places at once, that the defendants, wanting for reserves, were mastered. The storm began about one-of-the-clock on Saturday morning May the 31st, and lasted about two hours. The enemy were strongly resisted and three times beaten back, but then several bodies of foot stormed at once breaking in many places. Ours were driven back to the market-place, and kept up the fight in the town for almost an hour after, only some of them escaped.

At the enemy's first coming in, they slaughtered many, until ours had laid down their arms and yielded themselves prisoners. Then they fell to their plundering work, taking men to be their prisoners, and executing their accustomed cruelty to the women, stealing their money and best goods. The town committee are yet kept prisoners in the town, and many other gentlemen of the county and officers of the garrison were sent as prisoner with the best of the plunder to Newark or Lichfield.

I know their tender mercies are cruelties, but give the devil his due, there was indeed many slain at the first entrance, and some that made little resistance, and some women and children killed amongst the multitude by the rabble of common soldiers, but I cannot learn of any such order given to destroy all, as is said by some. It is confidently believed that not above 300 are slain on both sides.

The town was full of wealth which had been brought in for safety, including nine pieces of ordnance, great and small, above 1000 Muskets, near 400 horse and arms, and about 50 barrels of powder. The greatest defect was want of men. It was to be wished that garrisons of such importance might have at least 1000 foot soldiers in pay. Had Leicester had such, with the help of the townsmen, we might have kept out the enemy and made them pay for their boldness.

I pray God we may never forget to do the fallen the best good we can by our prayers, purses, and pains, knowing that nothing hath befallen them, that we are not subject unto, a sanctified use whereof both to them and us, is the earnest prayer of your loving friend.

Northampton, June 9. 1645.

26. Cousins and Lovers: Newport Pagnell, June 1645.

Here they shall weep, and shall unpitty'd groan,
Here they shall howl, and make Eternal moan.
By Blood and Lust they have deserv'd so well,
That they shall feel the hottest flames of Hell.
(Thomas Shadwell, *Prepare! Prepare!*)

An army had come to Newport Pagnell. Black Tom Fairfax had brought nearly fifteen thousand men in new pots and red coats to the village of Sheraton, just north of the town. The fall of Leicester had sent Parliament into its usual frenzied panic. Fairfax had been ordered to seek out the King's army and destroy it. The Yorkshireman had jumped at the chance. He wanted Cromwell as his General of Horse: the Committee of Both Kingdoms acquiesced. He wanted full freedom to command in the field: they gave it to him. If the new army lost, it would be the new army and Fairfax's failure. If it won, then it would be Fairfax and the army's own success. The House had envisaged and created this new weapon of war, and now they washed their hands of it.

Politicians are cursed with short-sight. At the least, most are. I recalled John Hampden's words before Chalgrove Field.[61] Would Parliament make a new Caesar out of Fairfax, just as the Senate of Rome raised up Julius to be consul? Would Fairfax cross a Rubicon? 'You are being ridiculous,' Everard told me. 'The new army is filled with the godly, it is a righteous host. Fairfax is a good man; if you were more devout mayhap he would regard you better.'

William had arrived with Fairfax. He was still dressed in his mismatched shabby, but looked happy and well enough. He was surrounded by fellow Independent zealots in his new unit, and it fired his enthusiasm. Since arriving, he had spent most of his time trying to persuade Sam and me to join up with the army. We were not accommodating him.

'Would you make an Anabaptist of me?' I said. 'It is such a self-righteous host that bothers. Non-conformist and Independent to the man. The majority of the country is not so inclined.'

---

[61]See The Last Roundhead

'Then the majority of the country should have fought for their ideals.'

'We have been,' I said, coldly.

He sniffed at that but did not contradict. He could not; I had shared every trial and tribulation, borne every sacrifice, and spilt as much of my blood as he for the cause. I was not the only one to complain of the rabid zealotry of the godly. Vermuyden had resigned because of them, claiming foreign business as an excuse, and it was the Independent Cromwell who benefitted in spite of the denying ordnance. Other Presbyterian and Anglican officers had resigned almost as soon as they were appointed, mostly Waller's men; they had all been replaced by Independents. The radicals had control of committees in Parliament, the senior officers in the army, and important positions in the country. It did not bode well for the future. [62]

'You should join us, Blandford,' said William. 'Watson would give you a commission, and Cromwell would welcome you.'

'Watson would use me then betray me, whilst Fairfax would spurn me and Skippon slander me,' I said. 'No thank ee. I am for Boston

---

[62]Vermuyden's resignation provided the perfect excuse for Cromwell's command to be extended and Fairfax was quick to utilise him. Samuel Luke recorded in a letter to his father than there were grumblings of discontent from Presbyterian officers in the army, but he had his own problems. Challenged with the threat of mutiny in Newport Pagnell, Luke's control of the garrison town was much diminished. Radical preachers defied his orders in the streets, and he received little support from either Parliament or the army. Cromwell had been sent to raise troops and defend Ely and the Eastern Association against any assault after Leicester. When no Royalist attack materialised, Oliver joined Fairfax and the New Model Army at Newport Pagnell. At the council of war there, it was decided to march after the King.

and the New World when this current business is over.'

'Sugar has heard tell of beautiful native women in the Americas,' said Sam, with a laugh.

'And you, Sam? Will you not join the army?'

William was persistent, at the least.

'I serve Sir Samuel. I will go with him back to Cople, and have already given my eye for this cause. That is enough.'

Everard looked at the boy.

'I am for the Americas,' said John, with a shrug. 'It means an ocean voyage and a great ship. I am looking forward to it.'

Indeed, it had been the only topic of conversation that lifted his humour from black dog misery to some semblance of normality. I actually missed his customary impudent, insolent, tongue. The New World would be good for the both of us, I had decided; a new beginning.

'I understand this not,' said Everard. 'You were there at the start, not the boy, but you two; you should be at the finish. The Lord of Israel walks with us. This army is the instrument of God and our victory is certain...'

I burst out laughing.

'Icarus, where are you? In what region shall I seek you?'[63]

His eyes narrowed at that. Sam spoke up.

'You took the Covenant to join this new army, William? Are you Presbyterian now, or was it a false oath?'

'The new Covenant allows for toleration of church independence.'

'Lillburne says it does not,' said Sam.

That was cruel: Lillburne was one of Everard's heroes and had refused to join the new army over the oath. The shabby poacher had no answer to that point; instead, he stood up and drained his cup of wine.

'And if it seems evil unto you to serve the Lord, choose you this day whom ye will serve,' he said. 'Whether the gods which your fathers served that were on the other side of the flood, or the gods of the Amorites in whose land ye dwell. But, as for me and my house, we will serve the Lord.'[64]

And with that, he put his cup aside and stalked out. We could hear him tramping all the way down the stairs to the taproom two flights

---

[63]Ovid

[64]Joshua 24:15

below.

'His temper is improved not at all,' I said.

A moment later, we heard the steps coming up the stairs once more. Sam and I looked at each other. Was William come back to harangue us? The door opened and Figgis poked his head around. Everyone, tense and expecting Everard, burst into fits of giggles. My manservant did not look impressed with our mirth.

'Sir Samuel requires ye, Master Blandford, and the innkeeper wants paying.'

I wiped the tears of laughter from my eyes and sat up.

'By God, Figgis, I love thee.'

If my uncle wanted me, it meant he finally had some employment. The last fortnight had been spent in idle recreation. There were simply not enough men or animals in the garrison for me to be useful. I grabbed my doublet and followed Figgis downstairs, flipping the innkeeper a silver crown for our board and lodge, and headed down the High Street to Uncle Samuel's quarters. It heaved with men from Fairfax's army, all seeking wine and women during their brief respite at Newport.

'Blandford! Blandford Candy!'

I turned at the voice: a young man, brown hair, blue eyes, and slender. He looked familiar but I could not place him. He started to laugh at me.

'My apologies, sir, do I know you?'

'I am your cousin, dunderhead.' He grabbed me and gave me a hug.

I realised then who it was. Richard Candy; my first cousin on my father's side of the family.

'Dickon, well met indeed, what do you here?'

'I took your advice.'

'My advice?' That confused me; I had not spoken to the boy in years.

'Your sister wrote and told me to go to General Cromwell, with your blessing.'

'My blessing?' What had Elizabeth done now?

'Aye, indeed, I am made Lieutenant in the Ironsides. All thanks to you. Cromwell sang your praises; he said you were a friend to his dead son. We brought letters from him to your Uncle Samuel.'[65]

---

[65]A Richard Candy was commissioned into Swallow's Troop of Horse at the start of 1645.

That be an interesting snippet.

'Dickon, I have a prior appointment with my uncle, but have chambers at the Swan. Figgis is there, he has wine. I shall be back soon.' My cousin knew Figgis well enough, and my manservant would make him welcome. He nodded and shook my hand. I turned and went to my uncle to see what he had for me.

Butler said nought to me as I entered the Saracen's Head. He was grown increasingly surly now that his employment was almost finished. My uncle was too generous to the man; he should have sent him down years before. Uncle Samuel was waiting for me. He wanted me abroad with Sam and John. We would be attached to Okey's Dragoons in case of battle, but mostly left to our own devices. We knew the local area (at least Sam did) and he wanted us to make contact with Meg.

'Mistress Powell has been in Oxford with her sister,' said my uncle. 'She has important information for us. You will need to head for Daventry; we have a contact there that will help you find her.'

Uncle Samuel gave me the details I would need, and signed a new commission. I returned to the Swan to give the others the news, and to finish the sack. It seemed William Everard had had his way, and we all joined the new army despite our misgivings.

There was little enough time before setting out, and only a bare few hours with Dickon. He told me about the family (not that I cared overly), of the Wiltshire Clubmen (troublemakers and upstarts to a man) and of home. He told me about the puppy, a grown animal now, brave and loyal, left home and waiting for his master away at the wars.

*

Three days in the rain. That is what our assignment had led to. First to Daventry, avoiding Royalist scouts all the way there, now to a lonely tavern in the middle of nowhere seeking out Meg Powell. It was late in the afternoon and we were soaked through, mudded and tired by the time we got there. An old cowshed set on the outskirts of a small village with a shingle roof turned into a taproom.

'Where are we?' asked John, dismounting.

'The hamlet yonder is called Welford,' said Sam, gesturing to a cluster of thatched roofs down the track.

I walked over to the cowshed, climbed the steps and pulled open the door. It was dark inside, lit only by a couple of tallow lamps; I blinked as my eyes became accustomed to the gloom. The odour of rotting fish assailed my nostrils; there was dirt and dank rushes on the wooden floor. A rough tapster with a scraggly red beard sat next to a barrel; badly hewn tables and benches filled the room. There was an open fire stinking peat smoke, making my eyes water, and only one customer: a figure seated in the far corner from the door with hood drawn over the face. The tapster stood as we entered.

'Wine?' I asked.

'Ale,' said the tapster.

I ordered a flagon and took cups for us all, and we sat down opposite the hooded figure.

'Hullo, Meg.'

'You are late, I was set to leave.' She was being serious.

'Better late than never. Do I get no kiss?' I puckered up my lips.

'Coxcomb.' She smiled at me.

John was watching the road, but Sam sat with Meg and me.

One's too few, three too many.

'You have information for us, Meg?' asked Sam.

'Aye, to business before Sugar charms me with his sweet lips.'

'That be not all I wish to do with my lips.'

She poked her tongue out at me and reached into her cloak.

'I have this for you. You must take it to General Fairfax, immediately.'

'What is it?' asked Sam.

'Some parts of the King's correspondence, letters to Goring. The Western Army is camped around Taunton and the King wishes for troops. His Majesty is in Market Harborough with all he has,' said Meg. ''Tis not so many.'

'How many?' I asked.

'No more than eight thousand in all, Foot and Horse.'

There was indeed little time to waste. This was the opportunity that everyone had prayed for. We outnumbered the Royal army by perhaps two parts to one. If we could bring them to battle, we could destroy King Charles' dreams of victory. Sam and John set to ready the horses. I kissed Meg holding, her in my arms.

'It is almost over,' she whispered.

'If Fairfax uses the information.' I had bitter experience of the apathetic passivity of our general officers.

'He will use it.' She touched my cheek. 'You have to go.'

I kissed her once more and bade my love farewell. She was correct, much as I disliked the fact; time was of the utmost importance. The others waited for me outside and we took the road south from Welford towards Guilsborough, perhaps a five-mile ride. A high ridge rose to our left, with a tall white windmill and village of thatched houses atop.

'What is that village up there?' John asked Sam.

'Naseby,' Sam said. 'A small place of little consequence.'

I took little note of their conversation; my mind was on Meg. It was exquisite cruelty to have spent such a short moment of time with her; a snatch at sweet nectar before the bitter aftertaste of parting. Mayhap it would have been better not to have seen her, I reasoned. Then the pain be not so raw. When this is all over I am going to talk to Megan Powell, and see which way the bed is made.

It was dark and raining again by the time we reached Fairfax's headquarters in Guilsborough. Leonard Watson took me to him as soon as we arrived. Another scout (Tarrant I think his name was; a good man) had intercepted letters from the Western Army to the King. It was the very reply to our letters from the King to Goring. When we arrived at the headquarters, Cromwell was already there, and Henry Ireton. We gave Fairfax the packet from Meg, and Tarrant the letter from Goring, but our brave general was reluctant at the first to open them. I could barely believe it. Here was the intelligence that could decide the war, and Black Tom prevaricated. I say this only because it was most unlike him, not because of our personal animosity. He was a decisive commander; he won battles with skill. I was fain to wonder if our leaders had some strange malady that afflicted them as soon as victory was within grasp.

'We are twice their number,' I blurted out finally, as Fairfax hummed and hawed about the letters.

They all looked at me, only Cromwell smiled.

'We should always try and listen to those beneath us, General,' said Oliver to Black Tom. 'Every man knows that gold is buried underground.'

Fairfax actually smiled at that. He and Oliver rubbed along well enough.

'Very well,' said Black Tom. 'This is the good Lord's bounty, as you say. It would be churlish to spurn such.' He looked to me. 'You are dismissed, sir. Get some rest, tomorrow shall be busy and hot.'

Letter from Charles I to Henrietta Maria. 8th June 1645.
Dear Heart,

Oxford being free, I hope this will come sooner to thee then otherwise I could have expected, which makes me believe, that my good news will not be very stale, which in short is this. Since the taking of Leicester, my marching down hither to relieve Oxford made the rebels raise their siege before I could come near them. They had their quarters once or twice beaten up by our garrison, and lost four hundred men in an assault before Bostoll-House.

I thought they would have fought with me, being marched as far as Brackley, but are since gone aside to Brickhill. I believe they are weaker we thought; whether by their distractions, (which are certainly very great: Fairfax and Browne having been at cudgels, and his men and Cromwell's likewise at blows together. Besides Goring hath given a great defeat to the Western Rebels, but I do not yet know the particulars).

I may (without being too much sanguine) affirm, that (since this rebellion) my affairs were never in so fair and hopeful a condition. Among ourselves have our own follies, but I am confident they shall do neither harm nor much trouble. Yet, I must tell thee, that it is thy Letter by Fitz Williams, assuring me of thy perfect recovery with thy wonted kindness which makes me capable of taking contentment in these good successes. For as diverse men propose several rewards to themselves for their pains and hazard in this rebellion; so thy company is the only reward I expect and wish for.

The Portugal Agent hath made me two propositions, first, concerning the release of his master's brother, for which I shall have 50000l if I can procure his liberty from the King of Spain. The other is for a marriage betwixt our son Charles and his master's eldest daughter: For the first, I have freely undertaken to do what I can, and for the other, I will give such an answer, as shall signify nothing.

I desire thee not to give too much credit to Sabran's relations, nor much countenance to the Irish agents in Paris. The particular reasons thou shalt have by Pooley, (whom I intend for my next messenger.) In the last place, I recommend to thee the care of Jersey and Guernsey.

Charles R, 8th June 1645.

27. The Last Battle: Naseby, June 14th 1645.

I am a man of war and might,
And know thus much, that I can fight,
Whether I am i'th' wrong or right,
Devoutly.
(Sir John Suckling, *A Soldier*)

Get some rest? That was a jolly jape. By the time we found Okey and his men it was past midnight. There were only moments to rest the horses and drink a watery onion soup, and we were back on our animals not long past two in the morning. We picked our way past Naseby village to the heights beyond in the darkness. As dawn broke, the regiment halted at the windmill atop Naseby ridge. The dragoons were the first unit to arrive at the rendezvous. North to Market Harborough was obscured by a summer morning's mist, blanketing the undulating hills and vales below us.

'The King is in that direction, then,' said Sam to me, as we sat atop our horses viewing the scene.

'Aye.'

More troops were arriving – Horse. They moved past us to take up positions in the fields beyond the village, facing northwards; every man's eyes strained against shadows in the mist. If the King came out of the fog we could be beaten before we began.

'He cannot get up this hill,' said Sam, reading my mind. ''Tis too sharp a slope. We would hear them, even if we can see them not.'

''Tis a sorry situation,' said John. 'Why are we here again?'

'I remember a lad, not so long past, who wanted nothing more than a sword and to see a battle,' I said.

'I have seen a battle since, 'tis no grand thing, and I am the champion blade of London Town.' He looked us up and down. 'You two are better protected than I.'

That was true enough: Sam and I both wore pots, gorget and cuirass, we had carried them on our animals in preparedness for battle, but John had only his blue woollen suit, a borrowed red coat and leather hat on his head.

'The champion blade of London Town? Prince Karl cancelled the result,' said Sam.

'Prince Karl can go swive a greased pig.'

I gestured to the rest of Okey's men. Only the officers wore any armour, the rest were dressed similarly to John.

'We are dragoons today.'

'Pish.'

More and more men were arriving: Pikes and Muskets with flags waving, pipes playing, drums beating, and men singing psalms. They tramped past us taking up positions in the field; two lines of Foot, with Horse in great bodies at the flanks. The artillery train was being dragged up behind them; twelve guns in all.[66] Okey ordered us to move over to them, behind our left flank.

It was perhaps eight of-the-clock as the mist evaporated in the morning heat, and the Royalists came into view. There was an audible gasp from the army along the ridge, like a gust of wind sweeping through our ranks. Then came the cheers and trumpet calls, drum rolls, and flags being tossed about in martial challenge. The festival before battle had begun.

'Will they attack?' asked the boy.

I studied the ground. Our army was still perched atop the steep slope with a brook across the front.

'There be no good reason for them to,' I said. 'We are in a strong position and outnumber them.'

The Royalists were also in a good place. We would be hard pressed to dislodge them, but even across the narrow valley, it was clear we had the greater numbers. I must confess that the normal pit of fear in

---

[66]Actually the New Model Army only had eleven guns at Naseby, and both they and the Royalist artillery proved ineffective with the limited visibility and close quarter fighting. Neither side was very well informed of their opponents position or movements, although Fairfax's scouts had told the Roundhead command the night before the battle. The Royalist scouts failed completely to find the 15,000 strong New Model Army only five miles away, and it wasn't until Prince Rupert himself rode forward that Fairfax's position was discovered.

my stomach that had accompanied all my battles was absent that day. I felt detached and without emotion. I was not the only one: others have told me they were overtaken by a deep sense of calm before the fight. I am not a devout man, you know this of me, but perhaps it was all the will of the Lord.

Orders came from General Fairfax for the whole army to move to the west, and down the slope to another rise below the ridge. The second line of infantry would be hidden from Royalist view (and their guns) on the reverse slope.

'Bugger!' I said.

'What?' asked John.

'We are trying to tempt them into an assault, like a pretty foreign maid tempts a rash boy.' That was cruel.

'Stones and sinners, sir.' John was not impressed by my wit.

There was much shuffling of our infantry frontage as the officers dressed them, bully sergeants beating them into place with cudgels. The whole army took up positions further west. The open vale of battle was bordered on our left by a ditch and great boundary hedgerow, running north from our left flank to the Royalist right wing of Horse. Our right flank of Horse was afflicted with a broken front of gorse, rabbit holes, hillocks and boggy ground. The poor Foot were squeezed into the space between, too many for comfort in such a small field.

Who would be a damned infantryman?

Okey's officers saw to it that shot and powder was readied, and that every man had some spare in his satchel. The three of us bore a brace of Scout pistols each, as well as carbine and swords. I checked my weapons.

'There is Cromwell,' said John, pointing. 'He looks pleased with himself.

I followed his gesture. 'That he does.'

Oliver was trotting towards us, helmet off and a wide grin on his chops, with some of his officers trailing in his wake.

'Okey! Okey!' The general called out as he arrived.

Okey always struck me as a melancholic type. A strangely formed fellow: long face and nose, and oversized eyes too high in his head. He was, of course, a radical knobkin, so Oliver calling him over was akin to a summons from Achilles. They sat atop their horses in earnest conversation for a moment, and Oliver gestured to the Royalist right flank of Horse. Okey nodded and turned to the dragons, as Oliver and his officers rode back to his own regiment.[67]

'Something be occurring,' I said.

Sam nodded.

The 'goon Troops were made ready to move: men mounting and checking their carbines, with cornets fluttering. Our little trio was off to the side, not members of any unit. Okey rode up to us.

'Captain Candy?'

'Yes, Colonel,' I raised my gauntleted hand.

'Stay close to me this day,' he said. 'You and yours will act as messenger should there be need.'

'Yes, sir.'

Okey trotted to the head of the regiment – Sam, John and I moved behind the standard – and led us in column down the Welford Road; through our own psalm singing soldiers along the rise. There was a way past the great hedgerow and stream that ran along the western edge of the field; a gap wide enough for two riders to pass through. The first troop of red-coated dragoons pushed their horses through and fanned out in loose formation, carbines ready in case the Royalists had a nasty surprise, but beyond the hedgerow was open

---

[67]John Okey (1606-1662) came from a prominent London family, and before the war worked as a brewer's stoker and ran a chandler's business. He joined the Earl of Essex's army as quartermaster at the outbreak of the civil war. He quickly rose through the ranks and by Naseby was Colonel of Dragoons in the New Model Army. His regiment later served in Wales in the Second Civil War. He was one of the commissioners to the trial of Charles I and signed the King's death warrant. During the protectorate, his religious radicalism earned Cromwell's displeasure, and he had retired by the time of the Restoration. Okey initially fled to Holland with the return of the King, but was captured and returned to England. Excluded from the Act of Indemnity, Okey was hung drawn and quartered as a traitor on 19th April 1662.

common clear of enemy.[68]

'They are sending us into the hedge to enfilade?' said Sam.

It was a sound plan; the Royalist right wing of Horse, thousands of them, could not get at us. The green walls protected us like a castle keep. From atop Apple, I could see the enemy flags and tops of helmets, but little else; we kept too close to the hedgerow to view them as we moved up to flank. I looked back to our army on the high ground behind us. They felt far away, we were exposed here; a forlorn hope. 'Twas typical, I mused.

'We ever get to empty the cesspit,' I said. 'Just for once, I would like

---

[68]Naseby battlefield is fabulously well preserved with the ancient enclosures largely intact, if less of a barrier than in the Seventeenth Century. The great boundary hedge along the western edge of the field that Blandford describes was known as the Sulby Hedges, dividing Naseby Parish from Sulby. A small section at the southern end is still the thick barrier that protected Okey's dragoons in 1645. Blandford's account of the New Model Army's deployment and position match the other primary sources (notably Okey and Joshua Sprigge). The early march, the mist, and Cromwell's good mood are all attested to. The New Model Army moved off the top of Naseby ridge westwards, taking up position on a lower rise with open fields to the front. Whilst the NMA left flank was fixed by the hedge, the right flank was faced with broken ground, gorse bushes, rabbit holes and boggy ground. It was not the best for a cavalry engagement. Cromwell himself commanded the right flank of horse, with his future son-in-law Henry Ireton commanding the right wing. Blandford's bête noir Phillip Skippon was in command of the Foot, which were squeezed into the small space with a front of about 2000 yards. The Royalists, with fewer men, were not so constricted.

another to get splattered with shit.'

Sam laughed. 'This is the last battle, Sugar. William assured us, remember? When this one is over, I shall buy you a bottle of that Madeira sack you like so much, and we shall get soused.'

'I will hold you to that.'

It was perhaps ten-of-the-clock and Okey's troopers were dismounting. Every tenth man took his fellows horses and fell back holding their reins. Some knelt in prayer before the fight began, others, less devout, took up their carbines and headed into the hedge on foot. I looked to Okey, but he remained mounted. Our dragoons kept in loose formation as they walked up to the hedge. They were only yards from the enemy flank. A slight breeze on the air came to us. Soon we would be choking on the white powder smoke of battle. Okey raised his hand and waited, as if for a signal from God, then dropped it. A great cracking of musketry broke out, smoke began wisping around us. Within moments returning fire was coming back from the Royalists through the hedge. I could see our men falling as shot hissed through the greenery. The enemy could not get at us, but their bullets could. The furthest troop, closest to the enemy, were taking heavy casualties. Bloodied men were being pulled out of the fight, wreathed in smoke and fire.

'They must have commanded muskets with the Horse,' said Okey. 'Candy get yourself to Captain Bridge and request that he withdraw away from the enemy.' Okey pointed at the low ground between the two armies rather than the hedge at their flank. 'To there,' he said. 'We can still put fire up at them through the hedge, but their shot will go o'er our heads.'

I nodded and spurred Apple into a canter. We rode through the musket smoke; I could feel the old familiar sting of acrid powder in my nose and throat. The enemy muskets were making it exceedingly deadly for our advanced troopers. Men fell with bloody wounds from their shot, dragged away by comrades. I found Bridges amidst his men, carbine hot in hand. I had to yell over the noise of explosion and shot to explain the orders. He nodded and turned to a sergeant. I rode back to Okey, perhaps one hundred yards to the rear under a lone oak tree. Bridges and his men fell back a way to the dip in the ground with the other Troops, then set up a storm of lead shot at the Royalist Horse once more. The enemy muskets could not bear down on them. Okey had been in the right with his summation of the field.

'They may not stand for long under such fire,' Sam said, as I arrived back.

The Royalist Horse could just be seen from our position, at least their heads and pots and flags. I could only imagine the murder being wreaked on man and horse as our lead balls tore into them, ripping bodies, shattering bones, punching through breastplate, leaving tattered corpses as if some giant had broken them in his rage.

'They are moving look, look.' John pointed excitedly.

The Royalist right flank (stung by our gunfire) began a great charge across the valley and up to our waiting cavalry on the hill. As the wave of battle rolled past our position behind the hedge, every man discharged his piece at them. Beyond the hedge, the roar of battle, muskets, men screaming, drums beating, pipes and trumpets. Atop Apple, with only enemy pots and flags in view, I took aim with my pistol and squeezed the trigger. I know not if I made a mark.

'Get in the hedge and find out what is happening,' I told the boy.

He dismounted and ran over to the hedgerow. Our men had ceased their fire, indeed we knew not who to fire at. The enemy had ridden out of our musket range, dressed their lines calmly, and charged uphill into our own horse. It was the same old story. The Royalist Horse swept through our men, putting most to flight, and galloped on past.

John ran back to us and explained all he could see of the battle. There were few enough enemies in range of our guns, but few enough friends in sight. Okey ordered his men to reload and make ready to move, but we waited, and waited, as the push of pike and battle of Foot began beyond the hedges. It must be close, I thought. I only heard one volley of cannon before the crash of pike phalanx. The screams of dying men, the wild cracking of musket and pistol, the kettle pot clatter of blade on blade. The sounds surrounded me with the smoke of the fight. Sam began to cough.

I handed him my waterskin. He took a great gulp, and nearly choked.

'This is brandy?'

'Yes?'

'Who drinks brandy for breakfast?'

'Someone who has no Madeira.'

'If we be lost,' said Okey to his officers. 'We shall make a stand here to the last.'

Sam, John and I looked at each other. All three of us contemplating when the best time to make a run for it would be. I was making no damned last stand. If we be lost, I was for London as swift as Apple could carry me.

We waited there for some time. The confusion of battle turns moments into hours and hours into moments, but I would wager we were not more than half-the-hour, listening, watching, and waiting.

'Make ready, we join the battle,' Okey's second called out.

Orders were given for the dragoons to shoulder their carbines and remount. Swords and pistols at the ready, we pulled back to the road from our green fortress. Coming out on the high ground above the left flank of the battle, my full view of the field was obscured by smoke and fire. Yet, it reminded me of old school texts of Cannae as it came into view. The Royalist Foot had charged into our centre, but with so many men in our line and so few in theirs, our infantry had not broken. Instead, the line had bowed like a shallow horseshoe as the Cavalier Foot drove on. At the flanks, the Royalist pressure was not so great and our pikes were pushing them back after the initial charge.

The enemy had surrounded themselves by charging too deep.

Over the far end of the field, to the north, I could see men on horseback battling. The flashes of pistol in the pan could be seen from where I was. There was a regiment of Royalist Foot stoutly moving up to the battle line (I heard later 'twas Rupert's Bluecoats).

'We are winning,' said John, he sounded surprised.

'It is a wonder to me, as well,' I said. 'I thought us lost.'

The remnants of our Ireton's Horse had gathered with us when we emerged from behind the hedge. Prince Rupert, as he was so oft to do, had charged on towards our baggage and the treasure. I will make a point here: Rupert of the Rhine knew what he was about, his men were capable and brave, and he ordered them well enough. At Edgehill, at Naseby, they made only one charge and one was never enough. Money and baggage were more enticing than victory. Had they turned on our Foot instead, Naseby would have been lost despite our greater numbers. Thank God for greed.

Okey's trumpeter started tootling up.

We dressed into ranks as best we could, more than a thousand Horse. Swords out, we started at a trot, picking up the pace; trumpets sounded and we spurred our animals, kicking them into a gallop. It was not an orderly charge, more a wild ride down the hill into the enemy flank. I gave Apple his head, thundering ahead of the others on their little cobs, wondering at the power of my animal as we crashed towards the Royalist infantry. Damn me, I adored that horse.

I discharged my first pistol in my left hand, and then I was amidst them, slashing in fury at their heads, parrying blades; hacking, hacking, hacking. Men fell under Apple's hooves, smashed and ridden down. John and Sam were with me, and the rest of Okey's men; the enemy line was thinning. I pulled on the reins turning Apple, and paused to draw breath. We were through them.

'They are broken! They are broken!' John yelled in delight at the wild charge. He had lost his leather hat, his black curls shone.

The boy spoke the truth. The Oxford Foot were broken.

Some threw down weapons and called out for quarter, others were cut down where they stood. Perhaps the greater part were running, back the way they had come, tossing away heavy pikes and running for the hills. It was mostly a confused mess, but some companies of muskets would turn and unleash a volley if our pursuit got to close. Across the field, the Bluecoats made a stand as brave as the Lambs at Long Marston.[69] They bought time for their fellows to flee. They paid with their bodies and lives, but 'twas not enough. I turned my face away from that murder.

Sam joined me, not a scratch upon him. He lifted the bars to his pot as he arrived.

'You know, Sugar, happen Everard was in the right. This war is finished.'

'Tell him not,' I said. 'He will be insufferably sanctimonious.'

What was left of the Royalist army was in full flight towards their baggage train. Our horns sounded, and I caught a glimpse of Black Tom as we moved off in pursuit of the King's broken army. There was no battalion or regiment; some were in Troops still, most others just loose along. Fairfax ordered us into vague bodies of Foot and Horse.

The enemy made one last stand, halting on a hill to the north of the battlefield. There, they made ready to receive us once more, but Fairfax held us back from the charge. Instead, he ordered the caracole, a constant round of fire-retreat-reload-advance from horseback. As muskets arrived he sent them to volley more shot into the remaining enemy. It was brutal destruction. They stood no hope, and the grass soon became stained black with their blood. A standard, tattered and torn with shot, still flew above them but they were finished.

'Blandford! Blandford! Sam!' We all turned at the voice.

William Everard on horseback, bloody sword in hand, attired for war in a buff coat, but no pot nor armour. We had not seen each other since the night in Newport Pagnell. His eyes were glazed, as if he

---

[69]See *This Deceitful Light*

were drunk or possessed. He gave us a strange smile as we turned to him.

'I knew you would be here. This is truly a sign from the Lord God Our Father. Come, come quickly. God be praised.'

Everard led us away from the Royalist last stand, down a hill and into a small lane. There were people running, women and men, our soldiers cutting at them. Screams of rape and murder; a richly dressed woman was butchered by two pikemen as we rode past. None of us paused. There was so much innocent blood being shed. In victory, we were corrupted. I kicked Apple to a canter, riding aside William.

'What is it?' I asked him.

'The King's carriage; I have found the King's carriage.'

28. The King's Cabinet: Naseby, June 14th 1645.

'Tis not in season, to talk of Reason,
Or call it Legal, when the Sword will have it Treason;
It conquers the Crown too, the Furres and the Gown too,
This set up a Presbyter, and this pull'd him down too.
(Traditional Ballad:*The Power of the Sword*)

The Royalist baggage had been pitched in a large enclosure with a gate onto a country lane. Thick hedges and tree line protected them from assault, but there was only one entrance for vehicles and animals, and that was blocked with a broken discarded wagon. We pushed past the dross on our horses, and into the field. Rich carriages, tents and carts, sumpters, pack animals, cattle, spare powder and shot, victuals; the whole paraphernalia that an army needs to move.

'This way,' cried Everard, and kicked his mare into a canter.

At the centre of the field were the King's own carriage and tents, awaiting a royal master that would never return to claim his goods. A grand carriage with back wheels the size of a hogshead lid, packed with boxes and baggage. There was more bloody murder here. Camp women, wives and whores, were being cut down by our troops with no mercy nor discernment. Royalist baggage guards running, some fighting, most killed where they stood. There was no order to it, no design, it was slaughter. The rage of a victorious army is a terrifying sight to behold.

And then I saw her; she was struggling with a red-coated trooper. I expected her to have left the Royalist train by now, not to be here. There was another woman behind her waving a pistol, and a bloodied man in shirt sleeves fighting with a sword against one of our troopers. I jammed my spurs brutally into Apple's side and he sprang forward, 'twas only yards but I was still too slow. The soldier's blade went through her stomach and out of her back. There was too much blood. It was a mortal blow, and I knew it. With her last breath, she stabbed a stiletto into the man's eye. He fell back losing his grip on his sword, and both collapsed.

'Meg!' I screamed at the top my voice.

In one bound I leapt from Apple's back to the ground beside her, not a thought of the massacre around me. I was too late; she was already gone. There was no final goodbye, no last words of love. I find there is rarely time when death strikes.

In that instant, I felt my heart break.

I closed her eyelids, covered the lifeless stare that has haunted me for seventy years or more. Even now, I weep as I write of her. No regrets? If I could have lived my life without the heartbreak of that day, I would.

It was a pistol shot close to my head that drew me back to my senses. Meg's murderer lay dead; her dagger had punched through the eye socket into his brain. I pray it was an agonising death. The pistol-wielding woman had killed our other trooper. Everard had dismounted and looked set to cut her down in return. The wounded Royalist officer was fallen to the floor, just alive.

'NO!'

I grabbed Everard's coat, and yanked him back in a fury, throwing him to the floor. Sam pointed his carbine at him from horseback.

'I have my good eye on you, William, do not test me.'

I turned to the woman. She was thin, and older than me by some time, mid-thirties perhaps. Her black hair was streaked with grey, and there were lines around her stunning violet eyes – Megan's eyes. I realised who she was.

'You are Lilith? Meg's sister?' A wave of grief washed over me but I fought back the tears.

She nodded.

'And this would be your husband, Major Lucius Wintour?'

She nodded once more.

'At your service, sir,' said Wintour, weakly from the floor.

Major Wintour had been run through and cut up badly on his legs. He must have charged a pikeline, I thought. This man served the King's secretary, and he had served the royal quartermaster. Major Wintour was a valuable prize indeed. The man had lost much blood and needed sewing up and bandaging, if his life was to be saved. I looked at Everard still glaring in fury at me from the grass. He was a wonder with potions and needle and thread. He had sewn me up often enough and saved my life.

'Fix him,' I told him.

'No... He is an enemy and a Royalist, probably a papist or Irish. What care I for his life?'

'Meg be dead; I will see no more death this day.'

'She was a whore, a godless sinner.'

I felt such cold hate as none would believe, but I was calm and clear headed. Other troopers were gathering; Sam and John had their carbines in hand. I pointed my sword at Everard and spoke loudly so all could hear.

'You will fix him, Ensign Everard. Else, I swear to the Lord God Almighty that I shall have you hanged for mutiny and murder. This man has important information for General Fairfax. If one hair of his head be hurt, I shall hold you responsible.'

One of the red-coated troopers came forward, as if to intervene. Sam shoved a carbine muzzle at him.

'I would not, if I were you, friend.'

The soldier stepped back, hands up. There was easier pickings to be had elsewhere in the field.

'Fix him, William,' I said again. 'That be an order.'

He stared at me for a second; a stranger. The man I had loved was gone, consumed with hate.

'I will fix him, Sugar, but you and I are finished now,' he said.

'We were finished a long time ago,' I replied. ''Tis my mistake not to have recognised such.' I looked to Sam. 'Make sure he does it properly.'

Lilith and Sam watched over Everard as he fixed the major. I ripped down blue velvet coverings from the carriage box and laid it over Megan. It matched her eyes, I thought. Grief would wait for me, it would slide up and plunge me into drunken darkness later, but I was calm still. I turned my attention to the King's carriage. An oaken frame, iron tyres with steel springs; there were small plate glass windows in either door (I noted a crack in one pane of glass). It should be said that the King's carriage was not as opulent as the Duchess of Marlborough's. Times have changed, but that was royal luxury back then.

I smashed the lock and pulled the door open, sword at the ready in case some hidden assailant came at me. Inside was dark and quiet; silks and lace, upholstered seats, cushions and comfort. The dull daylight revealed the greatest treasure of all, perhaps greater than the victory just bought with so much blood. All of the King's papers; boxes and boxes full of papers. I pulled a letter. It was written in open hand. This was his personal correspondence, everything. Some was in code, most was not.

In faith, I was stunned at such a haul.

We had won the war.

*

Not one man was punished for the murder of the camp women. One hundred died in the killing frenzy, more had their noses slit. Irish whores the newsbooks said. That was a lie; most were Welsh, most of good quality. When you give in to hate, murder is always the result.

Capturing the king's cabinet was a feather in my cap, no doubts, even Fairfax grudgingly praised me. It was, of course, William Everard's success (he had found the carriage, after all) but for once I felt not a pang of guilt that I had usurped the victory laurels. We did not see William after the battle. He treated Major Wintour well enough, saved the man's life, but then he left in silence. I cared not. I resigned my commission the next day and rode back to Newport Pagnell. Sam and John came with me.

'I have told them that I will not carry on as governor,' Uncle Samuel said. 'What will the three of you do now?'[70]

My uncle looked better, as if the decision taken to resign had freed the burdens upon him. Command is a lonely mountain to climb; I do not recommend it unless you have a surfeit of self-confidence and a damnably thick skin. His chambers at the Saracen's Head were already packed up. He could not wait to leave Newport Pagnell behind.

'I will come home, sir,' said Sam. 'If there is employment for me?'

Uncle Samuel smiled. 'There is always employ for a good man at Woodend.' He looked to John and me.

'I am for the New World,' I said. 'At least for a time. Elizabeth has concerns in New Amsterdam and Boston.'

'I will go to the Americas, Sir Samuel,' said John. 'He needs someone to look after him.'

---

[70]Samuel Luke finally resigned as governor of Newport Pagnell a couple of weeks after Naseby. He had arrested two illegal preachers (junior officers from the army) who had complained to Cromwell and Fairfax. They were released and Luke criticised by the Army command. Luke resigned in disgust at the Independents and returned home to his mansion at Woodend. He spent the next few years trying to recover the monies owed to him by Parliament.

My uncle smiled. 'How much are you all owed for your service?'

That was a good question. My pay had been some months in arrears when I had resigned my rank. So had the others. We all knew how much we were owed, but held out little hope for its payment.

'Four hundred pounds between us,' I said. 'At a best estimate.'

'I am owed over seven thousand,' said my uncle ruefully. 'I have spent my fortune on this command, but I have the means to recover it. I shall pay you gentleman all your outstanding monies and add it to my petitions.' He turned to me again. 'I have more sad news for you, Blandford, and your sister.'

I needed no more sad news.

'Your cousin Richard was killed at Naseby.' He continued. 'I received word today. My condolences.'

I nodded, but there was little grief left in me. I had spent the past week soused and weeping. I thought of the hound Goliath, waiting in vain for a master that would never return. That be something to ponder upon: the unintended consequences of a good deed. I saved a pup from drowning and a small boy a beating. Now the boy was dead and the hound masterless. Even in triumph, there was no joy. It was not, as Oliver would claim, a happy victory. It was cold misery and a broken heart. Do you wonder why I am so bitter?

There would be some more fighting, but no more great battles, no more risk of ultimate Royalist success. Naseby finished the King's cause. His best men were dead or captured, his cannon taken, his colours lost. All that was left were isolated garrisons and towns that would soon fall to Fairfax and the new army.

There was a crash in the chambers outside my uncle's room. We looked to him in askance.

'Mr Butler has discovered that his employment is to be terminated with immediate effect,' said Uncle Samuel. 'I fear he is not taking the news very well at all.'

That at the least cheered us all somewhat. We left Uncle Samuel writing letters for the new governor. Outside, Butler was packing his desk away. Whatever personal effects he had were being shoved rudely into a bag. He looked up as we exited my uncle's offices.

'Captain Candy, and Mr Brayne, well met indeed,' he said.

'Butler,' I nodded and moved past.

'I wonder,' Butler said. 'I find myself in need of employment. Perhaps your sister Mistress Candy might have some industry for me? You could talk to her, perhaps? Or Mr Thurloe?' There was a hopeful look on his flushed dish face. 'Or you Mr Brayne, perhaps?'

'Perhaps...' said Sam.

'Not even if hell freezes over,' I said.

I looked at Sam, and he looked to me with his good eye.

'I thought we were shooting for honesty?' I said.

'Not brutal honesty.'

I turned back to Butler.

'I would not employ you if you were the last pox doctor on earth and I the only syphilitic. Since the sad sorry day I first met you in Windsor, you have been nought but a stinking turdlet to we scouts. Do you ever think how much happier I would be if ugly old Mother Butler had swallowed instead of opening her legs? How much happier we all would be? You are only here because she did not wish to muss her makeup.' He went bright red at that, but I was not finished. 'Some drink from the fountain of knowledge, Mr Butler, you gargled and spat. You have the intellect of a brick and depth of a puddle. No, no, no! I will not speak to my sister on your behalf.'

'You will regret that, Candy.'

'No, when it comes to your sorry visage, I will regret nothing, you insolent cur. Your very speech makes me desire to tear off my ears and sew them o'er my eyes. Then I would neither see nor hear from you again. Remember your place, Butler. You are a supplicant seeking employment now, and I am a gentleman still. Nought you can do will ever change that.'

Time changes all.

John sniggered behind me. I was perhaps overplaying my hand, but three years of Samuel Butler was enough to make a man hammer a nail with his head. We left my uncle's former secretary red-faced and humiliated, and stepped out onto the High Street.

I linked my arms with John and Sam as we walked to the Swan.

'I cannot wait to get out of this hive of villainy,' I said. 'The sooner we are back in London the better.' I looked at Sam. 'You owe me some Madeira.'

He smiled. 'We shall drink it together before you two go home to London and sail off to the New World.'

The report of the Scout William Everard, that brought the news of the great victories at Isle Abbots and Langport.

On Wednesday the ninth of July 1645, there were 1500 of the enemy commanded by Lieutenant-General Porter, on whom Major General Massy fell upon before the enemy were aware of it. Accompanying

Colonel Massy were Lieutenant Bull, Major Sanderson, Colonel Webb, and some other officers, who with the common soldiers behaved themselves most gallantly.

At about three-of-the-clock in the afternoon, the enemy were grazing their horses at Isle's Abbot, and having made works about the Church, and in exceeding good quarters. They, little thinking that Massey was so near, had only set a small guard of foot at the town's end. Major General Massey drew his men into two divisions, for each end of the town. Massey commanded the main body himself, and Capt. Gutredge the other, which was but a small party. Massey's men marched with green boughs in their hats.

Gutredge, coming to the southwest end of the town, found the hedges lined with enemy musketeers. Cap. Fransway, a Dutch Captain, commanded a party to fall on the one side of the ambuscaders[71], and Capt. Gutredge on the other. The Dutch Captain, when he was charged by the enemy, began to face about, which impeded Capt. Gutredge's prosecution of the business. Yet, the rest of the officers and soldiers, with the wisdom of Capt. Gutredge, ended the business so well that they beat up their ambuscaders and drove them quite away.

In the meantime, Major General Massey marched up to the other side of the town. Colonel Cook, having the command of the forlorn hope, attacked the Cavaliers. They in like manner had lined the hedges at that end of the town, but Massey with Cook and the rest, raised them, and those with the rest at the other end of town. They chased so hard upon the enemy that they drove them all from the town, pursuing them within two miles of Langport, and took many arms in Isle Abbot's. Major General Massey's password was Wales, but the enemy did not give any word at all.

On Thursday the tenth of July, Sir Thomas Fairfax marched toward the enemy, and discovered them when he was with his body by the windmills, between Langport and Somerton. The enemy were on the Hills in Langport field about two mile and a half off, with a body of water being between them. About eleven-of-the-clock, they drew out, and about one-of-the-clock Major Bethel charged the enemy. The fight was very hot, and lasted about two hours, but about three-of-the-clock Goring himself fled into Bridgewater.

Prince Charles and the Lord Hopton have fled to Barnstable with three Troops of Horse, to raise what forces they could in those parts,

---

[71]Ambusher

to join those which were to come from Grenville. Rupert was gone to the King to send what strength he could to join with them, and Grenville's Horse. All these were then upon their relief march toward Goring, and also Sir John Barkley was before he was drawn off, upon some discontent or other towards Exeter. Sir Thomas Aston was with Goring, who hath a regiment in which are good store of Papists, but he ran away like a base coward, and the greatest part of his regiment are taken. The poor county men are not a little glad, for the Cavaliers have been extremely cruel in plundering.

Sir Lewis Dives was then in Sherborn, it seems he loves a garrison better than the field, and holds it more secure. The Cavaliers seem to be very sorrowful for their losses, we perceive from them, that they have lost some considerable men. Sir Thomas Fairfax quartered that night some miles from Bridgwater. Major General Massy is joined with him and Cromwell.

FINIS.[72]

---

[72]The Battle of Langport was the last major pitched battle of the war. General Goring's Western Army, whose failure to reinforce the King at Naseby had caused the disaster, had chosen a strong defensive position, but Fairfax relied upon the zeal of the New Model Army and launched a frontal assault against their position. Cromwell's cavalry took the hill from Goring, and then chased them to Langport. Goring retreated towards the West Country, but with few remaining troops or ordnance. The King's last field army was destroyed, and Fairfax would spend the next year mopping up increasingly isolated garrisons. Montrose was beaten in September, and the fall of Bristol to Fairfax broke the King's resistance. Charles I, realising his cause was lost, finally surrendered to Scottish Covenanter forces in Newark on May 6th, 1646.

29. A Reckoning: London, July 1645.

By what bold passion am I rudely led,
Like Fame's too curious and officious Spy,
Where I these Rolls in her dark closet read,
Where worthies wrapp'd in time's disguises lie?
(William Davenant, *By What Bold Passion*)

The victory at Langport had destroyed the King's last pitiful forces in the west. My home in Hilperton had been liberated by the army under Fairfax (I am not so certain all the natives saw it as liberation), and all that remained of the His Majesty's cause were broken hopes and corrupted crown. Fairfax would soon reduce the last Royalist holdouts to dust, and the King would become a fugitive in his own land. I cannot say I felt much pity for him. Too many good people were dead, and still more would die, because of Charles Stuart. I passed the pamphlet to John.

'William has been busy; it will all be over by Christmas,' I said.

'I have heard that said before.'

'You be grown cynical for one so young.'

The door opened and Figgis came into the cabin. The three of us were set in a tiny hutch under the half-deck. It was normally used as the chicken coop but had been given over to us (at extortionate cost). Four bunks alongside the adjoining wall, my apologies, the bulkhead, too short for even an average sized man; a small unstable foldaway table, and barely enough room to swing a rat. With our sea chests stowed in the top bunk, we all had spare shirts and stockings, but Figgis's fetid feet would be an odorous accompaniment to the voyage.

'All the trunks be packed away in the hold, Master Blandford. But the wine ain't arrived.'

'What do you mean the wine has not arrived? It was supposed to be here hours ago.'

He shrugged at me.

There were barely a few hours before departing with the tide. The Meeuwtje[73] was set for Boston and then New Amsterdam. That

---

[73]The Seagull

meant up to six weeks at sea bobbing around to reach the Americas. We carried no personal provisions, food and ale were eaten with the crew and passengers, but I had ordered forty-eight bottles of the Madeira to take with us. Six weeks of piss-ale would be worse than sobriety. The other passengers were from all over, Protestant exiles from France and Germany headed to the new world. Without wine, the journey would be one hellish sermon of fire and brimstone after another.

'I shall go and see the wine merchant myself,' I said. 'We still have a few hours.'

The ship was at anchor just below the Bridge. Boats were still bringing over goods for the hold from wharves by the Customs House, and provisions for the passengers and crew. I hopped onto one of them on its return to the land, promising the seamen that I would soon be back with baskets to be ported. There are a cluster of traveller's rests and taverns at the lower end of Thames Street (by Billingsgate) where passengers for the boats waited for the tides. I whistled to myself as I wandered to the merchant's there. I must confess that resigning my commission had a quite liberating effect. The first weeks after my return to London were spent in drunken misery, with John Coxon my fellow in cups. Elizabeth had finally put an end to our anguished wallowing, and arranged for our trip. Now we were set to leave, and I felt free. Free for the first time in years, perhaps. That does not mean I had forgotten Meg or did not still mourn her, but grief cannot stay raw forever.

As I turned into Love Lane, Sidcup Buttermeadow stepped out in front of me. I stopped in surprise at sight of the Fool.

'Sidcup? What do you here?' I had said my farewells to Beeston and the theatre hands three nights previous.

''Twas not my idea, sire.' He looked quite sorrowful.

I felt the muzzle of a pistol pressed into my coat from behind.

'Now, now, Sugar, do not start. My finger is twitchy.'

It was the Jack-a-Dandy.

'What do you fellows want?'

'The Burned Man wishes to see you.'

That was an invitation one could not refuse.

'I have to say I am most disappointed in you, Sidcup.'

'My apologies, sire.' His head dropped.

Jack-a-Dandy led me to a broken down old wooden house near Smart's Wharf. I thought nothing of escape. I wore my sword, but knew that a bullet will always beat a blade. Sidcup knocked three times on a side door. Another miscreant opened it and beckoned us in. Sidcup went first and I followed with the pistol still pressed into my back. It was dark inside; I blinked as my eyes became accustomed to the gloom.

'This way,' said the new scoundrel.

He led us to some rickety wooden stairs going down into the bowels of the earth, roughly cut planks hammered together. They creaked as we descended down into the depths. The cellar below was old (built by monks I would wager) with flagstone floors and stone walls. Small windows set high in the cellar walls, but at ground level, sent two shafts of sunlight into the room. Specks of dust hanging in the air glistened like diamonds in the shine. Sitting at a table in the middle of the space illuminated by the sunlight, was the Burned Man. He wore the same black Benedictine robes, but a different mask: white porcelain quartered like a harlequin's face in gold and black, the blood red lips painted into a deep smirk.

Once again, I wondered at the drama and staging of it all. I was convinced he was a former actor, and passing certain that he had served the King until Marston Moor. He had returned to London with all the other dispossessed theatricals flooding back to the city. I was also certain that there was some link to my former servant Jacob. And, it had occurred to me, that if he always wore a mask, none could be sure that it was always the same person.

The Burned Man sat waiting for me to speak, waiting for me to blurt out something foolish. For once, I held my tongue. I like to be unpredictable.

'I knew you would come looking for the wine.' There was a snigger behind the mask. 'Your vices make you predictable, Sugar. They make you weak. Sit.'

I was growing to heartily dislike this man.

The sunlight made me squint as I sat opposite him. I thought of the broken old rooms upstairs, rubbish on the floor, dust and grime covering all. It was empty of furnishings, bare boards and peeled pain, with this dry stone cellar beneath. Perhaps it had been an alehouse once, but not for years. It was the kind of premises Elizabeth would want to purchase and rebuild.

'What is this place?' I asked.

'This is the Pocket and Purse,' said the Burned Man, waving his hand through the shafts of light. 'Or it was once, and will be again.'

'What be the Pocket and Purse? A Gypt stew?'

'A beggar school.'

I burst out laughing.

'You find it amusing?'

'I did not take you for a schoolmaster?'

'I was taught here, as a boy,' he said. 'So was Haniel Boswell. And not just to read and write. Old Mr Wotton would beat us black and blue until we learned to pick a pocket and cut a purse. It was a school for sinners, for footpads, cutpurses, and scoundrels.'[74]

He was not jesting.

'What has this to do with me?'

He blinked behind the mask.

'Nothing, actually, 'tis merely a convenient place to meet.'

I noted that Sidcup and the others had gone quietly back upstairs

---

[74]As strange as it seems the Pocket and Purse was a real establishment. A letter to William Cecil in 1585 from the recorder of London leaves us with a description of Wotton and his school for sinners: *"Amongst our travels this one matter tumbled out by the way. One Wotton, a gentleman born, and some time a merchant of good credit, having fallen by time into decay, kept an ale-house at Smart's Key, near Billingsgate; and after, for some misdemeanour, being put down, he reared up a new trade of life, and in the same house he procured all the cut-purses about this city to repair to his said house. There was a school-house set up to learn young boys to cut purses. There were hung up two devices; the one was a pocket, the other was a purse. The pocket had in it certain counters, and was hung about with hawks' bells and over the top did hang a little scaring-bell; and he that could take out a counter without any noise, was allowed to be a public hoyster; and he that could take a piece of silver out of the purse without the noise of any of the bells, he was adjudged a judicial nipper. N. B.—That a hoyster is a pick pocket, and a nipper is termed a pick-purse, or a cut-purse."*

despite the creaking boards.

'Well, what want you? I am for the New World and have wine to find before the tide.' I pretended to be uncowed.

His blood-rimmed eyes blinked again behind the mask, and I was certain he was smiling. The fixed smirk on the porcelain was a most unsettling look.

'Your wine has already been delivered,' he said. 'As soon as you disembarked it was loaded up and sent on.'

'Oh, so what is this then?'

'You owe me a favour, as I recall, and I have a gift for you.'

My heart sank. I had been vaguely hoping to escape to the Americas, and then perhaps the Burned Man would be dead or deposed by my return.

'Which would you rather first, the favour or the gift?'

'I shall take the gift first.' Pleasure before pain.

'Sometimes pleasure and pain are one and the same, Sugar... Edward Boswell knows your man killed his father. His men are on the streets as we speak. I doubt they would storm a Dutch merchantman, but you will have to watch your back if you are to make it on board safely.'

'How be that a gift?'

'Forewarned is forearmed.'

I shrugged. 'What is the favour then? I trust it will not delay my departure?'

'Indeed no, quite the opposite. You are set for New Amsterdam?'

'After Boston, yes.'

He reached into his black robes and pulled out a copper tube, about six inches long, the ends soldered up and stamped. The Burned Man rolled it across the table to me.

'I want you to take that with you and deliver it.'

The tube was hollow and had something inside, but the only way to get at the contents would be to cut it open. I picked it up; it was light in the hand.

'Deliver it to whom?'

'A ship's captain in New Amsterdam that goes by the name of Billy Jackson. Tell him it comes from me, and he will know what to do.'

'What if I said no?'

Another blink.

'Then you would not leave here alive; we would cut up your corpse and dump it in the river. Coxon and your servant would assuredly come looking for you, and both would soon follow you to the bottom of the Thames.'

''Tis a fair point, and well made.'

He gestured to the stairs. 'You are free to go. Have a care to avoid Boswell's boys.'

I was about to make a retort about the weakness of kings, but I recalled Meg's words that the Burned Man was not a true Romany. He may have been the King of the Beggars, but p'raps he be not the King of the Gypts, I thought. That was Eddie Boswell's crown. I climbed the creaking stairs to the broken taproom above. Sidcup and the other two miscreants were waiting in the empty room. They said nothing as I went to leave. A thought struck me and I turned back.

'Make certain my sister comes to no harm whilst I am away, Sidcup Buttermeadow. Else you shall answer to me for it.'

He doffed his cap.

'Ye have my word on it, sire.'

The Pocket and Purse overlooked Smart's Wharf, but I could not walk along the river to the Custom House. There was a boatman, but as my good mood and trust had evaporated that afternoon, I dared not take it. He looked shifty. He could easily be one of Boswell's men. The supply boats for our merchantman were on a wharf by the Custom House. I turned back up to Thames Street, crowded and busy as always. Keeping close to the houses I walked briskly towards the Tower before turning back to the river.

I was nervous, watching every face, every bystander or passerby. My heart was beating so hard I thought it might burst pumping through my breast.

Was that a man watching me at the street corner? There was another on the other side of the road. Damn, damn, damn! I was certain that I recognised him, certain that he was with the Boswell crew. I started to run, thanking God that for once I had on light shoes instead of my musketeer boots.

The two men saw me take to my heels and started after me. I pounded down the street towards the wharves. I could see where the supplies to our ship were being loaded onto a longboat to be ported. I risked a glance back, and with horror realised there were three men racing after me, and they were closing.

They were pushing the supply boat away from the wharf. I cursed.

'Wait! Wait for me!'

There was another figure running at me along the waterfront from the left, another of Boswell's men. I ran full pelt for the end of the wharf. The supply boat was perhaps twelve feet from the shore.

Without pausing, I leapt. I was short. Plunging into the foul Thames water, gasping and spluttering as I came up for air. A beefy hand reached down and grabbed at me, hauling me dripping onto the boat. 'Right you are, master, there is time afore the tide yet.'

I gasped my thanks at him, as the other boatmen hauled away at the oars. Breathing a sigh of relief, I looked back at the wharf. Four scoundrels were stood in front of the Custom House cursing at me. They were Eddie Boswell's man; that was for certain, but they could not get at me now. The tall wooden walls of the Meeuwtje soon towered above us. Rope fenders were cast out of the longboat as we pulled up alongside. A knotted line was cast down for me to climb up as the goods were loaded into a net. I walked up the side and stood on the deck.

The sailors that bustled readying for the voyage took no notice as I went back to my cabin. John and Figgis were absent but there was a basket of Madeira wine packed with straw on the cabin's deck. I stripped off my wet clothes. Figgis had stowed out sea-chests in the unoccupied top bunk. I pulled mine out and put it on the floor. The keys were in my wet doublet with the copper tube. I took them out and opened up the chest. My dry spare shirt and stockings and a clean pair of breeches were grabbed and put on. Then, I opened up the small iron casket with my coin and papers and placed the Burned Man's copper tube inside. I locked the casket and put away the chest. Sitting on a bunk, I cracked open a bottle of the Madeira and drank deeply.

Damn me, I thought, and I was looking forward to the Americas.

Cross Deep, Twickenham 1720.

And now of blood exhausted he appears,
Drain'd by a torrent of continual tears.
(Ovid, *Metamorphosis*)

There have been celebrations and rejoicing throughout Twickenham and Cross Deep. The sounds of revelry carried along the river. Craggs the Younger was most extravagant in his entertainment by all accounts (my presence was not requested or desired). The idiot declined his invitation, and instead travelled into London to sup at Leicester House; to sup with Walpole and the Prince of Wales. He drinks with Whigs yet works for Tories. Nothing good will come of it.

Parliament has accepted the Company's proposals: all the nation's bonds and redeemable annuities will be transferred to Company stock, and the stock climbs ever higher. It is a tower of Babel built on sand. Whilst it climbs, the excitement builds, more and more invest, and up and up it goes. What is it Newton says? What goes up must come down (odious man). I think the same is true of stocks as well as apples. I am not a lone voice. The Bank understands; the Bank is worried.

My pensions will be converted not. The Crown owes me for my service, and I will not be swindled out of it by cornjobbery and corruption. Only months ago the idiot urged me to invest, now he tells me I must not. I never had any intention of investing in the first place, but he does not listen. The young always think they be so clever, so inventive. I can say this: age does not confer wisdom (I am the same spoiled and vain creature I have always been) but it does gift experience. The Dutch musician told me of the tulips in Amsterdam. The prices going ever higher but only so long as people are prepared to buy. At some point, they realise a field of pretty flowers is simply not worth the price of a good horse, or slave, or house, or the ship that carried them. At some point, the reality of one ship servicing the national debt through trade will be realised. What happens then?

'Does the name Von Königsmarck mean anything to you, Uncle?' The idiot passed me a cup of brandy and sat in a cushioned chair opposite. His wife has been abed for days.

'No,' I said it too quickly. 'Why? Where did you hear the name?'

'Last night at Leicester House.'

'Some German princeling then?' I took a great gulp from my cup.

'He was murdered, so they said, he just disappeared.'

He was murdered, I thought. They cut him to pieces and threw the parts in the river. I watched it happen. I watched him dance the saraband with the King's wife (Sophie Dorothea of Celle) earlier that night. I watched him creep from her chambers later flushed with love, and I watched them butcher him in the corridor.

'People disappear for a multitude of reasons, my boy. It does not mean they are murdered.'

'I was told that the Queen.'

'There is no Queen.' I reminded him. 'She may be mother to the Prince of Wales but she is no queen, whatever people said in Leicester House. The King is long divorced.'

King George was just the Elector of Hannover back then, not even heir to the throne. I did not consider his potential elevation. Anne was still popping out brats and the Stuart line was secure.

'Well,' the idiot said to me conspiratorially. 'Königsmarck was her lover and King George ordered his murder, and that is why they divorced, and why she is still imprisoned.'

A fair summation, but the King did not order the murder; his mother Princess Sophia did. I carried her command and saw that it was done. All the while George's mistress urged the killers on and dipped her fingers in the blood.

'The Prince is said to hate his father because of the affair,' the idiot continued. 'Mr Walpole hopes to end the feud.'

That be why the Duchess of Marlborough is so interested in Princess Sophia. It was all Sophia's design, after all. If the Duchess or Walpole could settle the royal feud, they would earn the gratitude of the current and future King. Clever bitch; clever bastard. Both are out of favour, both need royal redemption. Perhaps it is best that I do not see another monarch ascend to the throne. Six is enough, seven if you count Cromwell. Seven is enough.[75]

'This must have been years ago,' I said. 'The King has been divorced

---

[75]Blandford is either forgetting James I, who died when he was a baby, or dismissing Queen Mary, as his lifetime spanned eight monarchs including Cromwell.

for decades.'
'That is the thing, Uncle; it was twenty or more years ago, in Hannover. It was a great scandal. I was but a child when it happened and knew nothing of the case, but...' He paused.
'What?'
'Were we not in Hannover at the time? You took me to Germany with you back then, I remember. The dates seemed to tally. I thought with all your tales and stories you might know more.'
'I remember the tale, not,' I said.
Some memories are deadly, after all.[76]

---

[76]The disappearance of Philip Christoph von Königsmarck in June 1694 had been a notable royal scandal in the courts of Europe. Königsmarck had become close to Sophia Dorothea of Celle, George I's wife. Königsmarck was apprehended creeping out of Sophia Dorothea's apartments and murdered, according to deathbed confessions made years later. Over three hundred letters were discovered that were purported to be between the couple, exposing the affair (although there is some suggestion that they were forgeries made on the order of George's mistress to incriminate the pair). George later divorced his wife and kept her imprisoned, refusing to let her see her children (including the future George II). George I was only Elector of Hannover at the time and not likely to succeed given Princess (later queen) Anne was married and fertile. However, the murder and subsequent treatment of Sophia Dorothea caused a rift between father and son that would only get worse as time passed, particularly after George ascended the English throne. By 1720, the Prince of Wales and his wife were banned from court, and forbidden from seeing their own children by George I. The feud had obvious political ramifications in England, and Walpole and the Whigs were to be instrumental in resolving it. Sophia of Hannover had initially

opposed the marriage of George to Sophia Dorothea, only agreeing to it when the political benefits outweighed her doubts. Blandford is the first source to link her with the murder, but she was certainly very disparaging about her daughter-in-law in public and private, and supported the divorce in 1695.

Appendix I: Religious factions in the Civil War.

The different religious factions during the English Civil War are often confusing. The Elizabethan religious settlement had encompassed a middle way, between the austerity of Puritanism and the pomp of Catholicism. The Anglican Church had been a compromise between the two competing extremes, and had changed little under James I. Whilst there had always been recusants, (people who refused the Anglican Church) in the catholic section of the population, in the Seventeenth century there were increasingly recusants from the Protestant congregation. When Archbishop Laud implemented his reforms, he further alienated many who saw them as a return to the idolatry of Rome. This led to a fracturing of the Elizabethan settlement, and a number of competing groups vying for control of the English Church.

Anglicans were a group that followed the King's prayer book, and supported the reforms of the archbishop. Whilst they would not consider themselves Catholic, they accepted ritualistic elements of faith which appalled puritans, such as icons, statues, incense, and altars. They made up the majority of the population who, despite antipathy towards Catholicism, regarded the Elizabethan settlement as a successful compromise. Blandford's family, other than his sister Elizabeth, were typical Anglicans and unsurprisingly Royalist in outlook.

Puritans is a catch all term for those who felt the Elizabethan settlement had not gone far enough, or who had been alienated by Laud's reforms. They wished to reform the church and clear away any remnants of Catholicism. The Stuart Kings failure to address their concerns led some to leave England for the New World. Oliver Cromwell himself planned to sail for the Americas in the 1630's. Those that remained, became a vocal opposition to Charles I rule. However, there was a wide range of competing ideas amongst the puritans. A variety of Calvinists, Lutherans, Anabaptists, and later groups such as the Quakers, added their dissenting voices as religious control broke down during the Civil War. Politically, they tended to fall into two camps: Presbyterians (Covenanters) and Independents.

Presbyterians believed that there should be no established bishops, and opposed the feudal Episcopalian system. Favouring instead a national church on the Scottish model, with no Bishops, and elected representatives. James I and Charles I passionately opposed the abolition of Bishops, regarding them as vital in the administration of the country. James I declared memorably: *No bishops, no kings.* The Presbyterian faction in Parliament, was powerful in its opposition to Charles, but also later came into conflict with Cromwell and the army. The military was filled with much more radical and independent dissenters.

The Independents believed in local congregational control of church affairs, with no wider hierarchy, no bishops, or national structure. They were heavily represented in the army, especially after the reforms that led to the creation of the New Model Army. Cromwell and the other army grandees were ostensibly independents, and this led to the break with Parliament at the end of the first civil war. Despite their stern reputation, Cromwell and the Independents were surprisingly tolerant in religious matters (except if you were an Anglican or an Irish Catholic). The readmission of the Jews in 1656 is theologically consistent with the Independent view, if not necessarily an example of a caring tolerant Cromwell that some would claim.

Catholicism was very much in a minority in Stuart England, although there were influential nobles who wanted a return to loyalty to Rome and a re-established Roman Church. Certainly, after the Gunpowder Plot in 1605 Catholics were seen as the enemy within. Always relentlessly persecuted by both sides, they tended to support Charles I during the war, hoping for concessions from the King and his domineering Catholic wife Henrietta Maria.

Blandford himself was brought up as an Anglican, and would have attended church services at least once a week as a boy. Once in the army he was exposed to more radical preachers and independent dissenters, and he attended sermons by famous firebrand preachers of the time. Whilst not considering himself an atheist, he was certainly more influenced by Enlightenment ideas than religious devotion. The breakdown of authority and central control during the Civil War saw social bonds collapse. This included religious bonds, freeing many people from theocratic control for the first time.

Appendix II: Money.

Pounds, shillings, and pence were the basic currency of Britain until 1971, having a value of 12 pence to the shilling, and 20 shillings to the pound. A straight comparison with the cost of living is difficult, since the relative prices of various commodities have changed. In the case of foodstuffs a rough rule of thumb can be followed.

Blandford, as a Captain, theoretically earned about £5 a week and drew extra as a scout giving him an annual income of around £400, which was a sizeable amount in the Seventeenth Century. The inflated cost of troops during the war is clear. A horseman in the New Model Army earned nearly £40 a year. By 1688, they would only earn, according to Gregory King only £14. A junior officer under James II could only command a salary of £60-80. Of course, pay was always late, always short, and in the case of officers less likely to be paid at all. Blandford's allowance from Elizabeth of £160 a year put him firmly in the range of gentleman socially and was certainly more reliable.

John Bunyan gives us a price of *four eggs a penny* in *The Life and Death of Mr. Badman.* An egg today will cost around 25p – four eggs to a pound. Therefore, at the level of basic foodstuffs, the factor of comparison with the modern cost of living is around x 240.

Items such as clothes, jewellery, and furnishings would be much much more than that. For a fashionista like Blandford, keeping up with the current trends would be very expensive. Drinking, whoring, and gambling cost money after all.

Authors Note.

The novel is based on information taken from extensive sources. Some of these included: Samuel Luke's Journal, the Memoirs of Prince Rupert, Edward Hyde and Margaret Cavendish; collections of letters by Henrietta Maria, Charles I, and Oliver Cromwell; copies of original newsbooks, such as the Mercurius Aulicus, Perfect Diurnal, and Parliament Scout, and contemporary poems, ballads and plays.

Secondary sources included work by Christopher Hill, CV Wedgewood, Samuel Gardiner, John Adair, Julian Whitehead, Dianne Purkiss, Antonia Fraser, Brigadier Peter Young, Andrew Hopper, John Ellis, Eva Griffith, Julian Whitehead, Lucy Moore, Serena Jones, Clive Holmes and Richard Holmes. I have also taken account of up to date research in Battlefield Archaeology from the English Heritage website, and information on the British Civil Wars Project website.

All dates are given according to the Julian calendar. During the Civil War, the Julian date was 10 days behind the Gregorian calendar. Years are numbered from 1st January which was the method used by Blandford in 1719, although many 17th century writers numbered the year from 25th March.

I must give my wholehearted thanks to those that have helped me in my research and completing the novel: Nicola McLaughlin for checking my schoolboy French, Tim Pelham Williams, Kali Napier, and Abi Robbins (my wonderful beta readers), James Smallwood (the original Blandford), the brilliant Anthony Saunders, for pointing me to research on Cappo Ferro and Meyer and explaining the nuances of historical swordplay, and Nigel Williams (for regular bouts of inspiration). Particular thanks must go to Vaughn's Company of the Sealed Knot, and all the staff at The National Civil War Centre, Twickenham Museum, and Oliver Cromwell's House in Ely for answering my many, many, questions. I cannot emphasise enough that ALL the mistakes are mine!

*

Printed in Great Britain
by Amazon

62655744R00168